Whitley Strieber is the author of the bestsellers *The Wolfen* and *The Hunger*. With James Kunetka he has collaborated on *Nature's End* and *Warday*, bestselling documentary novels about nuclear war and ecological catastrophe respectively. He is also the author of the internationally bestselling account of alien contact, *Communion*.

By the same author

The Hunger
The Wolfen
Black Magic
The Night Church
Communion
Warday (with James Kunetka)
Nature's End (with James Kunetka)

WHITLEY STRIEBER

Catmagic

GRAFTON BOOKS

A Division of the Collins Publishing Group

LONDON GLASGOW
TORONTO SYDNEY AUCKLAND

Grafton Books
A Division of the Collins Publishing Group
8 Grafton Street, London WIX 3LA

Published by Grafton Books 1988

First published in Great Britain by
Grafton Books 1987

Copyright © Wilson & Neff, Inc. 1986

ISBN 0-586-07448-1

Printed and bound in Great Britain by
Collins, Glasgow
Photoset in Linotron Plantin by
Rowland Phototypesetting Ltd
Bury St Edmunds, Suffolk

TOM

This book is dedicated to something that may be a cat. He is enormous, black as death, and usually gone. He has a shredded ear and a kink in his tail. If he is around, he might enjoy being stroked, and then again he might hurt you if you so much as touch a hair. He never purrs. He likes to stare.

Foreword to the Paperback Edition

The relationship between *Communion* and *Catmagic*

I wrote *Catmagic* in 1984, well before I was consciously aware of the visitors who figure in *Communion*.

Communion is the story of how it felt to have personal contact with the visitors. The mysterious small beings that figure prominently in *Catmagic* seem to be an unconscious rendering of them, created before I was aware that they may be real. It could be that the message of the book – which involves respect for Earth and all her creatures, and the seeking of higher consciousness – is somehow derived from my inner understanding of the meaning of the visitors.

The American hardcover edition of *Catmagic* appeared under a pseudonym, Jonathan Barry, primarily because it was published too close to the publication date of another of my books and would have created a conflict. I am the sole author of *Catmagic*.

Catmagic concerns Witches and Witchcraft, also known as the religion of Wicca. It is about the spiritual path of real Witches. It has nothing to do with tomfoolery like alleged 'black magic'. The Witches I met in doing research for *Catmagic* were no more evil than Christians or Buddhists or Hindus, or the practitioners of any other perfectly legitimate religion, among which Wicca can certainly be numbered. They were good people, passionate in their concern for the welfare of the natural world and the growth of their own souls.

Certainly there are a few people who distort Witchcraft and mock its ancient rituals in ceremonies that glorify evil. I met two such people. They turned out to be associated with another religion. They were calling themselves Witches and engaging in painfully silly black magic rituals involving dead goats in an effort to discredit Wicca. Others who do evil in the name of Witchcraft are mentally disordered or, simply, charlatans. Such people should no more be counted Witches than practitioners of the black mass should be considered Catholics.

To learn more about the 'old religion', the reader is invited to write to: Circle Wicca, Box 219, Mt Horeb, Wisconsin 53572, USA.

Whitley Strieber
New York, 1987

Prologue

Stone Mountain is the only truly rough peak in the Peconics. Its grey, cracked ridges stretch for about three miles in that otherwise benign chain. They are so loose and treacherous that even the most obsessive rock climbers avoid them as offering too unsubtle a doom. The Appalachian Trail, deferring to the fact that old Stone has been known to slice a good pair of Beans to shreds, skirts the mountain and passes through the orchard-choked exurbia of the little town of Maywell, which huddles beneath the mountain like an Israelite at the feet of Pharaoh.

From the grand and crumbling Collier estate at one end of town to the dark Victorian buildings of Maywell College at the other, the ridges look down on the whole of Maywell. This is not an area of superhighways and roaring commuter buses; Maywell has been bypassed by the roads and the developers. Once again, old Stone is to blame. No highway construction company would bid on a road to cross that miserable expanse of cracked granite, so Maywell remains much as it was a century ago, a town as pretty as it can be, alone, and largely content with its own gentle self.

Maywell prospers in a quiet way, on the orchards and the farms whose produce is trucked off to Philadelphia and New York, and on the maintenance of Maywell College, an institution small in both size and reputation, but more than adequate to provide the town its full share of raucous students and middle culture.

Maywell does not really like the modern world. It has a tendency to look to softer eras with well-dressed, genteel longing. It is peaceful, moral, and respectable.

It is, in short, just the sort of place where peculiar things happen.

These things may be grim and awful, as was the raising by Brother Simon Pierce of his Resurrection Tabernacle, or pretty much the opposite of grim, such as the witchy goings-on out at the Collier estate.

They may be odd, as in the case of poor Dr Walker. He was a brilliant biologist whose abrasive personality and dogged obsession with his own bizarre theories made him tiresome to his peers at Yale. Eventually, when he raved to the newspapers about bringing frogs back to life, he was hurled out. So now he continues his career in this forgotten corner of the academy, teaching freshmen the intricacies of the zygote and plotting the breakthroughs that will vindicate his genius.

Besides its beauty and isolation and its smattering of eccentrics, Maywell has something else odd about it. This is a bit more serious. This is quite terrible and quite wonderful – if such words have any clear meaning. *Terrible* conjures images of huge, gaping beasts or sulking psychopaths; *wonderful* brings a silken princess and a thornless rose.

Both words might conjure a cat.

Certainly either suggests the great King of the Cats, a creature known almost exclusively to students of obscure Celtic mythology, and holding sway, according to Robert Graves, 'upon a chair of old silver' whence he gave 'vituperative answers to inquirers who tried to deceive him.' No doubt he/she accounts in part for the androgynous nature of Puss In Boots and was the progenitor of the first Cinderella story, 'The Cat-Cinderella,' which is itself a folk memory of the very ancient legend of the cat as friend of Ishtar, the fierce old mother goddess who once held sway over Sumeria.

Among the fragments of the old mystery religion of the Greeks is the identification of the goddess Diana with a cat. From deep time, the female witch has identified a male cat as her familiar. And, of course, there were the Egyptian cats, most of whom were mummified and persist to this day stacked in the basements of museums.

The extraordinary creature that inhabited the ridges of Stone Mountain, though, was no candidate for a museum. Indeed, at the moment it was very intensely alive, and not out on the windy ridges, but wandering far more delightful realms.

All was not perfect: long ago it had been touched by one of Constance Collier's spells, and something was tied to its ear.

This was an invisible thread, which led from the delightful realms all the way into Maywell, where it joined the other invisible threads being woven on the loom of the town's life.

The other threads turned and twisted constantly, crossing as the druggist married the grocer's daughter, slipping apart when he died, becoming knotted when she also passed on, and so on, the cloth never finished, its invisible patterns ceaselessly shimmering and changing.

Only one of the townspeople, Constance Collier, had both the wisdom and inclination to sit occasionally at the sacred loom and manoeuvre the threads around a bit, perhaps granting some indigent follower of hers a little good fortune or causing the business affairs of one of her adversaries to come unravelled.

She never touched the thread connected to the mythical cat's imaginary ear, and hadn't since she had first tied it, a deed she had done on a soft spring day when she was still full of hope.

Many long years had passed since then, while Constance had plotted and spelled and hexed and waited. But she had never needed to call the cat. She had gone from being a beautiful young woman to a wise old one, and had become patient with her lifetime of waiting.

If the thread was pulled, it would bring the cat back to Stone Mountain, and down into innocent, unsuspecting

Maywell. There was, however, only one reason to do this appalling thing.

Of late Constance had known renewed hope. There was a chance, after all, that the final chapter in a very old story would at last be written.

Constance, Dr Walker, Brother Pierce – three of the main characters are in place. There remains only one more, and she is already approaching the town, chugging along in her ancient Volkswagen Beetle. Even more promising, it is jammed with luggage and easels.

An observer of the invisible could see that the particular thread that is tied to the cat's ear has wafted down and fallen across Morris Stage Road. The old Volks wheezes, its gears grind, and it moves closer.

Hidden breezes blow the thread about, entangling it in the lower limbs of an autumn-fired birch. Now the thread is tight.

Closer and closer the car comes, its blonde young driver peering out. There are no exit markers here. She has been told to take the third right after the big crossroads. She is counting and staring as the car sweeps into the thread. She experiences nothing more than a tickle and a sneeze, but off in the cat's realm things are quite different. The cat is dragged, howling with pain and anger, all the way to the dreary, windswept ridges of old Stone.

For a moment nothing more happens, but that is only because the cat's eyes are shut tight.

As the shock wears off, it blinks, then begins to gaze.

Huge, golden cat eyes appear, hanging above an otherwise empty expanse of rock.

The cat glares down into the weave of Maywell's life, to see what fool has dared this conjuring.

BOOK ONE

Godfather Death

The glacier knocks in the cupboard,
The desert sighs in the bed,
And a crack in the tea-cup opens
A lane to the land of the dead.

– W. H. Auden,
'As I Walked Out One Evening'

CHAPTER 1

The frog wanted desperately to hop. But it couldn't hop. It jerked, then jerked again. It stayed where it was, clamped down tight. It flexed, tightened, jerked. The hot, dry hurting kept on. The frog worked its tongue. Pain. It tried to move its head. Pain. Things were piercing it. Again and again it tried to hop. But it stayed right where it was, in this hard white place with no leaves and no whirring wings and no sharp delicious bugs to wrestle from the air.

It tried to hop.

Still, it did not move.

It tried. Tried. Tried.

It hurt, it had to move, it had to *hop*!

'There we go – no – hell. Bonnie, the animal is still too slick.'

Painful, tormenting, scraping all over its back, hot and dry. It hopped hopped hopped.

'Thanks. Now . . . yeah!'

'That did it, George. The probe's well seated. I have a good signal.'

'Okay, Clark. Let's get started.'

On Stone Mountain the creature – which was still only eyes – began spinning itself a cat body so it would be ready as soon as the sun went down. Two sparrows, who saw something astonishing create its own solid presence out of thin air, took flight, screaming in the silence.

A raccoon stiffened and stared, and mewed.

What it saw had no taxonomic classification. No, indeed, for it belonged to a rare law, this creature of mercy. Pacing now, it waited for the sunlight to rise away from the streets of the town. And suffered along with the frog.

The frog understood nothing it saw around it. There were long strands sweeping out above its eyes. It could see every turn and wrinkle in the wires leading from its skull. But it did not understand the wires. It saw them as legs, and thought of bugs.

It liked to use its good eyes, to see sharp. Seeing sharp meant eating well. But there were no wings whirring, no fat bodies, no good scent connected with the sight of these long legs. The frog's tongue swelled with the blood of hunger. It wanted to see insects, to smell dampness, to be in green water. It wanted to hop.

But it was stuck right where it was.

'That looks like a good, steady electroencephalograph to me, Clark. The frog's normal. Not too happy, but normal.'

'Don't let it jerk out my electrodes, Bonnie. I hate frogs. Give me something big any day.'

'Like what?'

'Like a person, Bonnie dear.'

'Constance wouldn't like that.'

'No, and she doesn't like this either.'

'You're doing it.'

'She might not like our work, but she appreciates the necessity, at least. That's more than I can say for the Stohlmeyer people. Sometimes I think they're secret followers of Brother Pierce.'

'God, don't bring him up. I don't want my hands to shake while I'm working.'

A silence fell among the three people in the lab. They all knew the eventual object of their experiment, the goal given them five years ago by Constance Collier: to kill a human being and return him or her back to life. Her goal, her programme.

But Constance didn't like all the animal killing they had

16

to do to succeed. 'I feel every one of those deaths,' she had told George. 'Maybe I've made a mistake. Maybe you ought to stop.'

He would never stop. He had pursued this goal at Yale and destroyed his career there. He would pursue it at Maywell and drag his name up out of the mud. He was going to vindicate himself in this little backwater. One day this college would be famous because of what he had done here.

The technician, Clark, finally spoke. 'Okay, folks, I'm ready to proceed.'

'I'm set,' said Dr Walker.

'Bonnie, how about the audiovisual?' Clark asked.

'Up and running.'

'Right. Here we go. Beginning the count. Five.'

The frog felt heavy, as if it were buried in mud. Heavy and smothering. Its heart began to beat harder.

'Four.'

Something tickled inside the frog. It was terrible, this feeling, like nothing else the frog had known, tickling under its skin, like water spiders running there. The frog tried to move, to escape the tickling, but the weight seemed to bear down the more. Fear made its eyes bulge.

'Three.'

It was as if the frog were being torn apart. It had a vision of talons, of huge whistling wings.

Death came to it then, and its heart slowed.

The smell of water rose up around the terrified creature, then became a vision, water in darkness. The talons let go, and the frog fell into the quiet water, then it was dawn and flies were rising, and the frog was on a lily pad singing up the sun.

'Two.'

The dream sank to dark, and the frog felt itself falling into nothingness.

'One.'

The black parted, and the water dream of a moment ago lay before the frog, and this time it was real.

The frog was free. It hopped easily to the good-smelling water, and the water splashed around it and made its skin jitter with pleasure as it dived down into a black bass pool. Reefs of tadpoles swept past and sticklebacks darted in shafts of sunlight, then the frog went up again and broke the surface amid blooming lilies.

'We have complete termination. It's dead, George.'

Cloaked by darkness at last, the cat began to move down the mountain. As it did so, its form flickered and grew ever more solid. When it crossed the ridge, it was a shadow of a cat, a shudder in the light, a wisp of colder air. When it reached the edge of Maywell, it was a scampering, dark suggestion of something quite familiar.

By the time it came into the streetlight at the corner of Indian and Bridge it was quite clearly an old black tomcat with a torn ear and a proud, bent tail.

At least, that's what it looked like. Animals and children, though, were not deceived. They sensed the true shape of this vast and terrible being, and were filled with dread.

All over the town cats awakened and stared at darkened windows. Strays slid beneath porches or huddled under cars. Birds stirred in their trees and dogs at their masters' feet. Here and there a napping infant screamed. On the grounds of the Collier estate old Constance paused in her walk, closed her eyes, and entered the immense space within herself. She knew she should try to stop Tom, but she did not. George would manage, he was a survivor. And the poor frog!

In any case, her gesture would probably be futile. Such a deep violation of the laws of life was making the cat awfully mad. Constance's interference wouldn't even be noticed.

The black tom began his progress across Maywell, intent only on one goal: Animal Room Two, Terrarium D-22,

Wolff Biology Building. He hurried down the sidewalk on the right side of Bartlett Street, past the tall homes that had housed the same Maywell families for generations, the Haspells and the Lohses and the Coxons, families whose ancestors had seen the Revolution from those leaded-glass windows, who had leaped in the springtime fields and left mandrakes for the fairy.

The tom passed a red Mustang convertible beneath which an elderly and very arthritic tabby hid.

The tom heard its wheezing breath, saw the pain in its eyes. Frightened of the enormous spirit it saw stalking down the walk, the tabby yowled miserably.

The tom stopped. He lowered his head, concentrated on the neglected, dying animal before him. A sensitive paw reached out and touched the cowering tabby. *I give you the gift of death, old cat. You have earned it.* Instantly the tabby's body slumped. The tom watched its soul leap up like smoke into the starry sky.

None of the tabby's fleas crossed to the tom. They chose rather to risk the cold autumn ground.

The tom continued on its way, and everything sensitive to it took notice as they might the transit of a wendigo. As it passed the Coxon house, it brought a vision to the innocently open mind of little Kim, the eleven-month-old baby. She began to wail in her crib. She didn't know words, but in a painful, true flash from the enormous mind that was passing, she had seen her own end, far from now in a sleek blue thing she did not yet know was called a car, in the bellowing water of a flooded river, on another autumn night. And in the prime of youth.

Hearing the desolation in her cries, Kim's mother came into the nursery, picked her up, and clucked and sang and patted. 'Oh, had a burp,' her mother said. 'Such a big burp!' When the wailing passed, she put Kim down.

The frog found fat, lovely flies skimming along the surface of the water. It caught them, aiming with its keen eyes, darting its tongue.

Something the frog might have called a goddess, had it known of such things, marched the water, raining desire down on the feeding bull, making it forget its feeding and follow.

'Monitor the blood flow in the extremities. We'll wait until it stops completely before we bring our baby back.'

The frog was jumping and leaping for the green goddess, wanting to show that it was the greatest bull, the bull of bulls, huge and strong and thunder-voiced. It dived deep, shot to the surface, dived again.

'That's the last of it, George. No more blood flow.'

'So we can confirm one absolutely dead *Rana catesbeiana*?'

'By any definition. Even the Stohlmeyer Foundation's.'

'This time, Doctor, they'll accept our protocols. For sure.'

'Thanks, Bonnie.' George Walker kissed her straw-sweet twenty-year-old hair. He stood to his full height, six feet of slim but fiftyish male.

God, he thought, the beauty of her youth!

'I have ninety seconds of null readings, Doctor.'

'Good, Clark. I think we'll convince 'em this time.'

'For sure,' Bonnie repeated.

And if we don't, George thought, you kids are going to be out of Maywell State College on your tight little asses just like me. No Stohlmeyer grant means no professorship – and no assistantships either. But then again, what would Clark care – he had the Covenstead to return to. Bonnie was too wild to live in Constance Collier's witch village. As for George, he kept his house in town. He had his reasons for staying away from the estate, chief among them his career. It was one thing for people to commute into New York from the Covenstead, another for them to try and work in the town.

Any professor foolish enough to have open contact with the witches could forget things like tenure.

If the Stohlmeyer grant ended, Constance might find George some money for his work, but the grant was the validation that the college trustees needed to allow him to continue it here. Loss of the grant meant loss of career. George could not bear that thought: he had worked so hard, and been so misunderstood.

'Let's earn some gold, kiddies, and bring this little sucker back to life.'

The frog heard, thrumming in the whole air, a rush as of bird wings. It was low and large, too large even to be a bird. Was it wind?

The frog saw scud on the surface of the waters, saw the lilies tearing, saw the leaves of cypress and willow lift into the black sky, heard the thrumming rise to a scream. It waited no longer, but rather leaped for the dark, safe deeps.

A shimmering, golden goddess of a frog swam there. The bull's heart was captured and he went deeper and deeper after her, his loins tingling, his muscles singing in the quiet. She lured him farther and farther, deeper than any frog should go. Come, she said with her quickness. Swim, she said with her grace. Swim! Swim!

The wind was seething behind him, roaring through the lilies, ripping the green and quiet waters, the holy pond.

Swim, little one, the goddess called, swim with all your soul!

The black tom began to run. He rounded a corner onto Meecham Street. The neighbourhood changed from houses to a row of neat little shops. Bixter's Ice Cream was open, its video games clattering and buzzing. Beside it the B. Dalton bookstore was just closing up. Joan Kominski locked her register and turned out her lights. The passing tom, unnoticed by her, shot her a vision of her own future: she was in a hospital room dragging breaths that would not fill her lungs. The hallucination was so detailed that she could smell the oxygen, see a picture of a clown on the wall, hazy beyond the plastic oxygen tent, taste her own drowning fluids. And feel Mike's hand in hers and hear him calling 'Doctor, Doctor!'

She paused, stunned. With shaking hands she lit a cigarette. She stood in her darkened bookshop, smoking, calming herself down.

The tom trotted quickly down Main and crossed the Morris Stage Road. Mike Kominski was roaring home full of Amtrak martinis, late as usual from his job in New York, and it would not do to be caught in front of that particular Lincoln.

The wind was just behind the frog now and he knew it was dry and he knew it was hot. He swam and swam in the roiling, dirtying, darkening waters. Ahead the maiden frog, the goddess, glimmered, urging him to rush on and on, deep to her, deep to her!

'We're getting an electrical field!'

The wind touched his back and it was hot and ugly and hard. It must be deathwind, for it smelled of the man-place.

He must not surrender to it! Ahead she flashed her gold beauty. He swam as he had never swum before, the water hissing past his nose and eyes, his whole body surging with the effort of it. Her eyes shone and her skin gleamed.

The wind touched him again.

'Heartbeat!'

No!

The wind surrounded him.

'It's coming to rhythm.'

The wind sucked at him.

'It's getting steady.'

His whole heaven collapsed. But she did not abandon him. Alone of all that beauty, the most beautiful part re-

22

mained. When she saw him being dragged back, she turned and came, too, swimming fearlessly into the dry agony that had captured him. She ceased to animate his determination and concentrated on giving him courage. She went deep, deep into him, into the secret place where glowed the strength of his spirit.

Then he hurt all over and he was hungry and he was hot and it was white and there were no fly smells and it was bleak again.

'It's alive, George!'

'Damn right it is.' George Walker could hardly restrain himself. He stood up from the bank of instruments, he clapped his hands. And Bonnie leaped, a blonde streak of joy, into his arms. He kissed her moist lips.

He enjoyed the deliciousness of the girl while young Clark looked on, glasses steaming. Relax, Clark, let an old man get a little. What does it matter, you get all you need on the Covenstead.

George did not have that privilege. His relationship to Constance was too deep a secret; he could not go on the Covenstead except by dark of night, and then only in those rare instances when he was called.

And as for living among the witches – well, if his work here was ever done, maybe. He had never told Constance his dream of retiring to the hidden witch village.

He was afraid to. If she said to him what he feared, that it was not his fate to find peace in this life, he did not think he could stand it.

Sometimes the loneliness of his position was very hard to bear.

'We've got to get it out of the halter,' Clark said, his voice full of testy eagerness. 'It'll dehydrate. We really don't need a damaged specimen, do we, folks.'

Bonnie broke away from George's hovering presence. 'I'll bag it and return it to the terrarium.'

'The isolate,' George said. 'And band it with the date and time. Under no circumstances do we mix this little piece of gold up with the other beasties.'

The frog was soon in the awful, waterless pond with the magic walls. It knew what it had to do here. Sit. A hop meant a hurt on the nose. The magic wall could not be seen, but it was as hard as the skin of a floating log.

So the frog sat. Remembering its heaven was almost enough to make it turn itself inside out with agony. It begged the golden frog to help.

I cannot!

Take me back, please.

I cannot!

Dried, dead flies scattered down, sticking to its nose. The frog's tongue did not go to get them.

Please, please.

I cannot!

The frog felt a cleaving that in higher things is called love, for the lost green water. All it could do, though, was sit, inert and mute, silent.

Frogs are not made for anguish. Nor to have their deaths stolen from them. Nor to be dragged back from their humble paradise.

Frogs are made for joy.

The Wolff Building crouched dark and ugly ahead. Nobody saw the incredible way the tom entered the building, nor saw it slip down the corridor to just the right door.

But the instant the cat went through that door the frog knew.

The frog saw dangerous eyes on the other side of the magic wall. Once it would have hopped away from such terrible eyes, but now only sat, apathetic. In its brain there repeated the image of the deep water and the golden lover it had lost.

Even when the huge black head of the tom came oozing

right through the magic wall, the frog did not hop. Had it understood the miracle involved in a cat pushing its head through solid glass without breaking it, the frog might have jumped. But it did not understand the magic wall. As far as it knew, the only purpose of glass was to disappoint frogs.

The cat nudged the frog with its muzzle, then opened its mouth. The sharp frog eyes saw the tongue, the white fangs, the gently pulsating throat. And it saw more.

Instead of terror, the frog felt eagerness. For down in the cat's throat it saw its lost beauty, her skin touched by sunlight. She lay in a crystal pond, tadpoles swimming about her flanks.

Heaven was in the belly of the cat. The frog laid his head in the tom's mouth.

This was one death it did not have to suffer. The tom snapped its jaws down so fast the frog felt nothing.

But then it had already died once and that was quite enough. It saw a fierce flash of light and heard a sound like tearing leaves, and was gone.

The cat tasted the cold, sour flesh of the frog, gobbled, drank down the cool blood, felt the eyes sticky against its tongue, the skin slick and bland, the muscles salty. It swallowed the frog.

When it returned to the night, the moon had risen red in the east, its light diffused by haze from the Peconic Valley Power Company's plant twenty miles away in Willowbrook, Pennsylvania. The tom proceeded along North Street towards Maywell's one and only housing development, 'The Lanes,' built by Willowbrook Resources in 1960. The development's sameness had over the years been camouflaged by trees. Each of the streets had been named after a familiar variety. The birches planted on Birch were tall and blue in the moonlight, the spruce on Spruce dark green. On Elm there were oak saplings and one or two still-struggling Dutch elm victims.

The cat passed down Maple Lane until it reached the Walker house, a substantial raised ranch with pale yellow aluminum siding and a '79 Volvo in the driveway. Beside it was Amanda's ancient VW Beetle.

The tom went between the two cars, through the closed garage door, and into the games room beyond. It was indifferent to the fact that the lights were on; it knew that the room was empty. It slipped behind the sofa just as Amanda, nervous and hollow-eyed, entered. It cocked its ears towards her, and heard much more than her breathing, her movements. It heard the voice of her mind, the thready whisper of her soul.

She looked around, shaking her head. Here she was again, back in this awful house. She knew that this was a triumphal return to Maywell, but having to stay in this place cast a brown shadow on her victory. Too bad she couldn't afford the Maywell Motor Inn. But she was lucky to have managed to get enough gas for the Volks, given the present state of her finances.

This house . . . this town . . . the only thing about any of it that brought even a flicker of a fond memory was the thought of Constance Collier herself, with her wild colony of witches out on the estate, and her flamboyant seasonal rituals, the fires burning on the hillsides and the wild rides through the town.

It all seemed so peaceful now. As she had got older, Constance must have mellowed.

Sneaking out to the Collier estate to see the witches dancing naked in their April fields had been desperately exciting, one of the few thrills of being a child in this staid community.

Always, though, there had been this house waiting at the end of a happy day. She had come home to the resentments and the sorrows: this was a place of unspoken anger, where people wept at night.

She looked around her. Everything was brown and sad. Since George had bought it from his brother, it had – if possible – got even worse. There was an open chill on it now, as if hate was glaring into every room, from the walls, the doors, the very air. There was no more hypocrisy here, at least. The body of the house now reflected its soul.

Standing in the family room, Amanda felt the weight of the place. She remembered one awful night when she had come in from watching – almost participating in – the Halloween ritual on the Collier estate. Her father had slammed her up against that very wall. 'Never, never get near that place!' His voice had been desolate with sorrow.

What would he think now? In a few days she was going to be working with Constance Collier.

She wouldn't participate in witchcraft. She had no time for such fantasies. Of course, it would be interesting to learn more about what went on at the estate.

She dropped down onto the old couch, the same one that had been here in her childhood. She was twenty and living on her own when she discovered that it was not necessary to be sad. Life could be rich and fulfilling. There was an aesthetic to living that had to be carefully learned, though, or there was the danger of falling down the same pit that had swallowed her parents, the pit of spiritual bankruptcy and moral indifference.

Through the dirty glass sliding doors she could see the backyard. The old maple where she had spent so many summer hours was still here, and her throat tightened a little to see it. Ten years ago she might have been in that maple on an afternoon like this, sitting in the palace of leaves.

Ten years. The silences were growing longer. Her relationships with her parents continued, dragging themselves out in her mind. If she had to stay here, memories that were now no more than haunting would soon become unbearable.

She hoped that Constance Collier would have some space

for her out on the estate. Then this hard journey would become much easier.

The only thing that would ever have brought her back to Maywell was Constance Collier. Now she was here, chosen to paint the illustrations for the renowned writer's new translation of Grimm's. It was the biggest and best commission she had ever had.

Mandy had come a long way for a twenty-three-year-old woman. A long, hard way. Of course the Caldecott Award for her *Rose and Dragon* illustrations had helped. She believed that the work itself, though, was what had attracted the secretive and distant Constance Collier's attention to an anonymous former townie.

She could create whole, complete worlds in her imagination, and paint them down to the last strand of golden hair.

Hands dropped onto her shoulders. 'Oh!'

'Sorry. I didn't mean to startle you.'

'Uncle George.'

She could only feel kindness towards him, since he had been so willing to let her stay here. As soon as she came in, she had understood the reason for his eagerness: without Kate and the kids, this place was more grim than it had ever been before.

'You're looking lovely, Amanda.'

'Why not? I've escaped Manhattan, and tomorrow I meet Constance Collier.'

As he looked at her, his eyes brimmed with what she suspected might even be desire. Had she been a damn fool to stay with him? Perhaps she should have gone straight to the estate. But Miss Collier hadn't offered her accommodation. All of her old town habits came back. She dared not be forward with Maywell's leading citizen. Her agent had agreed. 'Don't jeopardize the project by making demands right at first,' Will T. Turner had advised.

'Have you got anything to drink?' Amanda asked. George

padded off in his big sheepskin slippers, across the chipped linoleum of the games room floor.

'Old Mr Boston brandy good enough for you?'

She took it and sipped. 'Mmm. Just the thing to relax me.'

'I'm glad you're here, Mandy.' He stood close to her. 'I'm sorry the house was such a mess when you came. I just completely forgot. We've been very busy over at the lab.'

'Doing good things?'

'I'm hopeful.'

She nodded, sipped again.

'It's just that I'm so damn tired.' He snorted out a laugh. 'We were very successful today. Very successful.'

'Do you want to tell me about it?'

'Not really. Except to say that it was rather a triumph.' His eyes regarded her steadily.

If she stayed in this house, George was certain to make passes at her. She did not need that. She would have to risk giving Constance offence and request a room at the estate when they met in the morning.

She was ready to ask George some polite question about his triumph, when something unusual happened. One of her most treasured talents was the ability to have detailed visualizations on demand. But they never came like this, unbidden.

And yet, despite the fact that she was healthy and not in the least tired, she found herself in the grip of just such an uncalled vision.

She saw a haggard George, crouching in a dark room, perhaps even the awful cold room in this house's basement. Her mother used to store coats there, in what had been billed in the brochure as a wine cellar.

It was where Mandy and Charlie Picano had gone for prolonged kissing behind the coatrack.

It was where their cat Punch had died, starved to death

while the family was on vacation. Nobody had noticed that he had been shut in there.

It was where the children had whispered tales of witchcraft in Maywell, and Marcia Cummings had insisted that witches were good.

In Mandy's vision a woman lay on a table in the room, which had been transformed from a place of mystery into a torture chamber. The woman was dead, but George was not sad.

At the moment George was smiling. Mandy recoiled at the sight of his cadaverous grin.

'Mandy?' His smile faded. He began watching her closely. She threw back her brandy.

'You're good at that.'

'I've become a city girl, remember. And I'm tired from the drive. I want to go to bed.'

'I'm sorry I forgot to make up the guest room.'

'Don't worry about it. I can make a bed.'

When she started for the room, he followed her. As they walked together through the quiet house, she hoped against hope that it would not be – but of course it was her old room.

He paused before the door and took her shoulders in his hands. He kissed her forehead. 'Good night, Mandy.'

She fought down the shaking. When he kissed her, his lips felt like two leather straps. 'Good night, George.' She turned to face her past.

George and Kate had raised two kids here and not even changed the wallpaper. Mandy remembered selecting it at Chasen's on Main, being torn between the cornflowers and these repeating rose arbours. She had chosen the roses and then planted a rose garden beneath her window. Over three years her roses had flourished, and she had secretly called herself the Rose Girl. Only Marcia knew. 'I told Aunt Constance,' she had whispered when they were naked beneath the covers of a soft June night.

'You told her?'

'She said to give you a message. "Tell the Rose Girl that I love her and watch over her."'

'Me?'

Marcia had squeezed her, and they had slept in one another's arms, two ten-year-olds so innocent that their nakedness meant only friendship to them. 'She loves us all. Let me take you to meet her.'

That was strictly forbidden. Dad hated Constance Collier, hated Maywell. He was only here because Peconic made him be here in his capacity as regional manager.

How Mandy had dreamed, lying in that bed beneath the window. Sometimes she saw witch lights on Stone Mountain; sometimes she watched the red moon rising, or the stars.

There was dust in this house, dust and loneliness. And something else, too, she reflected as she closed the guest room door. There was a place in the living room wall that had recently been patched, as if a fist had been slammed into it. Shades of Dad. 'George is a violent man,' Kate had told her. And Kate had left him.

Mandy brushed her teeth and lay down on her bed in the dark. The moon made a pale shadow across the floor. A hollow autumn wind muttered in the dry leaves. Down the street a dog howled.

The old tom came out of his hiding place and proceeded across the games room, through the big eat-in kitchen, pausing in the living room. Against the perspective of the furniture the cat seemed unnaturally large.

It had a weathered, surprisingly kind face. And that kinked tail was endearing. The shredded ear, though, was almost comical, making it seem as if the whole cat was lopsided.

The tom waited on the sun porch where Mandy's easel and canvases were installed, waited amid the smell of linseed oil and paint. It saw the skill in her brushstrokes, and drank in the energy of the young woman. Poor, confused young woman. She had no idea how dangerous this story would be to her, as it unfolded.

She had painted a haunted landscape with a fairy stealing down a moonlit path . . . painted it with skill and even passion, and more than a little of her own heart's truth. But what a relentlessly sentimental notion of a fairy. It looked like a bug, with those wings. And it was far too small. The picture had the fatal defect of charm.

Settling sounds began to come from the bedrooms. The cat grew still. It closed its eyes, concentrating on every nuance of their beings. It felt as they felt, sensed as they sensed, shook its dirty old body as they tossed and turned, gazed with George as he adored the mental images of his women, Bonnie and his lost Kate, and Mandy, felt the pulsing, stifled sensation in his loins, and knew with him the dreadful weight of time.

The old tom waited until the moon was at the top of the sky to begin.

Then it moved off to commit the next act of the story.

It stole into George's bedroom, listened a moment to his sleep. In one quick motion it leaped upon his bed. It heard his heart labouring softly and faithfully on towards its eventual breaking end, listened to his stomach digesting the day's meals, felt his dreams, haunted dreams of frogs and death and girls and loss.

The tom walked softly up his sleeping body, until its big head hung over his throat. It looked down at the pulsing artery in George Walker's neck. It opened its mouth, its fangs just inches from the flesh. George Walker sighed, as if inwardly aware of the death overlooking him.

The cat gagged softly and regurgitated. Something green and slimy slipped out of its mouth and onto George's face. By the time he had taken the first shocked breath of awakening, the cat was in the enclosed porch, passing the easels and paints. By the time George was gasping and fumbling for the light, the cat was going through the back door.

It slipped beneath the back porch as lights pierced the windows of the house and Mandy's feet pounded down the hall while George Walker screamed and screamed.

CHAPTER 2

One moment Mandy was asleep, the next she was running down the hall towards George's bedroom. His screams called her deep instincts, so high they were, so like a panicked baby's. Her first, hideous thought was of fire.

Then she saw him, crouched in the middle of the bed, his fists clutching his thin hair. Moonlight streamed over him, making him seem a dangerous shadow. She fumbled for the light switch, found it at last behind the door, turned it on.

The suffusing yellow light changed him to a crumpled old man. Something obscene and wet and green lay on the sheet before him. He was screaming at it. She went to him. Another bellow gushed out of him. His eyes were staring, oblivious to everything except the sticky mass on the bed. Each time he screamed, flecks of bloody sputum flew from his mouth.

'George!'

She grasped his shoulders, shook him. He was as rigid as wood. His skin was cold. He shrieked again.

'George!'

There were a series of broken gasps. Then another shriek, cracking, pitched like the cry of a bird.

'Hey!' She grabbed his cheeks, leaned into his face. His nostrils flared, his lips parted for another scream. She slapped him hard across the right cheek. The scream shattered, became a sob. She turned his face and slapped him on the left cheek. 'George, wake up! You're dreaming!'

He raised his hands to ward off her blows. For a moment they remained like that, she holding his chin, he seeking sanity in her eyes. Then he sank against her, sobbing bitterly.

She held his thin frame against her breast. 'George, hush now, it's all right. It's all right.'

'The hell it is!' His voice was hoarse. 'Look at that! You know what that is?'

It was green, blotched with brown, so wet that it had made an irregular damp spot on the sheet. 'What?'

'A skin.' He sighed. 'The skin of a frog. *My* frog!' Then he was crying, silently, bitterly, his shoulders shaking, the tears streaming from his eyes.

He could only be referring to the frogs he used in his lab. But what in the world would one of them be doing here? She looked at it. Lying there on his bed, in a place so wildly wrong, it made her feel all the power of the wind that soughed around the house. Her thoughts went to snapping clean sheets and sunny rooms and she shuddered.

'Why is it here, George?'

'It really isn't very mysterious.' He cleared his throat. 'I need a drink.'

'Now, you take it easy. I'll get it. You stay put.'

'Not in here.' He got out of bed. In four spider steps he was across the room. He took his robe from the closet.

She followed him into the games room, where he had already started pouring Black Label into a highball glass.

'Cheers,' he said. 'Here's to *religion!*'

She had accumulated a fair number of questions in the past few minutes. But she did not press him now. He needed space to calm himself down. Although he was talking instead of screaming, she saw the wildness of his panic still in his eyes. 'Come here,' she said, patting the couch beside her. He sat down. She laid her arm around his shoulders.

Soon enough, he began to explain. 'This was undoubtedly the work of a religious fanatic named Pierce. He has one of these fundamentalist churches here. Brother Simon Pierce. A Bible-thumping charlatan.'

'Yes?'

'He – they, I should say – they've demonstrated against

my work. He preaches against it. Death is God's business, that sort of thing.'

'The mess in your bed –'

He snorted out a bitter laugh. 'You don't understand, do you?'

'No.'

'That is the skin of a frog I killed and brought back to life this afternoon.'

So that had been the triumph he had referred to earlier. 'You actually succeeded?'

'You bet I did. Well-nigh perfectly.' He uttered a sharp laugh. 'Of course you know we're already virtually cancelled by the Stohlmeyer Foundation?'

He said it like it should have been general knowledge. 'I didn't know that. Why in the world would they cancel such an incredible project?'

'Precisely because it is incredible. The academic world doesn't like breakthroughs. It doesn't like upset and bother. It wants nice, safe confirmations of old theories. The unusual is frowned on, the extraordinary actively discouraged. So my grant money runs out in a couple of weeks. Unless, of course, I should produce a result so spectacular that it gets massive press attention. Then Stohlmeyer'd be forced to renew my funding or face embarrassment. This frog was to be my spectacular.'

'You can repeat the experiment on another frog.'

'Not in the time I have. It takes a lot of prep. To satisfy the protocols the review committee imposed on us, we have to prove the animal to be completely healthy before we use it. That takes a good week of observation and testing.' He paused, stared into his drink. 'Oh, God, when I think of how close I came.' His shoulders sagged. 'My problem with Brother Pierce started out so innocently. Three months ago I gave an interview to *The Collegian*. The very next Sunday Pierce was on my case. The seeds of ego bear bitter fruit, goddammit!'

36

She thought she ought to say something encouraging. She didn't much like George, but he was suffering now. 'You can keep going. I know you can.'

'The frog was just a first step. Next we were going to do a series on rhesus monkeys, then the big one. The experiment beyond the spectacular. It would have made me famous. Famous, Mandy! I would have rehabilitated my career. The Yale Sciences Board would have had to swallow their slap in the face. Maywell would have to stop treating me like dirt just because I've failed elsewhere. It's time that I got a little recognition, don't you think?'

Beneath her hand she could feel the bones of his shoulder. He was much too obsessed with his work ever to get any exercise. He was wasting away.

He slammed his fist into his palm. 'It's breaking and entering! Malicious mischief! I'm going to call the sheriff's office.' He got to his feet.

'You're sure it's your frog? Maybe it's another animal. Just symbolic.'

'That fanatic broke into my lab, killed my property, came over here, broke into my house, and assaulted me!' As he spoke, his voice rose to a pitch of renewed rage. He dialled the phone. 'This is George Walker, 232 Maple. Yes, I have a crime to report! Breaking and entering. Assault. Who's the victim? I'm the victim! And I know who did it. I know exactly who did it!'

He listened a moment further, then slammed down the phone.

'They're going to come by in a few minutes. Oh, *hell*!' He picked up the phone again. 'Bonnie? Hi, hon. Sorry to disturb you in the middle of the night. Look, will you do me a massive favour? I think the lab got hit by Pierce. Yeah, by Pierce. I'm 90 per cent certain. And I've got reason to believe he destroyed the frog.' There was silence, punctuated by a burst of language from the other end of the line. 'Go over there and check. And call me as soon as you can. I've

37

got to have complete confirmation before the sheriff gets here. That's a love, Bonnie. I'll repay in grades.' He put the receiver down. 'She's general lab assistant. Her dorm is just across the quad from Wolff. I ought to hear from her inside of ten minutes.'

Mandy had a strong feeling that he shouldn't have called the sheriff's office. 'George, try to calm down before the sheriff gets here.'

'Why? I've just been assaulted, I've had my experiment set back, maybe even ruined if I can't get another extension from Stohlmeyer. Why, pray tell, should I be calm? If anything, I ought to be raving mad. And I am!'

'Just stay away from the liquor. And brush your teeth. If they smell you've been drinking, they're going to ignore you.'

'Mandy, I was assaulted in my own bed!'

'Think about what happened, George. How is it going to look to a cop?'

She left him to dwell on that. Alone in her own room again, she fumbled through the closet for her robe. Deep tiredness weighed upon her. It was just after three o'clock. The moon had dropped low, leaving the room in shadow. By the moonlight that lingered outside she could still see the bulk of Stone Mountain rising behind the house, its thick coat of evergreens punctuated by grey-glowing tumbles of rock.

Mandy pulled on her robe and opened the window so that the cold air would refresh her. It smelled of the sweet rot of autumn leaves faintly tanged by old smoke. She could see Ursa Major wheeling above the dark high ridge of the mountain.

The Great Bear. Woman's stars. The little girls of Athens once danced beneath them, honouring Artemis the wild huntress, who prowled the autumn hills in the shape of a bear. As a child Mandy's favourite cuddly had been a stuffed bear named Sid.

Car lights shone on the back fence as the sheriff turned into the driveway. Mandy drew her robe close around her and went back to George.

He swept the front door open before the bell even rang. 'Come on in.'

'You the complainant?'

'I sure am.'

The deputy was a lean man, his face all angles and lines exaggerated by the porch light. At his hip he had a big pistol, too big for the thin hand that rested on its butt. There were dark glasses in his top pocket, one chewed fret dangling out. His lips were dry and cracked. There was what appeared to be a food stain on the crown of his hat. He moved forward into the house, and Mandy smelled chilli on his breath. He regarded George. 'Assault?'

'That's right.'

'You hurt?'

'Mentally I'm seriously injured.' The phone rang. George rushed to get it while Mandy stared back at the deputy, whose eyes had filmed in an unpleasantly intimate way the moment he saw her. Once she would have hated him, but too many whistles and whispers and unwanted touches had taught her indifference to men like this. As she had matured, their sexual insecurity had become obvious to her. She thought of them as frightened kids, unable to grow up, trapped on the rock of adolescence.

George's voice rose and fell as he talked into the telephone.

'Would you like a cup of coffee, Deputy?'

'Yes, ma'am. It tastes pretty good about this time of night.'

'Come on.' She led him to the kitchen, made him a cup of instant. She was just pouring the water when George burst into the room.

'Just as I thought, the frog's gone! That damn preacher got in there somehow and took it. And killed it. Shit!'

39

The deputy shot Mandy a questioning glance. 'There was vandalism at Dr Walker's lab,' she said.

'Now, that'd be a college matter. We don't go on the campus.'

'It started there,' George snapped, 'but it ended here. Come on.' He led the deputy into his bedroom. The remains of the frog lay on the white bed sheet, drying to dull green. 'There is where it ended. Brother Pierce or one of his robots came in here in the middle of the night and dropped that thing on my face!'

'Who did you say?'

'Pierce! That fundamentalist lunatic! He hates me and my work. He preaches against me! He's even led a demonstration.'

The deputy put his coffee mug down. 'You saw this man?'

'Of course not. I was asleep.'

'Now, if I understand you right, you're preferring a charge?'

'Of course I am! I'm charging that fanatic with destroying university property worth God knows how much, with breaking into my lab and my home, with throwing that thing at me with intent to harm me –'

'Brother Pierce is a respected religious leader in Maywell, Dr Walker. I don't think you ought to just go charging him like this, with no witnesses or nothin'.'

'He's the obvious culprit.'

The deputy glanced at Mandy. 'The Lord will be on Brother Pierce's side,' he said softly. His gaze returned to George, narrowed. 'You just ought to know that. Not to mention the law.'

'The law? I'm the injured party!'

'You're not hurt.' He ran his finger around the edge of the mug. Then he looked directly into George's eyes. He smiled. 'Not yet.' His voice was almost a whisper.

Poor George. No judge of men. Mandy saw his mouth drop open, then saw understanding slowly enter his face.

He shook his head. 'The college supports this town. You ought to be ashamed of yourselves.'

'You high-handed professors don't run Maywell. And the college ain't even the biggest employer. That's Peconic Valley Power. Anyway, I'm just givin' you some good advice. There's penalties against preferring false charges. Stiff penalties, Doctor.'

'Ah. So now *I'm* going to be arrested. That makes a great deal of sense.'

'Listen, ma'am, why don't you put him back to bed? And keep him off the hooch. It don't do him no good.'

The deputy moved to leave. In an instant George was on him, spinning him around, grabbing the front of his jacket.

And staring into the barrel of his pistol.

The gun had come up swiftly. It hung between the two men, its potential silencing them both. They looked down at it. Mandy could hear them breathing, could see sweat on George's brow.

'You take your hands off me, mister, and I'll put my piece away.'

Mandy closed her eyes in the long moment before the two men separated. She saw the deputy to the door. He was about to say something to her, but she closed it too quickly to give him the chance.

'Useless! Utterly fucking useless! I'm telling you, Mandy, I hate this godforsaken little town. These people get someone like me, do they care? Hell, no! I'm going to immortalize this place. That lab of mine will be a museum someday. People will come here to see where the mystery of death was solved at last! And this rotten little town spits in my face.'

Mandy listened to her uncle rave. Outside the deputy's car started up, its lights flaring briefly against the front windows. Then its sound dwindled into the night. 'It's late, George. We'd better get some sleep.'

'Sleep? I'm going to the lab. I've got work to do.'

Her impulse was to try to stop him, but she realized that

41

her efforts would only put him under greater pressure. She let him go.

In ten minutes his Volvo was cranking up, then rattling off down the street. She heard its tyres squeal at the corner, then silence fell about her.

She returned to her bedroom. Too bad the door didn't lock. The idea of staying alone in a house that had been entered as easily and recently as this one did not appeal to her at all. She hadn't been in bed five minutes before she thought she heard a noise.

It was a scraping sound, and it came from the sun porch. She sat up in bed, looking into the dark and listening. The night settled close around her. The moon had set, the crickets stopped. The world had entered predawn thrall.

Again it came. Definitely from the sun porch. Carefully she pushed back the blanket and sheets and swung to the floor. Her first thought was to go to the kitchen and get a knife. But she'd have to cross the sun porch to do that. She went instead down the hallway, feeling her way in the dense shadows, until she had reached the entrance to the porch. While the stars rode and dry leaves whispered past the windows she waited. There was a feeling of sickness building in her stomach; her skin sang with the tickle of dread. She could not endure the suspense of staying here; she had to act. She would turn on the porch lights. They would surely scare away whoever was lurking beyond the door.

The switch clicked loudly. And she clapped her fist to her mouth to stifle a scream. What she saw made her back away on shaky legs. Then she realized that those glowing eyes were an animal.

Only an animal!

She laughed around her knuckles. Her heart slowed its awful pounding. The cat meowed.

'You poor cold baby,' she said, coming into the light. 'Let me get you some milk.'

A stray cat at the door. What a joke. She had been

terrified. As she went across the sun porch, through the dining room, and into the kitchen, she turned on more lights. She opened the huge yellow refrigerator and found it almost empty. There was a dried-up sausage of indeterminate age and make, a package of Oscar Mayer cotto salami, a loaf of Pepperidge Farm Bread, and down on the bottom shelf a pint carton of half-and-half. That the cat would love.

She filled a saucer and went back to the sun porch. When she opened the back door, cold air came in, and with it a very fast, very large cat. She spilled a good bit of the milk jerking back as the animal made its rush.

It began lapping frantically at the spills on the floor.

'You *are* hungry, you poor creature!'

She closed the door behind it and put the saucer down beside its great head. It really was the most enormous cat. Black as sin, even its nose. It had a kink in the end of its tail and a ravaged ear.

'You poor, ugly old thing.' Gingerly she touched its back, half expecting it to bolt. But this was no wild creature. It arched to her touch, then drank all the harder. A starving, grateful, and very domestic beast. 'You're so sweet!'

She felt around its neck, but there was no sign of a collar. Her every touch drew a reaction from the animal. She found herself stroking it while it lapped at the milk, just to feel the undulating muscles beneath the soft black fur.

The cat finished and raised its head. When their eyes met, Mandy was fascinated. The eyes had a slightly sinister quality, the way they gazed so steadily back at her. They were sharply intelligent. The cat nosed her hand. It was silent; she could not seem to get it to purr, almost as if it was too independent for such an abject expression of gratitude.

'Are you still hungry?'

It stiffened, looked behind and above her. With the silence and grace of an angel it leaped over her head and into the hallway that led from the bedrooms to the sun porch. It was an amazing jump.

'Kitty?'

From the direction of her bedroom there came a loud meow, sharp with beckoning. Mandy stood up, feeling a twinge of fear in her confusion, and followed the animal.

Questions. How could a mere cat jump like that? And where had it come from? And what sort of cat was it?

And wasn't it beautiful, sharp-faced and glowing, lying on the foot of her bed, beckoning her with one open eye?

Fleas?

Ringworm?

Fever?

A meow, as soft as some heavenward breeze. And she *was* tired. She slipped into her bed. 'You be a good watchcat, now.'

Almost as if drugged, she slept. She dreamed she was Alice, falling forever down the dark well of Wonderland.

CHAPTER 3

George dumped the bedroll he had brought up from his car onto the floor of the lab.

'What the hell is this? You going camping?'

'Living here is the only certain way to guard this lab. Brother Pierce has flunkies at the sheriff's office. To be safe, we have to assume he's also got them among the campus cops.'

'I hadn't thought of that.' Clark touched the bedroll with his toe. 'I suppose you're right.'

'I am right. This is Pierce's town, not Constance's – a fact which we ignore at our peril.'

'Constance was unhappy to hear what happened. She sends you a good wish.'

'Why not an effective spell against that cretin? I'm telling you, Clark, Connie's got to either support me or abandon me. There's no middle territory with this.'

Clark looked steadily at him. 'I think a little equivocation is inevitable, given the personal consequences she faces if you succeed.'

George sighed. He couldn't really blame Constance Collier. He understood why she rejected him; his work involved the transfer of power at the Covenstead. Of course it was hard for Connie. One leaf falls, another takes its place. The tree persists, but for the blazing leaf autumn is a catastrophe.

'She has to accept it. She's getting old. God, they initiated her with a bullet to the head. She should be glad that science might take the risk out of it for Amanda.'

'Nothing will take the risk out of it. The risk is on the

other side. You might ensure that the body will come alive again, but nobody can be certain that the soul will find its way back.'

'So Connie says. But at least the inheritor's soul will have a body to return to. In the past that often wasn't the case.'

'The problem is, they don't always want to come back.'

'Well, that isn't our concern. We're only responsible for the body. Speaking of which, let's get to work and see if this lab's been booby-trapped or what.'

Clark moved to his station. He began testing their most important pieces of equipment, the devices that killed and restarted the intracranial electrical field. With this apparatus they were learning to turn brains on and off like electric switches. 'How seriously booby-trapped?'

George went to him. 'A problem?'

'Not yet. It just occurred to me that it might blow up in my face. A booby trap could be a bomb, if they're really serious.'

'Surely even Simon Pierce isn't a terrorist.' When he thought about it, though, George wondered if they might not be in greater danger than he had realized.

Clark obviously shared his concern. 'They've killed more than one witch, George.'

'The Gregorys?' It was supposed to have been an accident, the Gregory fire last winter. All four members of the family had been killed in their home. Libby Gregory was high priestess of one of the town covens.

George peered into the forest of wires that led to the isolation chamber where they had killed and restarted the frog. His gaze travelled along the red leads to each electro-magnetic coil. He was looking for a new wire snaking off to God knew what. 'I think it's okay.'

'Maybe we'd better stand back, just in case. And warn Bonnie.'

'Let's do more than that. Let's set the switches and then

hit the generator from the other room. And open all the windows.'

They went into the main control room. Beyond, in the menagerie, Bonnie could be seen cleaning cages.

'Hey, Bonnie, we're turning on the step-up transformer. Duck and cover, dearie.'

'What's going on?'

'Look at this. I say "duck and cover" and the first thing you do is poke your nose out. What if we were under attack? Do you realize that an atomic blast can vaporize you at four thousand feet? Unless you duck and cover, in which case you burn more slowly.'

'George, you're so weird.'

'Weird and wonderful, my little chickadee. If we live through this, let's go to bed together.'

'Clark, thrash that man.'

'Now, Clark, don't deny an old man his pleasures.'

'I'm not interested in Bonnie. I have other plans.'

Bonnie bristled at that. 'Constance going to marry you off to some pubescent priestess, eh, so you can mind the babies while your wife spends all night lathered with ointment balling the priests?'

'You could live on the Covenstead if you would accept its rule,' Clark said gently. 'It might do you a great deal of good.'

'I guess I'm too much of a rebel. Smelling all that health food when I go out there gives me an overwhelming compulsion to eat about four Big Macs. I'm best off being a town witch where I don't have to live by a rule.'

'We don't live by rules, Bonnie. We all agree on how we live.'

'Which means only that you're willing to push a broom for the anointed and take orders from teenage girls.'

'No, that's a complete misconception. There's no fixed hierarchy on the Covenstead. Bonnie, I wish you'd just give it a chance for a couple of weeks –'

47

'Okay, kids, let's not get into *that* discussion right now when we could be sitting on Brother Pierce's Fat Man on our way to Hiroshima. I've powered up the transformer. I'm going to open the lines.'

George stepped into the animal room with Bonnie and closed the door.

'George, is it really dangerous, or is your paranoia getting the better of you?'

'We've got to take precautions. They were in this lab, after all.'

'The other animals are fine, by the way,' Bonnie said. 'Just the one frog missing.'

George shook his head. 'The one frog.'

'I ran blood tests on Tess and Gort, to be sure there were no slow poisons or anything. They're in good shape.'

'Small blessings count in this impoverished place. We can't begin to afford new rhesus monkeys.'

'The lines are open,' Clark called. 'I'm activating the cage.'

'Wait. Get out of there.'

'I have to watch the readings. If we overpulse we'll burn out the whole thing.'

'It might be dangerous.'

Clark set his jaw. 'Constance assigned me to this lab.' He needed to explain himself no further. George understood the loyalty of the witches to their queen. As a member of a town coven, he felt it himself, although less strongly.

The lights dimmed when Clark turned on the extremely intense magnetic field that was the heart of the device. It was so powerful that electrons within it were forced to stasis. Electric motors in the field would stop, batteries cease to emit energy. And sensitive electrical systems, such as brains and nerves, would cease to function. A few seconds in this magnetic limbo sufficed to stop the animal's nervous system and render it effectively dead, although completely undamaged. As time passed, of course, cells would begin to deteriorate. Enough time and the deterioration would become irreversible. But before then the animal could be restarted by turning off the field and shocking its heart back into action.

The system was potentially safer than anaesthesia, and the suspension of critical body functions opened up undreamed-of surgical possibilities. George felt that his work was important even beyond Constance's wish to use it in the ancient ritual of initiation. If things went right, he had a chance at immortality here. He dreamed of a Nobel, a chair at MIT, himself strolling the byways of Cambridge in a ratty tweed suit, ripe in age and honour.

The witch ritual was the most important thing right now, though. He loved the craft, its spirit and its aims. And the danger and drama of true initiation, the walk in the world of the dead: that was the greatest possible human adventure, and he was excited to be a part of it.

The ancient ritual now persisted in the West only at the Covenstead. Animists such as American Indians had stopped practising it. Among the Apache, to become a shaman it had once been necessary to throw oneself off a cliff. Those who lived passed the initiation. Those who died, died.

George listened to the humming of the apparatus. It sounded fine. 'What kind of readings, Clark?'

'Looks like we're okay. No unusual power drains, no sign of damage.'

George returned to the main lab. He put his hand on Clark's shoulder. 'That was a brave thing to do, staying in here.'

'A calculated risk. I thought perhaps they wouldn't have the technical skill to hook a bomb into this system even if they wanted to.'

'Still –'

Clark powered down the field. The lights flickered again, and the cage made a faint crackling noise. A sharp stench of ozone filled the air. George pressed the floor switch that turned on the ventilators. He realized that he was shaking. He was surprised that there hadn't been any damage to the equipment.

Suddenly he was weeping. Most men would have looked away, embarrassed. True to the custom of the witches, though, Clark threw his arms around George and comforted him.

'You know,' he said softly, 'no matter how hard this is, we've got to keep going. I don't want to be maudlin, but frankly, an awful lot of people will be helped by our work. We have a mission, and that can't be forgotten.'

Bonnie came in and put her hand on his shoulder. 'George, we're with you. I'm with you.'

He wished she had been the one hugging him. But when Clark let him go, she judged the moment ended and also walked into the animal room.

This was followed by silence: it was not pleasant to know they were under siege. As it penetrated, this hard truth deepened their upset even more. 'What I don't get is, Pierce takes the exact frog we were working on,' George said. 'How did he know which one?'

'The isolate terrarium,' Clark replied. 'It's separate from the rest.'

'I guess. I hope we've seen the last of him.'

Clark stopped working. For a moment he appeared reluctant to speak. Then he seemed to gather some internal force to himself. 'Frankly, George, this Brother Pierce is a lot more powerful around here even than you realize. Oh, I admit he's been having his attendance problems lately, at least if you believe the paper. But the man has more charisma in his big toe than your average fire-breathing demagogue does in his whole *corpus delicti*. You oughta see this campus on a Sunday morning when Brother Pierce is working some big issue. Empty. And people are not sleeping it off, they are down at the Tabernacle for the Sunday Student Worship.

Even the drug scene at Bixter's is getting noticeably smaller. We're becoming a Bible college.'

'That's what we get for admitting all these Jersey rednecks. We ought to recruit out of state.'

'My point is, we're surrounded by the guy. He's everywhere. If a fundamentalist preacher can get something going on a modern college campus, he's all but unstoppable. And Brother Pierce owns Maywell State. Simple as that.'

'So what's our alternative? Shut down the lab and go home?'

'It amounts to a further impetus to work fast, in my opinion. Even beyond the funding problem. The longer we take, the more trouble he can cause us.'

'What do you suggest?'

'Damn the experimental protocols and go for the big win. I think the way to go is to move directly to the rhesus experiment.' Clark's eyes were hollow. 'Despite the problems we're bound to encounter.'

'But what about the Stohlmeyer people? We'd be violating our own experimental protocols.'

'We have an obligation.' His voice shook. 'Constance tells me that time is short. She can't wait much longer.'

'It's a hell of a risk.'

'What if this place is bombed or burned down? The risk of that could be even greater.'

Since the monkeys were already under health-status observation, it would take less time to work one of them up than to recast the frog experiment. In addition to proving an experimental animal's health, they had to measure the tiny voltages in its brain and adjust all of their instruments to them so that the creature wouldn't be in effect shorted out when they nullified its internal electrical field. It was a long, complex task. But they had been measuring the monkeys regularly for weeks. Clark had a point. It would indeed be faster to go straight to the monkeys and forget the frogs. The risks were clear: if they failed, Stohlmeyer would cut them off. Then there was the equipment difficulty. 'Monkeys are a lot bigger than frogs. How do we get money to expand the field?'

With a rueful look Clark withdrew his wallet, pulled out a VISA card. 'All I have.'

'Three thousand dollars on a credit card?'

'One thousand, sadly enough. And you're good for another, unless I miss my guess. Or did Kate pick your bones?'

George's bitter reply echoed through the dank, animal-scented lab. 'I'm good for another thousand only if I can get a loan on my car.'

'We could try Constance. It's just a little cash. Surely she can give us that without exposing the link between the lab and the Covenstead.'

Bonnie called from the animal room, 'You know how conservative she is, George. You'll never get it out of her.'

'She wants speed, yet she doesn't like us to kill a few animals. And she won't give us any money! Constance either has to commit to this or forget it. You tell her that, Clark. Unless she gives me the money to expand the cages, I'm throwing in the towel.'

'No, George. No, you aren't. You know we can't risk a financial link between the Covenstead and this lab. And you need your Stohlmeyer. Otherwise, how will you gain legitimacy in the outside world? Research funded by witchcraft? Come on.'

'Constance could find a way,' Bonnie called. 'She's just tight with money.'

Clark ignored her. 'We'll manage, George, somehow. I wish I was rich, I'd kick in the whole amount. Since she's so committed, maybe Bonnie can kick in.'

George's eyes brightened. 'Hey, Bonnie, that's a wonderful idea. You'll surely invest money in your brilliant professor.'

A loud guffaw from the animal room. George opened the

door between the two rooms, letting an even more powerful burst of odour into the lab. Swamp water and frog piss, sour bananas and monkey shit. 'It's our rice bowls, Bonnie. All three of us.'

'I seem to recall that I'm on a scholarship. Where am I supposed to get money?'

'You buy plenty of dope over at Bixter's, my dear girl,' Clark said. 'I've seen you score a quarter-k at a time.'

'What're you, the house dick? Do they keep conduct cards on us out at the Covenstead now? Eh, Mr Starch?'

'You poor woman. You're a witch, and you're still not free. We know that the difference between good and evil is illusion. We also know not to confuse the two.'

'Goody.'

'The real truth is that you know that nobody cares at the Covenstead whether you're a bad little girl or not.'

'Oh, no, they just get those condescending smiles on their faces –'

'They don't care! Your bondage is your guilt. But it's yours, Bonnie. You should take a lesson from Constance. She knows what it is to be free.'

'Bonnie's bound, Connie's free. Sounds like some kind of a spell to me.'

'I can't get through to you. You just do not understand that the evil *is* the guilt.'

Bonnie sneered. 'Drop the holier-than-thou condescension, will you? It bores me. I can be a damned good witch without your help, Clark.'

Shaking his head, he went into the animal room. 'Let's concentrate on the problem at hand. If we don't come up with three grand worth of coils for the rhesus field, we are out of business.'

George followed Clark. Bonnie was preparing a likely-looking frog for its physical. 'If we compress the observation time to forty-eight hours, we can be on-line with this beauty by Thursday night.'

'There's yellow gik coming out of its anus, Bonnie dear,' Clark said.

'That's A & D ointment. I just took its temperature.'

'Clark makes a good point, Bonnie. If we expanded the field we could go with a rhesus tomorrow morning. As soon as we get the coils.'

'I have no money. And we couldn't pry another purchase order out of accounting with a crowbar. So let me finish getting little frogger here measured.'

'Bonnie, we can get two thousand dollars between the two of us. Surely you're good for another thou.'

'Wrong.'

George went close to her. There were two ways to characterize this little witch: one, she was delicious and delightful; two, she was one stubborn lady. At night she swam through his senses. But only in fantasy. She wouldn't take her old professor seriously. 'Even in the animal room you smell like an angel.' She smiled. 'Bonnie, you know what this means to me. I'm past fifty, darling.'

'I'm well aware of that.'

'Aside from making me as sexually interesting to you as it so obviously does, it means that I will die a sad old man if I don't succeed with this experiment. You're young, you have your life ahead of you. This is my last throw, honey. After this, sunset and bye-bye.'

She put the frog back into its terrarium. 'George Walker, you are a hypocrite, a charmer, and a bastard. If I gave you a thousand, it would be out of other people's money. Their happiness money. And they would be so mad if they couldn't get high. Mad at me.'

'What do I have to do, go down on bended knee?' Even as he spoke, his eyes went to the two rhesus monkeys in their big cage. They stared back at him, sullen and bored. He could sense their hatred.

'It might be fun to watch but it wouldn't help.'

George went over to the rhesus cage. He was tempted to

make a face back at the ugly beasts. 'How much smaller is Tess than Gort?'

'Tess is eighteen pounds. Gort's twenty-two.'

'I mean in body mass?'

'Tess is 56.75 cubic centimetres of monkey. She's approximately 77 per cent of Gort's mass. What are you getting at?'

'Tess might fit into a three-foot field. That's only nine more coils. You wouldn't have to give any money.'

'Good. My customers would kill me very, very slowly if I stole their money. And that's what it would amount to. I've got about sixty dollars of my own.'

George put his hands on her trim hips. She did not move away and she did not respond. She simply became very still. Such plans he had for this slip of a girl! If the rhesus phase succeeded, she was next. Dear little Bonnie was going to be the first person to die and live to tell about it. Assuming he could convince her. Assuming the mere suggestion didn't send her running for the nearest bus depot. But the problem of convincing her didn't need to be faced just yet.

George wrote out a purchase order for the coils. When they were delivered, Tess, poor dear, would have a most extraordinary experience. Oblivious to her future, she sat in her cage delousing her mate and rolling her lips back. If George worked at it, he could probably get Techtronics to deliver before noon today. They had trucks up to the college all the time.

Dear little Tess. Not a big rhesus, not a scared rhesus. Not yet.

CHAPTER 4

Mandy didn't need a map to find her way to the Collier estate.

It took up the whole southwestern corner of the Maywell township and went beyond. The lands of the original grant included Stone and Storm mountains and the valley between them, an area of eighty thousand acres in New Jersey and Pennsylvania. Mandy drove down Bridge Street towards the entrance to the estate.

A stillness filled the morning air. Red and yellow and orange trees overhung the old brick street. Here and there children dawdled past on their way to school. Beside Bridge Street and sometimes beneath it Maywell Brook shimmered in the sunlight. Autumn was the slow season for water, and the brook sighed along its gouged, muddy bed. It was all so familiar, so peaceful, as if she had left only a few hours ago. But the years had changed the familiarity of Maywell. Once this place had been, simply, life. Now it hurt to be here.

Mandy glanced at her watch. 9:20. She was due to meet the great lady in ten minutes. The great and dangerous lady. As a child Mandy had been cautioned never to speak to Constance Collier – not that she ever had. Except for her occasional forbidden intrusions onto the estate with other kids to watch witch rituals, she had only once or twice glimpsed the legendary figure sitting regally in the back of her enormous old Cadillac limousine, driven to some local function by one of her earnest acolytes.

On one memorable occasion she and Constance had locked gazes, as the old lady was driven slowly down Maple in her big black car. That was when life at the Walker house was entering the deepest level of hell. A quart bottle of gin went into the garbage every two days, and the arguments made *Who's Afraid of Virginia Woolf?* sound like a Marx Brothers film.

High up in her maple, Mandy had observed the car. It was moving very slowly. As it drew near she realized that the old woman was watching her carefully.

Sometimes she dreamed of that car, coming unlit down the night street, and sometimes of the old lady drifting out of it like mist which would slip across the lawn, beneath the shadow of the maple tree . . . and then she would see the tall, severe shadow in the hall, or feel a bony hand on her forehead . . .

Once she heard her father screaming in the basement, and there was a low, sharp voice between the screams, and little Mandy had thought, She's in the house. Constance Collier is in the house.

In the morning she had decided that it had to have been a dream.

In those days Constance had seemed frightening. Now the fact that she was a witch was a matter of indifference to Mandy. What she was interested in was this illustration assignment. There was no reason Amanda Walker couldn't become the next Michael Hague or even the next Arthur Rackham. Beyond that, though, illustrating a Grimm's offered her a chance to express her craft to the fullest.

Mandy was convinced that her visions of the fairy tales were original and powerful and new. Surely they would stun the art world if they were ever painted.

All that stood between her and success was this final interview. It promised to be hard. How had Will described Constance Collier? Quixotic. Rude. Imperious. And you were never late to an appointment with her. *Not ever* was the way he had put it. From her own past, Mandy could easily imagine Miss Collier to be even harder to deal with than Will had said.

Soon the forbidding brick wall that marked the townside edge of the estate appeared out of the right window of the Volks. It was vine-covered but in excellent repair. Iron spikes jutted up from it, hooked out at their tops. Perhaps the incursions from the town had grown more aggressive in recent years. There was no scaling that wall now and dropping over, sweaty and breathless, knees skinned and heart pounding.

The main gate, which Mandy had never before entered, was securely closed. Mandy pulled up and got out of her car. The gate was simple, almost stark, made of wrought-iron bars topped by more spikes. It might as well have enclosed a prison. Along the top of it were the familiar brass letters, 'This Land of Dark,' from a line of Constance Collier's great poem, *Faery*: 'Entered she this land of dark, borne by the mist's own hand.'

How very quiet this place was, and how old. The trees soared huge and silent. The only sound was that of an occasional leaf whispering to the ground.

Beyond the gate was a narrow dirt road, curving off into a thick forest the kids had always avoided, preferring to go the long way around, by the fields.

Mandy pulled and pushed at the gate until her feet scraped on the brick paving. The hinges didn't even creak.

She looked left and right – and saw a small gateman's house with its iron door hanging open. Inside was a disused telephone on a frayed cord. She picked it up, put it to her ear. 'Hello?' Dead. 'Great.' It was now 9:30 exactly. 'Marvellous.' She was getting off to a wonderful start. She would be fired before she even met her employer.

But she mustn't be fired. This just had to work, it had to. Her alternatives were bleak: illustrating the covers of paperbacks or maybe getting into advertising. To Mandy there was no thought more horrifying than that of being forced to abandon her vision and just use her skill. She had seen such people, had even interviewed in a few ad agencies.

It had chilled her to walk down the long rows of trendy offices, each with its light box and drafting table, and see the grey people huddling there in frayed designer jeans and Yves Saint Laurent shirts.

She deliberated climbing the gate.

Then she saw that there was another door in the back of the gateman's house, one that led into the estate. It opened easily. As she pushed it, paper rattled. There was a note taped to the back, where it couldn't be seen from the street. 'Please be sure this locks behind you, Miss Walker.'

Obviously this was the way she had been intended to come. Nice of Will T. Turner to tell her. He really was a very marginal person.

Once inside the estate she went around to the back of the main gate and looked for some sort of a handle. There was nothing.

Furious that none of these procedures had been explained to her, she hurried back to her car and parked it as far off the road as possible, then dragged her precious portfolio out of the back seat and re-entered the estate on foot. All of her most important work was in this worn black case, everything she had ever drawn or painted relating to Grimm's fairy tales.

The portfolio was heavy. Mandy couldn't be too mad at Will. He tried hard. If she had been planning intelligently, she would have called Miss Collier last night to reconfirm, and found out about this hike.

A few moments after she started off she found herself slowing her pace, despite her lateness. Finally she stopped altogether. She simply could not help it. She was in a wonderful cathedral of trees, their black trunks stretching to crowns of brilliant autumn colour. Leaves littered the dirt road, marking the dust with bright splotches.

This was awesome. Too many months in Manhattan had made her forget the passionate silence of the woods. She began to walk again, now also noticing the rich scent of the air, cleansed by autumn rot.

This place was not only beautiful and dark and huge, it was also something else she could not quite name. The very slightest of shivers coursed through her body and she began to walk a little faster. It was as if the wood itself was not entirely unconscious.

She had no idea how long this road might be. In any case it was longer than necessary to make her thoroughly late. She marched along lugging the portfolio, trying to hum and not succeeding.

Her imagination was really too vivid for this. 'You know I'm here, don't you,' she whispered. Leaves stirred down. The trees filtered the bright morning sun to golden haze.

The colours here were magnificent: these must be very robust trees. Plants die gaily because they are sure of their own resurrection. Not so higher creatures. All things that share the terror of final death are brothers, from the microbe to the man.

The road curved upward, finally cresting a hundred yards ahead. Long before she was close to the top, Mandy was breathing hard. Even so the chill of morning had vitalized her. She felt physically wonderful, her whole body singing.

What, she wondered, was the origin of the legend of the watcher in the woods? This place was so alive, but not in a human sort of a way. Trees were enigmatic beings. She knew that man had once acknowledged this alienness by considering them the temples of his most mysterious gods, the forest spirits. Now those gods were cast low. Who once had been worshipped in the woods was today captured in fairy tales and called a troll.

Grimm's was the net, after all, in which the Christian world had captured the old gods, diminishing their power (or so it thought) by making them the stuff of children's stories.

Just this side of the crest she came to a darker place

in the forest, where the trunks of the trees seemed more enormous, the carpet of leaves thicker.

She saw a small face, very still, peering at her from a hole at the base of one of the trees. Her imagination, of course.

She bent close, and watched with horror as it took on the absolutely solid appearance of something quite real. She started away from it, giving a little, involuntary cry. The sound was rendered tiny by the immensity of the place. And the face was quite terrible.

It just didn't seem possible that something so small, so strikingly inhuman, could be there – but she could still see it in outline even from ten feet away. As she watched it, an awful coldness seemed to slide up out of the ground and possess her whole body. She dragged her portfolio around to the front, a fragile shield.

She backed to the far edge of the road. She was suddenly freezing cold, almost sick, fighting the impulse to panic flight.

Her mind worked frantically, seeking some way of explaining the impossible presence. A dwarf? No. Perhaps a statuette. Yes, that must be it.

But she could see the moisture gleaming on its eyeballs.

She decided to get out of here. She would phone Constance Collier from the safety of some coffee shop in town.

Her watch told her it was 9:45. By the time she got back to the car and drove into town it would be 10:15 at least. Over the phone Miss Collier could so easily tell her to forget the whole thing.

There really was no choice. Reason said that she was not facing some supernatural creature, not a troll, not one of Constance Collier's faeries. Such things were not real, not any more.

But a mad dwarf from some nearby mental institution could be very real. And wasn't there a Peconic Valley Institute for the Criminally Insane?

Either she walked past it or she gave up this job.

Shaking, her hands clutching the portfolio, she started off for the crest of the hill. More than anything, she expected to find that the apparition in the hole was gone, a figment of her vivid imagination. But it was still there – staring out of blank stone eyes.

She stooped to look more closely at what was now quite clearly a little statue. It was a sneering, evil little elf, a creature of the cracks and holes of the world. Perhaps a mandrake, or a little *fee* guarding the lands of Faery.

> A wood of fabulous spells,
> Old sticks and roots and holes,
> *Leannan*'s grand dominion . . .

When she remembered those lines from *Faery*, the menace of the woods evaporated like a rotten mist. As with new eyes she looked around her. What had been hostile was now suffused with wonderment. The little face was not sneering, it was grimacing to frighten any who might threaten its queen. One of her doughty fairy soldiers.

Mandy was delighted. These were the actual woods of the poem. Here a twenty-year-old Constance Collier had written the dream of *Leannan*, the Fairy Queen . . .

With a newly confident tread, full of gladness and awe, Mandy marched to the top of the rise.

Spreading before her was a magnificent vista indeed. The road had been carefully planned to take advantage of it. It meandered down across the rolling green fields to a long lake dusted with lilies and swans, and thence across the wide pasture that led to the house. How typical of Will T. Turner to describe this place simply as 'crumbling.' Had he been forced to leave his car at the gate and come on foot also? Probably trudged this very road, thinking that the gate was rusted closed, the leaves not raked, that there were rather too many lilies in the pond, and the green was high with cockleburs and dandelions.

And he never noticed that he was in the Land of Dark, where lived the Faery of Constance Collier's extraordinary creation. Poor Will T. Turner.

Emerging from the woods, Mandy set out across the fields, filling her nostrils with the dry, sharp scent of autumn brush, her mind flashing image after image of paintings that must be painted here.

Late or not, Constance Collier had an illustrator. Amanda Walker had decided that she would not be driven off, not even at the point of a gun.

I'll do Hansel and Gretel in the woods, of course. And Briar-Rose's castle from this vista, with the thornbushes choking the ramparts in just this light.

Everywhere she looked there were more glories, wonderful wooden fences all tumbling down, a shattered hayrick, a great rusting contraption of scythes that must once have mowed the lawns.

How exactly right Constance Collier was to let it go to its natural state. If ever there had been happy land, this was it.

Oh, Pollyanna, smile on. You are heading towards a rough meeting with a very difficult old lady. Constance Collier eats illustrators for breakfast. She had quite literally fired the great Hammond Morris by burning the pictures he had done for *Voyage to Dawn*. When she heard that story, Mandy had felt contempt for Constance Collier. But she hadn't been offered this job then.

As she approached the house, she began to see that it was indeed in serious disrepair. The architecture was Palladian and very elegant, red brick and white columns, a lovely curved side porch, tall empty windows. Leaves were everywhere, choking the gutters, matting the walks, blowing about on the porch.

There wasn't a sound. Despite the cool air, the bright morning sun was making Mandy sweat. Her portfolio had grown heavier, and she was glad to lean it against the wall when she finally reached the house. She went up between the tall, peeling columns and hunted for a doorbell. She settled for knocking.

Her blows echoed back from within. There wasn't an answering sound, not the clatter of feet, not a call. When she knocked again, though, there was a startling flutter of wings at the edge of the porch. Six or seven huge crows wheeled about in the front yard, then settled into an oak and commenced to caw at one another.

'Hello!'

The sound of her voice caused the crows to rise again. They rushed back and forth across the weedy yard, their wings snapping with every turn.

When she knocked, the door rattled. It was obviously unlocked. Telling herself that old people are hard of hearing, Mandy turned the blackened brass knob and pushed the door open.

Inside was a shadowy central hallway with rooms to the left and right. The hall runner was old but fine, the lighting fixtures elegantly fluted. When Mandy pushed the buttons on the switchplate, none of them turned on. She looked at them; bits of wax revealed that they were now used for candles. Halfway down the hall a brand-new Panasonic vacuum cleaner could be seen in an open broom closet. At least there was some electricity still in the house. This touch of modern technology gave her hope, until she saw that the machine was not only new but not even completely unpacked. Its body was still in a plastic bag; as a matter of fact, all the packing material was visible beyond the end of the hall, in the kitchen. Somebody had been wrapping it up, perhaps to send it back.

As she proceeded into the house, the crows crowded onto the front porch, cawing and bickering among themselves, their voices echoing in the silence. But also, there were softer voices, and they were nearby. 'You've got to be more careful,' said a man. An older man, whispering. An elderly woman: 'I *must* keep on. By the Goddess, I'm so close!'

64

'Miss Collier?'

A gasp at the top of the stairs, then silence. Mandy sensed that she had interrupted a very private conversation. She would have returned to the front door, but by this time she was closer to the kitchen, so she hurried towards the back.

In the centre of the kitchen was a heavy oaken table, its legs elaborately carved with gargoyles and grapevines. On it there was a toasting frame, of the kind meant to be held over an open fire, and a partially cut loaf of homemade raisin bread.

As Mandy crossed the floor, she noticed that there were candles in the lighting fixture that hung down from the ceiling.

And then she saw something really amazing: an ancient iron hand pump at the sink in place of the usual faucet. Attached to the wall behind it was a small hot water geyser such as Mandy had seen in the cheap hotels she had stayed in during her European days.

The stove, to the right of the sink, was a huge woodburning iron monster with eight burners across its massive top. 'Royal Dawn' was embossed in the ironwork on the oven doors. The witch could have cooked Gretel in such an oven and had room left over for a couple of nice casseroles.

A thrill of childhood fear touched her. She'd never seen this place, but Jimmy Murphy and Bonnie Haver had sneaked in and seen a beautiful young woman cooking at this very stove. 'She was pretty but her face was glowing in the firelight,' Jimmy had said. 'She was so scary I thought I was going to pee in my pants.'

That had happened ten years ago, half a lifetime for Mandy. If Constance remembered, it probably seemed like yesterday.

From beyond the kitchen window there came the first loud sound Mandy had heard at this house, and it more or less astonished her. It was a splash, followed immediately by the distinct *boing* of a diving board.

Could Constance Collier possibly be in swimming – a woman past eighty, and in autumn? Mandy hurried out the back door and down an overgrown brick walk, which curved around a tangle of cedars. She came now upon another surprise. The walk ended in some brick steps, which led into a formal garden – overgrown, of course – surrounding a swimming pool inlaid with elaborate mosaics which shimmered beneath the agitated water.

A young man, lithe and pale, his blond hair streaming like smoke behind him in the water, swam vigorously from one end of the pool to the other.

'Hello?'

Oblivious, he swam another lap.

'Excuse me.'

He stopped, touched the edge of the pool. 'Oh.' When he stood up in the waist-deep water, Mandy saw that he was naked.

She was instantly angry at him for flustering her, and spoke quickly. 'I'm sorry to disturb you. I'm looking for Miss Collier.'

'She's not in the house?' He showed no inclination to hide himself. She tried to keep her eyes on his face.

'I called. Nobody answered me.'

'She's supposed to be in there having an argument with my father.' He came out of the water, grabbed a towel from the grass, and began drying himself. 'Were her birds there?'

'Her birds?'

'The seven ravens. They're almost always with her. If they were there, so was she.'

As the boy approached, the towel around his shoulders, Mandy realized that he was younger than he had seemed. Perhaps he was sixteen. Adolescent down brushed his top lip. 'I'm Robin,' he said. Mandy knew she was colouring; Robin was very, very beautiful, in all the ways she enjoyed in the male. His muscles were firm but not knotty. His skin was smooth, yet he did not look soft. And his genitals were, well, very much there.

He had been waiting for some moments before she realized that he was holding out his hand. She took it, pumped it once. He held firmly to her hand, raised it to his lips, and kissed it. She felt the warmth of his breath on her skin. He smiled slightly, glancing down at his own turgidity. Mandy battled not to shake, and she inwardly cursed the heat she could feel in her cheeks. 'I'm Amanda Walker,' she said evenly. 'The illustrator. I'm doing the Grimm's project with Miss Collier.'

He shook his head. 'I don't know anything about it. Perhaps Ivy can help you. My sister.' He took a step closer to her. She could see his teeth behind his half-opened lips. His smile was so subtle that it managed to imply passion and politeness at the same time. Nothing could be read in his obsidian eyes, which contrasted oddly with the blond hair and sunny Nordic skin.

'My sister is sunning herself in the maze, where the breeze can't get to her.'

Mandy had not realized that the great tangle of cedar in the centre of the garden was, or had been, a maze. She was glad to turn away from the young man, though. He had a nerve not even wrapping his towel around himself.

Close up, the maze smelled strongly of cedar oil. Mandy found the entrance and went a short distance in. Robin's renewed splashes were absorbed by the thick and long-untended growth. There remained only the faint screaming of the crows. The creosote path was so overgrown that Mandy had to go on her hands and knees to make any progress.

It wasn't a difficult maze, because the way in was marked by a string. No wonder; there was no fun to be had struggling through these weedy corridors full of spiderwebs and sticky cedar balls.

At the centre of the maze was a complete surprise, a

delightful secret garden. It was perhaps thirty feet square, and peopled by statuary. All the figures were characters from Constance Collier's books: there was Pandoric, the wicked horned boy; opposite him his mother Drydana, who had the power to turn herself into a woodpecker. At opposite ends of the garden were Braura the huge maiden bear, rearing up, her bronze claws gleaming in the sun, facing Elpot, the King of the Cats, who had one shredded ear and knew among other things how to fly. In the middle, on a marble pediment, stood the Fairy Queen, the tiny *Leannan*, Constance Collier's greatest creation, beautifully sculpted, with her trim waist and alabaster arms, her firm nose and delicate lips, and her wide grey eyes. The sculptor had captured not only Miss Collier's description of her character but the deeper wildness that sent the *Leannan* racing through her forests, 'the wild huntress screaming so shrilly that it froze the footsteps of whom she sought.'

'Excuse me. Who are you, may I ask?'

'Oh, I'm sorry! The statue – I'm Amanda Walker. The illustrator. I'm here for my appointment with Miss Collier.'

'You were meeting her in here?'

'Well, not actually in this spot. But here, yes, at the estate.'

Ivy rummaged among the things that had been spread out around her, pulled out a blue-faced watch. 'It's 10:30. She's still with my father.'

'Do you know if she was expecting me?'

'I don't know. I've been here almost all morning.'

Ivy was every bit as handsome as her brother. Mandy found her presence, though, even more disturbing. There was something confusing about her looks, the strong-muscled arms and legs, the tiny breasts beneath the prim black bathing suit, the soft, gentle face with those dark humorous eyes. If such a woman were to embrace her, Mandy wondered, what would happen then?

'I'm afraid I'm terribly late. I was due at 9:30.' The girl stared at her, almost as if she thought her mad. 'A mistake,' Mandy added miserably. 'Please help me.'

The girl smiled at that. 'You sound like you're desperate.'

'I know she doesn't like people to be late. The job is very important to me. And I'm *so* late!'

'You she'll forgive, Amanda.'

'Where can I find her, can you tell me that?'

'Look what I have here.' The girl bent down and picked up a big, colourfully illustrated book that Mandy recognized at once.

'The Hobbes edition of *Faery*!'

'Signed and hand-coloured by Hobbes just for Connie. Isn't it wonderful?' She gave the precious volume to Mandy almost indifferently.

'But this – it's extraordinary. I didn't even know it existed!' She looked down at the leather embossed cover. Reverently she opened it. Tucked inside was a photograph of Hobbes sitting with a much younger Constance Collier on the pediment of this very statue. He wore a wing collar and a striped shirt, the cuffs rolled up to the elbows. She was in a long dress, its top of lace. Her dark Celtic eyes gazed merrily at her companion, who looked rather stunned.

This book was not illustrated with washed etchings as Mandy had assumed but with the delicate original water-colours that had been their models.

A Hobbes watercolour of this quality went for five thousand dollars. And how many were here? At least twenty. 'My God.'

'See *Leannan* sinking dead,
her eyes pearled by dew,
Falling all ruined upon
fearsome Braura's bed.'

Amanda was surprised at Ivy's erudition. 'You know *Faery*?'

'Of course. Why do you think we're here, Robin and I? We are students, just as you are a student.'

'I'm an illustrator.'

'That was only a pretext to get you here. You'll see. She's got all sorts of ideas for you.'

Just then a new voice cracked from among the cedars: 'There you are, you prowling ninny! Come out of there! Why didn't you come upstairs? You must have heard us.'

'Miss Collier?'

A tall, thin woman in a dusty suit appeared among the shrubs. She burst forth brushing spiderwebs and twigs from her tweeds. 'What in Goddess' name are you doing in here? Oh! What do you have in your hands, you stupid girl!'

Mandy was horrified. All she could do was hold out the priceless book and hope that Ivy would own up to her wrongdoing.

'Don't give it to me! I'll drop it on the way back. Oh, be careful, careful! Don't let those cedars touch the leather, they'll start acid rot going! How could anybody be so thoughtless! Come on!'

Mandy's heart pounded as she hurried along behind Constance Collier, the precious book cradled in her arms. Back in the maze she heard soft laughter and realized that brother had joined sister from some hidden entrance, and both were enjoying the joke together.

She followed Constance through the kitchen and into a tall library, its bookcases laden with calfskin and morocco bindings. A heavy silence descended, punctuated only by the crows. Finally Constance spoke.

'Put it on the table. There. Now, young woman, are you mad? You must be to come in here and take the very best volume I have and carry it out into the sun, and then you go into that dirty old maze – it's criminal.'

'I didn't –'

'No excuses! If you want to work with me, the first thing

you've got to learn is to stop making excuses. I consider excuses loathsome.'

Mandy knew she was turning scarlet, and hated herself for it. Blushing was a curse. But there was nothing she could do about it. She could only hope against hope and push ahead. 'I brought my portfolio, Miss Collier. Of the ideas I've had for the Grimm's illustrations.' Should she add that it contained *all* the really good ideas she had ever had for Grimm's, and amounted to the best of her life's work? No point. The sketches and paintings would speak for themselves.

Constance Collier replaced the Hobbes in a slipcase on the leather-covered library table. 'He killed my husband, in case you've ever wondered. Hobbes killed Jack.'

Mandy recalled that Jack Collier had died under somewhat sensational circumstances back in the early twenties. A hunting accident or something. 'I didn't know that.'

'Shot him. Shot us both.' She stared at the book for some moments. 'You come highly recommended.' She looked up, her face for the first time clear to Mandy. It had the startlingly simian appearance that is sometimes associated with great age. Here and there were vestiges of the legendary beauty of the twenties and thirties, the dramatically straight, thick eyebrows, the narrow, angled nose. Gone, though, were those full, mysterious lips and the amazing lusciousness of complexion that Stieglitz had captured in his portraits of her.

Oddly enough, the same years which had devoured her sensuality had granted Constance Collier a deeper mystery yet: despite the fact that she was slack and dry, almost a leaf of a woman, her eyes shone with intense light. Mandy found herself very badly wanting to know her. Such eyes must hide wonderful things, or why would they shine so?

Mandy could readily imagine herself becoming a student of Constance Collier's. All the childhood mystery would be dispelled. More, she was fascinated by this place, the ancient kitchen, the candles, the maze, the strange adolescents. She *had* to be allowed to stay!

'I think I left my portfolio on the porch.'

As Mandy went towards the front of the house, the cawing of the crows got louder and louder, until it was a bitter, crazy cacophony, full of inscrutable passions.

The flock rose like an angry belch of smoke when Mandy opened the door.

She stood, shocked beyond words. Her own scream was so naked with rage that it made her clamp her lips shut.

The crows had torn her portfolio and all of her drawings to tiny bits and scattered them about the yard.

She stood staring, disbelieving, shattered. Her whole past, everything she had done that was fine, had been destroyed by the brainless creatures.

She hardly noticed when Constance Collier stole near, a knowing and sympathetic look on her face, and placed a consoling hand on her hunched shoulder.

CHAPTER 5

The acid, frightened stink of Long-hands made Tess scream. Her voice woke Gort, who screamed with her. She ran the cage, feeling the wind rushing in her face, perch to far bars, far bars to back wall, bang against back wall to front bars, swing back to perch.

She had gone far, but she was no farther from Long-hands. There was stinking fear coming from him, and it infected her. Tess screamed. Again she ran the cage. Her own fear confused her, made her hands do what they shouldn't. She hit Gort.

At once he showed his fearsome teeth and she thought how great was this monkey and cast her eyes down an instant to say, I am yours.

In that moment Long-hands reached his fingers around her. She screamed and screamed and bit the fingers so furiously there wouldn't *be* any hard fingers anymore, but Long-hands only made a growl, 'Sheuht!' and kept on taking her out of her home.

She hated it outside of the place where she had all her smells and all Gort's smells, and where Gort kept his body. Out here she couldn't run the cage, perch to far bars, far bars to back wall, over and over with the wind in her fur and Gort running too the other way, and passing each other and then tumbling down on the floor in their good smells together so glad.

Long-hands had her now, had her good. She tried to twist around and bite his face but she could not; she was being carried by Long-hands far away from Gort. She screamed. Gort screamed. Then she was brought into a man-smelling place and there was a bang and the wall closed up and she was away from Gort and all alone.

'She's all worked up, Bonnie. What's the matter with her?'

'She's kind of high-strung, you know that.'

'We can't put her in the field like this. She's liable to crack the coils.'

Tess heard their growling, heard the fear in Long-hands' voice, and knew the truth that he might have Tess but he was scared of Tess, so she showed him her teeth. She bared her strong, sharp teeth to make him submit. But Long-hands did not fulfil the law, he only held her farther away and kept up his frightened growling.

'She'll have to be sedated!'

'The protocols –'

'Leave it off the report. Dose her or we can forget using her.'

'Stohlmeyer will never accept it.'

'Bonnie, don't you understand English? Dose her and do not make a record of it!'

'We're getting sloppy, George. That's very sloppy.'

'Do what I tell you! We'll let her sleep it off and then run the experiment when she's groggy.'

Little Yellow bared her teeth at Long-hands, but Long-hands did not submit to her any more than he had to Tess. She realized his power then, and understood that it must be so great that it smelled like fear. If Tess could not frighten such a monkey, and Little Yellow, the bringer of food herself, couldn't do it, then Long-hands was just too powerful.

She grew calmer, knowing that there was nothing for her but to submit to the power of the awful Long-hands.

'Well, well, Tess, you finally getting tired? You bitch. I think we can skip the Valium, Bonnie. She's just gone as limp as a dishrag.'

'Handling does that to them sometimes. But it'll only last a few minutes.'

Long-hands put Tess in a cage so small that she couldn't even turn around. Certainly she couldn't run it. All she could do was lie down and feel the hard bumpers push on her stomach and her knees and her hands and her head. But this was Long-hands' will, and Tess was not strong enough to break it.

'Okay, Clark, she's in the damn thing.'

'I'm getting a good reading. Nice and strong. It's a pleasure to work with something that has a decent microvolt level. Those frogs are almost below the threshold of observability.'

Tess soon realized that the little cage didn't smell like Long-hands. So that meant he had freed Tess. But Tess couldn't move, not unless she pulled and kicked.

'Hurry up! She's getting crazy again!'

'Ready on the countdown.'

'Forget the countdown! Just do it! Go!'

'Okay, power's up. I'm activating the field – now!'

The whole world collapsed on Tess. She lost everything, her strength, her voice, her smells, her sounds. She screamed and screamed and screamed but there was no noise, there was no calling to Gort or even Long-hands to help Tess out of this awful nothingness. And falling! Falling and she couldn't find branches, she couldn't clutch leaves!

To the ground, the leopards, the hyenas, the stinking monkey-eating monsters that slip as shadows in darkness!

Terror slammed her like a great hand, she saw bared teeth and heard snarling death-growls, and she clutched and climbed and kicked – emptiness.

Then she smelled the most beautiful scent she had ever known, the best and most beloved of all scents, from when she lived in the forest where they ate green pellets sweet off the trees and danced between branches. She smelled the milky-soft breast scent of her mother.

Mother, it's me!

She clutched soft mother fur and warm skin. And mother

took her between her legs where it was so, so safe, and began preening her.

Around them there arose the whole old forest again, the same trees, the same delicious green water, the same thunder-cold joyful waterfall, the sweet, fresh smells of monkeys everywhere.

Mother again. Forest again. And all around in the trees the gib-gabber chatter of the Roaring-water-nearby troupe, the Clown, the Great Grey, the Little Browns, all the girl squealers.

Her mother preened down behind her ears where the mites got itchy and thick.

'Beautiful! Bring her up.'

The voice that had resounded across the sky left a smoking yellow rip where it had passed.

Mother hissed danger and Tess grabbed fur and they were off! They swung with the troupe through the bending, sighing trees.

A white wind was following them. White, dead! It was crushing the whole forest, the tall trees falling before it like sticks. It gasped and wheezed, sounding like something enormous marching through the wood.

Mother swept along, faster and faster, raging as she went, screaming back at the huge monster that had come through the tear in the sky. Its feet stomped and thundered the ground, its breath washed over them.

Tess screamed when she smelled it, for it was the odour of Long-hands and Little Yellow and their awful place-without-monkeys where Tess never, ever wanted to go again!

Do not take me from my forest, do not take me from my troupe!

The giant came closer and closer. Mother was screaming, carrying her Tess now low to the ground, now high in the branches, darting and turning as only a mother could, rushing along beneath low shrubs and among the rocks, uncaring of her own cuts, then grabbing a branch and sweeping up higher and higher to the very top of the forest and leaping as if she had wings.

There was a great thud.

The forest evaporated.

Mother fell screaming away into nowhere.

Tess felt the hard little cage poking her from all sides. Agony exploded in her.

'Good Christ, Bonnie, tranq her down, tranq her down!'

'I'll get the gun. I can't do it by hand, she's too wild!'

'Oh, Christ, look at that – open the cage – Clark, give me a hand. She's going to crack the ceramics.'

Tess leaped up into the hateful stinking ugly place, her heart breaking for mother and forest and all the joys just tasted. She jumped to the floor and ran, crashing into walls, screaming so loud she heard Gort screaming back from the other room.

Not that hateful place again, not that poor old Gort when she could have mother and forest and the troupe! No no no no *no*!

Monkeys cannot beg for mercy. They can only make the gesture of submission. She made it. She made it to the walls, to the ceiling, to the floor, seeking the terrible giant who had dragged her back here, trying to somehow say, I submit; I, Tess, submit to your power.

So let me go home.

The monkey stopped moving. Bonnie went up and checked its eyes. 'She's unconscious.'

'I was afraid she'd break those coils.'

Bonnie gathered the creature up in her arms and returned her to her cage. She reconnected the electrocardiographic leads to the sockets in the animal room so that Clark could continue his monitoring.

'It's amazing, isn't it?' George said. He stared down at the sleeping rhesus.

'I have to admit it, George. Yes, it is. A higher animal.'

'Clark, are you okay on the readings?'

'She looks normal from here, George. Looks good.'

'Bonnie, I told you this job would be an adventure.'

'It's certainly that.'

George reached in and touched the fur of the comatose rhesus. 'She hates my guts, you know that? She nearly bit through those handling gloves.'

'You show her you're afraid of her. She tries to dominate you.'

George drew close to Bonnie. 'I wonder what she experienced.'

'Nothing too pleasant, judging from the way she acted when we brought her back.'

'I think we can be sure that was a side effect related to the re-establishment of the brain's electrical field. I suspect she'll be fine when she wakes up.'

'You might be right.'

'You don't sound convinced.'

'I'm convinced. I'll be even more convinced when she wakes up normal.'

'Let's go look over Clark's shoulder. The EEG ought to tell us a lot.'

Clark was standing before the electroencephalograph watching the readout. His face was sharp with concentration.

'How's it look?'

'Still normal in every way.' He smiled. 'The Stohlmeyer Foundation is going to like this.'

'What must that monkey know?' Bonnie asked. 'I wonder if death is like a dream or just black? Probably a sort of descent into zero.'

George was watching her closely. He realized that this was the moment to broach the subject of Bonnie's taking the journey herself. 'It's going to be the greatest adventure in human history to find that out.'

'Nobel Prize time, George,' Clark said.

'Assuming we proceed to a human trial,' George added.

There. He had said it. All three of them knew that two more coils would make the cage large enough for Bonnie's body mass. And they could get two more the same way they got the others. No money, just some more lies and another hot purchase order. All that stood in their way was Bonnie herself.

'Somebody's going to get the answer to a hell of a secret,' she muttered.

'Somebody's going to become very famous. A heroine.'

Her eyes snapped to meet his. She had caught the gender. 'I know I'm the obvious choice. But the cage isn't big enough for me.'

'If Tess wakes up all right, that'll be the deciding factor. I can get two more coils with no problem.'

Realizing for the first time what George was driving at, Clark went grey. 'Constance isn't going to be comfortable with this. We haven't done the testing we said we would do. She might forbid us.'

'Hell, don't tell Constance! Don't tell her a thing! Just do your job, Clark.'

'My job is to report to her, you know that.'

George could picture Connie's reaction to his precipitate scheme: 'Oh, no, don't let him do that. He's so impatient.' Then, next day: 'Clark, you must tell George to hurry. Time is very short.' George had to convince Clark not to report to her. 'Now, Clark, you and I both know what Constance will say. She'll say that time is short.'

'You'll never convince her to go to a human trial so soon.'

'It isn't her business! I make the scientific decisions. You go to her if you want to, but I won't be here when you come back. I just can't work with the Stohlmeyer people looking over one shoulder and Constance looking over the other!'

'I have to inform her.'

'Do it and the project is over. Cancelled.' Clark squirmed. Good, he was afraid to take responsibility for that. George pressed his argument. 'Tess is alive.'

'You're a witch, Clark,' Bonnie said. 'Be faithful to the needs of the witches. If Constance dies before her successor is initiated, what will become of the Covenstead?'

Good for Bonnie! There was a game girl. 'So make your choice, Clark. Report to Constance and I quit. Or do your job right here and now and we all succeed together.'

Bonnie put her hand to her throat. 'I wish we could smoke in here. I'd really like a cigarette.' She laughed. 'I've decided to do it,' she said. There was wonder in her voice, fear in her eyes. Now she whispered. 'I want to know . . . to be the first.' Her tongue moved along her lips. Once again George saw how very beautiful she was, the delicate lines of her face, the casual sensuality of her mouth, the frankness of her eyes. She was precious to him, and he ached to kiss her, and feel that mouth open to him. Her cheeks were flushed.

'You'll be an adventurer. Afterwards someone as beautiful as you – the press'll make you a star.'

'Constance will never allow press,' Clark put in.

'Constance will have no choice,' George snapped. 'If Bonnie wants press, by the gods she gets press!'

Bonnie went over to the apparatus on the lab bench. She touched the gleaming black coils of the electromagnets. 'I could sit in it as is if you could make it a little higher.'

'No. I want you lying down. Safety.' He did not add that, as a dead body, she would slump over from a sitting position and simply fall to the floor, taking the whole apparatus with her. She walked around the bench, looking at the array of devices. 'You know,' she said at last, 'I am going to know once I do this. I mean, you guys, I am going to *know*.' She smiled, and when she did, George thought her as soft as a newly opened rose. 'I'm a second-rate witch, but I'll bet I'd be a first-rate media sensation.' She smiled her brightest smile. 'I wonder if I can act. Maybe I could parlay it into a film career.'

'Not if you can act,' Clark muttered.

Privately George doubted that she would be all that famous outside of scientific circles. What she was going to bring back, after all, was the news that death was death. Nothing. Blackness. Not much newspaper copy in that. 'You'll be like an astronaut,' he said.

She came to him and kissed his cheek. The two of them drew closer together, the explorers.

In her cage Tess screamed once, her anguish surfacing even through the drug-induced sleep. Then she subsided, and slept on.

CHAPTER 6

It had been hours since she left the Collier estate, and Mandy's rage and despair had not subsided in the least. She had driven around town until she was no longer too mad to cry. Then she had taken to the privacy of her uncle's house and locked herself in her bedroom.

Now even the tears were exhausted. She lay on her bed listening to the evening sounds of the neighbourhood. A leaf blower roared, a child called again and again a name she could not quite understand.

She certainly wasn't interested in the banalities of a small-town evening. Her mind still orbited her loss: that portfolio had contained images from her soul. Without it she felt herself more alone than she could ever remember being, the centre of a very private circle of pain.

The big black cat appeared. She stared, confused. Where had it come from? The bedroom door was locked.

It leaped onto the bed and rubbed against her thigh. Its fur felt silky and nice beneath her hand. As she stroked it the cat stretched. She seemed to remember from her childhood that Uncle George disliked cats, but until he came home and demanded it be put out, this magnificent beast was staying here. The cat moved suddenly to the far side of the bed. 'Here, kitty,' she said, and patted the place beside her. Her words sounded silly: you didn't say 'kitty' to a near panther like this. It lay down and commenced staring at her. She found herself gazing back into its eyes. 'You're such a nice old tom,' she murmured. It really was very beautiful, with its night-black fur and green eyes. She listened for purring, but there was none.

One could look very deeply into this cat's eyes. If all cats were like this one, gypsies would tell fortunes by gazing into their eyes. But cats generally look away.

In his eyes she could see her own face. How did she appear to him? Was she lovely, ugly, or what? Did he think of her as a goddess or a child? She touched his shredded ear and got a throaty growl in response. 'Sorry.' In apology she stroked his back. His muscles shuddered beneath her hand, as would a man she was stroking to arousal.

As would a man. But she had no man. And she had no work. Some of those paintings had consumed months.

Constance Collier had been furious with her crows and most apologetic, but nothing could alter the loss of the portfolio. Given that Mandy was twenty-three, unmarried, childless, and most essentially alone those paintings and sketches had been her family, her centre, the reason and sense of her life.

The tears came back, stinging her eyes. Furiously trying to quell them, she told herself that the pictures were not everything. Of course not *everything*, but they were her best. Among them were her treasures: her portrait of Godfather Death, which in some miraculous way had captured the laughter as well as the menace of Old Nick.

How could she ever do that again?

Or Rapunzel shaking out her hair, all that blonde glory bursting in strands of morning sun – painted strand by delicate strand. Will T. Turner had made her laugh by comparing her technique with the masterful Van Eyck brothers of fifteenth-century Holland. But there was something in it: she had spent a great deal of time studying their work. Detail. Care. Richness of vision. Not the ideals of twentieth-century art perhaps, but she thought of herself as being from long, long ago. She was lost in this quick age. Her art belonged to the perfect grace of the past – even the very distant past.

Once she had dreamed of a time before the bison had left

the plains of France, when winter had the name of a demon and cracked his breath like a whip . . . and she had been a queen reigning in a reindeer-skin tent . . . and making paintings in the sacred caves, the brush gliding in her fingers as if by magic, and the bison and the ibex racing across the plains of her mind.

When she woke up from that dream, she had wept to be herself, and to hear the droning of a bus in the street outside, and smell the smell of coffee on the morning air.

She had hurled herself into her work, spending four months on the little painting of Sleeping Beauty's castle behind its wall of thorns. And in among the thorns she had hidden the old world, the running deer and the flailing mammoth, the fish snapping in the water and the men like ghosts among the protecting gnarls.

The Sleeping Beauty carried in her soul all the promise of the future; the potion that drugged her was the past.

An artist's work is the issue of her body, and Mandy felt as if her children had been killed by Miss Collier's crows. The Seven Ravens indeed. The Seven Monsters.

She imagined an image in the cat's eyes: herself dead, her sea-pale skin soft against a pale sheet. We trust our souls to such frail vessels, a bit of skin, a beating heart, paint upon paper.

Suddenly she came up short. That had been a very vivid image, and it was not the first image of her own death she had experienced in the past few days.

Was she somehow in danger here? There had been all sorts of rumours about the witches, but none that suggested evildoing.

'Is that what you're telling me, old cat? Be careful of Constance?'

No, she knew what the cat was saying: Be careful of George. Yes, of course, George. He might come to her in her girlhood bed, come with pleas that became demands and the gleaming of a knife in the moonlight.

Tom preened himself. He stared at her. He could certainly capture her with those eyes. She kissed his forehead. 'Who are you? Who are you really?' His cat face of secrets seemed to laugh.

Once right out under that maple tree, she had dreamed of being a mother. A vision had come, of leading children to the banks of a river and watching as they splashed at the lily pads.

Knights had come, plunging their horses into the water, and she had escaped in a silver fairy coach.

She had painted those children – who were really fairies – as Jack and Jill. Quick, passionate strokes, Mandy seventeen and flaming like a comet, the two jewels of children laughing down their hillside to eternity.

That painting had been destroyed.

'It can be a blessed thing to lose the past,' Constance Collier had said. 'Sometimes what seems a treasure can really be a burden. You oughtn't to hate my birds for giving you a chance to start fresh. Great paintings have been made on this land. Give it a chance, and it will nourish you, too.'

The ravens had circled and circled, then alighted in a fine old maple and stared at Mandy with their blank yellow eyes.

Abruptly the cat raised its head.

'What's the matter, Tom?'

The cat gazed long at her, then licked her hand.

'Surely you can't be hungry?' She had remembered only one thing on the tear-blind way home from Constance Collier's house, and that was to buy a bag of Cat Chow. Tom had eaten heartily not half an hour ago.

The cat got up and stood over her, looming, enormous, its breath coming in sharp little growls.

A patter of fear touched her heart. It was, after all, a stray. 'What on earth is the matter with you?'

For more than a few seconds the cat stared. Then a shudder passed through the animal and it went to the foot of the bed, jumped down, and moved off towards the door.

'No, you don't.' She had lived with more than one cat and she suspected she knew exactly what this was about. 'I fixed up a litter box for you in the mudroom.' She got up, unlocked the door, and took the animal by the scruff. It was heavy, but she was able to drag it across the linoleum floors of the dining room and kitchen. 'Litter!' She pressed its nose into the box she had set up for it. 'You stay in here for a while, Tom, you'll get the idea.' She shut the cat in the mudroom and went back to the kitchen. It was nearly eight; she had been lying in that bedroom long enough. A nice little meal would be just the thing to cheer her up.

She opened the refrigerator.

Until the accident she had been intending to clean up George's house for him, and to fill the fridge and the cabinets with food. He was not much of a bachelor. Without Kate and the kids his life had obviously lost much cohesion. Kate had left him so abruptly. One day here, the next gone.

As Mandy had not done any shopping for human food, her choices were rather limited. She touched the stiff old sausage on the top shelf. What might it contain, besides bacteria?

She was forced to settle for a very dubious sausage sandwich.

By the time she had gotten the big iron skillet out of the cabinet and put the bread in the toaster she had exhausted the small reserve of psychic energy her long brood had built up.

The cat yowled. In a while it would get desperate enough to use the litter box. Probably it had its own accustomed litter outside. Maybe she shouldn't domesticate it. Maybe she had no right. This might be as much of a country animal as the ravens.

'Those birds aren't pets,' Constance Collier had said, 'they just live here. I suspect the flock's ancestors inhabited this place long before the house was built.' She had paused then and regarded the birds. 'Animals are in eternity,' she had added. 'How long do you suppose ravens and trees have been together on this very spot? One maple giving way to another – how long? A hundred thousand years? It's been that long since the glacier receded from the Peconic Valley.'

Mandy couldn't be too angry at someone who thought such thoughts.

There came hissing from the mudroom. Loud hissing. 'Black Tom, Black Tom run from the fire, run from the fire!' Mandy chanted as she sauntered back to see what was amiss. 'What's your trouble, kitten-cat?'

The growl that replied clapped like angry thunder. Mandy drew back.

Then she peered through the glass panes in the door.

The mudroom was empty.

At last the calls of the suffering, bereft monkey had become too strong for the cat to ignore. Tom had paced the little room looking for some explainable route of escape but had found none.

Its patience exhausted, it soared up from the house, wheeling across the evening town, just touching the top of the streetlight at the end of Maple, swishing through the crowns of trees. Birds fluttered away as it came. Dogs and cats dashed about below, panicked by its passage. A rat, falling from a wire, died before it touched the ground.

Tom flew through the evening hush, feeling the sleepy breath of the sky, crossing streets and alleys and houses faster and faster, passing over Bixter's and through the frying-hamburger odour coming from its chimney, then over Brother Pierce's Tabernacle, from which there rose the high-pitched excitement of a man too frightened of death not to preach damnation.

Then it reached the campus.

It was full of righteous fury. This experiment was unlawful. Constance didn't seem to care. Why didn't she put a stop to it? Was Tom being used by Constance yet again?

Despite his great powers, she had outsmarted him more than once, the cunning devil of a woman.

Had it dared, it would have come here with a sword of fire. But it knew that it had not the right to destroy George Walker unless doing so furthered the overall plan of Constance and the *Leannan*. Those were always the terms of the spell by which Constance conjured the King of the Cats into a brief earthly life.

The tom entered the lab. At least it could take pleasure in relieving the suffering of the rhesus. Far from being forbidden, this was a required stitch in the weave of the story.

The King of the Cats swept into the laboratory where George Walker sat eating a Stouffer's pizza in his underwear, his sleeping bag arranged on the floor beside him. George did not even stop chewing as it blew past him and through the closed door into the animal room.

The beast with the raped soul lay on its belly in the bottom of a miserable little cage, its mate crouching beside it. They had been preening one another. Now they slept.

They did not see the air shimmer before them, roiling and flickering. First there was nothing but a fanged grin hanging there, then green eyes above.

To make this kill quick and quiet, the cat needed the dexterity of a human shape, and a silent weapon.

It concentrated, remembering the smell, the shape, the heft of the human it knew best.

The eyes shattered and re-formed, now hooded with pallid skin, and the lips became those of an old woman, proud and delicate and firm.

Then the whole of the withered old body, quite naked, appeared suddenly in the air, dropped a few feet with a gasp, and stood poised, its fierce, kind face working with the palsy of years, a long, bright needle gleaming between the thumb and forefinger of its right hand.

Because one of this mated pair had been so terribly

wronged, both could be blessed with death at the same time. They had earned that very special joy.

It was with the greatest pleasure that the shape of Constance Collier raised the long, sharp knitting needle and drove it deep into the eye of one of the monkeys, then through the heart of the other.

An instant later only the weapon remained to mark her swift passage, that and the thin streams of blood running to the floor from the bodies of Tess and Gort.

CHAPTER 7

Without the cat the house was unpleasantly quiet. Small signs of her own past were everywhere, appearing before her like carp in turbid water, rising with their accusatory eyes. Overhead in her bedroom was the light fixture she had bought with three months' allowance, the roses she had painted on it faded to ugly smudges. On the game room wall there remained a faint streak from the crayon mural she had drawn there when she was ten and home alone, for which infraction her mother had given her the only spanking of her life.

She had hated the path worn across the living room carpet, and she hated it now. There were still holes in the sun porch ceiling where Mother had hung her plants.

Through her adolescence she had heard the tired acts of her parents' bedroom from this sun porch, sitting out here in the night with her legs tucked up under her, swinging in the porch swing to the creaky rhythm that shook half the house. The only reason she came out here was that not only the squeaking but the groans penetrated her own bedroom.

She had the awful feeling that she had not lived her youth. Where were the passions, the loves? All destroyed, pecked to pieces. But those were no real loves, those paintings. Could she really love? So far she'd had only casual relationships.

It was awful here. She ought to go down to Bixter's and see if the Pong machine was still there. Of course it wasn't, but they probably still made their famous crème de menthe soda, and there was always the magazine rack.

She sat listening to the water drip, still trying to work the loss of her portfolio to the back of consciousness and still not having much success.

She wished Tom would come back.

The telephone tempted her. Maybe a good talk would help. But she had lost her most recent male friend from half-intentional neglect, and the thought of falling back on him now only made her feel trapped. She could count on him to listen, though. Richard. Tall, sweet, sloppy in love. A sexual sentimentalist, capable of waxing talkatively nostalgic about the most private moment of love.

His love might be sticky, but it was also simple, and that she respected.

When his phone didn't answer, she supposed it was fate and hung up.

Didn't George ever come home from his lab? Everywhere she looked in this house she saw evidence of more deterioration. She had found newspapers from over a year ago lying beside a chair in the games room. George's sheets were slick with dirt; she doubted he had changed them since Kate left. There was a stack of *Persian Society* magazines on the floor of his bedroom with, oddly enough, all the pictures of the cats cut out.

She imagined that she heard his tread, saw his gaunt, haunted figure. She remembered the hate and terror in his voice when he had found the remains of his frog.

George had wept. Afterwards, in his misery, he had stared longingly at her. He was full of tormented need. Any young, attractive woman, if she wished, could make him worship her.

Worship. A cold, distancing word. She would rather have passion from a man. But from George, nothing. The idea of being intimate with him made her want to bathe.

Even so, she wouldn't have minded a nice chat.

An hour passed. Nine o'clock and the old family clock that still dominated the living room chimed eight rusty hours.

The clock had been too massive for her parents to keep when they moved to their trailer retirement in Florida. It told the cycles of the moon on its face, the sickle, the half, the full. They rode a landscape dusted with small blue flowers. Dim within it there could be seen twelve shadowed figures dancing about a thirteenth.

Nine o'clock, Friday, 16 October, 1987. The silence that followed the chimes seemed invested with obscure dangers, as if it were there to prove the menace of the house. Mandy thought again of the cat.

A search for him wouldn't hurt. She went out into the backyard.

Overhead, stars cluttered the racing gaps in the clouds. A sickle moon had risen and rode the quick sky. Wind swept leaves to running like night smoke from the trees, rustling over eaves and dancing branches against windows. The cat was nowhere to be seen. Mandy drew the collar of her sweater close about her neck and went back to the house.

She locked the porch door behind her. All the windows were locked already; she had done that earlier. The house was as tight against intrusion as she could make it.

She found herself returning to the mudroom. The ceiling light darkened the windows and made the white walls glare. The mystery of the cat bothered her more in the dark. There was no place in here it could be hiding. Certainly not under the sink, which was the only enclosed space. Even so, she checked there, finding a mouldering box of Spic & Span and a pile of dirty, dried rags made from old undershirts.

Before the sink was the trapdoor to the cellar. She had not opened it earlier – what point, the cat could not have gone down there. She did not want to be alone here, not with the shadows and the moon clock.

Maybe the trapdoor had been ajar, falling closed as the animal passed. When she pulled the ring, the door came up with oiled ease. From below rose the familiar odour of the basement, unchanged since her girlhood. She peered down into the darkness. There was a click, followed by the faint roar of the furnace starting. Yellow, flickering light from the firebox reflected off the walls.

'Kitty?'

There was no other sound.

Mandy reached into the dark and felt for a light switch, then remembered that there was only a string at the bottom of the stairs. She began to descend the rough wooden steps in the faint shaft of light from the mudroom above.

She reached the floor, found the string, pulled it. No light: the bulb was long since burned out.

Once her eyes got used to it, the combination of the glowing firebox and the mudroom light made it possible for her to see a little. She glanced around, ducking beneath the fat tentacles that issued from the top of the furnace, the ducts carrying their heat to the reaches of the house. This was the way she had come on the most secret missions of pubescent love, a willowy, confident little girl, her nervous chosen boy in tow.

Opposite the furnace was a door set in a roughly made wall of cheap pine panelling, the builder's fifty-dollar 'wine cellar,' and the scene of those early experiments, one or two of which had left indelibly torrid impressions, the first, confused genital contact and the exploding pillow of pleasure that came with it. She had held his shaft in that room, too afraid and excited to move, listening with half an ear to *General Hospital* on the TV in the family room above.

On the door now was a rude sign painted in red ink: 'Kitten Kate Club. Keep Out!'

The sight of the rough letters pierced Mandy's heart: this must have also been George's kid's secret room. More evidence of lives departed. Did those kids also remember their little room, even now whisper about it?

It was not easy for Mandy to open the door, but she did it.

When she saw what was on the other side, she could not even scream.

She just stood, gasping, disbelieving, staring. The walls, the floor, the ceiling, were painted and scratched and clawed with images of cats. Panthers crouched, wildcats leaped, toms and pussies lounged and crawled and spat, and here and there was a photograph of a dismembered cat. Spiked to the wall were bits of cats, fur, and shattered bones, and in one corner a gape-jawed feline skull.

There was a dirty sheet wadded on the floor. The place stank of something like rancid grease. A votive candle stood in the centre of the mess.

There was hatred here that seemed beyond the capacity of a human being. She realized that this was no children's place.

Only an adult mind had the patience to create this. A tortured, confused mind. Profoundly insane.

No wonder Kate had taken her children and run.

Mandy shrank back, closed the door to the ugly secret, then returned quickly to the mudroom. Her cat wasn't in the basement. She wished she did not know what was. She dropped the trapdoor, went back to the kitchen, turned on a light. She sat at the kitchen table, her head in her hands, feeling the secret of the house like a festering, rotting sore on her own body.

> How odd the Girl's life looks –
> Behind this soft Eclipse –

She whispered the words into the yellow Formica tabletop. Emily Dickinson knew secrets of women. So perfect to call the predicament a soft eclipse. Emily . . . you knew so much, wise Emily. And you hid on your little farmstead, far from life, far from the madness of men. I wish I were there with you right now.

Behind this soft eclipse . . .

To George, womankind, it seemed, was a cat. Kitten Kate.

So sick. So sad. So dangerous. She must leave here at once.

She stood up, thinking to go and gather her things. But there was movement outside. As footsteps ran up the front walk, her flesh crawled.

'Mandy!'

The voice was high, shredded like that of a desperate woman.

'Mandy, let me in!'

'George?'

'Yes!' He howled out the word, rattling the knob as he did so. His voice was literally squeaking with rage. Miserably frightened, feeling trapped, Mandy unbolted the door.

He swarmed past her, muttering, stalking as dangerously as a spider through the shadowy house. 'Sonofabitch! Son of a fucking bitch!'

He disappeared into the bedroom. At once thuds and crashes started. 'George!' She found him hunting through the bottom drawer of the dresser. Scattered around him on the floor were shirts and belts and about a dozen fat bullets. 'George, what are you doing?'

'That sonofabitching Jesus freak killed my rhesus! My *rhesus*!' He produced a large black target pistol with a long barrel, began scrambling for the bullets.

'George, what's got into you? Put that stupid thing down!'

'I'm gonna blow that bastard away! I was right next door in the lab and somehow or other he got in and killed my monkeys with a knitting needle.' He stopped, every muscle in his body tensing, his eyes screwed closed, his lips twisted back from his teeth. He clutched the gun in white, trembling fingers. 'He stabbed them!' A huge, terrible sob tore through him, more a bellow than a cry.

He got up.

'Give me the gun, George.' He laughed, started for the

door. Had she thought about it, she probably wouldn't have dared to stop him. But her instincts were stronger than reason: she grabbed his elbow and spun him around. 'You don't even have any proof.'

'I don't need proof! There's nobody in the world who hates me like he hates me.'

'His whole congregation. You said yourself he preached against you. It could have been any one of them.'

'He may not be *personally* guilty, but –'

'You aren't a court of law. You have no right to take his life. Go talk to him, threaten him, even spit on him if that makes you feel better, because, George, I am sure he is a bastard. But you give that gun to me.' She fought down her terror. He was so crazy. She couldn't let him destroy himself and another human being, too. She must not fail to get the weapon.

He swayed, then bowed his head. 'You're right, of course. I really can't afford to be put in jail.'

'Of course not. Give it to me, George.'

Suspicion flashed through his eyes, to be replaced by an expression too mixed to come into a sane face: it was made of cruelty and love and something that might have been laughter.

He gave her the pistol, which she returned to its place at the back of the drawer.

'George, I want you to try and calm yourself down. You need rest, and I think you could use a doctor, too.'

'I need to frighten that maniac into leaving me alone. And I think I know how to do it.'

'Now, look, George.'

'I'll go mad if I don't confront him! I've got to do what I can for myself, don't you see that?'

There was no way out of this. The man was going to have his battle. 'Come on, then,' she said. 'If you insist on going, I suppose I can't object. At least let me drive you.'

'You don't need to get involved.'

'I said I'll drive you. I don't want you getting into trouble.'

'He ruined me!'

'You'll keep working! You'll find a way.'

She had hoped that he would calm down riding around in the Volks. Then they would stop somewhere, have a drink, and she would take him home. When he was asleep, she would leave for a motel. Tomorrow she would deal with the issue of the Collier estate and the job.

He looked all in, shivering, huddled in his seat. 'My only alternative now is to go to a human test and hope the Stohlmeyer people overlook the sloppy pretesting. That's all I can do to save the project.'

'A human test?'

'It'll be safe enough. Hey, you took a wrong turn. The Tabernacle's at the corner of North and Willow.'

Too bad he had noticed that. She took a right onto Taylor from Bridge Street, still trying to engage him in a diversionary conversation. 'I met the great Constance Collier. It was quite an experience.'

He couldn't have been less interested. 'I'll bet.'

Dull pain returned as she recalled her own tragedy, but she said nothing about it now. 'Her estate is perfectly beautiful. And she seems rather good-hearted, actually. Despite all I've been told.'

'Constance Collier is a great woman. She means an enormous amount to me. Since your time, Brother Pierce has become her sworn enemy. He came in 1981, after you left. Last year he and his minions tried to get Miss Collier to put her name on something called *The Christian Faery*, and she responded by suing them for using her characters. He claims she's a pagan.'

'That's part of being a witch, isn't it?'

'To some extent. At any rate, witches certainly aren't Christian. That's what's gotten him so worked up. Take a right on North Street. We're almost there.'

Too bad.

The Tabernacle was a low building, obviously a cheaply converted warehouse. Cars were parked helter-skelter in the dusty lot that surrounded it. Light shone from within through windows that had been covered by 'stained glass' Con-Tact paper. A wide sign, clean and bright and professionally painted, loomed twenty feet above the roof of the building. I AM THE LIGHT, proclaimed the black letters against the white background. Enormous carbon-arc floods crackled at the four corners of the sign, blasting it with preternatural brightness. From behind the stained-glass windows came a powerful roar of song: 'O God, our help in ages past . . .'

Mandy could tell by the cars that Brother Pierce's followers were working people, most no doubt unemployed and desperate in this steel and coal country, clinging to his simple answers for support in a hard time. Despite herself she was moved by the power and resolution in their voices.

'I didn't expect a service,' George snapped. 'But I guess the guy's always got a service going on here nowadays. The whole damn township worships at his alligator-shod feet. The ones who don't follow Constance, that is.'

'Why don't we go have a drink? Come back after it's over.'

George ignored her. Before Mandy could stop him he was through the door. She followed.

The church was not filled to capacity, but there was a very respectable crowd. Mandy had thought that the fundamentalist movement was on the wane – but easily three hundred people were here, and on a weeknight. There were many young people, no doubt students from the college.

'Welcome, brother and sister!' A puffy, sweating usher rolled towards them from his station near the door. He continued over the last bars of the hymn. 'I believe you're new, aren't you? Praise the Lord who has brought you into his Light.'

'I want to see Brother Pierce!'

The usher's voice dropped to a whisper as the hymn stopped. 'Well, now, he's the one with the white hair, the tall man right up at the front.' He smiled. 'That is Brother Pierce. If you're here to offer repentance, you're not too late. He hasn't called the sinners forth yet.'

'I want to see Brother Pierce!'

'George, keep it down!'

'Brother Pierce! I'm Dr George Walker of the Biology Department!'

Faces turned, some expressions quizzical, some darkening at his tone. At the front of the church the bright blue eyes framed by the white mane of hair flickered to intense life. It occurred to Mandy that both of these men might be psychotic. And yet there was something very different about them: where George seemed cruel, there was about Brother Pierce something of the terrible kindness of the ignorant – the sort of kindness that used to burn witches to make sure they would go to heaven.

'I want to know why you killed my laboratory animals, Brother Pierce. Why you destroyed my experiment! Was it because it would free people from the fear of death, which is what you use to enslave them?' His voice cracked and trembled, but did not die away.

Now accompanied by three much younger men, the usher rushed up the aisle behind George. Mandy came after them, her mind spinning. George enraged was a human fireball. It took courage to challenge a fanatic in the middle of a crowd of his followers.

'I said I am Dr George Walker –'

'*I know who you are!*' Brother Pierce's right arm came up, his finger pointed. 'And I know you cannot help being here. The demon brought you, for you are but his instrument. But I love you in Christ, George, we all do.' He raised his arms, nodded.

The entire congregation responded: 'We love you in Christ.' The joy among them, the warmth, was at once

99

overpowering and affecting. Mandy was not sure she would have recoiled had one of them taken her hand.

'You shut up,' George roared, 'all of you! You killed my animals and I want restitution. I demand restitution!'

'Good people, we have never done violence to this man, much less to the poor creatures he sees fit to torment in his heathen experiments.'

'You killed my frog, you killed both of my rhesus monkeys!'

'We did nothing of the kind. Satan has closed your eyes to the good of the world. I urge you to kneel and pray with us for the deliverance of your soul.' He turned and knelt to the cross that hung against the back wall.

'You lying bastard!'

'O Lord, we beg you to open your heart to this lost one, that he may be delivered from the spell of the Deceiver!'

'Shut up, you old shit! You *shit*!'

Two of the young men took George's shoulders. He shrugged them off, took a menacing step towards Brother Pierce.

Mandy had to act. If she didn't, these people were going to throw off the patina of loving-kindness and give George the beating of his life. 'Leave him alone!' She pushed past the ushers. 'I'll take him home.' She put her arm around his waist. 'Come on, George.'

'Go with her,' Brother Pierce said sweetly. 'Go with that unholy harlot!' His blue eyes were glaring at her, lit to shimmering coals by the fire in him. 'You pagan.'

George was most definitely not the only madman here. She must have given some sign of her thoughts, because Brother Pierce instantly sensed her dismay and raised his accusing finger. He pointed it directly at her.

'You demon! You dare to bring your filth up from the pit.'

She tried to reply through a dry mouth, but her words were only whispered. 'I'm a perfectly decent –'

Brother Pierce's voice rose in an instant to a spitting, overamplified bellow. 'Yea, you are a demon! For I see you as you are. Oh, yes! Yea, "they had tails like unto scorpions, and there were stings in their tails. And they had a king over them, which is the angel of the bottomless pit, whose name in the Hebrew tongue is Abadon!"'

Mandy was too astonished to make a sound, even to move. Why was this man suddenly so enraged, and at her? Why was he attacking her instead of George?

'You are the pagan's servant! You sit at the feet of the evil that we bear among us!'

Oh. He must know that she was to be working with Constance. Big deal. 'Come on, George,' she managed to say despite her fluffy mouth. 'These people aren't worth our time.'

'I'll get you, Pierce. I'll see you behind bars!'

'George, forget it. He's a superstitious fool.'

'I call down the Love of the Lord upon you, I lay your sins in his Light. Lord, Lord, help us to love these poor lost ones, help us to save them!'

Mandy turned away, her temper just barely under control. 'We oughta come back and burn this place down,' George murmured as they went together down the aisle.

'I couldn't agree more,' she hissed.

Back in the car they sat silently for a moment. 'Maybe we can have that drink now,' Mandy said as she tried to control her shaking. 'Then I'll take you home and put you to bed.'

George remained quiet until the car was in motion. 'I can't go home now,' he said suddenly. 'I've got to prepare for the next step.'

There was no need to ask what he meant; she knew. Having delivered his threat to Brother Pierce, he was going to go back to his lab and test his process on a human being.

Should she warn his co-workers of the state he was in? No. That would be pointlessly destructive. Maybe George kept the true depths of his madness in the basement of his mind as well as the house. Tonight's performance was quite understandable even in a sane man. She contented herself with an admonition.

'Be careful, George. Don't hurt anybody.'

'Just take me back to my lab. I've got work to do.'

Despite its gracious old homes, its broad trees, the elegance of its brick streets, Mandy now realized that in the years since she left town, Maywell had become seriously infected. There was no glib explanation for what had sickened it. The infection was hidden; it lurked behind the glowing windows of evening, drifted like smoke in the soft laughter of the night. Five years ago people had tolerated Constance Collier. Now, because of the coming of a single man, they were being taught to hate her.

Mandy could not return to George's house, and now for more than personal reasons. The thought of meeting Brother Pierce's people prowling the night made her go cold. Between them and the basement room, there was no peace for her in her old home.

After she dropped George off at his lab, Mandy drove for a time, trying to calm down. Once the town's beauty had also been its truth, but its bleaker corners, the impoverished houses along Bartlett, the run-down trailer park near Brother Pierce's Tabernacle, seemed its greater reality now. Had the Grimm's project not been of such importance to her career, she would have left right now, and forever. But as she rolled past Church Row on Main Street, with the town common on one side and the three churches on the other, the white Episcopal with its elegant steeple, the Presbyterian neo-Gothic, and the ancient Friends Meeting House that predated the Revolutionary War, she could almost believe that Maywell was healthy still, and that Brother Pierce's glaring, buzzing sign was not glowing just beyond the trees.

A black truck charged her lights. She swerved and jammed

on her brakes. 'Damn.' What was happening to her? She considered herself a steady and deliberate soul, and here she was drifting out of her lane.

But there was a reason, for a vivid imagining was sweeping through her. It came like the white wind that sometimes invaded her dreams, so powerfully that she just had time to stop the car before she lost all contact with Maywell.

The road in front of her disappeared, the trees lining it became a high stockade, the air grew thick with the stink of roasting meat and burning hair.

Screams of agony mixed with low merriment. She was no longer sitting in a car, but rather standing against a rough wooden stake. She felt a coarser cloth upon her skin and knew the weight of a thick, sputtering taper in her hands. Chains lashed her body to the stake. She heard the gobbling crackle of a great fire, then saw red glowing in the faggots that were stacked around her feet, almost up to her waist.

She remembered words of consolation from long ago, when someone had said to her, 'If you are to be taken to the pyre, never fear. Drugs will reach you, and you will feel naught!'

When was that? Not in this life.

She stared helplessly at an impossible, spectral crowd rushing at her, men and women and dirty little weasels of children, all bearing fiery torches and bunches of twigs, which they threw at her feet.

Then a long tongue of fire licked her legs, so hot it felt cold for an instant. Then it was as if somebody were whipping her furiously, as if she were being scraped to death with a red-hot file. With a hiss her hair flared up. She felt her face dissolve like a skin of milk.

Oh, they have ruined me, they have destroyed my beauty. And I was the most beautiful thing they had.

I was their witch.

As abruptly as if a projector had been turned off, Maywell reappeared around her, the lamplit brick street, the dancing shadows of the trees. She sat a moment, too stunned by the hallucination to move. She slumped at the wheel.

That witch-burning crowd had been *real*.

She recalled that modern anthropologists now believed that witchcraft was an earlier, pre-Christian religion, nothing more. Christianity had branded them evil and turned their Horned God into the Devil because they were competition. Too reverenced to be branded a demon, their Mother Goddess had become the Blessed Virgin.

Or so said some anthropologists.

There was a deeper mystery, though. Mandy saw in her mind's eye the rage coming into Brother Pierce's kindly face . . . she heard Constance's ravens screaming, remembered the strange, lascivious young man, Robin, his naked skin shining in the morning sun.

What was moving in among the trees? A great, broad-shouldered shape, gliding swiftly closer.

With frantic hands she restarted the car. She had to reassert the Mandy she knew and trusted. She thought of herself as a woman of strength and effectiveness. She had an excellent imagination, but she did *not* hallucinate like this, not out in a public street.

Nobody was going to burn anybody to death. No matter how neurotic this little town might have become, this was still the twentieth century. Maywell was no isolated medieval village; it was a modern town, linked to the rest of the world in thousands of different ways.

She remembered more the tone of Brother Pierce's voice than the words, that tone, and the hurt behind the hating glare in his eyes. They really were the saddest eyes she had ever seen.

Somewhere in her mind the hallucination was still proceeding, asserting its presence just at the edge of awareness. As dreams sometimes do, it had doubled back on itself. She had not yet been burned. She stood before a trembling, excited bishop to receive her sentence.

He put the red taper between her small white hands.

Quiet, you! That part of her, the wild image-maker, must not be allowed to surface at times like this. Where the devil was her self-discipline?

Be quiet, I order you, Amanda of the heart!

There now. With a conscious effort of will she directed her attention away from the flaming maiden within her to the cute old ice-cream shop she was passing. It was Bixter's, and she'd never seen a place that looked more like home, or safer. She'd spent an awful lot of good time at Bixter's. Right out there, in the alley where they parked the delivery truck, she'd smoked her first and last cigarette, a Parliament that had been given to her by Joanie Waldron, who had married the Kominski kid when they were in their late teens.

Beyond the front window she could see the wonderful old marble soda fountain, its spigots gleaming chrome and brass. There were the same wrought-iron chairs and charming little tables, and large numbers of students from the college. How she and her friends had enjoyed being mistaken for college girls by the occasional out-of-towner. How they had trembled when the college boys were attracted to them, cool, distant Bradley Hughes and men like Gerald Coyne and Martin Hiscott.

Mandy could not face Bixter's, not the Bixter's of this sadly changed Maywell. Home might have been hell, but Bixter's was a place a kid could relax.

She turned onto the Morris Stage Road and began heading back towards Route 80.

She could go back to New York easily enough. Her loft was waiting. Her friends were waiting.

Or she could turn up ahead on Albarts Street and drive over to the Collier estate. If she dared.

But of course she dared. She was going to illustrate the new Collier Grimm's! She herself, Amanda Walker. It was a book as great, potentially, as the Hobbes-illustrated *Faery*.

A poem came to mind. 'For too long you have gathered flowers, and leaned against the bamboo.' Nan Parton had sent her that, and those lines applied right now, on this junction between New York and the estate. A poem of Wu Tsao. 'One smile from you when we meet, and I become speechless and forget every word.' Romantic, intense Nan, so angry within that her canvases seemed to have been scourged.

She could hear Nan now: go to the estate, it's even more important than it seems. Don't retreat now. If you do, you might never have another chance.

'For too long you have gathered flowers . . .'

Brave Nan, *you* would go.

Albarts Street came up on the left, marked by a flashing yellow light strung across the centre of the Morris Stage Road.

God, Nan, I wish you were here to help me. The icons from the East Village: Robert when I'm lonely, Nan when I need courage. I loved her. 'My dear,' went the end of Nan's poem, 'let me buy a red-painted boat and carry you away.' In the night, in the heavy gloom of her Bowery loft, she had come back to find Nan there weeping, her brave Nan. She was crouched naked on the futon Mandy used for a bed, clutching the sheets to her face, kissing them. Mandy had crept out, shocked and embarrassed. When she had come back, Nan was gone.

Dry with fear, she guided the car between the stately homes, beneath the ordered arch of trees, towards the Collier estate.

The thought of walking up to the house through that forest at night gave her pause. She could turn a corner, but she couldn't possibly do that.

But cars must go there all the time, so somewhere in Maywell there must be another entrance to the estate, one that a car could take. Dimly, she remembered a way in behind the old town graveyard. Hadn't some of the kids once gone in that way on Halloween . . . and ended up at a wonderful celebration where they'd been given hard cider, among other things.

She turned onto Bridge Street and drove along the wall, past the high gate with its motto and the trees beyond, so great and so at peace that they seemed not to be plants at all, but the bodies of gods.

She stopped beneath the streetlight at the corner of Bartlett and rummaged in her glove compartment for the map of Maywell she had bought at the Exxon station on the way into town.

Yes, there was that road. It became a dotted line on estate property just beyond the graveyard. She went back to the end of Bridge and turned onto Mound Road. Soon she was passing directly through the public graveyard. The Indian mound that gave the road its name rose abruptly beyond the edge of the graveyard. Maywell had been burying its European-descended dead here for three hundred years. The Iroquois used to expose theirs atop the mound. Before them, the Mound Builders had buried theirs within.

How long had burials taken place here? Thousands of years, probably.

By the usual standards of the United States this was a very, very old place. Once outside the graveyard the road turned abruptly west, towards the bulk of Stone Mountain, becoming strewn with leaves and narrowing to a car-width strip of asphalt.

She passed a 'Do Not Enter' sign attached to a tree. As soon as she did, the road deteriorated, losing its asphalt and becoming a clay track planked here and there by rotting boards.

This was a desolate spot . . . the sort of place she might encounter – she did not quite know who, unless it was Brother Pierce with his terrible eyes and his spitting rage.

He seemed so familiar to her, as if, in some circle between the worlds, she and he had always been enemies.

Her firelit screams shattered the night.

Image of an owl alighting on the top of a charred stake, soft dangerous thing of darkness . . .

She was jarred back to reality when her head banged against the roof of the car.

You stupid dreamer, where the *hell* have you been? There wasn't even a road anymore. She was driving across naked heath. The Volks was struggling, bottoming and slurrying about in the soil.

The Volks began to skid. Mandy downshifted to second, then to first. The tyres caught again and the car lurched forward – only to get stuck even more.

She got out of the car and walked around to the back. The tyres had torn through the thin covering of grass to the boggy earth beneath. For all she knew she might have driven this Volkswagen back to the Middle Ages. Maybe Brother Pierce was on his way in his bishop's robes, trembling with eagerness to burn her.

She gathered dry grass and stuffed it down under the tyres. Then she tried again to get out of the mud.

The car shuddered, the tyres whined, then she lurched forward with a roar from the engine – and promptly sank again.

She turned off the engine. It was dark out here and she was at least two miles from Maywell, perhaps half that far from Constance Collier's house – assuming she could find it. She hit the heels of her hands against the steering wheel. Give a city person a few trees and an unpaved road and watch the fun. She'd grown up here, she knew the condition of these old roads. Why had she allowed herself to get into this jam?

There was nothing to do but walk. She didn't care to stay with the car all night. A VW Beetle is no place to sleep if you are much more than three feet tall. At five-nine Mandy would be tortured by knobs and bumps and corners.

She felt around the glove box for her flashlight, turned it

on, and was delighted to discover that it cast a beam. 'At least –' The beam faded and died. Better put new batteries on her shopping list, she thought bitterly. She slammed the hood and set out on foot in the general direction she had been driving.

She would eventually see the house off to the right if she could just keep going in a straight line. With Stone Mountain on her left that wouldn't be very hard. She hadn't gone twenty feet before the ground got mushy.

She might walk towards Stone Mountain on the theory that the land would rise in that direction. She took a step and almost pitched forward. That way lay actual open water, lying in a pool across a sheet of mud. Perhaps the other direction would be more productive. In fact she could see forest hugging the land like a black cloud over there.

It must be the forest of the guardian *fee*, the little stone fairy she had seen when she first came here. Well, what the hell, the forest was a lot safer than this bog. She should have left her car on Albarts and walked in as she had before.

Mandy strode along, her feet sucking busily, her eyes barely able to discern the ground in front of her. She hoped that the blackness ahead really was that forest.

If it was, she would soon see the lights of the Collier house off to her right.

When she saw lights, though, they were not to the right. They glowed with deep radiance, but so softly that they might not be there at all. She stopped and stared towards them.

Very, very faintly she could hear the rhythmic jangle of a tambourine. There was a tang in the air, too, of woodsmoke. This must be the village where Constance's followers lived. If so, she was deeper into the estate than she had ever come as a girl. The witch village was a place of dark town legend.

She could see the dim outline of walls of wattle and straw, heavy thatched roofs. Candles flickered here and there behind leaded glass. Mandy found her way between two of the cottages and into the muddy track that separated this row from its opposite.

Candle lanterns hung before doors. Round stones for walking jutted from the track between the two rows of cottages. It was a scene from the Middle Ages, but the peace of it was far, far deeper than had ever been known in that tormented era. Mandy stepped along the stones. Just when she was sure the village was uninhabited, she heard the tambourine again, and this time noticed that it was accompanied by a low chant.

She knew then that this was indeed the witch village. She had come to this place of childhood legend.

At the far end of the path was a round wattled building very different from the cottages. Mandy went up to it and paused before the shut door. The tambourine was quite distinct now, as was the voice of the chanting woman. Mandy couldn't make out the words, but the tone was pure and firm and full of love.

Then there came a cry.

The voice and the tambourine stopped.

Behind her on the path Mandy heard panting. It was loud and close; when she whirled around, it became deep, chesty growling. It began to advance towards her. She had the impression that she was being menaced by a huge dog and backed around the edge of the building. This was one of the reasons that the townspeople stayed away from the estate.

There was a sense of quick movement and Mandy could feel the heat of its presence where she had just been standing. Then, in the faint light of a candle she caught sight of a long tail with a kink at the end.

'It's you! You, Tom!'

He growled again, a most uncatlike sound.

'Tom?'

When she tried to approach the building again, he spat at her.

'My God.'

The cat was on guard here. It was very obvious that it wanted her away from the round building. How could that nice old cat possibly act this way?

Unless, in the dark, she had made a mistake. Maybe she wasn't facing Tom at all.

Maybe this was something else.

When it growled again, she trotted, then ran around the building and onto the heath behind it.

She listened as she moved. Of course it was just the cat. Toms are crotchety. If she'd held out her hand, he'd probably have rubbed against it.

Even so she did not stop. She had to climb a sharp rise. This must be one of the hummocks she had seen from the house. At the top she was forced to pause for breath. She stood, gasping, the night close about her, longing for just a gleam of saving light, listening for paws padding through the grass. She'd deal with that cat again, but not until daylight.

She tried to take her bearings. The little village was bordered on one side by the bog, on the other by these hummocks. It must be invisible from every direction except Stone Mountain itself.

Ahead, Mandy was soon relieved to see the lights of the Collier mansion. They were soft, but there were so many of them it could only be that great house. Her confidence renewed, she set off across the tumbling little hills, losing sight of the house in the valleys, regaining it on the hilltops. With the sliver of moon now free from clouds there was even a small amount of light. She had the luxury of being able to miss stones with her ravaged shoes.

She came suddenly to the edge of the gardens. The smell of the land changed, became at once more complex. Then she realized what was underfoot: she was walking through an extensive herb garden. Too bad she couldn't see well enough to find a path. She hated to crush the plants. Come morning Constance no doubt would rage at her about the damage.

She was soon crossing tall grass. Up a steep slope she found the swimming pool, its water reflecting the moon. The windows of the house glowed with the loveliest light Mandy thought she had ever seen. She mounted the porch steps. The whole place was lit by candles, in holders, in chandeliers, in the wall sconces in the hall.

There came from the library Constance Collier's voice, speaking with a gentleness and humour Mandy had not before heard from those lips.

'Miss Collier?'

The voice went right on. Mandy entered the kitchen foyer, then passed through the kitchen proper. There were no candles lit in here and she had to move carefully to avoid bruising herself against the big table.

When she reached the library, she paused at the door. The room was crowded; Constance Collier was obviously giving some sort of a talk.

And the gentleness in that voice! Where was Will T. Turner's harridan now? Mandy approached the doorway, emboldened by the sweetness of the voice to a greater confidence than she had felt here before. 'Miss Collier?'

'Yes!'

'I –'

'You're welcome here, Amanda. Take a seat and listen if you will.' There was a single candle glowing in the room, lighting Constance Collier's old face in such a way that the lovely young woman she once had been seemed to flicker in its shadows, ready to emerge again. As astonishing as Constance was her audience.

They were children, easily two dozen of them, arrayed at her feet, so rapt with attention that they didn't even react to the interruption. They ranged in age from perhaps four to thirteen or fourteen. All were dressed in simple grey homespun. Constance herself was in a white linen dress embroidered across the bodice with green vines and pink buds. A lovely effect, so simple that it was elegant. On a young woman that dress would have been heart-stopping.

Lounging against a far corner Mandy saw Robin. His sister Ivy sat on a chair beside him. They also wore grey homespun now. When Mandy's eyes met his, he smiled a very small, very audacious smile. He shocked her, and the shock was delicious – which annoyed her.

'Now listen,' Constance said. 'This is the story of God-father Death.'

'The thing you must understand is that this story is very, very old. It is far older than fairy tales, and fairy tales are ancient things. This story does not come to us from the fairy-folk but down the human line. I suppose it has been told since we were granted the right of speech. And before then – well, it was in our hearts.

'A long, long time ago, when this world was still young and we were younger still, there was a woman whose fields were not great enough to support her growing family. She had been blessed with many daughters, and they had all found men and raised families of their own, until not even the woman's best harvest-leaping would bring up sufficient corn to feed everybody.

'Then one Lammas night her first daughter came in with yet another child. The mother took the baby and praised her daughter, but when the daughter had gone she wept, for the child must be exposed. Her heart heavy, the mother stole out in the cold of the night to give the boy to the sky.

'She was going along the road when she met a tall man with great horns on his head and eyes as fierce as a wolf's. This was not a bonded man at all, but some great hunter come in for the season's Sabbat. The mother held out the child and said, "Please, stranger, take this child of your own kind, and be his godfather."

'The stranger took the boy and gave the woman a wand of rowan in return. "This is a miraculous twig; with it you can heal the sick. But be careful, for if you see Death standing at the head of the sickbed, touch the patient with the rowan and she will recover. If Death stands at the foot, however, say 'She will die.'"

'So she became a great physician and very wealthy, and her whole family prospered. One day the Queen called her to the bedside of her own child, a great and powerful hunter who had been gored by a stag. Death was standing at the head, and the boy lived. Then a second time the boy was gored, this time by a long-toothed tiger. Again Death stood at the head, and the boy was cured. But the third time, when the boy was sick with love, Death was at the foot of the bed and the youth had to die.

'The woman went then to visit the godfather and tell him all that had transpired. But when she went into the house, she found that things were most strange there. On the first floor a great black cat was fighting a dog and there was a terrible row. "Where does the godfather live?" the woman asked. At once the cat changed into the Queen's dead son and sang:

'"Rowan, rowan, silver twig of life
Cast my shadow on blood of strife."

'The woman went deeper into the house. On the walls were the shadows of the many animals the godfather had slain, stags and bear and bison. And there were shadows of men there, too. On the floor there were many dead babies, the children who had been given to the sky. "Where does the godfather live?" the mother asked these children.

'They sprang up and sang:

'"Rowan, rowan, silver twig of life
Cast my shadow on skull of strife."

'So the mother went deeper, for farther on she could see a room scattered with skulls. When she touched them with the rowan wand, they came alive and spoke:

> '"Rowan, rowan, curse me not
> For godfather has caused my flesh to rot."

'Deeper yet the mother could smell a dreadful odour. She came then to a rotting forest, all the trees blackening with death, all the animals fallen down, and the grass withered like the curled fingers of dead children. Only the rowan bush remained untouched, and it glowed with life, its little buds opening even as she watched.

'She knew then where to find the godfather. Indeed, he was hidden in the rowan bush. When she saw him, she said, "Godfather, what are these strange apparitions in your house? At the entrance I saw your animals become children."

'"And I saw your hair become grey, old mother."

'"Then I saw the shadows of all your kills on the walls."

'"Ah. So you know then why you are here."

'"Then I found a room full of skulls."

'"You found your own people."

'"Then a rotted forest."

'"The world to come."

'"Then the rowan bush."

'So he leaped out and made as if to grab her, but she was a quick old woman and she got away from him. When she looked back and saw his horns and his red eyes, she realized who he was and ran all the faster.

'She was so fleet that she came back into her own land, and when her people saw her they fell to rejoicing, for their old mother had become a young maiden again.'

Constance Collier stopped. She smiled down at the children. 'That story came from my grandmother, who had it from hers. I've told it now and again to some people who know, and they suppose it to be a survival of the time when we lived as often as not in caves. And that's what the godfather's house is, eh, a cave, and painted just the way they painted them at Lascaux thousands and thousands of years ago. So this must be a story about such paintings and the lives of the people who made them.'

Mandy was entranced. That story could well be exactly as ancient as Constance claimed. It bore a close relation to 'Godfather Death' in Grimm's. But this was a feminized version, sounding as if it was from the era when women were just becoming agriculturists, and men were still hunters.

Looking about her at these rough-clad children, at the beautiful wild boy in the corner, at Constance dressed like a princess herself, Mandy was filled with deep wonder and excitement. Something extraordinary was happening here, something that appealed deeply to her. And there was such love among these people that even when they were silent there was a sense of laughter.

'Now take the fire and off you go,' Constance said to the assembled children. There were a couple of pleas for one more short one, and one piped request: 'I want my dad to come live with us.'

Silence followed the words. The joy was for the moment suspended in a graver mood. Constance reached her hand out and touched the cheek of a ten-year-old boy. 'That is a matter for the circle, Jerry. Next time you're there you make a picture of your father in your head, and imagine him among us, and make sure you see him smiling and happy.'

'Will he come then?'

'The magic you do in the circle will help him.'

The children fell in behind an older girl who carried a candle in a brass lantern. Single file the group went down the hall and out the back of the house. Soon the lantern was bobbing along on the hummocks.

Now was Mandy's chance to warn Constance Collier about the crazy old preacher. 'I was at Brother Pierce's Tabernacle –'

She looked up sharply. 'Why?'

'It has to do with some trouble my uncle is having with him. He's a scientist, and – but that isn't important. I was there to help my uncle. And Pierce knew all about me, what I'm doing here and all.'

'He reads the paper.'

'I think he hates you.'

Constance Collier's expression gentled again. 'But you do not. You are attracted to us. You identify with me.'

'Well, perhaps.'

'Come with me, Amanda. We'll send those pesky ravens along to guide the children.' She went to the window and clapped her hands sharply seven times. Wings began to flutter and sleepy bird voices harped and shrieked. There followed a chorus of enthusiastic cawing and the crows burst up from the shrub beneath the window, where they had apparently been sleeping. Their cawing echoed in the sky and was soon greeted by laughter and cheering from the children. 'They are good sometimes, dear, when they feel like it.'

'What are you?'

Constance Collier laughed. 'An old woman who wishes to be young again. A dreamer, I suppose.'

'Excuse me, Miss Collier, but I know it isn't that simple.'

Constance looked at her a long time. 'In the end I will reveal every single secret to you. But only when I'm ready, so indulge your old benefactor.' She smelled more of minty incense than perfume. In the candlelight her skin seemed as alive as a girl's. She touched Mandy's face with unexpectedly warm fingers. 'I could love you like a daughter.' Then, as if shocked by her own display of feeling, she rushed off. She called from the dark of the house: 'Yours is the second room on the left, top of the stairs. We rise here with the dawn, which tomorrow will come shortly after six. Someone will be in to wake you.'

Mandy wasn't convinced that such a thing would be possible at that hour.

'I have something wonderful for you to do tomorrow. Something marvellous. But you must set out just at dawn or there's no point.'

'But Miss Collier –' There was no answer to her call. Constance Collier was gone.

Robin and Ivy began moving through the house with snuffers, putting out the candles. Mandy was too uneasy about the boy to question him, and she didn't trust the girl at all. In the end she went upstairs. Her room was candlelit, with a basin of water and a chamber pot peeking out from under the ancient curtained bed.

Mandy undressed, putting her jeans, blouse, and underthings across the back of the blue stuffed chair that sat in front of the fireplace. She went to the writing desk and picked up the candle in its pewter ring-handled holder. Crossing back to the bed, she felt as if she had slipped into some unfamiliar space in the world.

The time of mysteries in the night.

But this was Maywell, New Jersey, in the month of October, the year of our Lord nineteen hundred and eighty-seven.

It was also the time and place to climb into a wonderfully cosy curtained bed, curl up, and make sure she dreamed of peaceful voices and not strident ones, of children in candle-light and fabulous tales from long ago, and left the terrors behind.

She did not see Tom, who spent the night curled up on the canopy of her bed. And as he was not a purring cat, she didn't hear him either.

She was sleeping heavily by the time Robin came into her room. He drew close to the curtained bed, parted the drapes, and peeked inside. When he was certain that she slept, he reached down and laid his hand on her naked breast, feeling its fullness and warmth. He whispered softly to her, an ancient spell:

              'I'll come to thee in cat-time
              I'll come and make thee mine.'

And then, the necessary words uttered, he crept off to his own bed.

Tom watched him go, switched his tail a few times, then settled in for the long night's vigil. In the bed below him, Mandy breathed as softly as a sleeping deer.

CHAPTER 9

On the night that the demon-sent doctor and the beautiful young witch came, Sister Winifred had been leading what remained of the congregation in 'Rock of Ages.' Brother Pierce, winded from his last exhortation, surveyed the crowd. About a third were gone. They loved the Lord, of course, but in the absence of an intense issue their faith waned. They began to worry about money or work or just getting the washing done, and they drifted away.

He loved them so much, each one of them, and longed with all his heart and soul to see them on their way to heaven.

To keep them on the road, there had to be a great question before the congregation, something with drama and importance, that would threaten them, each one, personally, their homes and their children. *That* was the kind of issue that could be used to reinflame their faith. As they sang he prayed. At once he felt a stirring within himself. When he looked up he was surprised to see the shadow of a cat in the doorway at the back of the church. Cats made him sneeze. He was about to signal the usher to shoo it off when it went of its own accord.

Simon kept the faith of Christ as best he could. Of course, Christ was a long, long time ago. It took a little imagination to believe that the cruelties he had suffered were really enough to wash away the sins of the world. Christian belief was the only thing that Simon had ever found which would hold at bay the fiery wind of guilt that roared day and night through his soul.

He was so sorry for what he had done. A few moments of pleasure, a few moments of anger – then a lifetime of remorse and eternity in hell. He refused to confess himself publicly and to ask God's forgiveness. In part this was because he felt that he deserved hell for what he had done. There was, however, the other possibility, that the whole thing – religion – was a product of the human imagination. If that was the case, he would be confessing and going to jail for the rest of his life for nothing. He was a believer, but he preferred to cut the cards himself.

Tonight Simon felt exceptionally tired. He had been slaving over the leaves all afternoon and now he was working like a dog, trying to get that spark to come into the eyes of his congregation. It wasn't working. He was just losing his magic. Six months ago he'd had this whole town wound around his little finger. Well, not all of it: the old families and the college professors who lived in the elegant houses on Albarts and streets like that weren't interested. If they went to church at all, it was to places like Saint Marks with its dried-up Rector Williams, who looked like he'd been sucked up in a prune-making machine.

Simon got the poor, the welfare cases, the unemployed. Guys who used to work full-time over at the Peconic Quarry, which now ran maybe three shifts a month, others who once moved steel at the now abandoned Mohawk Fabricating Mill. These men had wives and children and souls and hopes, and they weren't getting anywhere. Simon's congregation had numbered two thousand souls at this time last year. Now he had about fourteen hundred, a thousand workers and their families and four hundred Maywell students. His campus ministry worked surprisingly well, perhaps because the Maywell college kids were, in their own way, as much rejects as the steelworkers. These were the kids who hadn't made Princeton by a long distance, who hadn't even made Jersey State.

It had occurred to him to stand up and give them a little hellfire. Guilt was what made them keep coming back. Guilt, or was it hell? Sometimes their eyes really sparked when he described his ideas of hell. From some deep place in himself he knew what it was to burn. As a matter of fact, he was an expert on agony, both physical and spiritual. He could visualize burning flesh, sometimes even smell it as he preached. The trouble with his congregation was that they did not understand hell. It could be as small as a grain of sand, as large as a whole lifetime. And it did not have to be flames; it could be another kind of burning, the blue fire that consumes the spirit.

He knew all of this because he lived with it every day. His greatest secret was this: hell was with and in him. It was here, right now. He carried hell in his pocket.

He could feel it there now, dry and gnarled and unspeakably horrible. Their sins the Lord might forgive. If he could save just one from the torment he was already enduring, there was at least some small sense to his life.

But to do his work he needed their faith. He must kindle and rekindle it, and keep it burning white hot!

Instead he saw it dwindling. Those who came here came more and more out of habit, not because they couldn't stay away. At first they had poured through those doors with eager faces. Then they had come more slowly, then out of duty. Now some of them didn't come at all.

What worked best to keep them was controversy. Simon had first come to Maywell because of the rumours of witches there that had spread through the underground fundamentalist movement.

Such a place seemed an ideal mission for a really committed preacher. They needed Christ in Maywell; not the sweet, empty Christ of Catholics and the Presbyterians, but Simon's Christ, a living Christ who would save you right then and there, in front of everybody, if you could feel it deeply enough.

Simon had built his church on the stones of controversy. Issues and public statements of protest had brought his people together, made them see themselves as a separate band, changed them from congregation to band of brothers.

They had collected evil books and records, stealing them from the library, buying them or shoplifting them from the Dalton's and the Record Room. Then they had made a bonfire of them out behind the Tabernacle and burned over four thousand separate items. Chief among these offerings were copies of the works of Constance Collier.

After the burnings Simon had seen an article in the *Campus Courier* suggesting that Dr George Walker was engaged in fantastically evil experiments of reviving the dead. To combat this man, Simon had scheduled a ten-week series and thoroughly condemned him. He had even discerned a link between Dr Walker and Constance Collier. One of Walker's assistants, Clark Jeffers, lived on the Collier estate.

The creation of *The Christian Faery* had been another massive project. The intention had been to replace Collier's demon-inspired *Faery* with the purified work. Getting godless children's books off the shelves of the library and out of the local bookstore was almost as important as book burning itself.

Constance Collier had reacted with venom.

She was a focus of pagan evil. He had heard rumours of the sinful activities on her estate, rumours having to do with odd sex and the raising of demons with magic rituals. It was impossible to be a witch and not a worshipper of demons.

Now the *Courier* had carried a story about Amanda Walker and her work illustrating the heathen, paganistic Grimm's fairy tales – for none other than Constance Collier!

Dr George Walker. Amanda Walker. A witch working for him, she working for a witch – this was a cabal, all of it, a pagan cabal right in the middle of this God-fearing Christian community!

God-fearing and clean-living . . . but it was no wonder that they were afflicted by pagans and demons, for they were not led by a clean man.

He touched the small bulge in his pocket that was his own

personal torment. But tonight the hand was only a hard, dead little knot.

The hymn ended. Brother Pierce cleared his throat.

He didn't know what he would say next. But he trusted in the Lord to help him. Closing his eyes, he took a deep breath. His whole being seemed to stir. Out of the corner of his eye he saw the outline of a cat against the stained-glass window nearest his pulpit. It was on the outside, pressing itself against the glass. He did not have time to be angry about it, though, for energy suddenly began pouring through him, coming from above, from below, from everywhere. His body seemed about to burst into tingling life. Then the words appeared, rolling off his tongue as if of their own accord. 'There is evil running as a shadow in these bright streets of Maywell. Yes, it even enters here, a place we have tried to make sacred! The evil doctor comes among us with his whore and makes lying accusations.' He pointed upward with his right hand, and felt to his deepest core the warm, the righteous, the sweet presence of the Saviour. By God's grace he felt this, for he could now speak directly to beloved Jesus Christ. 'I say to you, Lord, your people are innocent. Yea, even as the Lamb!'

People were suddenly back alive, their faces shining, their eyes quick with excitement. He heard whispers: 'He is here, the Lord is here.'

'We can feel it,' he shouted. 'O Lord, thank you and praise your holy name.' He smiled a great chasm of a smile. 'O Lord, what a night!'

People began to shout. 'Praise the Lord!'

But there was another reality in this church, and if he looked past his own joy and faith, he could see it. The ones towards the back of the room were not included in the excitement. They sat, their faces fixed in pious expressions. He knew that they couldn't feel a thing.

He was being prevented from reaching even to the last row in his own church!

He had to find a focus that would mean something to the

man sitting in the otherwise empty row at the far back, who was either deep in personal prayer or asleep.

He cooled his throat with the water Winifred kept behind his pulpit in a green plastic pitcher.

His mind turned morbidly to a vision of the Tabernacle dark and empty, a 'For lease' sign on the front door.

A family of four defected from a front row. A front row family and the service not yet ended. So much for his ecstatic moment. He hadn't even inspired the front sitters, beyond a few automatic praise-Gods. The ones leaving didn't so much as look embarrassed.

Fighting himself, he quelled his urge to scream at the defectors, to run after them. It was hard. This church was his life, his first and only success. He had known cold and hunger and despair. The Tabernacle was the only good thing that had ever come to him. He was a man of many pasts. He had been a nightclub comic in Los Angeles, working the toilets, telling sorry jokes to scabrous drunks for fifty dollars a week. 'Little Red Riding Hood gets stopped by the Big Bad Wolf. "Okay, Little Red," the wolf says, "pull down your panties and bend over. You're gonna get it up the ass." Little Red Riding Hood pulls a .357 Magnum out of her basket. "The hell I am," she says, "you're gonna eat me, just like it says in the story."'

Was his problem that they knew, that some of his past somehow clung to him, a stink of cigar smoke and cheap booze, of midnight bus rides and nights in motels without names? Humour. When he got a laugh, it was like a blessing from on high.

There were worse things, though, that clung to him, things far worse than the residue of a few scabrous jokes. During the seventies he had been a social worker for the city of Atlanta, specializing in home placement for unwanted children. There had been trouble, big trouble. She had been a lovely butterfly of a girl, soft and smooth and saucy. Once he had been proud of how he had helped her.

Despite the dropping of the charges, he remained the object of persistent suspicion in Atlanta welfare circles. His little twenty-second mistake – not knowing his own strength – had condemned him for all eternity, but it had also kindled in him this fire to save others.

Everybody in the church was watching him. It was up to him to keep them a little longer or let them go. He hated for them to leave on such a dismal note. One little flicker of life, hope springing up, the feeling of Jesus right here in the room, then this emptiness.

His mind flashed to a bright, gleaming image of Amanda Walker. That niece of the doctor's was so perishingly, delicately beautiful. And yet her eyes were full of firmness and intelligence. She was just the kind of woman he dreamed of, as lovely as an opening rose, yet strong enough to take him well in hand. Firmly in hand. When he imagined offering her his guilty heart and asking forgiveness, he felt a shaft of agonized longing in his breast, just as if some demonic arrow had pierced him.

The restlessness in the room was getting worse. What the devil had this service started out about, anyway? He couldn't even remember. To buy a few seconds he took another pull at his water. Sister Winifred minced across from the choir box and refilled it.

Nervously, feeling more and more helpless, he flipped the pages of his Bible. Sometimes this worked. Why had he thought of the woman now? Maybe the Bible would give the answer.

Then he saw a word flashing past, a promising word: harlot. What a friend he had in the Lord! He cried out the passage to which he had been led: 'Wherefore, O harlot, hear the word of the Lord: Thus saith the Lord God: Because thy filthiness was poured out, and thy nakedness discovered through thy whoredoms with thy lovers, and with all the idols of thy abominations, and by the blood of thy children!'

He paused. The faces were on him again, the eyes coming

back to life. He felt much better. 'Well, now, wasn't that some witness! Oh, yes!' His laughter, ironic, angry, crackled through the silent crowd. 'The very whore was among us, witnessing to the lies of the demon doctor.' He pointed straight down the empty aisle. 'And worse, she is going to the house of the pagan, to help her make more evil books for our children. Mark my words, that beautiful girl bears the mark of the demon upon her white flesh. And I warn you, she is here as an agent of the Dark One, come to spread corruption and confusion among the children!'

There was response then, a little shocked whispering among the older folk. The young people just stared. As good as it had sounded to him, this was obviously not quite right. Something was still missing, the focus, the damned *focus*! He plunged on. 'Is it not our duty to cast the abomination from our midst, to cast out the shadow of evil that so vexes us, that turns the hearts of our children from the service of the Lord? And who is the whore's helper and employer? That *woman*, oh, yes, the pagan of the hills, none other. Yea, they are the unholy, the denizens come up from the deep. Yea, they are of Leviathan's army, oh, yes!'

Faces hardened. 'Praise God!' came the shouts. This was a little better. Just a little.

'So I say to you, evil walks and talks in the form of woman, yea, even a woman dressed in the clothing of a man, in those bottom-wiggler jeans. "The woman shall not wear that which pertaineth unto a man, for that *is* an abomination unto the Lord!"'

Ah. There was a marked improvement in the interest level. Nobody was leaving now: the room was touched by new energy.

Were they only shocked by his fury, or did they believe the news he brought of the evil among them? He took a drink, stared from face to face. 'Repent ye,' he shouted at one, 'Repent,' at another. 'O Lord, give us strength!'

Instead of blazing up with righteous love, those he had eye contact with glanced away. Despite the improvement he wasn't reaching them really yet.

He needed a simple, incendiary *word* that they could rally to, a fiery word that would entangle all three demons in one net of truth.

A glance at his watch told him it was closing in on 10:30. The service had been going on far too long, given the restlessness of the crowd. It was bad psychology to have people feel relief when the service ended. They ought to be left uplifted and longing for more. 'Leave them feeling as children who have just been praised by their fine old father,' a mentor had said. He struggled, he prayed in his heart, but no word came. He would have to drop the matter for the time being and go on to the last part of the service. May the Lord find his word for him.

'So repent you now, good people, come forth, come forth and bring your sins before man and God! Come, have no fear of the love of God nor the ears of your brothers and sisters in Christ. Jesus *wants* your sins. So be free with them, and bring them to his Holy Altar!'

He signalled Winifred, who started the organ. The choir hummed obediently along, 'Amazing Grace.' Brother Pierce bowed his head.

A tall man stood up from deep kneeling. He wore a grey-striped suit and a vest. He looked much more prosperous than the run of the congregation. As he came forward, Brother Pierce recalled his name: Roland Howells, chief teller of the Maywell State Bank & Trust. Not a tither. According to Mazie Knowland, who worked at the regional IRS office, Howells' 1981 income tax return showed $28,000 gross salary. Contribution that year of exactly $600.

What would he repent, this secret miser?

Howells came to the place appointed for confession and knelt before the congregation. 'My name is Roland Howells.'

'Speak up! If *we* can't hear you, neither will the Lord!'

'I am Roland Howells! I have to confess that I have been cruel to my wife, I have shouted, I have taken the name of the Lord in vain, and before God I have struck her.'

'Thou shalt not take the name of the Lord thy God in vain, Brother Roland!'

'Praise God, brothers and sisters, forgive me and pray for me. My wife took my son and left my bed and board, because I was hard and full of anger.'

Something struck Brother Pierce as he listened to this man's trouble. Quite often lately members of the congregation had come forward to witness to the breakup of their families.

Very often. Sometimes three or four in a single service.

Maywell was a quiet, settled place of barely five thousand inhabitants. Not your divorcing kind of town. Brother Pierce shook the penitent's hand, wondering. 'The Lord will return them to you if you pray well, brother.'

'I hope so, Brother Pierce. I sure do miss them. They're out there on the estate, I know that, I got a phone call.'

Good God. Those words immediately brought another witness, a woman of perhaps fifty, her fingers nicotine-stained, her face slick and pallid. There was something *abolished* about that wasteland of fat, smelly skin, probably full of the kind of imperfections that ruined a kiss to the flesh, moles and seedwarts and prickly little hairs.

'My name is Margaret Lysander. I also lost my family to the estate. My husband, my daughter, my son. They didn't want me to come here, and when I got saved, they left for the witches.'

Another one, and even purer gold than the first. The witches were stealing wives and husbands and children from God-fearing Christians, and that was a fact.

Here was something as deeply personal as there could be. A threat to the family was a threat to the very soul.

Something kept entering his mind, then flitting away, an uncaptured thought. A word. He put his fingers in his pocket and wound them around the dry, sharp-boned little fist that lived there.

Maggie Lysander started in again. 'I was a good mamma to my kids,' she said. 'I didn't treat 'em except as the Lord lays down in the Good Book, and as you teach us, Brother Pierce.'

'Amen, sister.'

'It was like they was just bewitched.'

Brother Pierce fairly reeled. Of course, it was so *obvious*! Bewitched. Witch! *Witch!* It wasn't anything wrong with his followers that was making their families walk out on them, it was the witch! And who was a known pagan who would not give her work over to the service of Jesus Christ? Why, the very one who employed the whore and was behind the evil professor!

Brother Pierce waved his arms with excitement. The Good Lord was in him now, in him deep and in him strong! 'Oh, I *feel* the blood of the Lamb flowing in my veins, ohhh, I feel the Lord moving in me!' The Tongues were coming upon him. Maggie Lysander shrank away, the congregation sighed with suppressed excitement. This is what they came for, this was what made Brother Pierce special. Very well. Now they were going to get their money's worth.

He held his hands out before him, making them shake and tremble as if they were no longer his own. They were going under the power of the Lord. Then his arms, then his legs and his whole body. He felt himself spinning, saw faces whirl past, faces and rafters and linoleum flooring. He grabbed on to the pulpit.

His mind emptied to make way for the coming of the Word. 'Ohhhh Lord!'

'Praise his Name!'

'Praise him!'

'Ohhh, ye have the hand of the witch upon you! God's people are under the palm of the witch! The witch comes among you, oh, praise God, the filthy sorceress with her charms and dirty talk, she poisons the lives of your children and breaks up your homes, Ohhh Lord! And we cannot raise a finger against her! Ohhh Lord! We cannot do a thing on our own! We got to put down our human ways and let the *Lord God* do it his way! Ohhh, we got a witch in the dark of the night a-coming to poison your chosen people!' It was as if a fire had been kindled down deep in his soul, a white fire of the breath of the Lamb, a red fire of his blood. Brother Pierce stalked down the aisle. 'You and you and you, you got the witches' charm right on your forehead, Ohhh Lord, she's bringin' us division in our houses and death, Lord, we cannot free ourselves, come into our hearts, O Lord, come right now among us!'

Maggie Lysander was the first among the congregation to catch on. Good girl. She arched her back and clapped her hands to her face and shrieked high and savage. 'Lord! Lord! I got you in me!' She began to gyrate. Winifred started in on the organ, a syncopated 'Rock of Ages' to sort of encourage things along a little. Brother Pierce grabbed a man and kissed him on the mouth. 'The Lord is in *you-uh*!' The man shook and swayed and soon was joined by a dozen people around him, then a dozen more, then more and more. 'The Lord is in us-uh! Ohhhhh!' Then more and more, some were shrieking and crying, some were clapping, stamping. Brother Pierce felt climax in his soul, all his false vanity burning away before the fiery coming of the Lamb. The Word was upon him. 'Oh Lammaadossachristi! Ohhh rosto-leuroxisatime! Lestochristomentisator!'

Maggie Lysander screamed. 'Mathama! Lopadoa destona deutcheber!'

'Ohh, Laaaededmedema! Memkakopolesto, yeaaaoooh!' That was a good one! He shut his eyes and swayed and clapped. 'Praise the Lord God-uh! Pra-a-aise the Lord God Almighty-uh, yea though they walk through the valleassssto-mana! Ooohabeliatking! Ohhseettalbmen! Beestalthnot, statltnot suffer, belsaltnot suffer, salnot *not – thou shalt not suffer a witch to live-uh!* There it was, oh, beautiful and true and good! A rich bitch of a witch of a stuck-up Mrs Constance and her filthy whore of a too pretty-o goddamn girl!

'Thou shalt not suffer a witch to live! Oh, boy! Oh, the Lord has me! Listen to the Word! Oh, boy! Ohhhaletitme-anta!'

He was jumping and leaping, and they were all jumping and clapping in heady rhythm, oh, yes, and he kissed one and another, a fat face, a sweated brow, pretty lips, flesh of flesh, his people, his dear people, the people God had given him to make new in the Word. 'Lammasuckum!'

He fell among the surging crowd of them, and they were touching him, tearing his clothes, putting their hands against his naked flesh, and raising him high now on a sea of hands, 'Praaaise God! God! God!' They were not gentle, they hurt him, grabbing him and touching him, grabbing his hair, the flesh beneath his torn shirt, grabbing him so it hurt and felt good at the same time, and calling out in tongues, and embracing him among them, men and women and children with their hands on him, praising the Lord God and touching him.

They carried him forth into the cold of the night, beneath the bright enormous buzzing sign where the last white moths of the season fluttered, and beneath the night sky also, Ohhhh Lord! They loved him, they loved him, the Lord made them love him and he cried and they all cried and praised God together right out in the middle of the parking lot, and then they hugged each other. O God be praised and thanked, he was getting his people back!

The congregation linked arms. Spontaneously and without manipulation they began singing 'That Old Rugged Cross,' that old, old song from the past days, his boyhood of sorrow and pain, and all the sorrow and pain of them all, the sweet, decent, good, shamefully bewitched children of the Lord God.

One song followed another into the night. Sometime after

twelve a fine mist began to fall. They went to their cars then, with no particular plan to do what they did, to drive the night in procession, flashing their lights and honking their horns, out Bridge Street and past the high brick walls of the Collier estate, until the rain changed to sleet, and the sleet to snow, and with much honking and waving and shouted praises, the congregation returned to their homes.

An hour later Brother Pierce lay sweating on his own bed in the trailer behind the Tabernacle, listening to good old country music all the way from WSB a million miles away in Nashville, sucking a bottle of Black Label, his mind clattering with his success. Just like that his congregation was united behind him once again. United against the witch.

If he could keep this going, he guessed he'd even see a tithe from the likes of Miser Howells. This was real inspiration.

Towards morning he knew he was not going to sleep. He had to point up the seriousness of his new issue. Had to leave a message that people *cared*, that they *hated*, that they were with their good Brother Pierce all the way.

He put a can of gasoline from the toolshed into his car and drove off about two hours before dawn.

Soon he was out on the lonely road near the Collier wall. A huge cat arched its back in his headlights, then darted to the roadside. Brother Pierce stopped his car. He got out. In his left hand he was carrying a whiskey bottle full of gasoline. He lit a rag stuffed in the neck and hurled it against the wall.

The bloom of gasoline fire swelled and jumped madly at the trees. It was not strong enough to do damage, and was not meant to be. What Brother Pierce wanted was for people to see the black scar this would leave on the wall.

Snowflakes whirled among the flames.

It took less than five minutes for the fire to flicker out. But it left a nice, big mark behind.

People would see and it would make them think. Thou shalt not suffer a witch to live.

It was just a suggestion.

CHAPTER 10

Mandy awoke to a clink and clatter beyond the curtains of her bed. She had slept so heavily that for a moment she didn't remember where she was. Then she stuck her head out to a slap of cold air and the sight of Ivy building a fire in the hearth.

'Good morning.' Maybe it was the cold air or the amazing sight of the snow beyond the window, but her grogginess passed at once.

'Oh, hi. I'm sorry, I was trying to keep quiet.'

'I don't mind. What time is it?' The sky beyond the windows was grey, saying only that the clouds were low and dawn had not yet come.

'Onto six. You've another twenty minutes before the bell.' She put a bundle on the chair. 'Here are clothes.'

Ivy's voice was warm, and her eyes when they met Mandy's were full of friendship. Yesterday the girl had seemed so reserved – and so mean, creating the trouble with the Hobbes edition and all. She had certainly had a change of mood. Mandy remained angry with her over the business with the book. It wasn't unreasonable, she thought, to want an apology. Ivy cheerfully poked up the fire.

When it blazed she stepped to the centre of the room, hands on hips. 'How's your pot?'

'My – oh, I used it, if that's what you mean.'

'That's what I mean,' Ivy said. She reached under the bed, hauled it out, and glided away with the big blue porcelain pot cradled in her arms. 'Breakfast in the kitchen at 6:30,' she called over her shoulder. A moment later Mandy heard her tell Constance that 'the lady' was up. How old

136

was Ivy? Seventeen, perhaps. Certainly she was too old to be calling twenty-three-year-old Mandy a 'lady.'

It took no small amount of courage to step naked into the freezing-cold room. A curtained bed, she had found, was a most delicious luxury. Maybe the style had been abandoned because it was simply too comfortable. She dashed over to the chair and opened the bundle, finding a bra and panties, and some of the homespun that the others wore, what seemed a shapeless dress that, when she wore it, clung most beautifully.

The cloth was so cold against her skin it made her hop and gasp.

She had just tied the belt when she heard a meow at the window. There stood Tom, pressing against the glass, looking annoyed to be out in the snow.

Down at the village he had seemed dangerous. But now he was a cold old cat, and she couldn't resist letting him in. When she raised the sash, the burst of freezing air that engulfed her made her squeal. 'Come in here, you! Hurry up!'

The cat rushed past her and in an instant was curled up in front of the fireplace.

'You're a weird one, kitty-cat. How'd you get out here in the first place? Did you follow me?'

The cat stared at her. She wanted to stroke him but thought better of it.

'If you ever want a kiss,' she said softly, 'you know who loves you.' She puckered up and went 'mmmmm,' but the cool seriousness of the cat's gaze silenced her.

This was unexpected. Could an animal see into a human soul?

Nervously she returned to her preparations. She had to break the ice on her pitcher to wash. The soap was home-made and smelled powerfully of peppermint. It smelled, as a matter of fact, very much like Constance Collier, like Ivy, like Robin. It smelled like this house. And it wasn't only mint, was it? There was in it a hint of some more exotic herb.

After her wash she dragged on her muddy shoes and wished she had some heavier ones, and also a good jacket or sweater.

And she wished Tom would stop that staring! Could there be laughter in a cat's eyes? Either he loved her or he disdained her. Or worse, both. Even though she was dressed, she still felt naked.

It took the faint tapping of flakes at her window to draw her mind away from him. October 19 and already it was snowing. If such weather held, this was going to be a long, cold winter. She peered through the hazy glass. What magic she saw, the world transformed to philosophical purity, silent but for the hiss of snow against snow and the rattling of bare limbs.

As the sky lightened she saw that the snow had touched the autumn colours of the trees with white. The perfection of the colours together, the pillowy razor of white, the staring reds, the oranges and browns, went to the centre of her, for the scene the snow had created was truly a wonder of nature.

When Constance came along, swathed in a huge woollen robe, nothing but a face in the dark folds, Mandy was still motionless before the window. 'I know,' Constance said, touching her shoulder with long, light fingers. 'You'll need the clothes we got you. Why didn't Ivy –' She went to the door. 'Ivy?' Louder: 'Ivy!'

From downstairs: 'I'm in the kitchen, Connie.'

'We need Amanda's warm things. She's practically naked, the poor girl.' She turned around. 'Ivy's quite new to big-house responsibilities. But she has a good heart. A very good heart.'

Her footsteps sounded on the stairs. A few moments later she appeared with another stack of clothes topped by a pair of stout hiking boots. 'I'm sorry, Mandy. I completely forgot the rest – the important stuff, too. I think it's too cold for me today.' She looked down at Mandy's feet. 'What's your shoe size?'

'Seven and a half B.'

'Hiking boots have to be a little bigger to make room for the socks. I think I guessed right, though.'

'I'm glad you thought of them at all.'

'You need good shoes. You must learn every inch of this estate as if it were your own,' Constance said.

There was a beautiful hand-knit wool sweater of rich, iridescent brown, and beneath it something huge and dark and grey. Mandy put on the sweater and unfolded the mysterious garment.

It was a hooded, ankle-length cloak made of the tightest homespun she had ever seen. Down the front were mono-grammed a five-pointed star, a triangle, a sickle moon, and two other, more obscure symbols. It was tied about the neck with a red silk ribbon.

'This is wonderful.'

'You like it?'

She swept it across her shoulders and tied the ribbon. Ivy raised the hood. The cloak was heavy and warm and altogether magnificent. 'Oh, Constance, I love it. Really love it!'

'It took half a year to make. The weavers started in April. We made it just for you.'

Mandy looked at her. What she had just said didn't make sense.

'I've been watching you ever since you were a girl,' Constance added. 'And when I saw your work in Charles Bell's book, I knew it was time for you to come to me.' She smiled. 'Change your clothes and come down to breakfast. We're wasting time.'

The table, when Mandy arrived, was spread with a red-checked oilcloth. A fire roared in the huge old stove and the windows ran with condensation. Mandy sat down to a plate of pancakes and syrup. There was a side dish of blackberries and a pitcher of fresh cream. Tea of an herb unknown to her completed the meal. 'Everything you're eating came from this estate. It can feed you four seasons of the year. And if you like homespun it can clothe you, too.'

'The village –'

'It's an experiment. The villagers are trying to live really close to the land. Everything at the village comes from the surrounding fields and forests. The village lives by the breath of the earth, which is the weather, and the heartbeat of the earth, which is the seasons. And they live close to one another, too, unled except by the necessities that the land imposes.'

'Who are they, Constance? Are they witches, like we thought in the town?'

'Friends. Most of them are from Maywell. Some from farther away. They're people who want to be reinitiated into personal contact with the earth. The village is an effort to balance old ways with new.' She smiled. 'Because we have drifted so far from our relationship with the planet, many people have a tremendous need to rediscover their inner love for her. That's what the village is about. It is only the first of its kind, I hope and trust.'

Tom came into the room. He stood beside Constance's chair, looking up at her.

Mandy dug into her pancakes. They were sour and heavy and delicious, made of a rough-ground flour and raised by their own rot, with neither baking powder nor yeast added.

With one of those swift, amazing leaps of his, Tom jumped onto the top of Constance's head. Mandy was so startled she all but threw her fork. But Constance hardly seemed to notice the creature that had draped itself over her scalp like some kind of lunatic fur hat with eyes.

The eyes sought Mandy. Didn't he ever stop staring?

'Amanda, today I want you to begin your work. To try to do something very special and very difficult.'

Constance had leaned forward. Her tone was serious. But

she looked – well – fantastically odd with the cat on her head.

'I want you to take your sketchbook and go out onto Stone Mountain and find the *Leannan Sidhe* and draw a picture of her.'

Mandy remembered the statue in the maze. 'The Fairy Queen – do you mean there's a statue of her up there, too?'

'Go across the hummocks to the foot of Stone Mountain. You'll find a path starting at a grove of birch. Just a track. It'll be tricky to negotiate. Climb the mountain until you come to a big rowan bush. Really huge. Do you know what rowan looks like?'

Tom crawled down her shoulder and disappeared under the table.

'To me a bush is a bush, Constance. I have no idea.'

'Look for smooth grey bark, red-orange leaves, and clumps of red berries. You really can't miss it. It's the only one like it on the mountain. Just beyond it you'll find a large round stone that's got figures etched into it. But they're weathered, so you won't be able to make them out. You sit yourself down on that stone. Sooner or later fairy will come. The Queen is instantly recognizable.'

Surely her leg was being pulled. 'You mean – real fairies?'

'I mean real fairies. They're about three feet tall, very broad-shouldered the men, and they'll be wearing their whites because of the snow. White breeches and tunics, mottled white caps. And she will be in white, too. A white gown of silken lace. She's blonde, and she'll have rowan in her hair. You'll see.'

She was so serious about this that Mandy became embarrassed. Constance Collier must be senile. 'You see these fairies?'

'My dear, fairy are quite commonplace in the Peconic Mountains. They live all through this end of Jersey and Pennsylvania. And they are not tinkerbelles and tom-tits, either, they are very real. Don't look for pixies, look for small, solid beings who are very real. They are as much a part of the planet as people and trees and cats. Much more than we. They're a Paleolithic survival, dear. The fairy were exterminated in western Europe during the Middle Ages because they're pagans. They follow the Goddess. This country is so big the fairy never got discovered. Even to this day there are parts of Stone Mountain that man hasn't explored. And all a fairy needs to hide is a bush not much bigger than a pillow.'

Mandy felt cut adrift from reality. This woman was rational and sane and serious.

'They built the burial mound you drove past coming here. And the hummocks out in the back pasture – those are the remains of a fairy city built before the Iroquois conquered this valley.' She tossed her head. 'The same families that built those houses have been up there on the mountain for thousands of years, waiting for the day when they can come down and reclaim their city.'

'What are they – I mean – what about language? Do they speak English? What should I say? And what if she wants money to sit for me? Tell me what to do.'

'Show the Queen respect. Bear in mind that we have been on this land three hundred years, and the Indians two thousand years. The fairy have been here since before the ice. Think of that. A hundred thousand years, maybe longer. You are on their land, we all are. Their Queen is the highest and most sacred being you will ever see in your life.' She paused. 'Of course they may not show her, they're unpredictable that way.'

As she had spoken, Constance Collier's voice had rolled through the room, commanding, powerful, full of strength and assurance. It was the opposite of senile. This was the very voice of wisdom, and in spite of their incredible nature, Mandy found herself forced to listen to Constance's words.

'Time is short, girl. Go your way. And don't make a fool of yourself by getting lost.'

Ivy shrieked and jumped back from the table.

For an instant Mandy thought she was reacting to the wild things Constance was saying, but then Tom's head appeared from under the tablecloth.

'I'm sorry! He stuck his nose between my legs!'

'Honestly, Ivy. You're awfully edgy this morning.'

'His nose is cold.'

'You know to keep your legs crossed when he's around.' She looked at Mandy. 'Watch out for him. He can be a tricky devil.'

Ivy moved away from the table. With a glance at her watch Constance told Mandy to get started.

'But I have no idea what to do!'

'I gave you your instructions. I want you to fall back on your own ingenuity. Amanda, darling, this is only the second test, and it's not the hardest. Please get going.'

'Now, wait a minute. What test? You must be some sort of a lunatic if you think I'm going to go traipsing around snow-covered mountains looking for fairies! I was brought here to illustrate a children's book. *That* I'm willing to do.' And that was that.

'I can't tell you what I'm offering you, Amanda.' She looked at the cat, who was now sitting on the drainboard licking the lip of the hand pump at the sink. 'If I did he wouldn't like it.'

'The cat wouldn't like it?'

She nodded. 'Something very odd might happen. You'd be surprised at what he can do.'

He continued licking the drips off the pump.

'I don't mind if you're eccentric. In fact, I'm flattered that you trust me enough to be yourself with me.'

'Amanda, this is *not* senility or eccentricity. What's more, it's terribly important.' Her voice was pleading now. 'You must do it. More is at stake than you can possibly know.'

'What? What's at stake? I came here to illustrate –'

'Hush! Forget that book. It was just a pretext to get you

here.' She reached across the table, grabbed Mandy's collar with trembling fingers. 'You must trust me, just for a little while. Amanda, I'd rather kill myself than lie to you. Please trust me.'

Tears appeared at the edges of Constance's eyes. Mandy reached up and took the old woman's hands in her own. 'I can do with a hike. I'm sure I'll be fine.'

She simply could not turn down such a heartfelt appeal. The only thing to do was just open her mind and let things happen. Whatever she found on the mountain, she found.

If there really *were* fairies – well, what fun. She got up, drew her cloak around her, and went out. The door slammed behind her. She pulled up her hood against the gusts of snow. The flakes were small and very hard, and they rattled against the thick wool. Mandy set out, her boots crunching the powdery half-inch thickness that crusted the ground, her face stinging in the fresh wind off the mountain. The clouds were low and grey; the sun was a smear in the east. As she walked along, Mandy's heart thrilled. She was so gay she thought to sing. Whatever happened on Stone Mountain, it was going to be highest adventure.

Even if she was *really* intended to enlist her imagination and draw the most wonderful Fairy Queen ever created.

She went down past the maze and through the herb garden.

Beyond the garden the land sloped farther down, then rose abruptly up the side of the first of the hummocks. When she reached the top she saw a group of men far off to the south working on her car with ropes and wooden pulleys. They wore deep brown homespun, and she could just catch the edges of a work song, the rhythm of the chant but not the words. The tone of their voices fairly lilted. The joy in them, so open and unrestrained, carried clearly across the air.

Down the hummock she scrambled, trying to avoid getting her cloak caught in the bushes at its base.

'Amanda!'

A male voice. 'Who's that?'

A bush trembled. Instinctively Mandy backed away. There had been something harsh about that call, something that made her cautious.

A face, youthful, satyr-like, appeared in the shrubs. With a great shudder of snow Robin stood up. He came close to her. 'Where are you going?' he asked. He stood directly in front of her, dressed in a long wool cape, wool trousers, and a heavy coat belted at the waist. 'You're going to the rowan, aren't you?'

Mandy said nothing.

'You know how the fairies keep themselves such a deep secret? If somebody sees them they don't like, that person never comes back.'

Still Mandy said nothing. Robin seized her and kissed her with cold lips. 'I love you!'

He was still a boy, and the road between seventeen and twenty-three is a long one. It was years since she had heard 'I love you' uttered with such enthusiasm. 'Thank you,' she said. How pale and controlled by comparison.

'Connie didn't tell you anything about how to act, did she? About how to survive.'

'I didn't get the impression they were dangerous.'

'Oh, but they are. They're very dangerous. They have the fairy whisper. Nobody knows what it is, because it kills instantly. And they have tiny arrows made of splinters. The poison on the arrows gives you a heart attack, and no doctor can ever tell that you were poisoned. Hunters that die in the woods of cardiac arrest – half of them paid with their lives for seeing fairy.'

'Constance never even hinted at danger.'

'But there is! You're being tested. Constance thinks you're the Maiden, but they can't be sure until the *Leannan* looks into your heart. She has all the fairy knowledge. She'll read you like a chalkboard and either kill you or accept you. It's all the same to the *Leannan*.'

'You're telling me I could be killed?'

'If you aren't just exactly who you're supposed to be, the fairy can't let you go. Surely you can see that. They don't want civilization meddling in their affairs. Anthropologists after them, for heaven's sake. They saw what happened to the Indians, and they know that all their own kind in Europe were exterminated. They're very defensive, the fairy.'

Mandy began to entertain the notion of turning back. 'Can you answer me one question?'

'Probably not.'

'Why me? Why am I being put through this . . . initiation or whatever it is.'

'You mean you don't even know that? Constance is really playing it close with you.'

'She must be.'

'You're unique, Amanda. She's been watching you all of your life. Why do you think your father was transferred to Maywell? She brought him here so you would be close to her. What Constance knows – it's impossible to tell, but she had the help of the *Leannan* at her disposal, as well as all the traditional lore of the witches. She commands a high and rare science, and you have to be very careful around her. You are old in the craft, Connie says.'

'Which craft?'

'Oh, wow, you're really in a hole. Wicca, darling, witchcraft.'

'I thought that was it. All the town rumours are true, then. Everything.'

'Oh, not everything. By no means. All the good rumours, let's say, and none of the bad! We're learning the old ways again from Connie, and from the *Leannan* and her folk. And you are going to be our next Maiden, which is a sort of protector, especially if we're under pressure from the outside. And our group is growing so fast, it's only a question of time before the pressure starts. The very word "witch" 'conjures up terrible images in people's minds. They think we're evil.'

'The wicked witch.'

'A false impression. Witchcraft is – well, you'll see when you get to know us better.' His voice had taken on an edge of conviction. In many ways Robin was certainly a boy, but his love for what he believed was a mature emotion.

'Amanda!' It was Constance, calling from the edge of the herb garden.

Robin's eyes narrowed. 'She musn't see me! Run, run to the top of the hummock! Wave to her, tell her you're on your way.'

As Mandy found footing in the snow she heard his voice behind her, a barely audible whisper: 'Blessed be, my love, blessed, blessed be!'

Blessed be? The witches' greeting and good-bye. Mandy had read of it in Margaret Murray's famous book, *The Witch Cult in Western Europe*. Nobody interested in fairy tales could escape without reading Murray.

She remembered her own dreams of being burned . . . and of being in a cage – awful dreams. She shuddered and went on.

Constance stood like a fur-wrapped stick a hundred yards behind. 'Please hurry,' she cried. 'Plea-ase! The *Leannan* doesn't wait for anybody very long!' Her voice was snatched by the wind and carried off among the rattling trees.

Far ahead of her she saw Tom jumping through the snow. She looked past him, to the dark tremendous mountain.

And she found that she was at least as curious as she was uneasy. She wanted to see the fairy. Oh, *if* there were such beings. A nonhuman intelligence sharing the earth with man. It was so enormous a thought that she couldn't even begin to play out its implications, so she simply filed it in a corner of her mind to deal with later.

From where she was now she could see a few curls of smoke off in the direction of the village. It was interesting to imagine life there, wearing homespun and using candles within hiking distance of modern America. There was undeniable appeal in the idea of reacquiring ancient ways. The witch rituals, for example, were so very old and strange that they had been ultimately terrifying to the superstitious medieval world. Now anthropologists understood them as a remnant of human prehistory. The Old Religion, the way of the earth. Wasn't 'witch' an early English word for wise, or had that theory been discredited?

Crossing towards the tumbled, frowning face of the mountain, she heard off in the direction of the village a girl singing in a clear voice.

> 'Lost on grey hills, in autumn's dread splendour,
> The wandering one, wandering one
> Will the moon ever find her?'

The lilting, sweet-haunted song did not fade until Mandy was battling her way up Stone Mountain.

The more she committed herself to it, the more brutal the climb seemed to become. The 'track' was a miserable affair, twisting and turning, as often as not blocked by fallen stones or an outgrowth of brambles. But for the glowing snow there was little light, and would be no more unless the sun broke through the clouds that were coming down from the north.

As Mandy struggled along, her feet grew cold despite the thick woollen socks and the good boots. Time and again she slipped on an icy spot or was deceived by the snow into stepping into a hole. She had been climbing what seemed to be an hour when the incline finally grew less steep. She stopped to look for the rowan bush.

Everything was a jumble. She couldn't possibly tell one plant from another. She turned around and found that she hadn't come more than two hundred feet. She was just now getting level with the roof of the distant house, which stood on its dark hill among its trees, seeming most forlorn and distant at this empty hour.

The wind belled her cloak and made her remember the world within that curtained bed. And Robin. 'I love you,' he had said. How could he love somebody he didn't know?

She wiped the snow from her eyebrows and continued on.

Now the wind whispered, now it howled through the shaking trees. A fine hiss of snow made its way deep into her hood and reminded her painfully of her ears. She pulled the silken ribbon together. The track was now a mayhem of sharp rocks. To make any progress at all she had to crawl.

Paradoxically that very fact made her go on. The harder it became to climb it, the more she responded to the challenge of the mountain. She had not been given gloves, and her hands soon smarted from the cold and the stones. Her sketchbook, stuffed in her waist, jabbed her breastbone with first one corner and then the other.

If she had any sense, she would find some overhang, cuddle up under it, and make a few sketches of the Fairy Queen from imagination. Surely that was all Constance really intended. There could not be a Paleolithic species still surviving in these hills. And even if there were, they would be dirty, miserable, and scarce. Savages had none of the awesome beauty Constance had attributed to the *Leannan*. Savages living on a mountainside as rough as this would be little better than animals themselves.

The Paleolithic was thousands of years ago. Beyond memory. Beyond time. The whole notion was ridiculous.

And yet, Constance and Robin had both been so serious. Her whole life was dreams and visions and longing for miracles. Now she might be close to one – just might be. She struggled on. The wind roared without ceasing, like some immense tide restless in the rocks. Constance Collier had neglected to mention another little matter of some importance: the rowan must be on the very brow of the mountain, that dark, bare spine that got covered with deadly ice in the winter.

When she did come to the top, it happened so abruptly that she at first did not understand where she was. She almost staggered out onto a menacing slickness of ice as smooth as glass. She lurched and slid, then toppled amid her flapping, flopping cloak. Her sketchbook bent completely in two. She felt her pencils scattering out of her pockets.

Scuttling about, she retrieved them.

When she raised her head, she was frozen, but not by cold. This was a place of wonder. She could see to the north the long brow of the mountain, its gnarled trees huddling against it like warped children. The west wrinkled off forever. Beyond the Peconics were the Endless Mountains and on the haze the northwestern fastness of Pennsylvania.

This was the border of one of the continent's last empty corners. Below lay Maywell in its shield of snow, the steeple of the Episcopal Church marking the dead centre of the town. She could see The Lanes and almost make out Uncle George's house. The college's black buildings squatted beyond the diagonal line of the Morris Stage Road. Directly below was the Collier estate. Huddling almost invisibly at the very foot of the mountain, the witch village blended so perfectly with the landscape that even looking at it she wasn't completely sure it was there. After some time she counted twenty cottages, ten on each side of the central path. Foundations and walls for twelve more were in the process of being laid. The round building dominated the village. Occasionally a figure huddled from one door to another. Among the snowy hummocks tiny human dots raced about – the children of the village were out with sleds.

So very hidden, so secret, was the witch village. Through all of her growing up in the town, she had heard of only one incident of townspeople meeting villagers on their own ground – and those kids hadn't seen the village itself. Now

150

she was seeing the whole estate, village and all, and it was lovely.

It did not prove nearly as hard as she had expected to find the rowan. An imposing bush, it stood easily ten feet high, its northern side angled from the wind, the rest of it rich with berries, a gay-painted creature in this impossibly hostile place. The rowan was so very alive that Mandy loved it immediately. It stood fast in its bed of ice and stones. But it was also a great, gangling adolescent of a thing. When the wind made it gyrate, she wanted to laugh.

She made her way around it, touching twigs and berries as she went. Somehow she kept expecting to see Tom, but he wasn't about. Naturally not. There was a cat who liked a fireplace. A romp along the lower reaches of the mountain had been quite enough for him.

She found the round stone Constance had described. It was perhaps eight feet in diameter and two thick, standing at a slight angle on the surface of the mountain. It was black basalt, completely out of place in this granite geology. The surface was carved over every inch, but time and wind had worked it, too, so only the presence of the etching could be detected, not its content.

Basalt is a hard stone. Mandy ran her hand along the ice-crusted edge. The thing must be very old. What tremendous effort it must have been to bring it here, for it was certainly an import.

Just as she had been told to do, Mandy went to the centre of the stone and sat down. She folded her cloak under her and sat cross-legged, so that she made a sort of a tent and was at the same time insulated from the icy rock. She faced southeast, away from the wind. This cloak had been exactly the right garment for what she was expected to do, which was sit and wait . . . and wonder how crazy she was to have come here.

Some adventure to get this cold. Not to mention thirsty and hungry. An image of those delicious unfinished pancakes came to mind. She saw the dark-flecked surface of them, the slightly crumbly interior, the amber glow of the syrup oozing along the plate. The memory confirmed the fact that she had very quickly ceased to enjoy this. She was up here alone and this was a damned cold place and she was freezing.

No sooner had the thought of leaving crossed her mind than a bird, of all things, fluttered out of the rowan and flapped about her head. It wasn't in the least afraid. This place must be very little visited. The dusty little sparrow was what city people called a trash bird. First with one bright, blank eye and then the other it looked at her. She had the distinct impression not only that it was a girl bird but that it felt kind of friendly towards her.

If she had brought crumbs she could have fed it, the little thing was so unafraid. She had never fed a wild bird before. 'Sweet, sweet,' she said. It flew away.

The next moment a squirrel, its fur rich and grey-black, came ambling along. It stopped at the rowan and ate berries for a time. Then it, too, came over to the rock and looked at the strange creature there.

'Hi,' Mandy said.

The squirrel raised itself up on its haunches and wiggled its nose at her. Then, as abruptly as if it had been called, it jumped and raced away over the edge of the mountain. It had not been gone ten seconds before Mandy felt the pressure of paws on her back. She turned around and startled a raccoon, which tumbled about in the snow, righted itself, mewed at her, and went on with its casual sniffing of her cloak. Then it poked its frigid nose at her hands, smelling them carefully. 'Well, I like you, too.'

The sound of her voice made the coon look up at her. It mewed back, the cry so full of question that she ached to answer. But she could only smile, as she did not speak coon.

She began to understand Constance's sending her here. There might not be any fairies, but it was nevertheless a magical spot and a fine place to let the images flow in her mind. Despite the cold, the ice, despite everything, she could *create* extraordinary fairies here. There are places of life and places of death. Here on this inhospitable mountain between the sky and the rowan Amanda knew a feeling so strong it shocked her. Especially because it was not an aggressive feeling at all, but one of the peace and rightness of this world. No matter the fate of man, the loss or regaining of the old cup of kindness, peace abides.

A quick, hairy movement beyond the rowan brought her back to the present. She almost screamed when she saw what was there. Surely it couldn't be. But it was, and it had just noticed her. It moved like a great black furry rock, humping quickly along. There was nothing cute about the bear's black little eyes or the fog coming from its muzzle. She sat dead still, her attention fixed on the approaching beast.

The closer it got the faster it came. She could hear it breathing now, hear the clatter of its claws on the ice. A terrible, buzzing fear froze her.

When it bellowed she knew it, too, was a female, as the other animals had also been. If each animal could be said to represent an attribute of woman, this bear was the power of her protective instinct. Her greatest and most dangerous power. A she-bear protecting her cubs is the most fearsome of creatures.

Slowly, carefully, Mandy spread her arms, palms open. Why the gesture? She did not know. Now she could smell the bear, a thick odour of rancid fur. Its coat was shiny with secretions. Mandy found herself looking into the animal's eyes. She saw there a femininity so savage, so full of implacable power, that it drew a choked little sound from her throat. The bear grumbled in reply, stared a moment, then became indifferent to her.

It walked on past, crashing off into the fastness of the mountain. Perhaps this bear was without cubs, or they were not nearby.

While it had diverted her attention something else had

happened, something which filled her soul with a coldness far greater than that of the wind.

About the rowan there stood six small men in snow-white coats and breeches. On their feet were white pointed shoes, and on their heads close-fitting caps just as Constance had described.

It wasn't possible. And yet, here they were.

Robin's warning rushed back into her mind.

She screamed, a single, sharp cry, quickly controlled. These men had sharp faces with pointed noses and large eyes. Perhaps they looked so different precisely because they were so almost-human. But then one of them licked his lips, and Mandy got a glimpse of tiny teeth more like a rat's than a man's.

Together they raised bows, and mounted arrows on them made of twigs. There came then on the air the ringing of small bells and a whisper of tiny feet in the snow.

She appeared from behind the stone, all blonde, her hair as soft as elder blow, her eyes startlingly dark brown, her body lightly dressed in the very lace Constance had promised. She was wee, not nearly as large as her six guards. On her head was a garland of rowan, berries and stems and leaves. Seeing such beauty, how ineffable, how frail, how strong, Mandy thought she would simply sink away. By comparison she herself was coarse. All delicacy seemed to have concentrated itself in this single small creature. Around her neck there was drawn a silver chain, and at her throat hung a gleaming sickle of moon.

Mandy instinctively lowered her eyes. It was more bearable this way, just looking at the woman's feet, no more than two inches long, naked in the snow. Then the feet rose out of her line of sight. She looked up, startled. The girl was floating in the air. Wings flapped and she was gone. A great grey owl hooted from the top of the rowan, its horns darkly silhouetted against the sky. It took flight, racing round and round the rowan. Next hoofs clattered on the stones, and a black mare reared into nothingness, its neighs echoing off to silence.

An ancient woman, drooling, her teeth yellow, one eye put out, her hands fantastic with arthritis, scraped up on a stick. 'Oh, my God! Can I help you?'

She held out her hands then and was as suddenly gone, the maiden spinning forth from her flying grey hair. The girl took Mandy's large hands in her own tiny ones. She was grave now, her eyes limpid – and yet so very *aware*. They were scary. Her lips parted as if she would speak.

Mandy remembered Robin's warning about the whisper. The girl's voice was as much the wind's as her own. 'You're trembling,' she said.

'I'm cold.'

'Come a little way with me.'

Mandy started to stand up, but she was stopped by the astonishing sensation of being enclosed in enormous, invisible hands. Woman's hands, immense and strong and soft. They drew her close to an invisible breast, clutched her, enfolded her. It was a terrifyingly wrong sensation: there was nobody here, and nobody could ever be so huge. She struggled, she tried to scream, she felt her stomach unmooring with fright.

But she found herself being cuddled in warm perfumed folds that could be felt and smelled and even tasted, so rich they were. All of the tension, the discomfort, the fear in Mandy's body melted away. Then, just as she was beginning to enjoy herself, she was set down. She wobbled, she cried out, she flailed at the air.

Never had she felt so thoroughly explored, so – somehow – examined. She had the eerie feeling that whatever had held her had also been in her mind. And was still there, looking and discovering, moving like a strange voice in her thoughts. But it wasn't ugly at all, it was young and so very, very happy and so glad to meet her. She couldn't help herself, she burst out laughing.

The lady laughed, too.

'Who *are* you?' Mandy asked her.

But she was gone, they were all gone, as clouds upon the air.

BOOK TWO

The Sleeping Beauty

That such have died enables us
  The tranquiller to die;
That such have lived, certificate
  For immortality.

— Emily Dickinson

The tom moved quickly, nervously, through the silent animal room. The terrariums were empty, the bloodstained monkey cage was empty. Even though the animals were gone, the room was still full of the ammonia stink of captured things. The tom hated this room, but he hated more the people next door, hated them enough to use them mercilessly. Because of their guilty dislike of themselves, he did not consider Bonnie and Dr Walker capable of being true witches, and Clark understood enough to take care of himself.

He could feel the faint rush of microwaves from the newly installed motion detector in the centre of the room. Such things were not powerful in his world, and they neither surprised nor impressed him. When he wanted Dr Walker to come in here, he would trip the alarm, but not until then.

Despite his disapproval of her, the tom could not help but feel a little compassion for Bonnie. She was about to suffer a most interesting death.

George preferred to think of himself and Bonnie as wanderers in a deadly jungle. Somehow Clark was not with them, perhaps because he was so dedicated a technician, too realistic to have a commitment to the romance of the experiment, and no sense of the art of the work.

Unless at least one of them was awake and on guard, they had to assume their experiment would be ruined by Brother Pierce and his fanatics. There were various things George would like to do to Brother Pierce, chief among them being dismemberment. Slow, considered dismemberment, the lifting off of appendages.

No. Burn him. Do it with a candle. Or tattoo his crimes on him. People did not understand the politics of pain, how it must settle in the victim and remain there for a time. An image from his dreams, of cat claws, hung a moment in his thoughts. He could light a fire in agony's tower on behalf of all destroyed things. He raged, and he hurt, and felt a fine rush of guilt: he could have delivered his body to Bonnie's will just then.

But he enjoyed too much the intricate mechanics of killing her, enjoyed her trembles and the faint scent of her sweat and the coolness of the skin to which he would soon attach electrodes.

He surveyed this tangled technical realm of his and saw that it was well sealed against the rages of Brother Pierce.

It had taken a trip all the way to Altoona to find locks for the lab doors that were both secure and cheap. Somehow George had installed them, reading the sketchy instructions, going by trial and error. His fingers were thoroughly mutilated but the tumblers worked smoothly and the steel protective plates were tight against the doors. He had put bolts on the windows and had bought a fifty-dollar motion detector at Radio Shack. It sat in the middle of the now empty animal room, ready to give warning if anybody should come that way. He had tried to buy a closed-circuit TV camera for the hall outside the lab, but he couldn't afford the four hundred dollars.

'This is just wonderful,' Clark said. He was staring at a piece of interoffice correspondence. 'Really very nice.'

Bonnie was eating boysenberry yogurt; George had been staring at the coils that surrounded the outline of her body that they had chalked on the lab table. 'What?' she asked.

Her eyes, so green, so full of fire, regarded Clark calmly. George himself was shaking, not with excitement or desire, but with the thought of just how risky this was going to be for her.

'It's a very politely worded requisition for our lab space. "In view of the impending completion of your grant-related activities there," it says. You'll never guess what they're going to put in here.'

'A bar?'

'Fruit flies. They're going to use it as a fruit fly hatchery for Biology One.'

'I wish I had a Bio One assistantship. No offence, George, but it's a secure job.' Even Bonnie's voice was calm.

'I don't know,' Clark said, 'the work's too predictable. Boring as hell, raising generation after generation of fruit flies.'

'Some people,' Bonnie said around a spoonful of yogurt, 'are better than others at fruit flies.' She laughed, high and sharp, betraying a first sign of nervousness. 'Your trouble is you're not committed to your work. I don't think you care. Take me, I'm the opposite. I'm dying to keep my job.'

George looked at her. There was panic in there behind the brittle humour. He did not relish the prospect of her getting balky. What would he do if she tried to back out?

'I think we'd be best off if you went in with as calm an attitude as possible. I'd like to see you in alpha before we put you under.'

'In alpha! You think I can lie there meditating while you kill me? Look, if you want to talk about it, let's be completely frank with one another. Shall we?'

'Of course.'

'Then I'll drop my act and tell you the truth. Yeah, you guessed it. I am scared to death! Absolutely.' She laughed again, this time without even the pretence of mirth. ''S funny, scared to death. But what if –' She stopped. The silence thickened rapidly. She stared down at her yogurt container. On the other side of the room Clark muttered numbers and worked with calipers, positioning the coils so that the fields they created would touch without overlapping.

'Are you afraid we can't bring you back? I just want you to think of the principles involved. You *know* you'll be returning. The physics is basic, so is the biology. Nothing's going to go wrong.'

'Oh, George, you really don't understand, do you? Not at all!'

'Understand what? Tell me what you're driving at, then I'll see if I understand.'

'George, what if something is *out there*?'

He restrained himself from laughing with relief. He had been afraid that he was going to have to cope with real death panic. But this sort of fear wasn't that bad. 'Come on, now, you're a scientist and a witch. You *know* what's out there.'

'Oh, no. I don't think you understand. I've enjoyed the witch rituals and all, but I was baptized a Catholic. They brand your soul at birth.'

'Oh, Bonnie, come on. That's absurd. Belief is relative. Death will be exactly what you expect it to be.'

'I just keep thinking, what if there really is a hell? And then I think, what if I fall in and I can't get out? I know it's stupid, it's highly unsophisticated, but there it is.'

'That's what's scaring you?'

'That's it. I don't think I can help expecting some kind of Catholic hell. Or worse, a Catholic heaven, which is a form of hell where the good are brainwashed into wanting to sing at all times.'

'You know what it's going to be like? Shall I tell you?'

'I wish you could.'

'My dear, beautiful Bonnie.' He caressed her cheek. It was so warm, so soft – he kissed it. 'I would never do anything I thought might hurt you in any way.'

He imagined her hanging from the ceiling, himself at her feet, and she comes down from her garrotte transformed into

162

a virgin of retribution and takes him at last to the black chamber.

The chamber in his basement.

No! Don't think of that. Not now.

'You're going to kill me, and I'm going to find out I'm still a Catholic after it's too late. The Devil –'

'You know where that legend came from! The Horned God isn't a devil any more than the Mother Goddess is a virgin. The King of the Netherworld and the Queen of Heaven are the oldest of seasonal deities.'

'I'm being sacrificed for a lark. So *you* can find out what it's like.'

When he spoke, it was as if the words were formed by an outer mechanism, a device that had been made to seem human: 'Oh, that's low,' said the outer George Walker. 'That's a low blow. Let's get our priorities in order here. I think that's what we haven't done. First, we are performing this experiment for a reason, and it's an important one. The craft needs it. Constance needs it, and we all love her, don't we? Second, we will be giving mankind a new tool. A person killed in this way and cryogenically frozen could last indefinitely. What's more we'll revolutionize surgery, make ultra-long space voyages more practical.'

'Don't patronize me! I'm scared, that's all. I don't know what I'm facing.'

Clark came over. 'I hate to interrupt this charming conversation, but our electronics are ready.'

Bonnie stood up as if she had been sitting on a tack. Then she slumped. Clark caught her from behind.

'I know it's stupid but I'm so scared I can't move!'

George saw the tears brimming in her eyes. He had to act quickly. That was the merciful thing to do – and also, she might be on the point of changing her mind. 'Hey, now, take it easy.' He sat her back down on her stool. 'Clark, do you think you could bring in that swivel chair from the other room?'

When Clark opened the door to the animal room, the

motion detector started warbling. After a moment he cut it off and came back with the chair.

'Better restart the detector. Don't give them any chances at all.'

'Okay.'

As Clark went back, George moved Bonnie to the more comfortable chair. He stroked her hair.

'Because I'm a woman you think you can cuddle away all my fears.' Her voice was ugly and low. 'Get me my cigarettes.' She drew herself away from him.

'The no-smoking rule –'

'Get me my cigarettes!'

He got them from her purse, held them out to her. When she took one, he lit it for her. She smoked in silence for a time. Clark came back and stood over them with his arms folded, his expression dark and analytical. The only sound in the lab was the intimate noise of Bonnie's smoking, the crinkle of the burning tobacco, the blowing sound when she expelled the smoke.

'When I was a little girl, I went to Our Lady of Grace School right here in Maywell. It's a lovely old school, run by the Sisters of Mercy. Sister Saint Stephen, Sister Saint Martin, Sister Saint Agnes. And Mother Star of the Sea.' She laughed. 'Good old Mother Star of the Sea. I'm glad she's safely dead. Sometimes I still have nightmares about her.' Goose bumps appeared on Bonnie's arms. 'Oh, God, she's waiting for me. I can feel it, she is! Mother, I'm sorry. Please forgive me, Mother.'

George listened to her exploring her private fears. He thought she might be an angel, this lovely girl, an angel come to torment him with her innocence. If she had risen up and taken him and jammed him in the coils, he would have let her.

'The thing is, it's so easy for a Catholic to go to hell. I've got so many mortal sins. Hundreds.'

'You're a witch. You're in a coven.'

'Listen, a Catholic can go through a whole life, be all sorts of things. But when it comes time to die, the first thing that crosses your mind is "Dear God, where did I put my rosary?"'

'Sin is a relative thing, Bonnie. No church can tell you whether or not you've sinned. *You* have to believe it. That is one of the most freeing things I've learned from Connie.'

'You haven't learned it quite right. What she teaches is that the conscience never lies. I've sinned, George, by the lights of church and craft alike. What if some devil captures me and never lets me come back?'

George didn't like the drift of this. 'Ready,' he snapped.

Bonnie took a long drag on her cigarette. 'You wouldn't believe some of the things I've done. Poor Mother Star of the Sea. I'm still guilty as hell about her. I guess I always will be.'

'What happened?' Clark asked. George could have choked him.

She snorted. 'Baby boy, I've done things you would not believe. Things that would blow even your wiccan mind away.'

George laughed, trying hard to lighten this conversation. Casting about in his mind, he thought he had come across a way to reassure her and regain control of the situation. 'Bonnie, do yourself a favour and forget Catholic sins. How about the real sins against humanity? I mean, like murder. Have you ever murdered anybody?'

Clark shifted on his feet. 'Let her talk about her sins. It could be important.'

'Clark, please be quiet! Bonnie?'

'It depends entirely on your definition of abortion. If you say it's murder, I'm six times guilty.'

That was a bad move, Georgie boy. Still, he kept fighting. 'You're as innocent as any other accidental mother! Abortion isn't a crime, is it? An aborted foetus is simply somebody who didn't happen.'

'Mother Star of the Sea always taught that hell is very, very small, because the souls in it are so turned away from God, so concentrated on themselves, that they've literally gotten tiny.' She looked at her cigarette. '"The whole of hell could be hidden in one corner of a little coal" was the metaphor she used.'

He had to pull her back to their shared hopes or he was going to lose her. 'This is science, Bonnie. Our morality is that of science and craft.'

For the longest time she kept looking at the glowing end of the cigarette. 'I think I see it,' she said. 'Hell has come for me. It's hiding in my cigarette.'

'I told you not to smoke. Now let's get going.'

'It's waiting for me.'

In a desperate effort to distract her, George took her cheeks in his hands, turned her face to him, and kissed her full on the mouth. He probed against her teeth with his tongue. She resisted, then she opened her mouth to him. He concentrated on the pleasure of the contact. No matter the circumstances, a kiss is a kiss.

'Bonnie, I love you. I love you too much to let anything happen to you. Let me tell you –'

'George, with all respect this isn't going to work. I don't think –'

'Hush! Don't say another word. It can work and it will. You know in your heart just what will happen when I turn off your electrical functioning. You are going to go to sleep. Black sleep. Emptiness. Nothing. Gone.'

'George, how do you *know* that? You can't!'

'But I do! And so do you. And so does every human being. We live a little time and then we die and that is the end. Why do you think we're so afraid of death? Because in our heart of hearts we all know it's the end. No more George, no more Bonnie. Over. Done. That's what scares us, not some medieval mumbo jumbo about hell.'

'So I'll just be – like – asleep? That's what you're saying?'

166

'Exactly.'

She stubbed out her cigarette. 'I don't believe you.' A flicker of smile crossed her face. She drew George close to her, pressed her lips against his ear. 'You be sure and bring me back, because if you do I am going to take you to my room and take off your clothes and love you senseless.'

'I'll get a heart attack!'

'That's the general idea, you old fart! I just want to make sure you don't give up on me. I want total motivation.'

Here was the old Bonnie again, sexy and tough and humorous. Her words had really steamed him up. Getting into her would be quite an experience. Quite remarkable.

He hoped it would actually happen. As time went on and he became more and more a beggar to the altar of womanhood, he had learned to control such hopes. But Lord, not even as a twenty-five-year-old Lothario had he ever received such a hot proposition. Not even from Kate, and he had married her. Married her because she was soft and hard at the same time.

He wanted someone to twist the guilt out of his bowels even as they caressed him. As well as a woman, he wanted a judge.

Bonnie touched the chalked outline of her own body. 'That lab bench is cold.'

'Think of how famous you'll be. You'll be on the cover of magazines. Personal appearances. TV. Lecture tours. For a while you'll probably be the most famous person in the world.'

'Maybe I'll even get to meet a few people where I'm going. Bring back the rest of *Answered Prayers* from Truman Capote.'

'Funny girl.' He glanced at Clark, gave him a quick nod that said let's go.

Clark responded instantly. 'I'm ready to wire you up, dear.' Bonnie was wearing jeans and an MSC sweatshirt. She pulled off the shirt without even a trace of embarrassment. She wore no bra, and her breasts were as succulent as the pears of autumn. Clark hardly seemed to notice, making George wonder for a moment if they might not be old lovers. But they weren't, of course. They simply belonged to the unfortunate new generation, which took bodies for granted. Sex for them wasn't dirty, poor suckers.

George helped her onto the lab bench. 'It's really cold in here,' she said. 'Put a towel over me after you're finished, okay, Clark?'

'Yeah.' He greased her ankles and wrists and attached electrodes, then taped others down on her chest, forehead, and neck. George wished he was the one doing it, especially that blushing chest. 'All right, lemme see here.' Clark went over to the array of monitoring instruments. 'Is the tape rolling, George?'

'No.'

'It's set up,' Bonnie said. 'I didn't turn it on. All you have to do is press the "play" and "record" switches on the front of the machine.'

George found the buttons on the videotape recorder. When he pushed them down, the machine whirred. He could see the tape inside begin to spin. 'It's running.'

'Right,' Clark replied. 'Here I go. This is life signs monitoring for Bonnie Haver. I have the following metabolic signs. Heart rate 77, blood pressure 120 systolic, 70 diastolic. The subject weighed at the beginning of the experiment 128 pounds. She is a blonde Caucasian female, eyes green, distinguishing marks a crescent-shaped scar on the left breast below the nipple. She is twenty-three years, four months, and eight days old.'

Clark was an efficient man. George nodded to him from his own station before the instrument bank. He ran the quicktest on the coils, sending a brief jolt of current through it to test connections.

'Oh! I felt that!'

'Just the test burst. What did you feel?'

'Like I fell right through the table.'

'Good. That means it's working.' George began to adjust power to the coils, making certain that there would be uniform voltages at all points around her body. He did not know quite what would happen if some part of it was not correctly nulled. What, for example, would be the implication of a dead heart and a living brain? He certainly did not intend to perform that experiment on a human subject.

Clark continued. 'I am now going to read out the electrical status of the subject. Microvoltage loads are well within the normal range. Brain readings are as follows: alpha, .003 microvolts; beta, .014 microvolts; delta, .003 microvolts; lambda, .060 microvolts; theta, .0014 microvolts. Oscillation rate is nineteen. The brain is in deltoid activity level. All indications are normal, and suggest a resting person, somewhat tense. That completes this statement of the subject's current physical condition.'

Now it was George's turn. 'Thank you, Mr Jeffers. The condition of the null-electric apparatus is as follows: the coils are all at uniform resting voltage of .00012 microvolts, equal to the ambient charge of the atmosphere present in the laboratory, as measured by the Forest-Haylard atmospheric voltmeter, calibrated to standard zero 19 September, 1985, in this same setting. Since calibration no variances have occurred and no adjustments have been made. Thus I conclude that the instrument is accurate and the null-electric field is completely inactive at this time. A brief operational test confirmed by instrumentation and by subject perception that the field can be activated. That completes my statement of the condition of the instrumentation.' He paused a moment. 'I think, at this point, we might have the privilege of hearing from the subject.'

'I feel more or less normal. My stomach's slightly acidic and I must confess that I'm tense. My breathing feels normal and unrestricted. I'm cold. I guess I'm also a little scared.'

'Bonnie, are you willing to go ahead with the experiment?'

A tiny voice. Hopefully audible to the microphone. 'Yes.'

At that moment the motion detector in the animal room began warbling. George felt a surge of blood; Bonnie jerked and gasped; even Clark raised his eyebrows. 'Visitors?'

'I'll go,' George said. 'Just stay calm. Odds are it's a false alarm.' His lie was mostly for Bonnie's sake. 'Remember, that motion detector was cheap.' He had not told them of the pistol he had brought from home and he did not tell them now. But he drew his windbreaker on. The gun was in the pocket.

The door to the animal room was closed. George watched the knob to see if it was being turned from the other side. He reached into his pocket and grasped the pistol. Then he put his hand on the knob and began slowly turning it himself. He was scared, but more than that he was mad. If he found any of Brother Pierce's crazies in there, he just might start shooting.

Clark appeared beside him. 'Take it easy, George. If you're planning to use that gun, take it out of your pocket. It won't do you any good where it is now.'

George was impressed not only that he had noticed the pistol, but that he seemed to know how to handle a situation like this. 'You an auxiliary cop or something?'

'I'm a Burt Reynolds fan.'

George hefted the pistol. 'Ready, Burt?'

'Ready.'

He opened the door.

And saw something so impossibly dreadful that it made him jerk back. All the anger boiling in his soul threatened to erupt. He hated, hated, and yet –

Cat of fire, burning across a summer night of youth, cat of torment –

It sat, as black as space and enormous, on the windowsill. The window behind it was locked.

'Maybe it's a stray,' Clark said. He went over and turned off the motion detector.

George managed to force words from a chalky mouth. 'What's it doing in here?'

'Maybe it's been here all along – in a cabinet or something. Sleeping.'

George stared at it. The thing was really huge. 'What is it, some kind of a throwback?'

'Probably got a little wildcat in its genetic mix.'

'Well, I'm going to get it out of here. I hate cats. They're vermin, as far as I'm concerned.' He stuffed the pistol in his pocket and moved towards the animal, which promptly arched its back and hissed. Loud.

'Unwise move, George. That cat prefers to stay.'

'I can't use the motion detector with that thing wandering around in here.' He held out his hand. 'Kitty?'

Sssst!

'Most unwise move. Maybe if we went over to the gym and found a badminton net, we could throw it over him –'

'All right! I get your point. We'll lock the door between the rooms and worry about it later.'

'My thoughts exactly. The experiment will only take three minutes. Nobody's going to stop us in that short a time. They couldn't even get the door broken down. So we're home free, right? If we stop delaying.'

George closed and locked the door. He kept his wind-breaker on, though, with the pistol close at hand. When he brought in the motion detector, he had checked every nook and cranny in that room for stray frogs. He had looked in the cabinets, even under them. The room had been empty.

'Okay, Bonnie, we are going to start. Please report your out-of-the-ordinary sensations, if any.'

'Nothing so far.'

George flipped the seven switches that activated the coils. He began turning the rheostats. 'Establishing a voltage base at .17 microvolts.'

'Oh. Ohhh! I definitely feel that. It's a tingling.'

'Blood pressure down to 110 over 68.'

'I'm sort of – all floaty. Oh, this is weird!'

When she stopped talking, George was startled to hear the distinct growl of a cat. He frowned, tried to look over the top of his instrument panel towards the door to the animal room. Although he could only see the top half, he could tell that it was very certainly closed. God, did he ever have the jitters. Cats were loathsome creatures. They needed to be drowned, every one of them. Or to be set afire and left to run like meteors in among the old sycamores of home. How his own cruelty disgusted him.

'Microvolts to .50.'

'Blood pressure 80 over 66. Brain to alpha.'

'I'm kind of sleepy and I sort of have this tickle in the middle of my chest where my heart is. And it aches a little.' Her voice cracked. 'All of a sudden I feel sad.'

'Microvolts to .75. Damn!' Just for an instant he had seen the eyes of a cat hanging in midair over Bonnie. Glaring down at her.

'What is it?'

'No – forget it. I thought I was getting a bad reading. But it's okay. Fine.' He tried to slow down his own thundering heart, to control the sweat tickling his top lip. 'Bonnie, can you hear me?'

'Mmm?'

'She's showing theta peaks now, George. Oscillation is only five. She'll be unconscious in a few more seconds.'

'Microvolts to .90.'

'Blood pressure dropping. Theta dropping out. Oscillation null. Intercranial activity null.'

'But you still have some blood pressure?'

'Twenty over five. Dropping slowly.'

'Microvolts to 1.00.'

'The heart and blood have stopped. The brain has stopped. Dr Walker, clinically Bonnie has died.'

George looked across at the still form on the bench. She

was staring sightlessly at the ceiling. On her face was an expression that stunned George silent.

Had she, too, seen the eyes of the cat?

CHAPTER 12

Bonnie fell out of the world. She felt her blood forget her, her heart forget her, her brain forget her, her bones forget her.

Throughout life the body holds on to the soul. Death is a forgetting, and when the body forgets, it loosens its grip, and the soul falls out.

That is the simplicity of death.

It was so dark and so hollow here. There was no noise, no smell, no *feel*. And yet its hollowness was very, very huge.

Something was chasing her.

'Why am I still awake?'

She answered her own question, and at once: because you expected to be. Death is whatever you expect. If you expect heaven, you get it, or hell, or nothing. And you are also your own judge: you give yourself what you deserve. The fundamentalist creates his own hell, the Catholic his purgatory, the agnostics wander empty plains, muttering to themselves.

As she had died, a cat had come leaping out of the ceiling. Now it was behind her, stalking her. She sensed that it was dangerous. If she refused to believe in it, maybe it would disappear. Maybe it would stop chasing her down the hall to hell.

Torquemada burns, Sartre stalks in grey oblivion, Milton ascends dismal glories, Blake leaps with his demons.

It is all the same to death.

Helpless to change her own deepest beliefs, Bonnie joined her fate to that of the human majority. This was the death she contrived for herself: the big black cat came leaping and snarling towards her. As it got closer it got bigger and bigger and bigger.

She could not scream, not even when its face was the size of the risen moon, and she saw galaxies behind its eyes.

It roared, and she looked down its throat. She did not see a black carnivorous maw, but rather a long corridor, somehow familiar. A woman was walking this way along the familiar green linoleum floor. Bonnie opened her eyes wide, staring in disbelief at the absolute reality of the linoleum, the glossy green paint halfway up the walls, the jittering fluorescent fixtures on the ceiling.

This was Our Lady of Grace School, circa 1973. 'No, please, it can't be.'

The oncoming nun was a juggernaut of black and white, the wimple framing a face made of prunes and daggers. Bonnie wanted to hide, for she knew who this skeletal creature was.

'Mother Star of the Sea!'

'Exactly, my dear. Come with me.'

'What happened to the cat?'

'Never mind that.'

Bonnie looked at the hand held out to her, the awful hand made of weathered, gnawed bones, glowing inwardly with fire where the marrow should be. 'No! Get away from me!'

'Deep in thy wound, Lord, hide and shelter me!'

'I hate "Soul of My Saviour." Don't sing it to me.'

'Why, Bonnie, I'm dismayed. Our war really ended with "Soul of My Saviour." Don't you remember?'

'I don't!'

'Oh, yes, Bonnie, you do.'

With a rattle of tiles and jangling of fixtures the hall swayed and re-formed itself into the seventh-grade classroom.

'I tried hard,' Mother Star of the Sea snarled. 'I've been

eagerly awaiting my chance to deal with you. Now, watch this.'

The classroom spun into full existence. They were all there, Stacey and Mandy and Patty and Jenette, the whole gum-popping crowd.

Bonnie sat in the next to last desk, Stacey behind her. 'Having fun, Bonnie?'

'Shut up, Stacey, Mother will hear you.'

Mother in her glory sat reading, officiating at study hall. Bonnie was enjoying herself and did not want her fun to be ruined by Stacey's meddling. She fixed the image of Zack Miller in her mind, the image of him sweating over his mop and bucket in the girl's bathroom just when she happened to be peeing and sort of left the door open and –

'Oh, Bonnie, you're *doing* it.'

'Shut up! Mother might hear you!'

'She can't hear or see.' Then Stacey's cool, fat hand was reaching around the back of the desk, slipping under the elastic of her skirt, going down to meet her own fingers. 'Where is it?' Her whisper seemed to Bonnie to carry across the study hall. Mother SS remained engrossed in her Breviary.

'No! This is a sin!'

'I can make it feel really marvie, ask Ellie and Jill how good I am. I'm the best in the class.'

'Get out of here! This isn't even youryouryour . . .' But it was her business, the intimate touch.

'This is a sin!'

'Only for Catholics. I'm a Unitarian, remember. My mom and dad tell me it's okay if we're in private.'

'The seventh-grade classroom is private?'

'The back row. She can't even see this far. Consider us behind a curtain.' The other girls tittered and glanced, and Jenette stared openly, cracking her gum in rhythm to the jiggling of the two desks.

Stacey was terribly good, so good that it was some time

176

before Bonnie became aware of what all the other girls had known from the moment it began to happen.

There was a shadow cast across her desk where no shadow should be. 'Mother Star of the Sea!'

The punishment was severe: you may not continue at Our Lady of Grace, no, you will be left forever to your sin and struck down in anathema for your sin. In the eternal agony to follow, God will remember how you did this *unattractive* thing in study hall.

– But it's not a sin! This is the twentieth century!

– You go to Our Lady. Therefore it is a sin.

The worst part of the punishment was the first note home, the sheer disgust of parents, the sneering laughter of the despised younger brother.

'In view of the fact that we do not have the budget to provide a psychologist, we simply cannot allow students with these tendencies to attend Our Lady. We would suggest that Bonnie enter PS 1 as soon as possible, and that she take advantage of their counselling programme.'

The expulsion lowered her in the estimation of her father, it embittered her mother. It would mean spending the balance of the year in the virtual prison that was PS 1, a girl with a history of the unspeakable, watched constantly by the human raptors who circled those bitter skies.

Bitter Bonnie did a worse thing to her tormentor: 'Mother SS was in on it!'

'What's that?'

'She – she –' Burst into tears, play it for all it's worth. 'Mother taught us how. She does it to herself. She made me – made me –' Another burst of tears.

Her father stormed over to Our Lady, had a fiery meeting with the principal, Sister Saint Thomas. Poor Mother Star of the Sea. Once she had been principal, had been demoted on some hazy canonical basis. Now this new cloud.

Bonnie was reinstated. Her first day back, what pleasure, she walked the halls surrounded by a surging pack of girls, while Mother Star of the Sea wept silently, standing against the wall near the chapel. The old lady could not even continue out the year, she who had loved the girls and had such hope for them.

Retirement will be a form of execution, slow but certain.

Still, at this moment in time she remains a teacher, will be until the end of the week: she must teach the killing child her music:

'Oh, brother, Mother, not "Soul of My Saviour" again!'

—'Twas on a cold and rainy afternoon in October, dear. You had already destroyed me, but it remained my responsibility to teach you. How I prayed for a miracle. "Let her confess," I prayed.

'All right now, girls, in the key of G, and briskly, please.' Snick, snick, snick, ruler against the edge of the desk. 'Ah-one, ah-two, ah-three!'

'Blood of my Saviour, bathe me in Thy tide;
Wash me ye wa-ters, gushing from His side!'
(Olay)

'Stop! Who said that? Who said that horrible word! Olay, indeed! You dare to *mock* Our Lord's suffering? Who was it? You? Was it you, Stacey Banks? Or you – yes, *you*, Bonnie, you black-souled beast! Bonnie, that was a *sin*! No, don't put out your hand, dear.' Mother Star of the Sea smiles. 'Live with your sin!'

Bonnie can see now, she can see Mother Star of the Sea's face, and it is the face of despair, so infiltrated by hate that it lives on even though – 'You're dead!'

'So what? So are you. We're both as dead as doornails.'

'I'm going back! George is going to bring me back!'

'You sinned against me. You destroyed my career and my life with your accusations. I wasn't the best teacher, God

178

knows, not the best nun. But you *destroyed* me. Don't you want to atone for that?'

'George has a machine, he's taking me back.'

'You, my dear, are falling through nowhere at the rate of ten million light-years a second. No human agency has the power to get you back to your body. You are dead.'

Bonnie tumbled over and over and over through all the terrible deaths of her memory, the death of her mother with the stone weight of the cancer in her stomach starving her crazy and making her throw up at the same time, through the deaths of her own babies interrupted in their amniotic heavens by long steel, then more deaths and more: people burning, drowning, falling, the life being crushed out of them, knives hacking their guts and bullets shattering their thoughts, ruin racing through the body of the world as cheerfully as a capering clown.

Merciful God, does death mean this?

Bonnie realized with a shattering burst of passion that she *wanted* the hell towards which she was falling. She looked at her own soul, looked closely at it, and thought she must never, ever look anywhere but at that one flickering dot because it was something, after all, something in this horrible black hollowness. Its light was so very cold. But it was not *nothing*, not like what she was falling through.

She wanted to atone. Poor Mother Star of the Sea!

'So, children, that is why C. S. Lewis described hell as tiny. The souls within it are so concentrated on themselves, to the exclusion of God and all else, that the whole of Satan's Lair could fit in a single crumb of the coal on Father Flaherty's cigar.'

'Yes, Mother Star of the Sea.' (Olay)

'Who said that? I'm getting awfully *bored* by your olays, Bonnie. Please, haven't you done enough?' In the eye, a tear.

'Olay!'

'You impudent little – go stand in the hall.'

Confessional, Our Lady of Grace Parish: 'Bless me, Father, for I have sinned. I – am – Mother Star of the Sea's – *lover*!' Another nail in an already sealed coffin. Just for the fun of it.

'Whaa-a-at! Who's this? What'd you just say?'

'Even though she's been caught, she still won't stop. Father, she – she –'

'Yes, my dear, pray to Our Lord for guidance.'

That was the end of Mother Star of the Sea, right then, that day. Pack your two black bags and off you go.

No more music class, no more 'Soul of Our Saviour.'

'You wretched girl, you not only got me retired, I was anathematized by the Order. How I suffered! I didn't have anything to eat!'

'You were strict. You were mean.'

'Not as mean as you! You ruined my life. All I did was make your palms sting. Because of you I did sin. Yes, I sinned. By my own lights, I sinned. I got mad at their refusal to listen to reason, and I did break my vows. I spent the last four years of my life working in a Woolworth's and going to the movies on Sunday. In my bitterness I denied the Church, I denied the Risen Lord, and I did it because of the cloud your accusations had spread over my life. Now I'm here, because I cannot believe that my denials weren't sins.' Her long, thin fingers came forth, skilful narrow things that twined in Bonnie's hair and slipped coldly behind her ears. 'I'd really like a vacation. Now you've come, I get one.'

The cat surrounded them like a shadow, its flanks seething, its eyes everywhere, in their hearts, in the most secret places of their souls.

Mother Star of the Sea's soul shivered and shifted, becoming a cloud of hot needles that swirled about Bonnie's head. 'I've got to get free,' the needles whispered and hissed. 'Just for one delicious, precious second!'

'But you're here for the long pull, aren't you?'

'You'd deny me my respite? You don't know what this is like!'

'I'm going to be leaving soon. Just passing through.'

'You've been here a million years already. The world's gone. It ended. The sun blew up thousands of years ago!' She rasped and swirled, crazed by her passion to escape. 'Hell is being condemned to time for all eternity. It never ends and it is never pleasant. Of the two of us, you committed the greater sin, and you must pay the greater price.'

Bonnie tried to back away. George had told her this would be like sleep! How arrogant of him, how absurd.

It is not what the mind thinks that creates the afterlife, but what the unconscious believes.

And the unconscious never lies.

'George, where are you? George!'

Mother Star of the Sea reappeared out of the snickering, jabbing swarm of needles. 'Yes, George, I want my vacation and I want it now!'

As if behind the screen of the cat's eyes Bonnie saw George tinkering in the lab. 'Hurry, hurry.'

'Oh, yes, George, I've got my valise packed. Ah, what fun!' The electric wind of George's device shattered into the nothingness, negating for a moment the whole primacy of death.

Somebody was carried back into Bonnie's body on that wind. But it wasn't Bonnie. No, Bonnie went down deeper, to a charming place centred by a certain gingerbread cottage with a particularly vile stove inside. Yes, indeed, Hansel and Gretel aren't the only ones to have visited there.

It was somebody else who reinhabited her body, fitting into the glimmers and flickers between the nerves where the soul is hidden. She came to do the will of her tremendous master.

The cat had a use for her. Just for a little while, she would slip through the weave of life, doing the bidding of the gods.

It was not Bonnie who returned to that lovely body on the lab table. No, it was Mother Star of the Sea, of course. And she had not come back for fun.

CHAPTER 13

George stood over her, looking down at Bonnie. As the last of her living flush faded, he touched her face. When she was this still, he could really see her beauty. His body stirred as it had not since Kate. Kitten Kate.

'George?'

Bonnie's hair was golden, very beautiful.

'George, she's been down long enough.'

Bonnie, Bonnie. Pretty Bonnie. How cool her skin was becoming, how like alabaster. How perfect.

'The blood's going to pool.'

George bent down between the gleaming black coils, drawing closer and closer to her face. He inhaled the fading sweetness of her skin, then kissed her cheek, lingering his lips against the softness. Bonnie had the nicest down on her cheek. He laid his lips on hers.

'For God's sake, George, we've got to bring her back. There's going to be irreversible brain damage in a minute.'

Bonnie was perfection.

'George! It'll be murder, I swear!'

Clark could be a hell of a bitch. George went back to his instrument panel. 'I'm going to go with a slowly ascending level rather than the quick jump we used on Tess. I think maybe we'll get a more stable electrical response from the brain that way.'

'Just do it. Right now!'

He began raising the voltage levels in the brain.

'Am I supposed to get a reading?' Clark called from his station.

'Of course.'

'I'm not getting a thing.'

'Christ.' George glanced over at her. What on earth had made him wait so long? She had been unexpectedly beautiful . . . dead. He had not been prepared for that. He raised the voltages to their full output levels. 'Now?'

'Leave it on! Try artificial fibrillation. Maybe if the heart would restart –'

George rushed to the lab bench, pulled the fibrillator out of the wooden case on the floor. The thing wasn't even plugged in. He had been that careless. He felt like a criminal. Shaking, fumbling, he got the plug into the socket and held the electrodes against Bonnie's chest. 'Give it a shot, Clark!'

The device snapped and jerked in George's hands. Bonnie's lungs expanded with a whoosh.

'No heartbeat!'

'Hit it again. Oh, *Jesus*!'

The fibrillator snapped again. This time there was a gargling sound from Bonnie's throat. 'Clark?'

'I think I got – yeah, there's one. There's another! She's starting! We have a heartbeat.'

'Bonnie! Bonnie!'

'D-d-d-'

'Bonnie, come back to us! Come back!'

'Heart rate 45. Blood pressure 55 over 30. She's responding, George. I hope to God there's no brain damage.'

Her eyes were fluttering, her mouth working. She coughed, gasped, jerked her head from side to side.

'Bonnie, baby, Bonnie, *baby*!'

'I'm gonna –' She tried to lift herself, failed, then made a mess all over George's beautiful equipment. He groaned to see it.

'Bonnie?'

'Yeah?'

'Come on, honey, let's get you out of there. Clark, give me a hand.' While Clark removed her electrodes George got some paper towels and cleaned her up as best he could.

Together they sat her up. She swayed, dangling her legs over the edge of the bench.

'My feet are asleep,' she said.

Had George heard correctly? Was that Bonnie's voice?

'My dear,' he said, 'what a low voice you have.'

When she looked up at them, George was confused. In a way that was hard to define, her face was not right. Her cheeks, which had been rounded, were now drawn inward by a tension that had not been there before. Her lips were held in a prim, angry line. And her eyes – she had a predatory look.

'Oh, my God,' Clark whispered.

'Bonnie – what strange eyes you have. Do you feel all right?'

'I'm a little woozy, but I think my circulation's getting better.' She stepped to the floor. 'There! See, I'm okay.'

Something was not right here. The voice was radically different. And her face, her eyes . . . he didn't understand.

'George,' Clark said, 'come in here.' He nodded towards the animal room.

'What about that cat?'

'Never mind the damn cat, just get in here!' Clark closed the door behind them. 'What's wrong with her?'

'I don't know.'

'Something's terribly wrong with her.'

'I – what can I say?'

'Look, man, we're getting in trouble here, you and me. Careers are on the line.' He paused. 'The whole damn thing is videotaped.'

George saw where he was leading. 'We've got to help her. She's the main consideration.'

'I'm a biologist. I can't help her. George, I'm telling you right now I'm pulling out of the project. Right out. I don't care what happens with my degree. I don't care what Constance thinks. In fact, I'm reporting to her that the whole experiment is a failure and we've got to shut down. If you ask me, you're going to end up in jail or sued by outraged relatives before this is all over.'

'Clark, just take it easy! It isn't that bad.'

'That isn't Bonnie in there, you know it as well as I do. It's something else – something we've unleashed.'

'That's an unsupported value judgment. The only thing that's definite is that there is a change of expression.'

'A change of expression? The woman has another face, somebody else's voice. She sounds like an older woman. A different woman.'

'There's no proof that these effects are related to the experiment. They might have happened anyway.'

'What a load of – you can't seriously advocate that! The girl was fine before we did this to her. Normal in every way!'

'There was nothing in the experiment that could have caused the effect we're apparently seeing. And I must stress that we've hardly had a chance to evaluate her. Probably we're dealing with minor sequelae to the blood pressure changes. My guess is they'll pass off –'

A scream pealed in the lab. When George threw open the door, Bonnie was reeling around the centre of the room with the cat on her head. Its claws were in her hair, and it was trying to reach her throat with its teeth. 'My *God!*'

George was revolted. A human being touched by a cat. And yet the suffering involved in being bitten by those teeth would be so extreme that it would be fascinating. He fought to get his hands under control enough to grab at the loathsome thing.

At last he did it, felt muscles pulsing beneath its skin, heard its hissing, smelled its breath like an electrical fire. He got the head and pulled it back away from Bonnie's neck. Claws savaged his hands as he dragged the cat off her. It writhed furiously, screaming, its head turning and twisting, claws slashing. Clutching the scruff of its neck, he took it into the animal room and tossed it into the empty monkey cage. 'This is crazy!'

He returned to the lab to find Clark standing at the door, staring down the hall. Bonnie was gone.

Mother Star of the Sea had to get moving. The damned cat was going berserk with impatience. There was no time to waste, not a single second. You took hell with you, even on vacation.

She did exactly what she was supposed to do – she ran. She did not know where she was going or even why she was here. That wasn't her business. She just had to run. It that had brought her here would direct her movements.

There was one thing, though, she wanted to do on her own, and she wanted it so desperately that she risked the wrath of the cat for it.

For all the time she had been dead, she had been longing for one simple thing that was only available in life. Her last one had been stolen by a nurse's aide on the cancer ward at Perpetual Light Hospital. Her very last one, and she had done her terminal suffocation without even the small pleasure it would have brought.

Mother Star of the Sea fumbled in the pockets of Bonnie's jeans for some change. Thirty cents. Good.

She crossed a two-lane highway and went down into the familiar old town, looking for the right kind of store.

Bixter's. Of course. She went in. At the counter was a display so beautiful she almost wept to see it. With a trembling hand she picked out from among the stacks of M&Ms and Hersheys and Oh Henry!'s a lovely, fat, fresh Snickers bar. She shook as she held her coins out to the girl at the register.

'Thirty-two.'

'Excuse me?'

'Thirty-two cents. A Snickers is thirty-two cents.'

Mother Star of the Sea wasn't really surprised. Her guilt didn't miss a trick. She was here, sure, but she had no intention of letting up on herself. Her suffering would stay with her. She knew better than to try and steal the candy. What would happen then she couldn't even guess, but it would certainly be worse than not getting the damn Snickers at all. 'Too bad,' she croaked. She put it back and left the store.

As she walked down the street, a little bit of hell amid all these happy souls, she found she hated them. They ate, they slept, they fornicated – and she couldn't even have a goddamn candy bar. Mother Star of the Sea begrudged them their silly, complacent lives. What a joke it all was. They thought they'd die, most of them, and face some sort of judgment. Saint Peter or whoever.

You could say not guilty, but it didn't matter a bit if you *knew* otherwise.

I am now walking around in a body I once hated with a passion so great it drew tears to my eyes. She looked down at the hands. They were smooth and pretty now, but in 1973 they had been plump, warty little things. Had she ever rulered them? She didn't recall, but she certainly hoped so. She raised one to wipe her nose. The arm was stronger than she had thought it would be, and she almost knocked herself out. Staggering, she recovered.

She was in here and she couldn't get out! How *horrible*. How funny.

Maybe I'm crazy. Perhaps I'm really Bonnie, but I *think* I'm the old dead nun. I'm Bonnie, and I've become my own guilt.

This speculation made her hate the people around her even more. In a few minutes the distance between her and her fellow human beings had become as wide as the black eternal pit into which she had fallen.

How she hated them, those bright faces, those innocent eyes, those sexy curves and jutting trousers. Two children passed. Their faces were smeared with chocolate. She smelled the aroma of Snickers on their sour children's breath. She would have gleefully roasted them over a slow fire.

As she walked along she noticed a trail of ants winding its way across the sidewalk. They were helpless. Unlike the people, they could be hurt. She pranced up and down, stomping them to ant butter.

'Are you all right, miss?'

A cop. 'Yeah. I just don't like ants.'

'We got a lot of 'em this year. I been puttin' out them ant motels at my place all fall.'

She crossed the street. Wherever was she going, anyway? Hell if she knew. Let the cat take care of it. The cat always knew just what it wanted. If you refused or hesitated in hell, the damn thing became a real tiger.

Something buzzed in her left ear like an enormous wasp, or perhaps a cat struggling to make human sounds.

The words were clear enough, though. They told her just what was next. Cross Ames and walk a block farther on. Then take a left on North Street, down a block, and there it would be, huddled up against the back of the Tabernacle, Brother Pierce's shabby old Airstream trailer with 'God Is Love' painted down the sides.

She arrived panting.

'Brother Pierce? Brother Pierce, are you in there?'

She hammered on the screen door that had been attached by coat hanger wires to the frame. The interior of the trailer was dark and quiet, warm from the sun despite the chilly day.

'Brother Pierce?'

She opened the screen door and stepped in. The trailer was not large. One side of it consisted of a reeking, unmade bed, the other of a desk and plastic-covered table littered with dishes.

She was careful to close and latch the door. The places where the cat's claws had penetrated her scalp burned like fire. She didn't care to encounter that creature again.

This was certainly a dreary little hole. Hot. Stinky. She cast around for some cigarettes, found a stale-looking pack of Saratoga 100s, put one in her mouth. Amazingly enough, she also located a book of matches. At least she would be allowed *some* small pleasure. But when she saw that there were just two matches left in the book, their phosphorus tips crumbling, she didn't even try to light one. What was the point? Without further ado she tossed cigarette and matches over her shoulder.

The voice had not told her what she was supposed to do here, so she stood, as inert as an undirected zombie.

As the minutes passed, Mother Star of the Sea came to seem less a self and more a memory. Bonnie was returning, the old nun dissolving away. It occurred to the reappearing woman that the Mother Star of the Sea delusion could be an unexpected consequence of her temporary death.

It made her feel cold and clammy to realize that she had memories from the time she had been dead. Death hadn't been blackness or emptiness, not at all.

It had been Mother Star of the Sea and . . . oh, dear.

That problem. But she hadn't – or had she – ruined Mother Star of the Sea's life?

She certainly had. And she had gone to hell for doing it. In a little while she was going back. Forever.

Mother Star of the Sea was standing in the back of the trailer, her habit billowing like great wings. There was a great pile of whiskey bottles behind her.

Bonnie rushed wildly from the grim apparition – and into the arms of a short, fat gasping man who was on his way in the door. 'I got to see Brother Pierce,' the man wailed.

'He's not here.'

The man wrung his hands. 'I got to see him!'

'You'll have to wait.'

'I can't wait! No time.' She heard brakes squeal around the side of the trailer. 'Oh, Jesus! Tell him there's gonna be a witch ride through the town tonight. Big secret, we ain't supposed to know! Tell him!'

Three more men hurried around the trailer. Then fatso

was off, puffing and blowing, his pursuers close behind. Their car came swinging around the corner raising dust, driven by a fourth man.

A witch ride? She could never say that!

'May I help you, daughter?'

'Oh!'

'I am Simon Pierce.' He did not smile so much as reveal his teeth.

'I –' She wanted to tell him she was just leaving, but she couldn't very well do that. This was his home and she was standing right in the middle of it.

'I ask that members of the congregation never come in here.' He chuckled. 'I am an inveterate bottle collector and some of my prizes are very delicate. Worthless, of course, except to me.' He stared at her, his eyes full of calculation. 'Who are you, daughter?'

'I'm – a messenger! I have a message for you from, from –' She waited for the buzzing voice in her ear. There was only silence.

'Bill Peters? Bill sent you?'

She had to think up something. 'That's it,' she babbled. 'Bill sent me. He said to tell you there's going to be a witch ride tonight.' It had burst from her on its own.

'Bill said that? Where is he?'

'Some men were after him –'

'Say no more. Bless you, daughter! You have brought me gold. *Gold!*'

So this was why she had been sent here. The cat of hell wanted to be certain that Brother Pierce knew about the witch ride.

He strode past her and got on the phone. Her last sight of him was of his back as he bent over the instrument, talking with excitement and relish. She had to get to the lab right now. She was remembering an incredible wealth of detail, and she had to tell George. Mother Star of the Sea, indeed. Guilty secrets of the dead.

She hurried up North Street to the place where it forms a triangle with Meecham and the Morris Stage Road. Bonnie was a careful girl. She negotiated the Meecham part of the crossing and paused on the pedestrian island, waiting for a break in the MSR traffic. She waited for some time. This was the commuter hour, and there was a steady stream of cars coming back to town from their day's journeys.

There was a loud feline growl behind her.

She whirled, shocked. All she saw were eyes and teeth, hanging in the air. But the eyes were glaring things, and the teeth curved like tyrannic fingernails.

She hurled herself away from the horror – and into the middle of the Morris Stage Road. The last thing she saw was the onrushing grillwork of a huge Lincoln. Mike Kominski didn't even have time to swerve.

Her message delivered, Tom returned the messenger to its eternal abode.

CHAPTER 14
The Wild Hunt

The moon had risen high, casting its light upon the mountain. Mandy stood beside the house with Constance, holding her cold, dry hand and watching the golden sickle in the sky.

'I want to stay here forever, Constance.'

'Yes.' There was shyness in her tone. Despite the march of years she had much still of youth in her. 'But you must be certain. Would you give your life for it?'

Mandy raised her eyebrows, regarded Constance. 'I've learned to be suspicious of questions like that.'

'Well, no need to answer just this instant. You've been given a reprieve. The ravens are announcing a visitor.'

Mandy heard their gleeful blaring babble of half-aware voices. She could detect the pleasure and excitement in their tone. 'They know the visitor. Somebody they're glad to see.'

'Very good, dear. You're learning how to listen to them.'

'Just the tone. Not the words.'

'The two are one and the same among birds. If you're careful, you'll hear the celebration in their greeting.' She smiled. 'Ravens only celebrate one thing, and that is food. So we will find that our visitor is feeding them as he comes up the road.'

'He?'

'The females' voices are sharpest. It's a he.'

They went back inside and down the long central hall to the front of the house. Ivy had not yet lit the candles. That wouldn't occur until the moon cleared the trees. 'It's nice to do things that remind us this old planet *rolls*,' Ivy had said. 'It's going somewhere, and we're going there, too.'

Rise of moon, setting of sun, tumble of stars, all were noticed on the Collier estate.

A man in hat, down jacket, and snow boots was just mounting the final rise to the house. As he walked, he tossed bits of something to the darting, gleeful birds.

Mandy was no longer so desolate about the work they had destroyed. One glimpse of the *Leannan* had made her past efforts seem callow, at least the efforts at fairies. Their destruction was a grace; she would not have been able to bear them now.

'Well, look who it is. Ivy! Robin! Your father's come for a visit.'

As she and Constance watched him making his way up the walk in his cloud of ravens, Mandy heard a rattle of footsteps from the house. A moment later Robin and Ivy burst past them and met him at the steps. With a cry of happiness Ivy threw herself into his arms. 'Dad!'

'Hey, baby! Hiya, Bill.'

'Their outside names are Margaret and Bill,' Constance commented. She offered no further explanation as their father stomped the snow off his boots on the wide front porch.

'Lord, Connie, why don't you get somebody in to plough that road? Turnbull'd do it for a hundred bucks.'

'Hello, Steven. Come on in and dry your boots by the fire. We've got some hot mulled wine.'

He tramped through the door rubbing his hands. 'Nobody mulls wine like you people,' he rumbled. Mandy was fascinated. Robin had talked about the danger of outsiders learning too much, but here was one outsider who seemed familiar enough with them.

Ivy soon brought wine in steaming mugs. 'Oh, that is good,' Steven said, leaning into the warmth. His face, reflecting the firelight, communicated strength and gentleness. His eyes were set in tangled brows, but the way they twinkled suggested that he did not take the witches quite as seriously as they themselves did. He seemed so at peace, so accepting. She could understand why he was trusted here.

'Snow in October! We had three inches down in the town.' He looked askance at Constance. 'Sure is unusual, snow in October. I wonder if *she* was as surprised as we were.' He chuckled. 'It is beautiful, though, the white against the autumn colours.'

'It'll melt.'

'Good! I can get my compost finished. Say, she didn't tell you when, did she?'

Constance tisked. 'That is no business of the Episcopalians.'

'Hell, Connie, I'm not just a church deacon. I'm also a gardener. I need to know. And you got my kids, you old witch. I think I'm entitled to a few favours.'

'Steven, I'd like you to meet Amanda Walker. She's going to be with us from now on. Amanda, this is Steven Cross. He's my neighbour across the road.'

Mandy smiled. She knew the name Cross, of course. It was one of the old Maywell names. There had been Crosses in the Founder's Excursion in 1702. Mother Star of the Sea had drilled that into their heads in History, along with the equally important fact that two of the founding families, the Sternleighs and the Albarts, were Roman Catholic.

'My Lord, you do get the pretty ones.' His big hand lingered in her own. Then he turned his eyes on Constance once again. 'I thought I'd better come up.' His voice lowered. 'Something happened last night.' He cast a significant glance in Mandy's direction. 'Pretty serious.'

'She can hear. She's going to learn it all.'

His eyebrows shot up. 'You mean she's the new –'

'That's right. But don't congratulate her yet, she only just survived the first challenge. Now, why did you come? What's happened?'

'About midnight last night I noticed a lot of traffic out on

Bridge Road. I went down the front walk and took a look. There was a regular procession, Connie.'

'Who?'

'Brother Pierce has gotten wind of something.'

'Maybe he's managed to slip a spy into one of the town covens. I wouldn't be surprised. That's the way it usually happened in the old days.'

'I hope none of the ones who use our facilities.'

'I doubt it. The covens that meet at Saint George's have been going for years.'

'How about Leonora Brown's group –'

'The Priestess Quest. She is rather new at it. Have you met any of her coven?'

'The rector says it's a good group.'

'And your Charlie knows people. No, I don't think my problem is there. I'd be more inclined to nose about the Kominski group. She's got three covens now. I cautioned her about growing too fast.'

Steven smiled. 'You folks sell ecstasy. That's a hard thing to beat in this day and age. People want to join, Connie. I don't think you realize how much you're affecting the life of Maywell. Far more than you did even five years ago.'

'I realize it. Never assume I don't know what I'm doing. And my people can keep their secrets.'

He tucked his chin into his chest. His eyes were no longer twinkling. 'Please forgive me, but I beg to differ. Not only Brother Pierce but everybody else in town knows there's some kind of a big do on tonight.'

'Of course. They have to know.'

He rocked back with surprise. 'What? Oh, Connie, come on!'

'The essence of the ritual is danger. If it wasn't dangerous it wouldn't work. To be real, magic must be serious. We aren't playing games here.'

Mandy listened with the utmost care. She believed these words.

Cross's voice rose as he spoke. 'Connie, I don't think you understand what your people are doing. They're *recruiting* all over town, even in the churches. Even from Pierce.'

'They aren't recruiting. We don't recruit. Witches are rare. It takes a very special person to become a witch.'

He shook his head. 'Whatever, you're going public. Connie, you people are way out in never-never land and this is a very conservative little town.'

'There's a long tradition of toleration here in Maywell.'

'Maywell is a Christian community, of course it's tolerant. Except for Pierce, that is. And he is far from tolerant.' Steven stopped, looked a long time at the floor. Finally he spoke again. 'You're in danger. All of you. This business of public rituals is highly irresponsible. And the recruitment –'

'We do not recruit!'

'Whatever it is! It's going to get you in trouble, mark my words. You've got families breaking up over this thing. Let me tell you how Maywell thinks of you. The tolerant ones – us, the Catholics, most of the established churches – still figure live and let live, but the more noise you make the more uneasy we get. As for Brother Pierce's followers, watch out. They're running around with torches in the night, my dear.'

Connie smiled softly. 'We have to do what we do and be what we are. Nobody really has a choice in such matters. If it means that we lose the toleration of the town, then that's what must be. But we love you and respect you. Carry that message to your congregation, Steven. Will you do that?'

'You know I'll do what I can. But my strong sense of it is that things are about to get out of hand. Pull back for a while.'

'I'm sorry, Steven.'

He drank deeply of his wine. 'What's in this mull, anyway?'

'Stool of toad, leg of worm.'

'Thank you. I'll have to write that down. There was more

than a procession out there last night. There's a big burned place on the wall about a hundred yards from the gate, back towards town.'

Constance's eyes narrowed. 'A burned place?'

'The grass is scorched, the wall is covered with soot, and the overhanging branches are blackened. Somebody's awful mad at you, Connie.'

Constance's eyes twinkled. 'Pierce, of course.'

'Probably. But you've got plenty of enemies besides him. Could be some husband whose wife has moved to your village. Could be a whole group of 'em.'

'There are only two families affected by the village in that way. And one of the husbands is about to come around. The other is too obsessed with his work to bother about us.'

'Then blame Brother Pierce. From what I hear he's out to cauterize this place to a cinder. Burn out the witch infection.' He coughed. 'This wine is loosening up my chest as well as my tongue. Your darned snowstorm gave me a cold, dear!'

'We don't affect the weather. That's just a superstition.'

Steven answered with a deeper hack.

'Ivy, what do you think your father's cough needs?'

'Well, it's bronchial, a lot of loose phlegm. Not very serious. I'd say onion broth.'

'Very good. But why are you sure it isn't serious?'

'There's no rasp in it, so not much inflammation, and none of the thickness associated with pneumonia. And it doesn't have the crack of a tumour cough.'

'See there, Steven. Your daughter is possibly going to be a quite competent herbal doctor. Ivy, give him the recipe.'

'Cut up six small white onions and boil them in a cup of honey. Boil them down for two hours. Strain out the liquid and take it hot, in small doses. You'll cough a lot at first –'

'I'm sure.'

'Then it'll stop, Dad. Your cough'll be cured.'

'I'll use up my Robitussin first, baby. I love you dearly,

but I don't think Mom's gonna let me boil down onions in the kitchen.'

Ivy went and sat on the arm of his chair. She stroked what he had left of hair. Robin, sitting on the floor before him, took his mug and refilled it from the pitcher they had left by the fire. Mandy was for a moment conscious of the depth of the love that flowed between this man and his two children. He looked again at Constance. 'Please tell me you're at least going to be careful.'

'Tonight is a bad night for us to be careful.'

There was that suggestion of danger again.

'Don't go down in the town.'

'We go wherever our ritual leads. The essence of the hunt is danger.'

'You've said that! Now, look, if you're going to be crazy, at least do me one small favour. Tell Sheriff Williams your plan.'

'I did that, of course.' She laughed. 'I even had to pay a hoof tax of fifteen cents.'

'I'm glad he knows. I don't want the poor guy to get a heart attack.'

'Johnny Williams is a good man, Steven. We used to dance together out at Rollo's Road House.'

'You remember that? When did that place close down — during the war?'

'Before the war. The reason I remember is that Johnny reminds me every time I see him.' There had come into Constance's face a fey expression. To say she had once been a coquette would not be accurate. She still was one.

On the distance came the single boom of a gong. 'The moon hangs two fingers over the mountain,' Constance said. 'We have a lot to do before midnight.'

He slapped his palm against his head. 'I'm telling you half of this town is *up in arms*, Connie, and you propose to go thundering through its streets on horseback at midnight? You must be mad!'

'Half the town may be up in arms, but the other half is mine.'

'Not half, dear. Perhaps a quarter.'

'Many of the others are friends.'

'Oh, come on. You act like you haven't heard what I said. You make a spectacle of yourself and you're going to lose the friends you do have.'

Mandy saw something fierce in the look Steven gave Constance, something he himself might not even have been aware of. The gong boomed again.

'I gather that means I have to go.'

'That's what it means, Steven.'

He got up. 'Thanks a heap for the wine. And don't say I didn't warn you if you have trouble tonight.' He tromped out, his children trailing behind him. 'Your mother sends her love. Her apples are ripe, and she says to tell you she's going to have thirty bushels. All grown without spells.'

'That's what she thinks,' Ivy said. 'I first spelled the orchard on Beltane Day.'

'I'll tell her that. I'm sure she'll throw away her fertilizer.'

'I wish she would. She doesn't need it. It shocks her trees. They're getting old before their time.'

'We've got a good harvest, too,' Robin added. 'Pumpkins and corn and squash and wheat and oats. And an incredible blackberry crop. We're going to be making the herbal stuff again.'

There was an awkwardness now between the three of them. 'It'll be a good harvest, then,' Steven said.

'The best,' his son said. A pause grew, spread into a silence.

'Your sisters miss you.' Steven paused at the door. He opened his arms to his son and daughter. 'You know.' An instant later he was off into the night. Soon the calls of the ravens began again, diminishing with him as he departed. 'Hey! Lay off that hat! I'm outa bread!'

Then he was gone.

200

Ivy went about with her taper, and soon the house shone with the deep light of the candles. Mandy saw Robin hurrying through the kitchen. The slam of the door made her gasp. She was alert with anticipation. She understood that she was at the centre of this ritual. Naturally she was apprehensive. She told herself that was all it was – apprehension. She would not admit to deep fear, the curdling terror that comes when one faces a true unknown.

'What am I going to do tonight?' she asked Constance.

Her mentor took both of her hands. 'You are the huntress, dear.' She wasn't surprised. 'I hope you know how to ride bareback.'

'I couldn't possibly! I haven't ridden a horse since I was sixteen.'

'Well, give it a try. You'll have to go sky-clad, too.'

'What's that supposed to mean?'

'You'll see. Now, come on, the moon doesn't wait.'

The next thing Mandy knew she was following Constance down the path through the herb garden. The idea of hesitating never crossed her mind.

When they reached the village, they slipped between two of the cottages to find the place most wonderfully transformed from Mandy's brief visit when she first entered the estate. There were candles everywhere, making pools of light along the snowy paths, gleaming in the windows of the cottages, in the lanterns before the houses, too. Holly decorated all the doors. 'You're to hunt the Holly King tonight, my dear Amanda,' Constance said. 'As usual the rules of the game will be simple. Just do your best.'

Here she went again with the vague instructions. Mandy remembered struggling up Stone Mountain, not knowing where the hell she was going. 'What if I fall off the horse?' she muttered, knowing there would be no reply.

She was being tested. Very well. She raised her chin. Fiercely she determined to pass every test they could give her.

Constance stopped in the middle of the village. She looked most wonderful, hooded, her cloak touching the ground. Her face was lit by the candles, and the moon rode high above her. 'If at any point you fail, my dear, we burn this village and go home. We quit.'

A stone seemed to knock in her chest. 'It's that important? Me?' Now all of her posturing seemed hollow.

'This is *your* night, my dear. You have taken your place with the *Leannan* as I took mine fifty years ago. To further prove yourself, you must capture the Holly King and make him your own. It symbolizes your strength. The Holly King is all of us, our covenstead, our way of life. If you want to lead us, you must first catch us.'

Mandy's mind was still battling through the possible meanings of what she had just heard when Constance marched up to the doors of the great round building at the head of the town and threw them open.

The room within was an astonishment of light and odour: it appeared to be a combination barn and ritual chamber. Around the walls were stalls full of horses and cattle and goats. Mandy saw fine mounts, their rumps gleaming, their tails beautifully curried. The smell was not unpleasant, just intensely animal. The stalls, though, formed only the outermost circle. The greater part of the space was taken up by a beaten-earth floor, upon which sat perhaps four dozen people – men, women, and children.

In the centre of the circle was Robin, his head crowned by holly, his body gleaming as if it had been waxed. He was, as were they all, quite naked. When he smiled at her, she was glad.

A familiar black tail hung down from a rafter, flicking occasionally.

There was a skirl of bagpipes and a rattle of bones. Six couples came into the circle around Robin. A young woman of perhaps eighteen dashed round and round it with an enormous broadsword, pointing it at the ground. The bagpipes wailed wildly. Mandy thought of all the movies she had ever seen of Scotsmen in war, and knew the sense of this magnificent noise. In hands such as held them now, the pipes were an instrument of courage.

Brother Pierce's face, sharp with hate, seemed to swim before her.

The group in the circle began to dance round their Holly King, clapping and chanting:

> 'Fire of life,
> Pass, pass, pass!
> Fire and flame, in Goddess' name,
> Pass, pass, pass!
> Heart and hand of Holly King,
> Pass, pass, pass!'

She understood it all now. They were going to make her ride a horse through a hostile town in the nude, chasing a guy with weeds in his hair.

She was thinking to get out of here when strong hands suddenly grabbed her and whirled her away among swirling chains of people. They snatched at her cloak until it was swept off, then at her jacket, at her blouse, at her jeans. Soon she was naked above the waist. There was so much laughter that the violence of the undressing was almost dispelled. They lifted her at last over their heads, and in passing her from hand to hand finally got the jeans away from her.

She was shrieking from all those unexpected touches when she found herself delivered to the centre of the inmost circle and laid at the feet of the Holly King.

Robin's eyes were big with desire. She could see, between his crossed legs, his standing flesh.

Close to him there was a strange smell, like mildew and rancid lard and menthol cough drops. A moment later she knew why. He dipped his fingers in a bowl of thick salve and dropped a huge glob of it on her belly.

'Hey!'

They held her arms above her head, put their hands around her ankles. In their faces was such love, though, she made no attempt to escape them.

When Robin began spreading the salve up and down her stomach, she discovered that the touch of his hands could be pleasant. He spread the slick stink over her whole body, leaving only her private parts untouched. She tingled, grew warm. The sensation was not unlike that of Ben Gay, but deeper and not in the least relaxing. On the contrary, she wanted to run and jump and yell; she fairly could have flown.

The young woman who had wielded the sword came and knelt beside Mandy. 'There's a little sting,' she whispered. 'Don't mind, it soon ends.' She took some of the salve and rubbed it smartly into Mandy's privates.

A little sting! It was all she could do not to shriek with the agony of it. As if anticipating her problem the bagpipes wailed again and the bones were joined by drums.

No wonder there were legends of witches flying. This salve made her feel as if she were floating. More than floating. If she closed her eyes, she just might sweep up into the rafters with Tom.

They got her to her feet and danced her about, clapping, turning, twisting to a new music. The pipes were gone now, replaced by flute and drum and bone, the old instruments of such dances, softer perhaps without the roaring pipes but in their way just as exciting.

> 'Corn rigs, an' barley rigs,
> An' corn rigs are bonnie;
> I'll ne'er forget that happy night,
> Amang the rigs wi' Mandy!'

Happiness filled Mandy Walker. The hell with her concerns, this was *fun*. She really danced for the first time in her life, naked and free amid the smells of animals and the sweat of people – and her own phenomenal stench – round and round and round till the rafters garlanded with holly spun and the Holly King on his throne of floor spun, with his smiling lips and dark wonderful eyes, the gleam there so intense it made her burst with laughter.

There was the feeling that she had danced this dance before.

Just then the dance stopped. Annoyance flashed through Mandy. Then she heard what had frozen the others. From far away the long sound of a horn. A hunter's horn.

Constance. She was out there somewhere, calling them to the hunt.

The stillness was only momentary. There followed a great roar of excitement. Mandy found herself astride a huge black horse, a snorting, excited, stamping giant of a stallion.

She was naked. She had only the mane for reins. Then they had drawn her through the doors, so quickly that she almost hit her head.

'I've got to have my cloak!'

Somebody gave the horse a swat and like blazes they were off through the middle of the village, the hoofs of her mount shattering candles as he galloped. In another instant they were out in the night, pounding along, her fingers frantic in his mane, her body slipping and sliding around because of the salve, the horsehair skinning her legs. And, she felt sure, they were heading towards the bog.

'Whoa! Hey, horse, come on! Oh, stop!' She tugged at the mane. The animal gave a snort and thundered on.

All she could do was clutch and hope. Maybe she would only be knocked out when she fell. Not killed. Please not killed at such a prime moment.

The salve was having a more and more powerful effect on her. For example, she wasn't in the least cold. And she could hardly feel the pain of the horsehair against her thighs. Even while she clutched and cried, the swiftness of the animal's flight began to seem less a terror.

It became exhilarating, scary in the same sense that a roller coaster is scary. She put one hand along the beast's pumping neck. It was a lovely creature, this horse.

It snorted.

'Take it easy, horse.'

She felt beneath her its muscles surging, its blood singing in its veins, its sweat mingling with her slickness as they pounded down the night.

She found that she could sit up for a few seconds and, while she did, actually enjoy the wind rushing past her face.

Then she could sit up longer. She could press her knees against the horse's flanks and sit straight.

It was more than good, this ride. She tossed her head and dug in her knees and shrieked out all the joy and wildness and power that had sprung up in her soul. And her mount neighed reply. She heard the maleness in his voice and knew he had responded to something in her own that she had never before known was there. She was a *woman* upon this creature, no passive cipher but a woman full of strength and pride and beauty.

She felt an intimacy with the animal flesh beneath her so raw that it startled her. He neighed again, a rich, delighted sound, and literally burst forward. They pounded, pounded, pounded, his foam flying back in her face, his smell filling her nostrils when the charged air didn't, pounded and pounded but were not spent, never that, never tired, only growing stronger and stronger together as they hunted down the night itself.

Hunted, yes! She was here to hunt Robin. She tossed her head and screamed again, screamed from the bottom of her belly to the top of her head, a high, slicing sword of a cry.

Far off she heard the huntsman's horn reply. Far, far off to the north.

She had not even to say whoa this time, nor to touch the mane of her horse. Only transfer the pressure from the knees to the ankles and he dropped back to a trot. Lighter pressure made him walk. Raising her legs altogether made him stop.

The horn pealed out once more. Behind her, wasn't it? Her horse turned his head back, met her eyes in the moonlight with one of his own. He was blowing hard, slick with froth, trembling with eagerness.

This was no ordinary horse. He *knew* where to go, she felt it. He knew how to find the Holly King. All she had to do was surrender to his simpler, clearer mind and his instincts.

For all she knew no horse was ordinary. Maybe there was no such thing as an ordinary horse or an ordinary ferret or an ordinary duck, for that matter, no more than there were ordinary fairies or ordinary people or ordinary cats.

She gave him knee and they were off again, rushing around the edge of the bog, up through the hummocks with the house gleaming in the distance, farther north in the valley than she had ever been, through acres and acres of fields, some smelling cut and rich with the blood of the land, others still ripening, corn and grain and pumpkins and squash, earth weighted with fruit. She wondered if the snow had destroyed much of the crop.

They trotted down a path between sentinel rows of corn, which clattered with their passing. Now the land began to rise and they went through an orchard, the horse's hoofs crunching the culls and adding cider to the thick, delicious chaos of scents.

'Holly,' she whispered, 'King of Holly . . .'

No, still farther north. Low in the sky she saw Polaris, hanging above the dark mystery of the land. That way lay the Holly King.

But how far? They were passing houses now, with electric lights and dogs reduced to hoarse yapping by the bizarre sight and even more fantastic odour of the intruders.

They approached a house lit by candles, which were quickly snuffed out. People came bursting out of the door, running after her, cloaked against the cold, racing up and touching her legs with a slap, then dropping back into the dark.

Her mount's hoofs clattered on the brick streets, echoing in the stillness. She was acutely aware of her nakedness.

Then a car gunned its motor and shot forward. She was impaled by the lights; she heard a powerful engine crying out the rage of the driver as the lights bore down. She dug her knees into her horse's thighs and pulled his mane sharply right. He burst into a gallop, climbing a steep lawn. The car followed, engine growling and tyres screaming, then whining as it came to a stop at the kerb.

She shrieked as her horse leaped back fences, stormed through porches, and jumped empty swimming pools. Then they were in an alley, then through it to the next street. Perhaps there had been a cordon arranged for them, but they were out of it now. She was glad, she felt the wildness again, the freedom, the sheer mad, sweating, gasping thunder of the ride.

And she knew she was closer to the Holly King. By long habit she wanted men, and waited for them. Never before had she allowed herself the feeling of just taking what she wanted.

They went past Church Row and across the town common beyond. 'Find him,' she whispered to her mount. 'Find him for me!'

Behind them other cars were muttering and growling, their lights prowling the streets that surrounded the common.

Then she saw the blazing sign of Brother Pierce's Tabernacle. People were running in and out, cars were coming and going – the place was like a wasp nest disturbed by a stick. She knew, at the same moment, that *he* was close by.

Her horse stopped. 'Come on.' She pressed with her

knees. He turned his head and looked at her. 'So this is the place,' she murmured.

She dismounted, stood a moment on shaky legs, getting used to the ground again. Snow crunched beneath her feet. The salve was not so strong now; she felt how icy cold this night really was. Half a block from the Tabernacle there was another candlelit house. More witches. But he was not in that house. No, he was outside. They were to meet in the night.

He was a clever boy, to go so close to Brother Pierce's Tabernacle. Clever boy. But she wasn't afraid of anything anymore, not even this.

She would have ridden right down the aisle of the Tabernacle if necessary. Maybe it was the ride or the salve or being naked in the streets, but she was very excited. She had never wanted anyone like she wanted the Holly King.

Her horse turned its head, pricked its ears towards a sound behind them.

And did not even have a chance to scream when the blast of a shotgun shattered its brains. The great body shuddered and collapsed. 'Okay, whore, put your hands up!'

She started to run.

'Stop!'

The hell with that. She had darkness on her side at least. She ran. A shot thundered behind her and something hissed past her right shoulder. Buckshot. Keep going.

'I got the damn horse!'

My horse, my horse, my beautiful magic friend of a horse!

'She's headin' towards North Street!'

'Get her, man!'

She flew, forcing herself not to shriek the cry that came to her throat. There would be time for rage later.

My horse!

In their thirty minutes together she and that stallion had become friends in passion, fellow celebrants of gender.

A flash of white ahead of her, a stifled cry, and she realized she had flushed the Holly King! Her beautiful horse had been taking her right to his hiding place.

When he sprinted across North Street, she saw him clear in the streetlight, his skin pale, his long legs pumping, his holly on his head.

Others saw him, too. Car lights flared and engines roared from both ends of the street. By the time Mandy was crossing there were only seconds to spare. Then brakes squealed and furious voices were all shouting together, 'It's the witch, it's the witch!'

Behind her she heard clumsy crashing in the shrubs. She knew she was back on estate land, beyond the far limit of Maywell. North Street, where the estate's wall ended, was also the border of the town. Here were the ruins of Willow-brook, an unfinished housing development that had been started and died after Mandy had left Maywell.

She stopped on an overgrown street to listen for the Holly King. The crashing behind her got closer only slowly, accompanied by a steady smoke of curses. Then, just as she was certain she had lost him, a shrub moved almost at her feet.

Instantly she pounced – and connected with his hot skin and pricking crown. She ripped it from his head and tossed it high in the air. He gasped, started to run again, but she grabbed his wrist and screamed out her triumph with all her victorious soul, uncaring of the people behind her, even of the flashlight beams that were probing for her position.

He pushed at her, he tried to break her grip. Her blood was so high that she raised her fist and slammed it across his face. He made a long, rattling groan and sank down.

'Oh, God, I killed him!'

But no, he was crawling. It was another trick! She leaped at him, grabbed him around the waist, straddled him, sat on him, pinned him to the ground.

And felt, to her infinite delight, his bursting rigid essence jamming up between her legs.

A flashlight beam skimmed her head and there was a brutal shout of triumph.

She could not move for the spear of pleasure he had thrust into her. 'We've got to run,' she whispered, but she simply sat there, staring down at his blood-running face, feeling him in her, and knowing joy so extreme that it almost made her lose her senses.

Then she heard ravens. And yells, frantic yells. The flashlight beams began to flail about in the sky to a great roar of the most fierce cawing Mandy had ever heard. The cacophony retreated rapidly towards the Tabernacle.

When the Holly King was spent beneath her, she got up, put his crown on her own head, and found herself surrounded by other witches, all gasping from their long run. They were wearing ordinary clothing, caps, jackets, hiking boots. Apparently only the principals in the rituals were expected to go naked in the town.

Without a word they clustered about her, tied her cloak around her, and gave her a sweet, delicious drink of hot wine and honey.

She walked with them all the way around the western edge of the town and beneath the cliffs of Stone Mountain, back to the estate. Gentle hands carried her lover.

She sat in the centre of the circle. They laid him, quite asleep, before her.

Her people then indulged in the revels of the night. There was so little she understood of their rituals, except that the bodies flashing about her in the circle meant ecstasy.

There were twelve of them, six men and six women, dancing about the inner circle of which she and the Holly King were the centre. They moved to the right, dancing and clapping, chanting a single word:

Moom, Moom, Moom, Moom.

They shouted, they whispered, they danced until the chant merged and changed and grew into another word, which she at first could not quite understand:

Moomamaamannamuaman adamoôm amandoom.

Then she heard it – her own name. Amanda. She listened to it weaving about in the chant, and watched the sweat-slick nakedness of the people dancing in her honour, and wondered, Whom do they take me for?

Who am I?

CHAPTER 15

For George, Bonnie's death was a great, black boulder, crushing him as a foot might crush an ant.

Clark had called him mad and disowned the project, then had gone back to the Covenstead to tell Constance all that had happened.

They had been together in the faculty commons when they got the news.

'There's been a student killed out on MSR,' Pearl Davenport had shouted, her head popping in the door.

Clark went a dull shade of grey.

The long call of the sirens swept up and down the room.

'George, where the hell did Bonnie go?'

'Oh, Christ, oh, Christ.'

'Pearl, who –'

'Clark, it was a girl. She got hit. I was coming across the damn road, there was an awful crunch, and this – oh, Jesus – this little rag goes flying halfway to heaven.'

'It was a girl! Who, Pearl, honey?'

'Blonde. Petite. I didn't see her clearly. I think she had on a college sweatshirt. Spacy-looking, that's all. Then she's in the road and oh, I don't want to think about it.'

Clark: 'Pearl, come here, sit down. Henrietta, bring her some coffee.' Bustle at the courtesy counter, grey Henrietta, Snow Queen of Frosh Bio, darting over with a Styrofoam cup.

Clark grabbed George's arm, grabbed it hard: 'It's her, buddy.'

Clark's rusting Datsun slipped and slid along, past the snowy playing fields and the track house, out the gates to the blue flashing lights of the Highway Patrol and the red shuddering ones of the Sheriff's Department.

There was a scar in the road, maroon, mix of blood and rubber. The driver had tried hard to stop. 'This goddamn corner!'

'Clark, we don't know!'

'The hell. She was crazy. She wandered into the street.'

'We do not *know*!'

He slammed on the brakes, clutched George's shoulders, his red, sweated face plunging into George's own, screaming, 'You fucking *asshole*! We know! It was her and we killed her. You and I in our arrogance killed her! Jesus, to do an experiment like that on a human being without so much as a *single* successful animal test, without any safeguards – we ought to be horsewhipped, both of us. Connie is going to ask us, where was your conscience?' He made a sound like shaking leaves.

'Now, hold it. Calm down. We've got to think this thing through. We've got to be rational. Assume it is Bonnie. There's no way this can be attributed to us. It was an auto accident. Happens all the time. We're in the clear.'

'My conscience is far from clear. I might end up spending the rest of my life in atonement.'

'You speak of Connie. She pushed us.'

'She never asked us to be careless.'

'She pushed us! If anybody should atone, it's Constance Collier.'

Clark did not reply. When George finally looked at him, he was laughing, but in total silence, his shoulders shaking, his face expressionless. 'George,' he whispered, 'if you don't get out of my car right now, I am going to kick your head through that window.'

'Please, Clark –'

'George, I'm warning you.'

'We've got to work together.'

'Go.' He swivelled in his seat, raised his legs to his chin.

His feet were inches from George's head. 'I'll kill you, you self-serving bastard, I swear I will.' Then the man cried, bitterly and long, heaving, his eyes staring, and George knew who it was that quiet Clark had loved, and that he had given his beloved to the demands of his craft.

They were two lost men, George Walker and Clark Jeffers. Clark's tears, though, told George that they were lost in different forests. The depth of his own sorrow was so great, he could not bear these tears. If he cried, he knew, he would go into his basement and light his candle, and die there.

George got out into an autumn evening brisked by the crackle of police radios, rendered urgent by the guttering of motors and the low voices of uniformed men with measuring tapes. Stone Mountain had a halo of deep orange. The mountainside itself was black. Clark did not drive away. He was watching George from inside the car, and George knew what he had to do. He walked up to an officer who was taking up a flare. 'Excuse me.'

'Yeah?'

'I'd like some information. Was –'

'Look, I don't have authorization to talk to reporters. Anyway, next of kin haven't been notified yet.'

'No, you don't understand. I'm Dr George Walker from the college. The girl – I'm afraid –'

'She was a student, if that's what you mean.'

'I know that. But you must, if she was identified, you must – was her name Bonnie Haver?'

'You knew her, then. I'm sorry. She didn't suffer. It was instantaneous. I'm sorry.'

George couldn't move. He wanted to somehow show grief, but there was only this awful, dead coldness within him.

He walked. One foot before the other, across the rest of MSR and the pedestrian island, across the last hundred feet of Meecham where it angled into MSR, then down North Street.

He knew Clark was watching him go. He could feel his

own end as the fall of an angel, wings dissolving in the thin moonlight.

Maywell was soft in the evening, so soft it seemed to want to seduce. As soft as a caress. Wind stirred from the north, rustling down the valley, drawing whorls of snow from the lawns that lined the street.

A cat appeared down the street, a huge black thing every bit as ugly as the one that had menaced him in the lab. He stomped. 'Move!' The animal darted towards a house.

'Bonnie, Bonnie belle beauty, Bonnie belle, gone to hell. Bonnie belle beauty-o. Oh, shi-i-t!'

He had to laugh, really. What an absurd career his had been, not even big enough to be a cosmic joke. It was just a dreary reality, the smell of Lysol on the lab floor, the deaths of frogs and monkeys.

She walked in beauty, died in God knows what kind of horror. 'Oh, Constance, why did you want it? What was it for!'

In his mind's eye he saw the old woman, serene, regal, standing before him in the formal drawing room of that tumbledown old house of hers. 'George, I must challenge death. I must be able to kill, and then return to life, a human being, and to do it no later than December of 1987. Do you think it's possible?'

'Constance, the research is just in its infancy. There isn't all that much money.'

'I can't give you money. There must be no traceable connection. Please, George, it's vital to the future of the Covenstead.'

He could not say that it was impossible. Tears filled his eyes again. Soon he would have to go to Connie and tell her everything. How could he ever ask forgiveness?

He passed Brother Pierce's Tabernacle, heard him roaring within. Cars were arriving, people were hurrying up to the doors. Here and there a pickup stood with rifles racked in the rear window. Honkies. Rednecks. Slime.

'Slime! Hey, Brother Slime!' He gathered a snowball and hurled it up at the massive sign. God is Love, indeed. God is a sphere with no circumference and no centre. God is nowhere. And God doesn't give a damn.

People had paused in the parking lot, big people with ugly little faces punched into the fronts of their fat heads. 'Hiya, boys. Praise the Lord!'

'Amen, brother.'

George continued more briskly, passing Stone and then Dodge. Going home. All of a sudden, he couldn't breathe. Going home? His house was dark and cold. 'Kate? Please, Katie.'

Kitten Kate and the kids. The gone.

She had cried and he had laughed. But he cried now, on his way down Bridge Street, past Elm with its shadowed houses and onto Maple. He struggled to his own shadowed house, to the front door, then the cold, dark living room.

What the hell are you crying about? Remember Saul Jones: 'She's moved out? Good. You'll go for an uncontested. She gets the kids and you get the house.' That was not a completely undesirable outcome. The other way around would have been disastrous. Truth be told, he could get along without his caterwauling, whining, wheedling, disappointed kids. The disappointed generation. Let them all live on the Covenstead. They even had their own school out there, fully licensed and accredited.

'*You* are leaving *me*, baby,' he had said. 'And unless you give me the house and the car I'll put up a fight for the kids.' That worried her enough to stop trouble before it started.

'They're already gone. They left last night. It was their idea in the first place.'

'You seduced them!'

'You get psychiatric help and we'll come back.'

'I'll get a girlfriend.'

'How about a cat instead!'

'You bitch.'

'You're crazy, George. I'm going to tell Constance. She'll assign you a counsellor and make you go.'

Constance did nothing of the kind. She was too practical. She needed George's work too much to risk his rebellion.

'Why, Constance? Why!' He had never been told the reason his research was so important to her. Now he wanted to know. It might help to dampen this fire in him. He could feel the red gargoyle of his anger turning on him, and it scared him. 'Why! You tell me, you have to!' Constance stood before him, her smile sad and enigmatic. 'Your grief is your chance to grow, George. I never said it was easy.' Miserable at the memory, he jammed his fists into his eyes until he saw green stars. He sank to the middle of his dusty living-room floor bellowing as hard as Clark had. Long sobs wracked him. He poured his misery and grief and defeat out into the indifferent house.

Oh, Kitten Kate, I need you now. I was so glad the day you left. That wonderful morning when I slept until noon and watched the Miami game and drank eleven Buds. Lord, what a day! I was a laughing angel boy again, my mamma's genius. No longer was I your husband, the accused failure.

But we were young together, Kate, and we shared some things. Remember that line, Kate – 'Something amazing, a boy falling out of the sky.' Oh, baby, something amazing all right. I loved you and I threw you away, and I fell, baby, right out of the sky. Okay, I confess. I fell right out of the sky. 'Something amazing . . . a delicate ship passing by saw something amazing . . .' He could never remember all of her favourite poem. 'A delicate ship passing by saw something amazing, a boy falling out of the sky.' Just that one line.

The house smelled faintly of linseed oil from the box of paints Mandy had left on the sun porch. He liked that odour; it reminded him of the six weeks of the summer of 1968 he had spent in Florence. There had been college students from all over the world there, art students, working on

218

the restoration of the Uffizi masterpieces which had been damaged in the flood of the year before.

He had met Irish magical Roisin, with whom he had cohabitated for weeks, before he had found, jammed into her suitcase, the terrible rubble of a dead owl.

He had run terrified from her. Roisin, lost in the dangerous clutter of time.

Upon the dead waters, the last leaf finally sinks.

This snivelling had gone on long enough. It was time for the scum to be punished. He owed Kate, he owed the kids, he owed Constance, and now he owed Bonnie, too. He went to the mudroom.

He opened the trapdoor.

He descended to Kitten Kate.

Here he sometimes slept, with the cat eyes he had pasted on the wall staring at him, with the cat faces glaring at him, with the marching, running, jumping cats all around him, the long cats and the slinky cats, the cats of death and hell.

He had burned one once, he and his dear childhood friend Kevin. They had burned a cat named Silverbell, a huge black cat with a loping walk and a kinked tail. Cat of Claire Jonas. They had massaged Sterno into its fur and touched a match to it.

He slammed his head against the back wall, the one that had cinder blocks behind the thickness of cutout cats and drawn cats and pasted cat parts, the tufts of fur, the crisp bits of skin. This was the painful wall.

'Jenny went in there today, George. I told you what'd happen if you didn't tear it down and the kids saw it.' Kate's foot went *slam* against the floor.

'Look, I'll get help.'

'How many times have you said that? Fifty? I want a divorce, George. I cannot stay here any longer. I do not want the kids exposed to whatever the hell's going wrong with you.'

'I told you, I'll go to a shrink. Constance will know somebody.'

'You'll never do it. Anyway, you probably need an exorcist more than a shrink. That room is evil! Evil, George, and horrible and completely crazy and your daughter has seen it. You know what she said? "Gee," she said, "is this why Daddy hits me so hard?"'

'I always knew it. Somehow or another cats would destroy me.'

He looked around his room. This room *was* a cat. It was in a sense all cats.

It was Tink Tink reeeoooowww! across the green lawn a streak of popping blue fire, reeaaaaooooo poppop *crackle* rrreeeeeaaaaooooo!

What the hell, it was funny, she goes to the door, Claire opens it, and there's this burning cat all wound up on itself, rolling around on the porch.

They took her to the vet, and George couldn't forget it even now: one yellow eye staring, the other burned away.

Put to sleep. Lullabye and okay, close your goddamn eyes, Bonnie! Golden slumbers fill your – oh, crap, I am missing my chance, somehow or other. Come on, honey, wind of the western sea, blow, blow –

Oh. Go to sleep. Jenny, please go to sleep.

Not for you, Daddy!

George undressed. He knelt. He lit the candle. He arched over it, bending low, feeling the warmth rise to heat, to small pain. His chest was marked by a dozen round, red scars, the after effects of similar torments.

In the Kitten Kate Room, before the marching, the jumping, the yellow-eyed and creeping cats of the world, George knelt and forced his shaking, jerking body into the crackle-hungry flames, until a spot just below his left nipple, a fresh spot, spluttered and oozed red.

'God.' He pitched back from the flame, clawing at the agony of the wound, rolling, rubbing his filthy basement sheet into the crisped skin. Bacon chest. Is that funny-haha or funny-weird?

Very fine. Shirt back on, tuck it in nice and neat, do a good job, oops, no oozing through allowed. There was a stack of old newspapers back behind the door. Let's see. September 14, 1983, *The Collegian*. Picture of Dot Chambers, Sorority Mavin, 'Hazing Rituals to Be Reviewed.'

The SAOs had to cut out their Long March, and the Phi Zetas their paddling.

There is so much anger in this world. He plastered Dot Chambers down on his leaking flesh, then winked out the candle between thumb and forefinger and climbed back up the ladder to the mudroom.

A little torment could cure so much anger, so much grief. Bonnie was a volunteer. She took a risk in a noble cause and lost. The witches would give her body back to the earth. He would be forgiven. The experiment would be forgotten. Whyever Constance had needed it, this would be changed. The world would roll out and the Covenstead would live on, without anybody ever having returned from the dead.

He got a beer and went prowling about, wondering after little Mandy dear. Doing illustrations for Constance, was she? She'd be a witch soon, that was for sure.

Witch. Bitch. Kate gave good head once, back before the beginning of the end of time. Bobbing Kate – head down there giving head. You could make a lifetime of memories of Kate, had ye the inclination.

When he sighed, Dot crinkled. Okay, all right, you win. He threw back the Bud and went to the kitchen for another.

No?

All done. The refrigerator light filled the gloomy kitchen with an even gloomier glow. Gloom and glow, gloom and glow, Edelweiss, Edelweiss . . . remember *The Sound of Music* and Kate a girl then, the old Chevy II, back in the days of Martin Luther King and Bull Conners and the Yippies and oh what a fine ringing, singing time.

Bang.

One brief shining moment. Shamalot. A-a-a-y! I was gonna be a great scientist. Man, I won the science fair. I won a Westinghouse scholarship. (Almost.) I won tenure. (Almost.)

Bang.

'So in the very moment of defeat he says to himself, wait a second. The experiment has been troubled by external conditions. There is as yet no definitive reason for shutting it down.'

Once the death was connected with his lab, everything would be impounded, his records and his equipment both.

George put on his jacket, zipped it, went out through the mudroom to the garage. All right. He was entitled to take his own property off the campus. They were his goddamn coils.

He didn't need the monitoring equipment, not really. Just the video camera. He'd take his own VCR down from the game room. Dear me, reduced to home experimenting. Down among the cats, where the air smells like burned beef jerky.

All right, okay, home experimentation isn't totally invalid. Here's some precedent: synthetic rubber was discovered on a wood stove. Penicillin was an accident.

As he guided the car down the driveway, he looked back at his house and thought, one day this place will be a museum. And that basement window there, the one between the rosebushes, people will point to it and say, that is where subject X took the ultimate journey, right behind that window. And in the end Constance will thank me. Yes, she will thank me for what I am going to do.

The streets were dark and surprisingly empty. He thumbed the knob that lit his watch. 12:47 A.M. A hell of a lot of time had passed unnoticed. He must have been in

Kitten Kate for considerably longer than it had seemed.

Well, good. He needed time there. Good. It meant he had suffered longer, and therefore put himself back together for more time. The longer he suffered in the Kitten Kate room, the more chance he had for a happy life. He was filled with strength. Power. The power of pain. Dear little Dot, plastered to my breast, who will it be?

Must be a she, of course, because only a she will fit my seven-coil array. Mandy was not enormous, and sooner or later, she would come back here.

Mandy, dear, you're five-nine if you're an inch. You'll fit. Just barely, but you'll fit.

Wasn't there a song somewhere about Amanda? 'Farewell, Amanda . . . de de dah . . . sweet Amanda.' He smiled. 'Farewell, Amanda . . . remember me when you're stepping on the stars above.' That was it. You'll step on the stars, Amanda.

I think.

He turned onto Ames, crossed the little bridge there, and saw glaring in his car lights a most unusual sight. A huge black horse, a nude woman astride it bareback, the two of them surrounded by a flock of dark, darting birds. Hoofs clattered and crows cawed and the woman let out such a shriek that George screamed, too, involuntarily, screamed until his throat would break.

Hazing ritual? Too late in the season for that. Streaker prank? Fad was over.

George followed in his car, bearing down on the whole apparition, horse and woman and birds. The horse was not three feet in front of the Volvo when it leaped high into the air, across the sidewalk, and into the middle of a lawn. It continued on, snow clouds rising from its hoofs, around the house and into the backyard.

George sat there, staring after it. He was sobered. Again he heard the woman scream. Engines were roaring, lights rushing past. Pickup trucks, shotguns, guys with beer cans and cigars. Must be college revels, however improbable.

It grew much colder.

George drove onto the campus, went to the lab, and began loading the coils into cardboard boxes. Four trips back and forth and his car was full. There remained only one thing to get: the tranquilizer gun. There was enough scopolamine in one of those cartridges to close a human being down for a good hour.

He pocketed it. His pistol was nowhere to be found. Clark, no doubt, making sure the doctor didn't do himself in.

No, not yet. The good doctor had been in a tailspin, yessir. But the good doctor was now flying again.

He had a fine plan. He was going to become the spider of the house. Do a little web sitting.

Sooner or later, dear little Mandy would be bound to return, if only to get her things.

When she did, he was going to kill her.

Farewell, Amanda.

And bring her back to a normal life.

Hello, again. (Applause.)

Together they would share their triumph with the world.

CHAPTER 16

Mandy awoke to the sound of dripping water. She opened her eyes and found herself looking across a dirt floor. Her shoulders ached, her thighs ached, and greasy male flesh wrapped her body. Robin, in the truth of the morning, needed a bath.

As she became fully conscious, she was struck by powerful, pounding emotions. There was sorrow over the horse that had been killed, but at the same time something new moved in her, a sense of tautness, as if a little steel had impregnated her bones, and her muscles had been filled with the energy of a coiled spring. Robin was not a large, distant model of her father, but somehow smaller, and she knew that she could share power with a man, or even take it from him if she wished.

Beyond these newly discovered feelings and powers, though, there was something much greater. Over the past twenty-four hours it had emerged as the new centre of her understanding, revising everything. It was her memory of the *Leannan Sidhe*, the Fairy Queen. To lie back in the straw and know she had seen the *Leannan* and that the fairy were real gave her the most exquisite possible joy. For her the meaning of the world had deepened and grown much richer. The joy that filled her extended itself beyond love of the *Leannan* to include Robin and Constance and the whole Covenstead. She had reached, she thought, the centre of the world's beauty.

She indulged in an elaborate stretch, feeling every muscle, every limb.

The water was gurgling, tinkling, pinging all around the

outside of the wattled building. Here and there a drip came through the thatch. The unseasonable snow was melting.

Around her people sighed and snored. She was the only person awake, but the animals were snuffling about in their stalls. Across a tossed expanse of sleeping humanity a soft-eyed goat was munching hay.

Besides her enormous sense of personal well-being, there was a physical reality she could not ignore. She felt sticky and clammy, dirtier than she had been since the days of tattered sneakers and sand piles. She could not recall wanting a shower quite as much as she wanted one now. The dripping sounds made her long to feel a warm stream sluicing across her skin, to smell the gentle billows of Ivory as they washed away the battles of the night.

She stared back at the eerie lozenges floating in the goat's eyes. Somehow it did not seem entirely innocent, this goat. Who knows what is in the mind of the animal – the simple emptiness that seems to be there or a silent, motionless intelligence? Its ears pricked forward. Her staring had made it curious.

There came the memory of thunder in the dark. The hard flash of the shotgun, the quivering of her devastated horse.

Her horse? She hardly knew his name.

But for a little while that horse had been part of her. He was the shaded man she had touched once or twice inside herself. In every woman, she thought, there lives a father and a bandit of a man, who is somehow reached through that mad love of horses that affects many an adolescent woman. Mandy could remember owning pictures of horses and going to the county fair to see the trotters.

You do not just kill a magnificent horse.

Robin's hand dangled across her thigh. She took it to her lips and kissed it. How unfamiliar it was. She decided that she did not actually love him. She felt passion for him. For her, this was a very rare experience. Her relationships with men were not straightforward. There had been too much

226

anger between her and her father for her to ever trust herself to a man.

Idly she ran her fingers in his hair, touched his sleeping face. Would she love him, this man who had been given to her, or did the gift preclude that desperate, clinging thing?

Through the smoke hole far above came a blast of light. Outside chickens were cackling, and a rooster set up a lusty crowing. A cow kicked her stall and something made a chortling sound.

Something else moved in the far shadows, disturbing the dark near the wall. When Mandy raised her head to look more closely, the movement stopped.

She was not deceived, though. Even her brief experience with raw nature had already changed her perceptions. Animal cunning did not fool her so easily. She knew something was there.

Stillness settled, and as it did, the shadows began to move again. Something slid along, changing the curve of a leg, the thickness of a thigh, the length of an arm, as it moved among the sleepers.

Mandy understood all at once what she was seeing, and when she did she jammed her fist in her mouth to keep from screaming. It moved steadily across the room, its head held just above the floor, its tongue darting, its eyes polished knobs.

Mandy watched it come into the centre of the circle. Midway down its length was a lump about the size of a rat. It was at least six feet long, a great red and yellow creature, fairly glowing with reptilian health. It was on its way home after its predawn hunt.

The snake was no fool. It did not attempt to go near the animal stalls, but rather headed towards the door, crossing sleeping people with impunity, staying strictly away from the hoofed things. As it slid across a child's bottom, she giggled in her sleep.

Not ten seconds after it had disappeared into a crack

in the wattling beside the door, the great gong boomed. Somebody coughed. The child awoke laughing. Other shadows began rising in the half light. Cloaks and jackets and shirts were found. Mandy chose to watch the activity out of half-closed eyes. She didn't want to miss any chance, however small, to learn more about these people. She was now able to accept that she was important to them, and thus it bothered her all the more that they were such strangers to her. She had already learned that direct questions didn't help much. Ask them their names and they would say Flame or Wild Aster or Garnet or some such thing. But never a legal identification.

As if he existed half in her imagination and half in reality, she saw Tom clinging in the rafters, a vividness fading. He had done terrible things, that cat. You could hear his fury in the way he breathed.

The general shuffle in the room awoke Robin. He shifted, stretched, then groaned.

'Hi,' she said.

'I must be alive. I ache all over.'

'You aren't alone. I'm hungry as well as sore.'

He laughed. 'You're lucky you don't have to eat and run. I've got to commute all the way to New York.'

Surely he was joking. The Holly King couldn't possibly be a commuter.

'Don't look so amazed. You make me feel like I've got two heads or something. I go to the Pratt Institute. I'm studying design. It's no big deal. A lot of us commute. The Covenstead has to exist in the real world, after all. And it's out there, believe me, belching smoke and vomiting a continuous stream of Big Macs and VCRs.'

He stood up and took a couple of halting steps. 'Damn. I might be cutting class this morning. Look at my feet.'

She touched the cuts, the swellings, the bruises. He had run barefoot as well as naked last night. Considering which, his feet were actually in fairly good condition.

Now that she was fully awake she recalled the Wild Hunt in exact detail. And she wondered about the morality of such an escapade. She and Robin had abused their bodies. Above all, there was the death of the horse and the terrible chase that could so easily have ended in their murder. One of the things the Wild Hunt had given her was the willingness to ask hard questions. She did not know it, but she was beginning to take the first, hesitant steps towards rule. 'Why did you go into the town?'

'The Wild Hunt would hardly be wild if there was no danger. And the town covens would have been bitterly disappointed.'

'You could have found danger in the woods.'

'Safer danger? Come on. Our enemy lives in Maywell.'

'I lost my horse.'

'Raven was a great creature.'

'I loved him.'

'He was part of you last night, wasn't he?'

'More than you realize.'

'Then he still is, Amanda. Now and always. And you should thank Brother Pierce for that. He gave you Raven.'

'That's ridiculous!'

'No air is sweeter than that we breathe after we have escaped our enemy.' Robin touched her face. 'Come on,' he said, 'let's find us some breakfast.'

She found herself willing to accept his touch and the consolation in his voice. The Wild Hunt was over. Nobody needed to tell her that she had passed that test as well. From the new power and assurance she felt within, she knew it.

They went out into a mild morning. The ground was sodden, everything wet with runoff. The temperature was easily fifty. The air smelled of hot bread and wood fires, with a colder breath coming off the mountain. Robin inhaled, looked around. 'If the snow had come a week earlier or stayed a day longer, it would have destroyed our crops.'

'You're lucky.'

'Some people around here think the *Leannan* can control the weather. All the covens cast spells for a thaw, though. Maybe that's what did it.'

'Show me some spells.'

'Soon.'

'Oh, come on. I'm sick of being kept in suspense by you people. I want to know now!'

'Look – quick!' He pointed towards a tangle at the base of the mountain.

'What?'

He laughed. 'Fairy. You have to be quick to see them.'

'I'd like to see them up close again.'

'They don't let you do that.'

'I'd like to see the *Leannan* again. Really see her.'

'Except for Constance, you're the only human being who's ever seen the *Leannan*. Unless there are some who saw her and didn't survive the experience.' What he said both chilled and delighted her. She tossed her head, laughing somewhere deep inside. She remembered the silver-blonde hair, the face with its laughing, sultry smile. 'Do you wonder what she's like?'

'Of course.' His voice was sharp, she thought a bit disappointed.

They came to a cottage near the centre of the village. Inside Ivy was making oatmeal in a kettle over the open fire. Mandy had never actually been inside one of the cottages before. It was low-ceilinged, with rush beds against two of the walls. They were concealed by dark brown draperies of homespun. Each bed was wide enough for two. In the centre of the room was a large table on which there were four earthenware bowls. A loaf of black bread sat on a board in the middle of the table. Beside it was a large wedge of pale cheese and a pitcher. There were earthenware cups and wooden spoons. A young man in a grey pinstripe suit laid plates out beside the bowls.

'Morning, Ivy,' Robin said. 'Morning, Yellowjacket.'

'You both look like hell,' Ivy replied. 'And you smell worse. Go down to tl.e sweat lodge, please. There'll still be plenty of food left when you're endurable.'

Robin took Mandy's arm, guided her out. 'It's her house,' he said. 'Better not rile her.'

'I'd love a bath anyway.'

'You know about the sweat lodge? I was hoping it'd be a surprise.'

'Whatever are you talking about?'

'The sweat lodge. I designed it, you know. The structure, all the equipment. Everything.'

She had not noticed the long, low building hugging the edge of the village before. Smoke came from tall chimneys at either end. It was made of brick, with a roof of cedar shakes.

There were shoes and boots lined up along the doorstep. An overhang protected articles of clothing from the elements. 'Hang your other clothes under your cloak.'

'I'm not wearing any other clothes.'

They disrobed together. She stood, feeling the prick of the morning air, her hands touching her breasts.

'I hope it's warm in there.'

He opened the door into a steamy wonderland. The odour alone was unforgettable, a heady ambrosia of pine and cedar and soap. Cedar beams sweated above. There were three tubs made of glazed bricks. Under them fireboxes glowed. People sat up to their necks in the water. A woman lay nearby on a wooden table being gently massaged by another. Two men did stretching exercises together on the wet slate floor. People talked quietly, laughed. Men shaved before a long, dripping mirror, their faces lathered light green. A girl, blonde and tall, tossed wood into the fires, then went to a large canvas mechanism. She dipped the canvas bucket in one of the pools and raised it by a winch to the ceiling. 'Shower's ready,' she said to Robin and Mandy.

At last, a wish granted. The soap, however, wasn't Ivory.

The bars were heavy and green, and flecked with herbs. They created dense lather that smelled of mint and left Mandy's body feeling smooth and very clean, almost as if her skin had somehow been penetrated and renewed from within.

'Get rinsed,' the girl said. 'Your water's almost over.' As Mandy finished she heard the girl telling some of the people in the tubs to hurry.

'Maywell has only one bus into New York,' Robin said as he dried himself with a huge, rough towel. 'If we miss it we miss work. So we do our ritual sweats in the evening. This is just your ordinary garden-variety communal bath.' Saying that, he got into one of the big tubs. Mandy followed, slipping down into the delicious water. The other soakers were just getting out, and she and Robin soon had the tub to themselves.

'What do you people do in New York? My impression was that you were living out here in isolation, farming and things like that.'

'We've got a great farm. But people have jobs, too. Careers. Some of us don't choose to give them up. In addition to this, our economy isn't completely internalized. We have to go outside for a few things.'

'You mean matches –'

'We don't need matches. We use rushes and waxed tapers and take from fire to fire.'

'Candles, kerosene?'

'I doubt if the whole Covenstead uses ten gallons of kerosene in a year. Wax comes from our own bees. We have fine hives, and Selena Martin is an outstanding mistress of bees.'

'Medicine, then. Surgery. Advanced diagnostics.'

The attendant interrupted. 'I'm going to damp back the fire now. It's past time and you have your bus, Robin.'

Robin only nodded. 'Would you believe me if I told you that modern medicine is to some extent an addiction. The

232

more you rely on it, the more you need it. When we get sick, really sick, the medical team goes to work. We use herbal remedies extensively and effectively. As far as diagnostics are concerned, Constance is extraordinary. And she can heal, too. When a witch chooses death, the whole Covenstead celebrates. It is sad to be saying good-bye, but we're also happy for the dying witch. You will learn about the Land of Summer, where we believe we go to await rebirth. Witches do not deny death. For us a death is as rich and joyous an occasion as a birth or a marriage.'

'I always think of it as a tragedy.'

'That's just a cultural habit. Death is just another stage of life, perhaps the fullest, best stage.'

'But what if somebody – some female witch – is dying in abject agony from breast cancer? What then? Do you dance and sing?'

His eyes filmed for a moment, then cleared. 'A hard death is a blessing also. Anyway, we have powerful drugs for pain, not to mention hypnosis. All of that is Connie's province. I don't know much about it.'

'What is she, beyond leader?'

'Oh, she's not a leader at all. Connie is much closer to being a mother than a ruler. She's where you go when you have need – advice, encouragement, medicine, whatever your need is, she is there for you.'

So that was to be her own role. Life was turning, Connie had grown old. 'She wants me to be her assistant. That's why they call me Maiden.'

'She has no assistant. She is Crone. Once she was Maiden. As she matured, the character of the Covenstead changed. When she was Maiden, things were much wilder, more intense. Then in her Motherhood we were builders, knitters, carpenters. Now she is Crone, and we are a contemplative covenstead. When she passes –' He stopped suddenly, and she held out her hand to him. 'I'm sorry. She will die, or she would not have brought you here to be initiated. You will never be anybody's assistant. When you are Maiden, we will belong to your will and your will only, just as we belong to Connie now.' He raised his head, smiled. 'You will not rule us, though. We rule ourselves, each one of us. The only hierarchy of the Covenstead is that of heart and hearth.'

'Robin, this is just fascinating. But I have to admit that the water's getting awfully cold.'

'Yeah, that's a fact. Maybe we'd better go for breakfast, assuming Ivy's saved anything for us.'

On the way back to the cottage they passed women and men hurrying off in the direction of the main house. They carried briefcases, wore topcoats, even some hats. Others had gathered into a work gang and were marching towards the fields. These wore plain homespun trousers and jerkins, men and women alike.

'What about taxes?' Mandy asked suddenly. 'And those suits and ties. Surely you didn't weave those.'

'The suits are bought. As far as taxes are concerned, the IRS knows where we are, and we pay our taxes. You have trouble writing off Bell, Book, and Candle as a business expense, though, so don't even think about it.'

'It's been tried?'

He looked at her, his face expressionless. 'It's been tried. Many of our priestesses and priests are recognized by the IRS as clergy. At least they were, until this year.'

'What happened this year?'

'Senator Stennis happened. He tacked an amendment on the Postal Appropriations Bill forbidding the IRS to grant tax exemptions to people who practise witchcraft.'

'What! That's government interference in religion.'

'Fundamentalist Christians are not interested in preserving the Bill of Rights when it comes to people who disagree with their religious beliefs. The amendment passed by voice vote. Senators were afraid to go on record as supporting witchcraft.'

This cold wind from the outside world made Mandy remember her own dream life, the intense vision – almost a hallucination – of being burned to death.

She was to become responsible for these people. Would there come a time when the senators and the fundamentalist preachers would gain power in America and the flames would rise again? She knew already that she loved the Covenstead and wanted it to persist. If she had to burn she would, to ensure its survival. She would do whatever she had to for them, and in the end she was sure she would defeat people like the fundamentalists, whose very lives seemed to imply the existence of real evil in the world. If there was a Satan, Mandy thought, fundamentalist Christianity was one of his central means of capturing souls. They prayed to Jesus but did the work of their demon hearts, burning books, trampling the rights of others, spitting on America's noble and ancient tradition of tolerance. She thought of Brother Pierce, of his kind, sad eyes. There was a man in service to evil, and not a bad man, either. A trapped man. And the sadness in his eyes told her that he knew the truth of his false religion. How different it was from the ever-opening flower that is the true spirit of Christianity.

As they walked through the Covenstead, Mandy noticed as much as she could, trying to form true impressions of this society. If she was to be their Maiden, she had an enormous amount of homework to do.

The village was different from every other place she had ever experienced. The very air seemed different. There was no subtle message of oppression here in the way men strode and women walked. Rather, there was a sort of disciplined openness that was hard to characterize. Women managed it, she knew that. But there was no sense that one of the sexes had been overpowered by the other. The irritant of sexual politics had been subdued.

The moment they re-entered Ivy's cottage this impression strengthened. The almost indefinable sense of possession rested somewhere between Yellowjacket and Ivy. Although it flowed out of her, it stifled neither of them.

Robin was on his way to the kettle when Ivy handed him a chunk of bread and a slice of cheese. 'Drink some yogurt and you're off,' she said. 'There's no time.'

'I'm not so sure I'm going. My feet are a mess.' He poured thick, brown liquid from the pitcher into a cup, drank it down, and took his bread and cheese. Yellowjacket got up to leave. 'Good-bye, Ivy, and thank you. Good-bye, Amanda.'

He and Ivy kissed at the door. 'Lawyers turn her on,' Robin whispered. 'She's no fool. Utopian communities may disintegrate, but law degrees last for life.'

'You're not a very convincing cynic, Robin.' She kissed him, a pert, shy little kiss that surprised her almost as much as it did him. It was not love that made her do it. It would be most accurate to say that she felt poetry for Robin. She watched him eating, his long hands working the utensils, his rough homespun sweater revealing his strength. She had made love to that man last night.

Or had she? No, she had made love with the Holly King. And that was the difference between them: he was the Holly King only in the dark, on the Wild Hunt. But she was always Amanda.

'Let me look at those feet, brother.' Ivy knelt before him.

'The right one's the worst.'

'I can see that. Broken blisters.' She felt the lesions. 'Fortunately the puncture wounds are from thorns, not nails. But just to be safe I think you'd better get Dr Forbes to give you a tetanus shot before he goes to town.'

'How delightful.'

Amanda was interested to hear this exchange. 'Who's Dr Forbes?'

'A witch,' Robin said. 'His witch name is Periwinkle Star, which is why we all still call him Dr Forbes. He does all our vaccinations and immunizations and such. I think I forgot to mention him because I don't like shots.'

'I'll make up an arnica salve for you when you come back,' Ivy said. 'But you'd better be prepared to show me your needle mark.'

Looking disconsolate, Robin left the cottage.

'He'll be fine in a couple of hours,' Ivy said, banging about in the kitchen. 'As soon as he's sure he's missed the bus to the city, he's probably going to improve tremendously.' She regarded Mandy. 'I've got bacon,' she said. 'It's from a village hog, and it's great. We're very proud of it.'

'Bacon?'

'Thick bacon. Don't you like bacon?'

'I do, but somehow I formed the impression that this place was vegetarian.'

'Some of us are. But *I'm* not, and I didn't think you were. Plus, you're eating like you're really hungry. I think you can use the protein.' She commenced serving. Mandy moved to help, but Ivy wouldn't let her. 'You're practically Maiden of the Covenstead. Let me express my respect by serving table, if you don't find it too uncomfortable.'

Her first impulse was to say that she did feel uncomfortable, but the truth was different. Deep inside herself, the position they were putting her in seemed very right.

She worried, though. The challenges of the past two days had made her aware of a passivity in her personality she hadn't even known was there. By thrusting her into one incredibly difficult situation after another Constance and the witches had shown her how rarely she really took charge of her own life, and how good at it she was when she did. The trouble was, she had seen the passivity, but she had not surmounted it, not completely. If she was to take responsibility for all of these people and their remarkable way of life – especially during a time of persecution – she had to reach deep into herself and transform the passive into the strong.

She had spent her life placing herself in situations and waiting for things to happen, and that was not enough. Now she was to be Maiden of the Covenstead. Not President or Queen, but Maiden. To her it was a beautiful word. Not as cold as 'crone' or as warm as 'mother.' Maiden. It had a suggestion of home in it, but also another element, one that was fierce.

Maiden was a word of both love and power. She remembered herself on the hunt, how she had screamed.

Maiden meant woman's softness. It meant tentative beginnings. But there was also the connotation of the Maid of Orléans, and Athene the Maiden of Battle, and the Maiden Huntress Diana. The Maiden, singing softly, seated on a creekside stone . . . the Maiden astride Raven, galloping to the battles of the night. It was a long, long time ago that women had such a role in this man's world. She remembered reading a hymn to Ishtar, written at the dawn of time:

Ruler of weapons, arbitress of the battle
Framer of all decrees, wearer of the crown of dominion,
Thou merciful Maiden . . .

She sat down to the meal Ivy was making for her. Alone in her own place Ivy exuded loving decency. The bitch of the maze was no more. In fact the whole incident – everything that had happened to Mandy on the Collier estate – was obviously part of this great testing of her spirit. The choreography of it all was subtle but not invisible. She knew the object: to help her find her strength and live from it so that she could be Maiden.

'I've got to get out to the farm,' Ivy said as she laid a plate of brown bacon before Mandy. 'We're harvesting pumpkins.' She laughed. 'The Vine Coven is going to be making a *lot* of pumpkin pies and pumpkin bread and pumpkin soup this year. We've got a great crop.'

'The farm is organized according to covens?'

'There are three farmer covens, one shepherd, and one husbandry. The others are all more generalized.'

'What are their names?'

'Well – we're Vine. And there's Demeter. They do the grains. And Rowan does the orchard and stuff. Hard labour is Rock Coven. Io is the husbandry coven. They raised the hog that gave the bacon that's in your mouth. His name was Hiram, by the way. He was a very friendly guy. He used to root in the kids' pockets.' Mandy stopped chewing. '"Who eats flesh must do it with conscience, otherwise the weight of death will enter your blood." Constance always says that when she sees us eating meat.'

Slowly Mandy began to chew again. This time the bacon tasted very different, much richer and more succulent. The hog had given its life. Its sacrifice was somehow present in the meat and could be tasted by a sensitive palate. All of her life she had eaten meat and never thought twice about the suffering that went into providing it. Never before had she thought to honour the animals who gave their lives for her. There was something strange here, strange and terrifying, that seemed to hover at the edge of consciousness. Mandy was afraid, and ate no more bacon.

Ivy continued. 'Besides those of us in the covens, there are people like you who haven't been initiated into the Covenstead yet, or taken into a specific coven. They – not you – are sort of outsiders. They live in the two end cottages.'

Mandy smiled. 'You've told me more about the organization of this place than anybody else.'

'Well, since you captured the Holly King –'

'I've passed muster?'

Ivy smiled. 'Let's say that Connie's very pleased with your progress.' Her cheeks coloured. 'The rest of us, to tell you the truth, are awed.' Her face became grave. 'What was the *Leannan* like?' she asked in a low voice.

'Very small. Pale, blonde. Her eyes were dark, almost the colour of sandalwood. She was beautiful, but not in a simple way. Her face was gay and sort of light – that's the best way I can describe it. But it was also very *aware*. It was the loveliest face I've ever seen. Also somehow the most dangerous.'

Ivy stared a long time into Mandy's eyes. 'What a wonderful experience that must have been. I'd give a great deal to see the *Leannan*.'

Mandy could only nod. It was not easy to talk about the *Leannan*. Sometimes she seemed like a memory, then like a dream. Ivy began to clatter in a chest. 'I've really got to mix Robin's salve and go. Please make use of my house. And if you want to, you can handle my tools. In fact, it'd be a privilege if you did.'

'Your tools?'

She gestured towards the hearth. 'My witch things. Just don't touch the drying herbs. Connie'll be furious with me if I don't pass my herbals exam this term.' A silence fell between them. Ivy looked at Mandy with the very plainest sorrow in her eyes. She continued, but with effort. 'It's really a good day for harvest. We needed that. Grasshopper counted over four hundred good pumpkins!' She busied herself at her hearth for a few minutes, crushing dried herbs in a mortar, then mixing them with purified fat. She left the salve with a note for Robin, and an admonition for him to get out into the fields since he wasn't going to New York. 'His feet aren't that bad. And we need the help.' Then she was gone, the door closing behind her with a creak and a decisive click.

Mandy stood in the middle of the compact room. Deep silence settled. Soon the smell of the bacon made her forget her misgivings about eating Hiram, and she sat down again. She was in a state of great sensitivity. Her whole body was tingling with life. Her senses were preternaturally acute. She noticed, for example, that she could actually hear herself eating. He jaws creaked, her teeth ground, her lips smacked. They were not unpleasant sounds. She also began to notice, very faintly, the music of a harp mingling with her own sounds. Maybe it was next door, maybe farther away. She couldn't tell. But it was sweetly done, a tune that reminded her of a thousand tunes, of moments and days that were lost.

Normally Mandy did not think much about her past. Life had been too hard to dwell upon. Nobody in the family had cared about her or been interested in her desire to be an artist. She was an encumbrance to her mother and father, an interruption in the titanic duel that defined their marriage.

One hot afternoon when she was seventeen she had seen some framed canvases tucked away in the garage rafters. She had climbed up and discovered six paintings of her mother, all enormous, all profoundly awful. They managed to mix sentimentality with bad technique and ghastly colour choice. In them Mother looked like a corpse with the hands and thighs of a hairless gorilla. She was a voluptuous woman, but not coarse.

The fact that the paintings were by her father had revealed a lot to Mandy, crouching up there in the dust, a secret witness to his failure. Their ignoring of their daughter's talent wasn't a side effect of a failed marriage, it was purposeful.

She had left that attic furious at her parents for their tragic self-absorption and their indifference to their own child. She became sullen and hostile, then openly rebellious. There were blows, and Mandy had screamed out her contempt for the hidden paintings. Dad had wept then, and Mother had crept away, her cheeks blazing. It was not until some time later that Mandy understood what had been behind their reactions. They thought of the paintings as a sort of personal pornography, but they did not destroy them because they were their only link to the time when their marriage had been good.

Not long after that Mandy moved to New York.

She finished her meal and got up from the table. The harp

had faded, and with it her painful memories of the past. They had been teaching memories, though. She saw that she should have been more compassionate towards her parents. It was too late now, though.

She didn't know quite what to do with herself. Should she explore the village? Could she? And what of the library up at the main house – what did it contain?

Before she left, she stopped to look at Ivy's ritual tools, which were lying on a piece of white linen on the mantelpiece. Chief among them were a long silver sword and a shorter knife, hooked at the end. There was red cord neatly wound, and a small cauldron. Mandy could see things in it, but she did not know what they were and she dared not reach in and touch them.

'It's a fine cauldron.'

'Constance!'

'Good morning, dear. I brought you some clean things.' Constance strode into the middle of the cottage and put a bundle on the rough table. Mandy unwrapped the clothes.

They were beautiful – a cream-coloured silk blouse, a tweed suit, hose, Gucci shoes. A small makeup kit completed the package. 'Constance, these clothes – what's it all about?'

'You should dress your part. You're a princess now, to half the people of Maywell. Soon you'll be their queen.'

'Maiden, I thought it was called.'

'That's the first turn of the cycle. Maiden, then Mother, then Crone. I am, obviously, Crone. And I'm at the end of my time.'

'Constance, you're healthier than most women half your age.'

'Don't you patronize me, girl. When a woman in my position says she's near death, you accept it. As a matter of fact, you don't have much time before I go across. Now, don't stand there like a scarecrow. Dress!'

'I can't wear these things – I'm on a farm.'

'You'll be going down to the town this morning.'

Mandy dressed. There was even perfume in the makeup kit. Norell. Constance did everything right.

'Why am I going to town?'

'You'll see.'

Mandy would have none of that, not anymore. 'I am not as passive as you think, Constance. So far you've done pretty much what you wanted with me. But I'm afraid from now on I'm going to need reasons before I agree. I could have got my head blown off last night.'

Constance shrugged. 'You want to be Maiden of this Covenstead, don't you?'

'Do I have a choice?'

'Certainly. Fail one of the tests and you won't inherit your birthright.'

'What would happen to me if I did fail? For example, say I hadn't found the Holly King last night.'

'Oh, you were going to find the Holly King no matter what, as long as you stayed alive. In these tests the only way you can fail is to get yourself killed. So if you'd been shot dead instead of my horse –'

'My God. Do you mean to tell me that the purpose of all this is to see if I can stay alive? Oh, Constance, that's awful. It's downright immoral. I won't do any more. I quit.'

'No, not you. You've got too much determination, my little warrior. You'll see it through. All your instincts make you want to protect the Covenstead. I know, I'm the same type as you.'

'Constance, this is absolutely crazy. I won't hear of it. I won't!'

'Don't you ever call me crazy, you little whelp. If you had any idea how hard this is for me – what sacrifices have *really* been made for you – you would go down on your knees to thank me.'

'So tell me! Why *should* I thank you for trying to get me killed. I'd very much like to know.'

243

'Oh, what force you have. Reading your history, I've wondered what you were like.'

'Don't try to change the subject. I want to know, and I want to know now.'

'Well, what you really want to know is why you should risk your life. You cannot love the Covenstead like I do, more than your own life. You hardly know the Covenstead. But you will come to love it exactly as I do.'

'I can see that.'

'You must prepare yourself.'

'I know. Find my inner strength so that I can rule. I've understood that. It seems to me that I've also done it.'

She looked Mandy up and down. 'Yes, perhaps so. You did well with the *Leannan* and with the Holly King. In the sense that you're still alive.'

'The *Leannan* . . . the fact that she exists is what I cling to. No matter how I feel, that tells me something about this is very real and very important.'

'Oh, little creature, how innocent you are. I suppose there's still enough arrogance left in me to make it impossible for me to see how anyone could take my place. Then I see the fire in you, and I think: you can do it. And I'll tell you something. You're going to have a terribly difficult reign. There will be persecution of witches, environmental disaster, perhaps even a world war that will burn us along with the rest. But somehow, if you survive the initiation, I think I agree with the *Leannan Sidhe*. You are well chosen.'

'I guess I'm complaining because I'm not used to this constant sense of jeopardy. I sort of see the need, but still, haven't I proved myself yet?'

'Do you know the story of Persephone in Hades?'

'Of course.'

'You haven't proved yourself until you have gone to the world of the dead and returned to tell the tale. And I won't say another word about it, except that a young woman – not a very good witch, but a witch – died for you yesterday, and I want you to respect her memory and not be such a complainer.'

'Died for me? In the Wild Hunt?'

'Before that. In an entirely different part of the process, one that relates to the Great Test.'

'I wish you wouldn't be so darned cryptic!'

'You haven't complained before. If that woman's death is to have any meaning, don't complain now. And don't overdo that eye shadow. The Vamp look went out some time ago.'

'I wish I was in control!'

'The only one in control around here is the *Leannan*. She knows something about you of which you're totally unaware. The *Leannan* knows who you really are.'

'I'm me. That's the long and short of it.'

'You're an ancient and very powerful witch.'

Those words seemed to explode in Mandy's brain like a white slash of lightning. She cringed, such was the power of this fiery internal bolt of recognition.

Constance continued. 'You're terrified of your own history. That's part of what makes you such a passenger in your life. You will drift until you begin to do what you were born to do.'

'You say the *Leannan* is in control. She's like a ghost. We hardly see her, let alone talk to her. Most of them have never seen her.'

'She's not fifty feet away from this spot. She's even played her harp for you. Haven't you heard?'

'The music was very nice.'

Constance snorted. 'It was designed to evoke conscience, and it did. You learned from it. Now, listen, you must act. You must begin now, immediately. Show yourself in the town. The town covens need a boost of morale.'

'Who's my armed guard?'

'You can't use a guard.'

'How about Raven? *He* could have used one.'

'Let's go up to the house. Your car's there and you're due at your uncle's within the hour.'

'At my – since when? I don't want to go to my uncle's. Has that ever occurred to you?'

'You've got canvases and frames and paints there. Clothes. Books. You need to pick them up.'

'I don't want to leave here. If I'm so important, I must be able to make a few decisions. And my decision is, I'm staying right here on the Covenstead.'

'The prospect of Maidenhood is making you imperious, Amanda. I'm not sure I like you imperious.'

'Then don't come in here and order me around. I've had more than my share of terrifying and difficult experiences orchestrated by you, and I have no intention of having any more.'

'What possible terror could your uncle hold for you?'

'I just don't want to deal with him. He's disturbed, and he's not going to become my problem.'

'After what happened to Raven last night, and the business of the young woman, I just want you to give the town covens a morale boost.'

'Why don't you go?'

'You're the one they're excited about.'

'How can you be sure of that? My impression is that I'm quite the outsider.'

Constance looked a long time at her. 'You were born to your role.'

'You hardly know me.'

'You say that! You're naked in your work, dear girl. I know you from your painting. And I *know* that your visual skill is more than ordinary, or even extraordinary. It's almost unique.'

'I'm not that good.'

'As a painter, no. There is something inherently banal about fantasies of elves and such, I'll grant you that. But the detail with which you render them, the depth of vision, suggests an imagination of great power. I know, I've spent time over your work.'

'So have I.'

'The *Leannan* says you have the birthright and I say you have the power. If you can visualize, you can do magic, which is a matter of making the real world run parallel to the inner one of images and dreams. You have the strength to visit the House of the Godfather and come back. I did it, and I am less than you.'

Visit the House of the Godfather?

In the story Constance had told the children the other night, the Godfather was death.

The visit to the town suddenly seemed even more dangerous.

She wished she could just be left alone to wander around and learn more about the Covenstead, maybe even do a little painting. Some portraits of the witches, sketches of Raven before the memory grew too static.

Constance looked straight into her eyes. 'That, my dear, is not your fate. The days of painting and dreaming are behind you. You have a great work to do.'

What could Mandy say? Constance had just read her mind. 'What are you, Constance?'

'You've asked me that before.'

'What are you?'

'The best friend you ever had!' Her voice rang through the cottage. In the silence that followed the harp started again. This time the tune turned Mandy's heart, for she had not heard it since she was very small.

> Sweet and low, sweet and low,
> Wind of the western sea.
> Low, low, breathe and blow,
> Wind of the western sea . . .

The harp notes were from a small instrument, plucked by fingers able to touch the strings with great precision. Behind the gravity of Constance's expression was hidden a smile. 'The *Leannan* wants you to go, Amanda.'

The music, Constance's loving expression, Mandy's memories, all combined to create a moment of great beauty. Mandy found that she had not the heart to refuse them what they asked.

'Your uncle needs you now. Help him. He is your father's brother, after all.'

Her father's brother. Maybe in another age that would have meant a lot.

The harp whispered, the harp sang.

Mandy dressed in the clothes. Constance embraced her and kissed her, and wished her well. 'Blessed be,' Constance whispered.

Mandy started on her journey.

CHAPTER 17

High morning was relentlessly bright, with water and melting snow sparkling off every twig and tuft of grass. Amanda guided her little Volks along, aware of the expensive crinkle of her suit and the creamy scent of her perfume.

She understood that she was entering the world of death and that there was great and ancient precedent for her journey. In the passage of the seasons Persephone moves through the netherworld to return to life in the spring. She is the corn seed hiding in the winter field, springing up alive again in the summer, giving humankind nourishment and prosperity.

Amanda was to make Persephone's passage, and she was to do it now, dressed as if for a sacrifice. Constance had obviously walked death's edge herself when Hobbes shot her. Among ancient cultures everywhere: the Indians, many African tribes, the peoples of Siberia – wherever the old religion persisted – it was necessary to make this journey in order to become a guide for others.

The Volks hummed on. Nice of them to pull it out of the mud for her. Nice of them to tell her how to leave the estate by car. She was supposed to follow an almost hidden track through the hummocks and northward into the farm.

It was eerie in among the sharp little hills, especially considering how old they were and what they were said to contain. What must the fairy city have been? Were there silver towers, or painted gates, or pearl-white roofs sweltering under the prehistoric sky? Or had the fairy come from some far place, from the stars, even recently?

Did their ancient cities exist only in the minds of their

human followers? Somehow she thought they lived in structures very much like the round meeting hall of the witches. Theirs was a whole civilization of magic, based on the simplest of goods. Their glories were those of thought unbound.

To them the mind of man was easy to control. Thus the *Leannan* could seem to change her shape or even become invisible.

The fairy would never emerge, though, into this world, not as it was, a place of illusions. They would do no more than watch from their far hills and their flights in the sky.

The goal of the witches was to create a world where even fairy could be understood, which meant one where men no longer thought of the earth as something separate from themselves, but viewed humanity as one organ in the living body of the planet, and could see the universe all in its truth, without the self-deception that the human species was separate from the deeper continuity of the planet to which it belonged.

The *Leannan* was without question the loveliest form Amanda had ever seen or imagined. She almost wept to remember the music of that tiny, perfect harp, to imagine those fingers working the golden whiskers.

Just in time she downshifted to compensate for a length of muddy sand, and found herself out of the valley of the hummocks and on the witch farm.

Riding through it last night, she had known that it was fertile, but by day the fecundity of the place was startling. There were no tractors rattling here, and the air smelled of the sweat of the plants, not the sharp odours of fertilizer and insecticide.

The scent was an intoxication, pouring in her open windows as she drove along the narrow road between rows of corn. It was mixed of wet hay and cut stems and the rot of the season. Among the fallen stalks and the brown vines the farming covens worked. Amanda came to a group of women labouring with scythes in wheat. They moved along the roadside, their tools whistling in the air, the stalks falling with a hiss and a swish, and the rattle of the wheat berries dropping onto canvas. They chanted as they worked:

'Where have you gone, John Barleycorn,
Where have you gone, John Barley?

'I've gone to the fields where the stalks are grown,
You'll find me in the fields, John Barley.'

The chant was whispered, as if to the stalks themselves. Rapture moved in the faces of the reapers as the wheat fell. Nearby a group of children rolled and laughed in the stalks, and three men bundled hay.

Never before had Amanda had such an impression of how very old some human things have become. Mankind has been farming for a long time now. She did not sense the presence of actual deities in these fields, but the mystery and the energy of the old gods seemed very real indeed. Demeter was the Goddess Earth, also called Gaia, known among Catholics as the Blessed Virgin Mary. Out of her rich belly her daughter Persephone emerged, escaping from Hades. Among the Romans Persephone's name was Proserpina, and she was the goddess of health and well-being, as well as death.

Amanda had to learn what Proserpina knew. That knowledge was to be found in the world of the dead. With it she could bring prosperity to the Covenstead.

There were chants going among many of the teams, the round voices of the workers harmonizing with the roar of insects and the bright calling of the children. As Amanda drove carefully along, she became conscious of how rich life in fields really was. How was it that such magic had been forgotten?

Where is mankind going, that we would choose to leave

farms such as this behind? Too much of the joy of working with the earth has been sacrificed. No prayer is needed to assist the fertilized plantings of Iowa and Kansas and California, but without prayer we are less human than we were, and our farms are less alive, our food less true to the needs of our flesh.

And yet, our flight from the magical and the prayerful was not without sense: there was terror somewhere here, beneath the swelling light of the sun.

'Hello, Amanda!' A tall woman held a huge pumpkin aloft, her figure tiny in the sweep of the land. Amanda waved from her window and tooted her horn. The woman, though, had put down the pumpkin and was running across the field. Amanda was stunned to recognize Kate, George's former wife. She stopped the car and got out.

'Amanda, look at you, how you've grown!'

She embraced Kate, whose hair had gone grey, but whose face was radiant, flushed with sunshine and work. She wore a loose homespun dress tied by a black cord. On her feet were thong sandals wrapped to her ankles. In her hair was a silver pin of the quarter moon.

'Kate, I didn't realize that you'd come here.'

'We all did. George became impossible.'

Amanda nodded.

'Constance has told us many times about the coming of the Maiden, but I had no idea that it was you. When I heard your name I thought, is it possible? Then I saw you. Our Amanda. I just can't believe it.'

Silence fell. There was obviously something else on Kate's mind. She was still smiling, but there was pain in the smile. 'I spent a night at your house,' Amanda said. 'I'm going there now to pick up my things.'

'You've seen him? Constance won't let him on the estate anymore. Is he well? Or is that the right question?'

George was certainly not well. 'You're forbidden to see him?'

'God, no. Connie doesn't do that sort of thing. Afraid to see him. Amanda, something happened to him, something dark that has to do with Constance. Don't think she's all sweetness and light. She isn't! She drew him into an involvement with death. She saw things about him that made him become obsessed. It was like death entered the house. We were in one of the Kominski covens. We were so happy. It was new and it was fun. Then George started these sessions up at the estate with Constance. The next thing I knew, he had started that series of experiments, trying to kill things and bring them back to life.' Suddenly she stopped, looked around. 'Let's continue this in the car.' Amanda followed her in. They rolled up the windows. 'I think Constance did something to his mind. He changed. All of a sudden he wanted a ritual chamber in the basement.'

'The Kitten Kate Room?'

'God, yes! It was so crazy. What in the world do cats have to do with it? He went in there and performed acts of self-abuse. He injured himself with candles. I trusted Constance and I sent him to her, and he got even worse! His work came to dominate his life. He'd spend literally days in that lab with that awful girl, Bonnie Haver, a tramp and a drug addict.'

'Bonnie Haver? You mean the one from Our Lady?'

'Yeah, you must have been in the same class, or close to it.'

'I remember her. She was involved in a horrible scandal. More than one horrible scandal.'

'She's no better now than she was then! She had a terrible effect on George. The more he saw of her, the more time he spent in that hideous, demented room. My God, Amanda, I could smell the burning skin. It was hideous, hideous!' She slammed her hand against the dashboard. She was crying too hard to go on.

There was certainly a dark side to Constance. Dark and subtle.

The words of what had once been a favourite poem of hers came to mind.

> I am the mower Damon, known
> Through all the meadows I have mown.

For a moment she could see him, huge and dark, straddling the fields with his great scythe like a fiery ray of sun. I am the Godfather Damon –

'He was such a brilliant man. Now he's crazy.' Known in all the meadows –

Snick. Snick. Snick. Down go the stalks.

To his cool cave descending . . .

All the meadows he has mown.

'Why did you come here?'

'I wanted to, I was desperate to live here. So were the kids! Poor George – it's terrible what's happened to him, but still, I love the Covenstead.'

'Have you confronted Constance?'

'Of course! She listened, then she embraced me and sent me on my way. End of story. Amanda, they're all saying that you're going to be Maiden of the Covenstead. Please, if you are, remember what I've suffered. My husband has been destroyed for some scheme of Constance's.'

'I'll remember, Kate. And I will make Constance tell me what it's all about as soon as I get back from town.'

Kate kissed her cheek. Her eyes were big with sorrow. 'I want my husband,' she said. Then she went back to her work.

Driving along, Amanda had the sense that something larger and darker even than she had thought was occurring. The trouble with this play was that the actors were not allowed to know the plot. Thus they were not actors at all, but puppets. She didn't like being a puppet, not in such a fierce and dangerous mystery.

By the time she began passing the vegetable patches she

was trembling. The warm, pellucid air was pearl-white with haze from the rapid snow melt. She sensed the close presence of a terrible contrivance of magic, terrible and beautiful, as sweet as light, yet so very dangerous. She recalled the *Leannan*'s guards, with their rat teeth. The *Leannan*, too, must have such teeth. Were they evolved from rodents, the fairy, as we are from apes, or had they come to earth from another planet? And Constance – what did she really know, and what did she really intend to accomplish?

She thought, as she rounded the last quick turn in the road, that she heard a horse galloping. Just here she had cried out for the sheer exhilaration of it, upon Raven's back, when they were flying together. Oh, horse.

The border of the estate was marked by a neglected wire fence, a few posts, and a faded sign warning against trespass. There were blackberry thickets full of human laughter – the gay laughter of men picking berries together, and from the sound having a good time of it.

Then she crossed a rickety wooden bridge into the outside world. Beyond a mowed field there was a row of shuttered houses. She remembered their lights darkening down last night, the cloaked people running out, the excited voices, the rustle of feet in dry grass, the snapping hiss of quick-drawn breath.

They had touched her for luck as she rode by.

The road went from gravel to asphalt as it passed through the field. Then there was a yellowed wooden sign: Corn Row. Beyond that was a brick street, neatly curbed, overhung by nearly bare trees. There were tall houses set along either side, fanciful Victorians with curved porches and towers and widow's watches edged by gingerbread. A man with a cap pulled low over his face peered at her from one of the yards. He had something fat and green in his hand. His face was rigid.

As she picked up speed, she saw him lean far back, raise his arm, and throw the thing. She jammed on the accelerator.

The car roared, and at the same moment what he had thrown hit the roof with a thud and a splash.

She turned on two wheels to Bridge Street. Her car filled with the reek of gasoline. She thought, no, no, not that, they mustn't set me on fire! More than anything she hated fire. The idea of being consumed by it haunted her nightmares. She prepared to stop and jump.

For whatever reason the gasoline bomb did not ignite. As she picked up speed again, she saw in her rearview mirror the man dash across the street.

They must wait there, she thought, just at the edge of the estate, for anyone who dares to come out. No wonder the nearby witches' houses were shuttered during the day. They must be under virtual siege for their beliefs.

As she proceeded down Bridge Street towards The Lanes, the peaceful life of the town surrounded her. A blue delivery truck from Hiscott's Drugstore went past, followed by a small school bus full of kids. It turned onto Main Street, heading for the red brick school which took up one side of Church Row. In the distance bells rang. Early yet: 8:30.

Under the larger trees the melt fell like rain, and Amanda had to turn on her windshield wipers. The stink of the gasoline slowly faded. Amanda kept her speed high; she felt dreadfully exposed in the streets of this town. There was a strong temptation to turn around and go back to the estate. But she could not. She did not understand the whole of what she was to do in the town, but she intended to follow Constance's instructions. Deep within herself, she sensed that she understood very well what she was doing, even though her conscious mind refused to recognize the sense of it.

Her plan was to go to George's house, get her things, and get out as quickly as possible. If that was all that happened, then the visit could be seen as a further test of courage. Maybe the man with the gasoline bomb was really a follower of Constance's. Perhaps that's why the bomb didn't ignite.

'The essence of initiation,' Constance had said, 'is the confrontation with the Godfather. To lead people in the ways of the hidden world, we must know death.'

The shadow of the mower seemed to darken the whole town, Damon in the field of souls. Constance had said that Amanda did not love the Covenstead as much as her own life. But she was here, allowing herself to be acted upon by Constance, delivering herself to whatever new danger her teacher had devised.

The mower mowed, his scythe whistling.

She came to the corner of Maple Lane and turned left. Leaves cluttered George's lawn. No curtains blocked the windows of his house, which were black from the darkness within. His Volvo stood in the driveway. Amanda pulled in beside it, turned off her car, and set the brake. With the shrubs mostly bare the Volks could be seen all the way to the end of the street. It would not take somebody with a gasoline bomb long to discover where she had gone.

She ran a finger through the oily film on the roof of her car.

The house was silent. She went up to the front door, tried the handle. The door swung open.

The front hall was dark, the living room off to the left empty. She went in, intending to cross the dining room and see if George was in the back.

Halfway to the bedroom she heard Jane Pauley talking about French green beans. George was in the kitchen huddled over the little portable TV, absently stuffing Fritos in his mouth. An RC cola stood open on the counter beside him.

'George?'

'Oh, Good Lord, Amanda! You scared the hell out of me!' His smile was stiff on his face and he seemed very tired. 'I assumed you had gone to live on the estate.'

'I do think it would be more convenient for me to stay there. I'll be doing all my work there.'

His eyes had gone all alight. The suddenness of his movements suggested nothing so much as stifled rage.

'The estate is really very quiet,' she said carefully.

'No, Amanda, it's not quiet. Just last night they had a ritual. Surely you know about it. I was coming up Stone when I saw a naked girl riding a big black horse. Beautiful. She took off across the lawns before I could see her face.' He laughed, and the laughter changed to a wheezing cough.

How should she respond to him? He seemed to know nothing about her, yet he was supposed to be a witch, too. She decided to be careful. 'Constance mentioned that there had been an event last night in the town.'

'Everybody from here to Morris Plains is talking about it. And you remember Brother Pierce. That beauty. He's having a conniption. There was a run-in. Some of his people shot this girl's horse and then got themselves mauled by a flock of trained crows over in the Willowbrook ruins. Oh, boy, the whole town's going crazy! I was looking for some news on the Altoona station but they didn't mention it. It's a local sensation, though.'

It wasn't like him to chatter. George had not struck her as being any more of a talker than her father, whose speciality was the long silence.

The sooner she understood the nature of this latest test, the sooner she could go back to the safety of the estate. 'Never mind the town, George. I want to know how you're doing.'

'Me? Extremely well. My experiment could hardly be going better.'

'Brother Pierce leaving you alone?'

'Your friends've made sure of that. He's thoroughly preoccupied with witches now.' He smiled a little. 'You ought to see what they've put up in front of the Tabernacle. In a way it's funny.'

Why was George so uneasy? Why was she so scared? 'I

have a question for you,' she said quickly. 'Are you my Godfather?'

'It's been years since I thought about that. But yes, I am supposed to be responsible for your spiritual well-being.'

'So you are.' (Known in all the meadows you have mown.)

'The one and only.' He grinned.

This test was about death, all right. Her death. Constance had gone too far. 'I've got a lot of work to do up at the estate. I think I'll just get my canvases and stuff –'

'Brother Pierce and his people have erected a stake in front of the Tabernacle. A stake surrounded by piles of wood. It's a most dramatic display.'

She could still smell the gasoline fumes.

'Hardly surprising.'

'They shot that horse. Beautiful thing. I heard it. I was the first person there after the sheriff. He's a witch, too, people say.'

Amanda remembered his fundamentalist deputy. That department must be a tense sort of place. 'How horrible, to kill an animal that way.' She kept her voice as steady as she could. She had the sense that if she moved too suddenly, he was going to make a grab for her.

'I saw it. Fine animal. The poor thing didn't die right away. I hate to hear a horse scream. Sheriff had to put it out of its misery.'

She stared into his jack-o'-lantern smile. Until now she had consoled herself that Raven hadn't suffered. A vision swam up of his whole end, as it had really happened:

For a few seconds he lay in silence, confused, not understanding what had happened to him. When he realized that the ground was under his side and he was no longer running, he tried to get up. That was when the pain hit, the thrumming, pounding pain that flared from his nose to his neck. When he screamed, laughter replied and a vicious kick to the muzzle. He shrieked through bloody, shattered nose bones. He could only see out of one eye. Even so, when he could quiet himself he had looked for her.

Then he had seen the North Star. And he had begun galloping into great, snowy mountains. The sheriff's shot of mercy had sped him on.

'Amanda, I'm sorry. I didn't mean to upset you.' He made a clumsy movement towards her.

'I'm not upset. It's just that I don't like cruelty to animals.'

'Amanda –'

'George, I have to go now.'

He laughed sharply, then suddenly stopped. 'I'm nervous. Sometimes I think Maywell might be hell.'

'Maybe you have a point.' She wanted to get out of here.

'Give me your hand, darling.'

'No, George.'

'You're my goddaughter! I want us to be friends.'

She had to play for time. 'What's troubling you, George?' As she spoke she stepped away from him.

'Troubling? Nothing at all. I'm fine.'

'You look terrible.' She took another step back. The point of the test was to go into the cave of Godfather Death and bring back something precious. She was here, and the treasure was the tools of her art.

'I've been working late. And I don't eat well on my own.' He waved his bottle of cola. 'Amanda, I'm awfully glad to see you.'

How could someone so pitiful be so frightening? 'Take it easy, George.'

'I'm not going to hurt you.'

'Stay right there, George. Don't come any closer, please.'

'Amanda, you don't understand. I'm offering you a place in immortality.' What was this? It didn't sound like part of the script. 'Immortality! You'll know the secret of the ages!'

'George, calm down.'

He waved his cola. Saliva flew from his mouth. 'They might hate me and they might laugh at me and they might destroy my work, but they will never kill my ideas! No, my ideas will go on and on down the halls of time and in the end they will triumph.' He smiled as a marionette smiles. She saw his truth in that smile. He had failed, totally and completely, and his failure had driven him crazy.

Her only thought now was to get away, but he had placed himself between her and the front door. She was forced to try and talk her way out. 'George, get hold of yourself. If something's wrong, you and I can sit down and discuss it like two civilized people. I can help you, George.'

'You certainly can! You're young and strong and just the right size!'

What did he mean?

When he lunged at her, she managed to make a dash for the door.

He moved with tailored grace. His long arms came around her neck. Such was the force of his manoeuvre that the cola bottle slammed into a thousand pieces against the far wall.

Rape must be on his mind. Just the right size, she thought bitterly. Indeed. She might put up more of a fight than he expected.

He moved so suddenly, though, that he dragged her right off her feet. 'We're going to the basement now. Oh, you idiot, don't struggle so! Everything's going to be just fine. You don't have a thing to worry about.'

'You bastard! You try to rape me and I'll kick your balls off.' She would, too.

'Rape? I'd never do that. I've got too much respect for women.'

'Look, George, you're – stop pulling at me! Where are you trying to take me?'

'Basement, dear. My equipment's down there.'

She writhed, remembering the room full of cat pictures. The lair of Hades.

God, this *was* contrived. He was Hades, and he had

surprised her despite her caution, just as in the old myth. He was dragging her down into the netherworld.

'Come on, quit that kicking. You're not going to get away from me.'

'Let me go, George, I'm warning you!' She couldn't quite get into position to hurt him. If he got her down there, she had failed the test.

'It's a gift I'm giving you. You'll know what it is to die and come back to life. Think of it, you'll *know*. You'll be famous, Amanda.'

It took a few seconds for her to understand what he was planning. When she did, panic overwhelmed her and she screamed. He was about to kill her in his machine! Kill her! This was no game. Constance had literally sent her to her death.

'It's not tested! You might murder me!'

'It works perfectly. It's safe.'

'Then why is it in the basement and not in your lab? George, please listen to me. You've got to get yourself together.'

She was babbling and she knew it. Her body, her bones, her young blood, were panic-stricken. She exploded with effort. Twisting, contorting herself, she managed to dig her nails into his cheek. As he reared back she kicked behind her, jamming her heel again and again into his shin, tearing and pulling and twisting.

And suddenly falling free.

She stumbled to her feet and rushed to the kitchen door. He was not three feet away, snarling, a flap of bloody skin dangling from his nose, plunging towards her.

Then she was through the door, running as fast as she could around the back of his Volvo, slipping in the wet grass, falling down.

He leaped on her so hard her breath whistled out of her mouth. Even so she wriggled free of him and managed to stagger to her car. She got in, fumbling frantically with her

262

key. Just as she jammed it into the starter his arm came snaking in the window and his fingers twined her hair. 'Immortality, you little beauty! You're happy about it! Happy!'

It hurt so much when he yanked her hair that she saw flashes. But she started the car. With her last bit of strength she engaged reverse and let out the clutch.

Something pricked her shoulder. When she looked he was withdrawing a syringe. She bellowed, grabbed at her arm. 'It's just scopolamine, Amanda,' he said, his voice full of apology. 'It won't hurt you.'

She stared in horror at the shoulder. It was as if a warm tropic wave washed over her. In the distance she heard the car ticking over. Quick! You're too slow!

She pressed the gas pedal. From far, far away there came kindly laughter. 'I've got the key, dear. I took it out. You can't drive the car, the engine isn't even running.'

What happened to the engine?

'Let's go back in the house now.'

'No-o-o . . . no thank you . . .' Was that her voice? So empty, so distant.

'Come on. Right now.'

He opened the door. Then his hand was under her elbow.

'Let's go, Amanda. We have a lot of work to do.'

She rose up out of the car even though she didn't want to. There just didn't seem to be any way to resist. As he took her into the house she cast a sorrowful look back. Then he closed the door and began nudging her down the long hall towards the mudroom.

'Tom?'

'What's that?'

He was in the games room, lying like a long black python along the back of the couch, his kinked tail switching, his eyes gleaming.

'Tom, help me! Tom!'

George looked around. 'There's nobody here but us, dear.' For some reason he could not see the cat.

Tom kneaded the couch and yawned.

'Please, Tom, please!'

'Be careful, honey,' George said, 'you have to climb down a ladder.'

'Oh, a ladder.' Please . . .

'That's it. All the way down, now. Right. You stand there. Stand still.'

She couldn't move if she wanted to. His voice was the only command she could respond to.

'Oops, you were swaying. Did you realize that? I had to give you quite a dose of scope, honey. You'll be out like a light within the minute. Come on, now, hurry along.'

The Kitten Kate Room again. She didn't like the Kitten Kate Room. On the ceiling was a picture of a galaxy spiralling through eternity. Superimposed on it was a lean black cat. Black and dangerous and lovely. 'Tom, help me!'

'Cross your wrists in front of you, please. Sorry I don't have any straps, I know they'd be more comfortable. But I can't risk you moving in your sleep and wrecking the coils. Also, when you wake up you're going to be a tad upset, I think, so it's better this way. Isn't it better, dear?'

Dimly, distantly, she felt her wrists and ankles being bound, felt rope swinging round and round her body, felt the world swinging away.

She dreamed long, vague dreams of the beautiful lady of the mountain, and the Holly King and Raven, and all that new world.

And Tom . . . yawning while George killed her.

The first thing she saw when she was conscious again was the terrible face of the panther in the ceiling.

'Hello, Amanda. How do you feel?'

'I've got a headache.' She tried to move, realized she was still tied. Her confusion was complete. She was bound down tight, surrounded by shining brown ceramic devices of some kind. She tried again to move, but the ropes held fast.

'I was killed! You killed me, didn't you?'

He put his hand on her face. 'We're going to begin the experiment now, dear. I had to let the drug wear off first. You've been asleep all day.'

The blackest despair covered the little sprig of hope that had started to grow in her. 'No! *No!*'

'Not so loud, dear. These houses are close together.'

'Help! *Help me!*'

'Hush, now!'

She heard a buzz, felt the table sway. A terrible tickling swarmed in her chest, centred on her heart.

'See you in a few minutes. Toodle-oo!'

The dark took her.

CHAPTER 18

Red Moon

moom moom
hear my call
moom moom
speak to me

– Anselm Hollo,
'Troll Chanting'

No wind passed her and she impacted nothing, but she knew she was falling. She heaved and twisted. It was excruciating to anticipate a splattering end that never came.

She screamed, but there was no sound. She called out, 'Don't kill me! George, please, please.' Her voice was dead.

So this is what it was like. This – this billowing emptiness. Her body was not a body anymore. It seemed more smoke than flesh, thick and cold. But aware, and conscious and very scared. George had succeeded in killing her. Of course he'd never bring her back. If he could, he would still have a lab and official approval. She had come into the cave of Godfather Death and got herself killed. The final test was over, and she would never inherit the Covenstead.

She began to cringe in her falling, waiting for the shattering crunch, her ribs jamming full force into her shoulders. If terror was a creature, she was dropping down its throat.

But she had no ribs, and there would be no impact. She was falling into nowhere, and she herself was becoming nothing.

There mumbled in her mind the ragged thought: I'm dissolving.

She didn't think she could bear it, not falling and falling and never hitting, in absolute silence and absolute dark.

'Please, I can't die. I've got to get back.'

A terrible, thin face flickered nearby, as if in response to her cry. She batted at it, a starved husk of a face with white worms for eyes. But it had delicate eyebrows and a familiar pale shape. Amanda rejected it with all the force of her soul.

'Daughter,' it said, 'welcome to hell.'

'Mother! My God, what happened to you?'

The face shifted and congealed, wrinkling and collapsing on itself. 'I lived,' it gargled, 'I lived wrong . . .' And then was gone.

'No, Mamma, no.' How horrible, how hideous, what a tragedy. She said she had lived wrong – but how wrong? What had she done?

'Mamma!'

The face reappeared, dissolving, just inches before Amanda's eyes. The skin was sloughing off the bones, and the hair was growing long and ragged. Decay that must have taken a year in Mother's coffin was being re-created in seconds. Amanda screamed and hit, and her blows went right through the apparition.

'Mamma, why?'

'I need this. I chose it. I must atone for my life.'

'*What?*'

'From the time you were six I hated you.'

'You didn't hate me, Mamma! You –' But it was true, wasn't it? Remember the hot sorrowing nights when she would not come, remember how she scorned your art, remember how she sat, as still and rigid as a wooden mother, that time Dad beat you up? 'Mamma, I forgive! I forgive you!' Worms, get out of her eyes! Skin, come back! Hair, stop growing!

'We judge ourselves when we die, honey, and we are never wrong.'

'I forgive you.'

'I have to forgive myself, and that's going to take some time.'

'You don't deserve to suffer like this!'

'I told Mother Star of the Sea to discourage your interest in art.'

'Mamma, I know that. And she ignored you.'

'You got into the Pratt Institute. And I threw out the letter of acceptance.'

'Since then I've taught at Pratt two semesters. I'm beyond caring about Pratt.'

'I wanted to destroy you. I wanted to hurt you.' The face glowed as it spoke, as if with fire from inside.

'Mamma, I forgive.'

'I was jealous! You were beautiful and talented and I was – me.' Something was moving behind her, something complicated.

'I forgive you!'

'I can't forgive myself.'

Amanda saw it more clearly now, a huge black hulk of a thing with piercing green eyes.

When it opened its mouth, a great mewing scream filled the still air. Mamma recoiled, her rotted flesh fluttering from her brown bones, as the cat came closer. He was tremendous, but his face was familiar: there was that shredded ear.

Amanda was stunned to see him. Tom must be death or the devil or something. But he had been so cute, lapping milk and cuddling in her bed.

There came a crackling sound as he took a chunk out of Mamma's skull. Amanda could see the brain within, as crunchy as a sponge that has been dipped in bleach and let dry. When Tom's long pink tongue scooped it out, Mamma made a sort of babbling sound. Then her eyes became blank.

While Amanda shrieked, her stomach twisting, her throat burning, her skin tickling with dread, Tom ate. At last there remained not even a tuft of Mother's rough hair.

Then Amanda saw that Tom was staring at her.

There was a new sensation involved in facing those eyes. She could actually *feel* his stare driving like wild snow into her soul, seeking every hidden crack and cranny of her being.

Was this the Last Judgement? Did a cat – no, it couldn't be Tom, not sitting in judgement over her.

'Please –'

The eyes grew bright and fierce.

'No. No! Keep away from me!'

The mouth opened.

Down Tom's gullet Amanda saw fires dancing, and a vast legion of tragedies, each as immense and personal as her own.

Hell was inside him.

'Who are you? Why are you after me?'

There was no answer but the oily gush of his breath and the burnt-hair stink of the cooking dead.

He was getting larger and larger, so large that she could walk into his gaping jaws if she wished. But she didn't wish! 'I'm not guilty of anything! I got murdered and I'm not going in there! I've got to get back because my life isn't over and they need me!'

At once the jaws snapped shut.

Then she landed, as lightly as a feather, upon a grey and silent field. Her body felt substantial, solid. Or rather, almost solid. When she looked down she could see herself, but she had the feeling that she could have walked through a wall. She peered around her at the storm-turned line of the horizon. This was empty country. Tom curled about her legs. He looked up at her out of his little cat's eyes and seemed ready to wink.

After what she had seen, she was afraid of those eyes. Maybe they would become big and menacing once again, and those jaws would open –

He carried everlasting tragedy in his belly.

And yet he was the only other thing here, so in a way she

was glad of his presence. Without looking at him she bent down and stroked him. His fur was full of electricity. 'I wish you could talk. I wish you could tell me what's going on.'

He didn't speak, but a gentle force turned her head. She was stunned at what she saw: the quietest, most perfect landscape of trees and green hills, blue sky flecked with white clouds, and in the shadows of the sky something wonderful that had no definite shape. It was, rather, the presence of a condition – an emotional colour – as if goodness filled that air. Amanda's first love, a boy who had died in a fire, came walking towards her. 'I remember you,' he said, and there was something eternal in his voice. 'I've been waiting for you.' He opened his arms, and what flowed from him was as a fine old song.

Other voices soon joined the song, then overwhelmed it. They were soft and yet solid, chanting: 'Moom moom hear our call. Moom moom hear our call . . .' The chant went on and on, splitting and filling the soft air of summer that caressed her.

She recognized those voices – it was Ivy and Robin and Constance and the others. 'I can hear you!'

Her heart almost broke: before her lay heaven, behind her life. The name the witches were calling evoked in Amanda powerful, hitherto hidden feelings. Moom! So familiar. How Moom had loved her life.

'I've got to go back. The witches need me.'

Her old friend laughed very gently. 'Tom guards the line between here and life, Amanda. You can't make it past him. And nobody who goes down his throat ever comes out again.'

The chant went on.

'Hey! I hear you!' It tore her soul. Despite what her dead friend had said, she turned back from heaven.

The air around her shivered and began to fade. And she knew it was doing that because she had just made a firm and unshakeable decision: she was going back to life, somehow, if she could.

A cold wind sprang up. Ugly grey clouds swarmed across the sky. Her first love became a black, dancing skeleton in a bombed landscape, and replacing the song of heaven there arose a great multitude of sorrowful cries. They echoed out of the clouds like high thunder, and Amanda saw that the grey hid monstrous flying things.

Terror began to grow in her. The things in the clouds had wings and black scales and long red nails. She knew that they were demons.

Above their banshee cries there remained the chant: 'Moom moom moom moom,' on and on and on.

She wanted to somehow open the sky, to part those dreary grey clouds, to get through to the chanters.

Tom had returned, sullen and slinking, mewing loudly. 'Tom, they're calling me back, I can hear them! Please, Tom, tell me how to get to them! They need me! Oh, God, I can feel how bad they need me!'

She ran, she jumped, she clawed the air. When she scrambled up the gnarled remnant of a tree, she could hear the sucking eagerness of the demons in the clouds.

How absurd, she thought, to have chosen this. Nobody ever came back from the dead, not with all of hell barring the way. The dark once entered . . .

Guardian: a great maroon scorpion with the blue-eyed face of a little girl.

Guardian: a white bird that warbled lies.

Guardian: something that once had been a nun. Mother Star of the Sea.

Amanda hadn't thought of her since sixth grade.

Tom spoke, a fierce, rasping voice in her head. 'They are death's soldiers, the demons.'

'Then death is evil.'

'Death is death, neither good nor bad. It's just there.'

She ran. It was brutal, simple instinct, the reaction of the monkey to the slinking panther. The ground beneath her was spongy and had the slickness of skin. Maybe it *was* skin.

This hideous place could easily be on the back of some inconceivable monster. She slipped and slid in the soft, glittering folds of it, and smelled the sweet stink of it.

The cat ran along beside her for a while. Then she saw it prancing in front.

Then the clouds spat a drop of hot, sticky rain.

The drop tickled her face. She raised her shadows of hands and touched the ooze. It was full of hair-fine worms. The tickle on her face changed to an itch, then at once to a dull ache. She reached up again and pulled away a great gout of skin. It was seething with the threadlike creatures. She threw it down in disgust and wiped her hands on the rubbery ground.

The sensation in her face was awful, an ache and a salty cut and the itching of a scab. She raised her eyes to the sky, which was tossing and bulging down at her, as if great fingers punched behind the clouds. 'Let me go home! I don't belong here and you're not going to keep me!' She would have thrown something but she had nothing to throw.

Somebody whispered in her ear, and she knew it was a demon: 'You've got a lot to learn, baby.'

'Don't you dare call me that! I'm Amanda Walker and I'm not your baby.'

The clouds twisted and stormed, became a great, dark skull filled with lightning, and began to draw closer to her. The grinning jaws bellowed thunder so loud she held her ears and screamed, but her own voice was lost.

And she had an odd thought: the demons in those clouds don't hate me. They're just doing their job.

'Your body can't receive you back. Dead is dead. The ones who do return end up as ghosts, useless victims of the winds.'

This was a new voice, not big like the storm. Rather it was soft and small and full of peace. Amanda had heard something like it before, at the fairy stone. If a voice could be called sacred – she went to her knees. 'I thought death

272

was something like going down a long, hollow tube and then meeting my grandfather or somebody and being welcomed, and –'

'Each person creates his own death.'

Amanda was increasingly sure she knew that voice. And if she was right – then maybe things were going to get better. 'Who are you?'

For just an instant Amanda glimpsed a bright, tiny woman, quite perfect, with rowan in her hair.

'*Leannan*, it *is* you. I was hoping it was. Listen, please help me get out of here. I've got to find a way to go back without ending up in hell.'

The *Leannan* regarded her. 'You've set yourself a difficult problem.'

'But I don't deserve hell. I'm not guilty of anything.'

'If you want my help, then come with me.' Tom was at her side, looking large indeed next to the Fairy Queen. 'Don't worry about your demons. They won't stop you going deeper into death.'

'Oh, no, that's not what I want. I'm going to get out of this. I've got to go back to the Covenstead!' She turned – and found herself facing a narrow man with a sneer on his face and rape in his eyes. He grabbed her throat with a wet hand. Suddenly both he and she were as solid as living bodies. She could smell his rancid skin, see his oily tongue, hear his breath bubbling in his nostrils. 'Hey, baby,' he said, 'let's dance.'

'Oh, God! Oh, God, help me!'

He brought out a long, serrated knife. 'This is God.' When he started squeezing her throat, she suffered very real agony. 'This is just the beginning, you stinking bitch. I'm gonna 'cut your heart out and eat it right in front of your eyes!'

The blade caressed sensitive skin, and she saw a long spike of flecked drool start in the corner of his mouth. '*Leannan*, please, you said you'd help me!'

273

'Then you must follow me.'

'I'm sorry. I will.'

At once the rapist began to change. His form wavered and he rolled his eyes. His knife fell into dust, his whole body shivered, twisting back on itself.

Then Tom was there, swishing his tail.

'It was you! All the time, it was you! You're evil, you're a monster. A *monster*!'

'He obeys the law, Amanda. And so must you.' A hand so small it felt like a little, warm mouse came into her own. 'Come with me. I want to show you your past, so you can learn what's drawn you so against your better judgement to your witches. Perhaps then you'll see that you should go to what you think of as heaven, which I call the Land of Summer. You've long since earned your peace.'

'I want to go back. I've *got* to.'

The *Leannan* sighed. 'You're very strong,' she said ruefully. But the small hand squeezed Amanda's fingers.

Amanda walked along with the *Leannan*. She wasn't at all sure she wanted to, but every other choice seemed worse. She had expended her last bit of resistance facing Tom the rapist.

She suspected that he was only the first in a long line of guardians of the gates of life. The scorpion, for example, was worse. And the little bird far worse. And then there was Mother Star of the Sea. Dear God, she was the very personification of guilt. In school she had managed to make Amanda feel hell-bound for having an untied shoe.

'Will you please hurry up, Amanda? I'm having trouble with my damn fire.'

That was Constance Collier – and this place – they weren't on the field of skin anymore, they were – oh, God, this was all familiar. 'Oh, *Leannan*, thank you, thank you!' All the time she had been bringing Amanda back to the Covenstead. Deeper into death, indeed.

'The veil between life and death is thin here. But make

no mistake. I have not brought you closer to the resurrection you seek. Let Constance show you your first life. Perhaps then you'll see that you have the right to the summer you have earned.'

The meadow was clear and bright, and Constance was sharply outlined by the sun. Things were still very strange: there were people around her, for example, but they were mere shadows, seated in a vague circle. Connie was stirring a great, iron cauldron, and that was very clear, too.

She smiled at Amanda. 'You're slow as molasses, girl!' Her voice renewed Amanda's determination. Despite what the *Leannan* said, she could hear how very desperately Connie wanted her to return. The old woman waved her long staff for emphasis. 'By the very Goddess we've got to get you back.'

Amanda ran up to the edge of the circle. 'Constance, am I really dead? This is crazy – if I'm dead how can you be here?'

'Go round the circle once widdershins and you can come in. Then I'll tell you.' Amanda began to walk. 'Not that way. That's sunward. Widdershins is the other direction.'

Inside the circle even the air was different. It had less of the sparkle of spirit air, and smelled of fields and farm. She could just see, if she looked very, very closely, the faces of the people huddled around its edges. She recognized Ivy, and her heart panged to see Robin. But they certainly did not see her. 'Where is this place?'

'We can meet here for a time. The witches' circle lies between the worlds.'

'I'm on the estate?'

'The circle is in both places.'

'What places? Have you given me some kind of a drug?'

'Oh, little baby, the drug is death! You are really and truly dead. And we don't even know if your lunatic of an uncle will get himself back together enough to return you to life. He doesn't *want* to, that's for sure.'

'But you sent me to him! If you knew this would happen –'

'To be the witches' guide in life, you must learn the secrets of death. And to do that you've got to die. Unless there's a chance you won't come back, you aren't really dead.'

'The *Leannan* said that you were going to show me why I don't need to return. But you seem to want me back so much.'

'I'm going to show you your first life. How you take what you see is your business. Now I'm going to swirl the cauldron and you lean over and look into it. Be mindful of what appears, young woman!'

The cauldron gurgled and gargled almost like a living throat; it boiled and bubbled. Soon Amanda began to see things rolling about in the murky waters. Shadows, faces . . . things that made her look more closely.

'That's right, that's good!' Constance swirled harder. 'The tennis shoes you wore when you were ten, some snapshots of you then. Baby treasures, too, Holly your dolly and first friend. And Old Moll with her nose askew, and calico Kitten Stew – remember them?'

'I remember.'

'Look, then. Look at life in the classroom.'

Something was wrong with this picture. Her childhood had not been a time of such terror. Or had it?

The waters turned and turned. She remembered sixth grade. There was Daisy O'Neill and Jenny Parks sitting by the window, and Bonnie Haver in the back, plump Stacey behind her.

Two swishing rows of girls came down the chapel aisle behind Mother Star of the Sea. They chanted to the *Stabat Mater* tune:

> 'Touch your lips to a weenie on Friday,
> And you are doomed.
> Be a whiner or a masturbator,
> And you are doomed.

276

Drown a baby or steal Mother's eraser,
And you are doomed.'

'Now, wait a minute,' Amanda said. 'Eating meat on Friday isn't a sin anymore.'

Bonnie Haver: 'But you did it when it was, so you are doomed.'

'I'm not even a Catholic! Mother Star of the Sea might have secretly baptized me that afternoon I fell asleep at my desk, but –'

'You are doomed.'

Just at the edge of the circle Amanda saw the blade-faced man again. He was wearing a long slack coat. In his hand was a smoking soldering iron. He held it up. 'How about some scars, girl?'

Constance brandished her staff and shouted: 'Away, Tom! Come as her friend or don't come at all.'

'He's a demon, Connie, and I think the *Leannan* might be one, too!'

'No, Amanda, they're not demons, not those two. They're gods. Or angels, your Mother Star of the Sea would call them. In any case, they're a couple of whores. All gods are. They'll be whatever you want them to be and do what you want them to do. If you declare yourself guilty, they'll take you to hell and give you to your demons. Or they'll sing with you in heaven. It's up to you.'

Despite herself, Amanda found that she was looking deep into her own soul, where the moss of forgetfulness grew. And under the moss she saw: 'I *did* tease that nun. And I did it on purpose, because I wanted to make her suffer. Oh, God, I did it for the sake of hate.'

The man with the soldering iron stepped right through into the centre of the circle. With a shout Connie pitched back and fell among the shadows of her witches. Amanda looked at the blue, smoking tip of the iron.

'Now, my dear, open your legs.'

She would not. She was guilty, but not *that* guilty. 'I was just a little girl. It was the innocent anger of a child.'

The man twisted and hissed at her, then in a yowling instant was Tom again, curling about her feet, his tail low and sullen behind him.

Connie came shambling back, brushing corn silk from her cloak. This field had just been harvested.

'The particular deity you call Tom is your familiar, dear. You must learn to control him. Until you do, be careful. Remember that he follows your wishes. If you stay on this guilt trip, watch it.'

Amanda looked at the cat. He winked one green eye.

'No, dear, ignore him. Look into the cauldron again. See what you've suffered on behalf of the witches. You needn't feel guilty if you don't wish to make such a sacrifice again.'

'I thought you wanted me back, Connie.'

'Not out of guilt. Out of love. Now, look. Look deep!'

There was somebody in the cauldron, a tall and furious somebody from a far place and a farther time.

'You're beginning to see who you were. You've been a witch for a long, long time.'

'That other one down there – I remember him, too. He burned me!'

'He always does. But don't be attracted by his bishop's robe. Go back farther, to when he wore simpler things.'

Amanda looked deeper into the cauldron. Just then it shook as if someone had kicked at it. She seemed to slip and slide away from the edge. The waters, which had been clearing, grew murky again.

'What's going on?' Constance rasped. 'Who's messing up the chant?'

'I'm sorry.'

'What's the matter with you, Ivy? Can't you tell she's here? Can't you see her?'

'Connie, I'm trying my best!'

'This is the most important circle we've ever cast! Don't you dare break it. Now, chant, girl, *chant*!'

'I said I'm trying.'

When the chant became smooth, the cauldron cleared again. But it lasted only a moment. Soon the waters were more turbid than before.

'Ivy, you are breaking the chant.'

'I'm sitting in a damned ant bed, Connie. They're swarming all over me.'

'*Chant!*'

The waters came clear. Amanda peered in. As before, her childhood floated at the surface. Below came the various colours of other lives, whole finished worlds swimming in dim old seas.

Back Amanda went through the babble of time, to a tiny brown village huddled beneath something vast and tumbled white, a mountain upon a mountain of pure ice, a glacier.

'This was the first life, Amanda. You had just fallen from the eyelashes of the Goddess. You were new then.'

Too late Amanda realized that she had leaned beyond the limit of balance. She fell into the boiling cauldron.

There was a shock of intense pain, then she was suddenly sitting in a reeking tent. It smelled of rancid grease and human filth, sour breath and sweat. She gasped, shocked that she had suddenly reacquired weight and substance. Her mind bumbled about in an unknown tongue. Her body was smaller but heavier, her breasts enormous pendula, sweaty and jiggling with milk. She was swinging them back and forth over a fire.

Upon her head was a crescent of horn, around her neck a necklace cunning-twined of last summer's vine, the one upon which the Red Goddess Flowers grew.

She was Moom, Daughter of the Red Goddess. Moom, the happy, the rich, the good! Round her thighs were fastened leather garters, one on each, made of the softest doeskin, well chewed. They were marked with the waxing and waning phases of the Red Goddess and signified the rule of the wearer, who could dance in them, work in them, give love in them, and never need for an instant to remove them.

Wearing them, she *was* the Goddess. Without, she was only Moom. She kept the knots tight, never mind that it made her feet tingle. Other women envied the garters and liked to lie upon her lap and gaze for hours at them. Chief among these was Leem, who would have been the great queen ahead of Moom had she not stolen a cave bear cub to keep her warm at night. Its mother came in a rage and bit off her hand. No maimed woman could keep hold of garters.

The ritual of the raising of milk went on. As she swayed and wove herself about above the flames, Moom heard the leather of the tent slap against the frame. The whole tent shuddered. A frigid gust leaked in, making the men and the children in the outer circle press against the women who surrounded the fire. Moom felt the milk oozing out of her bones, sensed it running along the milk channels in her flesh, knew it was filling her breasts.

They soon became huge and tight, brown-gleaming in the firelight, their nipples rigid and dripping.

The women sat back on their haunches now. All were engorged. They began to clap. Three times sharp, three times soft, three times fast, three times slow. They hummed the music of the bees, to bring summer luck to the family. First their daughters and their sons came to them and took each according to his age, the youngest as much as they willed, the older less, and so on. Through this the men waited.

Then each man brought to the fire something of their mysteries, a great black haunch of bison, a liver from an ibex, a mammoth's stomach still stuffed with flowers and roots. All of these things they set in the immense earthenware cauldron, the family's greatest treasure. They dropped brands in it until it hissed and smoked and filled the tent with wonderful smells.

Moom chewed the blue flesh of the stomach while her husbands took breast upon her, and then ate the flow of her monthly blood.

Thus Moom's family shared the food of men and women, in the lost winter of a long time ago, not too far from what would one day be called Alesia, then later Eleusis, the central place of the mysteries of antiquity.

It was there, in the hard spring of her fifteenth year, that Moom met the most terrible of ends.

The water had flooded their lands that Maymoon, running down from the White King's icy haunches until the men said, 'The White King's piss is going to drown the world.'

Moom said, 'We belong to our place.'

The men said, 'We cannot live in the White King's piss. We've got to get out of here.'

As a portent a great piece of the White King, so large that it reached far past the top of the sky, toppled into the meadow with a roar that loosened teeth and sent the leather tent flying about in tatters.

So they left, all but handless Leem, whom they abandoned to the winds. They went down the long stone ridges, into the forests where the little animals lived. Life in the forest was hard, for a hunter could spend all day seeking a beast not large enough to fill a single mouth. Moom, though, had been granted the secrets of mushrooms and berries, so they did not starve.

Beyond the forest there were plains so full of bison that the very air smelled of them. Moom wondered if they were not a single beast with many bodies, so closely did they cling to one another.

In the centre of these plains, where there flowed water, men had made many leather tents, and even some of grass and mud, more tents than Moom had ever imagined in one place.

'I am Alis,' said the man of the place, when Moom brought her family down among the dwellings. 'We are Alesians.'

'We are Moom.' She slapped her belly. 'I am *the* Moom! The powerful! Full of milk and blood and babies!'

Alis laughed. He was tall and greybeard. 'Eighteen times I have brought back the sun! Oh! I am *the* Alis! The most powerful!'

She was confused and amazed. Challenged by a man, who could not even let the Red Goddess Moon into his baby closet? How could it be that he was so foolish? She did not know that Leem had come here ahead of them, travelling fast because she was alone, and contrived this treachery. 'You might dry up the Goddess! I wouldn't risk that if I were you!'

The lands of the Alis, she noticed, were yellow and dusty despite their river.

He threw her down and took her garters and put them on. Then he strapped a leather flap to his loins to cover his bull. He danced the women's mystery dance, slapping his belly and shrieking the birth cries. Then the Alesians made cages of strong saplings and put Moom and her women inside.

When hot stones were piled high around it, Moom ran her cage, and shouted and shrieked in agony unspeakable. All one day as the sun crossed the sky of Alesia she suffered. And she saw Leem, jeering among the men, waving her stub of an arm. The bars at the end were covered with Moom's roasting blood, and she was purple. She was cracked. She smelled like the last of the cauldron. Her hair was nubble that crumbled off in her hands.

She called at last: 'I am Moom!' And died.

The Alesians ate Moom and her women. They remained beside the river a full season after that, but the men made no milk and birthed no young. In time other women came and took Moom's garters off Alis's legs, and the Alesians went away with them.

Amanda lay weeping, exhausted, in the shimmering, dying circle. The figures around her were exhausted, too, dwindled from ghosts to embers. Somewhere a bell was ringing.

'Amanda! By the four winds rise! Amanda!'

She couldn't. She was too tired. Black fingers came from the sky, sweeping down around her.

'Amanda, you must wake up. The demons are taking you.'

The voice was dulled by the thick, black clouds.

'You're innocent, Amanda. You've sacrificed enough!'

She was becoming heavy and dreamy. She remembered summertime and cherry Kool-Aid and Mamma's delicious gingerbread, and her own little backyard playhouse.

'I used to pretend it was made of candy . . .'

'Amanda, you fool! You're letting them deceive you! They can't take you to Summer. They want to destroy you!'

'The cottage in the forest . . . gingerbread . . .'

'They're monsters. They want to eat your soul.'

How silly Connie sounded. 'Oh, Connie, it's just Tom and another one of his tricks.'

'Tom's a friend! But these things – oh, God.'

The smoke smelled like honeysuckle. Amanda remembered the backyard, the sprinkler ticking, Mamma humming an old tune.

'Chant, witches! Chant with all your hearts and souls! Can't you see what's happening to her? She's *not guilty* and they're going to take her to hell anyway, because she dares to try and return to life. Please by the Goddess chant!'

The smoke had become a crowd of dark shapes. One of them shifted and focused, and grew into the solid form of a very pretty girl of about twelve, wearing a blue dress. One hand was hidden behind her, and in the other she held a leash. There was a bear on the leash, a bigger, more friendly bear than Amanda had ever seen before. It leaned down when it saw her, and regarded her with eyes so intelligent that their stare was a kind of song.

The bear said: 'I am a very special bear, my dear, for I

283

can give you visions. And they're better than that cauldron nonsense.' With that it followed its mistress off into the dark beyond the circle. From Constance's throat there came a last, fading cry: 'Don't forget, Amanda, you are not guilty . . .'

Amanda followed the girl, and her wonderful bear.

CHAPTER 19

Simon Pierce stood surveying what he could see of the Collier estate from across a tumbledown fence. He was looking into a blackberry patch, beyond it cornfields. It was lovely land, and tended with love, too. Most of the nearby fields were already harvested. The nearest thing worth burning was a stand of uncut corn three hundred yards away.

For hundreds of years the people of Maywell had kept away from this place. There wasn't even an occasional hiker. Nobody came onto the estate without an invitation from Constance Collier. Most would say that it was out of respect for her privacy, but Brother Pierce had heard darker rumours. There had been spells and curses that worked. Early Jones, back in the 1820s, had tried to cut wood in Collier land. His wife gave birth to horribly deformed twins. He himself died of a strange, progressive weakness of the limbs. More recently the Wilson brothers had hunted Stone Mountain. They had reported glimpsing 'little men' who scared the animals away. Two years ago they had been found back in the Endless Mountains, far from the estate, lying dead around their campfire. They had both had heart attacks while they slept. Natural causes, or Constance Collier?

Simon did not want to cross into that woman's land. But he had to. He had driven his congregation to a high pitch of excitement. They had to do something, and he had to lead them. Burn the cornfields. It was simple and practical, and he thought they could get away with it. The ethics of doing it bothered him a good deal, though, especially now that he saw with his own eyes how honourably tended was this land. It was painful to burn good land. He had been brought up to think of the land as the great source of prosperity. Still, this land was good because it was witched. Beneath its fertility was a foulness.

Simon motioned to the man behind him and started down the road. At first he moved along beside it, but the absence of opposition emboldened him to step onto the strip of grass between the ruts.

'Careful, Brother Simon. Better stay off the road.'

'We're here to do the work of the Lord. We have no call to skulk and hide, Brother Benson.'

'This is private property. If we're seen here the sheriff'll have a reason to fire me.'

'Wherefore, if God so clothe the grass of the field, which today is, and tomorrow is cast into the oven, shall he not much more clothe you, O ye of little faith?' Simon felt sad for the poor, mistaken pagans, and found the deputy sheriff's whining a disappointment. 'You put yourself in the hands of God, Brother Benson. If the Lord wants you fired, you'll be fired. You walk proud now, for you are on a mission of mercy, to teach these ignorant ones the power of the Lord.'

His mind turned and turned with the complexity of the situation. Simon liked things clear, but they were far from that. He needed the witches as a galvanizing issue; he also felt terribly sorry for them. He was not a man to hurt others.

He felt down deep in his pocket for the shrunken, brown talisman of his own wrongdoing. It was nestled there, reminding him for life of his terrible sin. Its presence gave him satisfaction: often he prayed with it, 'Lord, take me soon. I want to burn for what I did to her. Please, Lord, send me down to the deepest fire.' While awaiting his descent into his own richly deserved hell, Simon Pierce saved the souls of others.

He grasped the hard nubbin that was the hand. Once it had been white. Once soft and sweet to kiss. The hand had been connected to the precious body of one of the Lord's finest creations, an innocent little girl. Before he found the Lord, Simon had been so confused, so disturbed and angry. His mother hadn't been a good mother. After his father had disappeared on a Bible-selling trip that never ended, she had whored, bringing man after man home, and he would hear her bed banging against the wall between the two rooms, and once one of the men came to him naked, and she hit him in the side of the head with a steak mallet and pushed him out on the fire escape.

She would drink and take diet pills and whip Simon, cursing him while she did it, then subside into long states of suppressed fury.

Sometimes even now he dreamed that he had been brought up in an orphanage. He had to work to remember his real childhood. In his teens he'd been impoverished, living in a slum with his wasted old ruin of a mother, and she went crazy one night and tried to set them both on fire. At the age of fourteen he lost her. It was bitter because he was so lonely without her, and yet she had been so bad.

As he grew older, moved from one foster home to another, he found that his exploding adolescent sexuality was all twisted. He could not love women, not even those his own age. He just couldn't face them. His feelings concentrated on little girls. They were so helpless, and he felt so safe with them.

Then had come Atlanta, and his conversion, and this stern life of remorse. He was doing two good things today: strengthening his own people and bringing the witches a chance to see the error of their ways.

If this was so good, though, why did it feel so bad? Sometimes he saw Christ as a red-eyed monster of his own making, and he wondered, Do I worship the Lord, or have I been deceived by a demon in a beard? He fought the tears that had appeared at the edges of his eyes.

The air was warm, the sun spreading long shadows across the fields. He glanced at his watch. 4:30. To throw the witches off, they had decided to come in broad daylight, when they would be least expected.

Indeed, all was quiet. There was the familiar melancholy of harvested fields, but there was something else, too, something awful. You could smell it. The place was just plain *too* fertile. It looked good until you really looked, then you saw the obscenity. God never intended His land to work this hard.

This richness was a gift from Satan. Thinking thus, it would not hurt so much to burn the land.

'Hey, look here.'

'What is it, Brother Turner?'

'Just about forty quarts of blackberries.' The short man was smiling, standing next to a massive blackberry bush to the right of the gate. He held up a steel bucket. 'We can have a feast!' The other men laughed. Turner took a handful of berries and began to eat them.

Simon knew just what he had to do. He leaped at Turner, grabbed his wrist, and flung the berries aside. 'Don't be a fool! That's witch poison!'

'They smell fresh.'

'I'm tellin' you, if you want to eat the produce of the Devil's farm you go swear on the Devil's Bible! You eat only of the garden of the Lord.' He snatched the bucket from Turner. 'Do not *ever* put this sort of foulness to your lips!'

Now would come the first test, for Simon and for them all. The blackberries were fat and had been picked with proper care. None were broken. Simon knew how meticulous the work of blackberry picking could be, with the thorns and the delicacy of the berries. So much effort was in this bucket. To lay it waste took strength.

'Jesus,' he whispered, 'I love you.' He poured the berries out onto the ground. He kicked the sodden mass. 'Come on, this is what we're here for! This *garbage* is probably going to be sold right in Maywell. Your children might be the ones to eat these devil's berries!'

288

There were several full buckets by the bush. He took another and raised it high over his head. For a shivering moment, he held it there. The bucket was heavy. When he flung it to the ground, it hit with a thud and a splash of fat, ripe fruit.

Simon stood, surveying the rest of the buckets. A curious feeling, almost of relief, replaced his former regret. He recognized this as the Spirit of the Lord working in him. 'Praise God!' Sad it may be, but this was certainly labour in His vineyard.

But the other men hung back. Deputy Benson still stood near the gate, his hand nervously resting on the butt of his pistol. His badge, Simon noticed, was not on his chest – as if people wouldn't recognize him without it.

Simon shuddered. Now the Spirit of the Lord twisted and turned in him, and met up with the softer spirit of the hand. The hand had belonged to a wonderful little person, a saint, Simon was sure, and it did not like these evil fields. The hand revealed to him that death itself swarmed in the stubble, as if the borderland of the Lord's world was back there at that gate. Brother Turner stooped over and picked something up.

'What's this?'

Simon examined the plump little packet of cloth. 'Open it.'

'I don't want to open it.'

Simon took it from him. He undid the thong that held the package together. Lying within was a withered image of a fat little man with roots growing out of it every which way. He threw it down. 'Mandrake,' he said. 'They put them in the fields to get the Devil's blessing.'

'I'm gonna take that little thing home –'

'Leave it, Turner. This isn't a game. They've charged that thing up with so much satanic force it just might come alive at night and get down in your throat.'

'Lord.'

'You don't know what it'll do. People these days have no

289

idea of the Devil's *power*. Just sheer power! You take that thing, and it will drag you right down to hell, mark my words.'

The men backed away from the poppet. The hand told Simon to get out of this foul place. The hand said, 'Do God's work, and do it fast.'

'We will baptize ourselves here, my brothers. We will each of us take a bucket and cast it down.'

Let blood, and blood will flow. But first the knife must slash the skin. After they participated in the destruction of the berries, Simon knew that his followers would grow more bold. And then the next act would embolden them further, and so on until the grand plan that God had given him could be fulfilled.

He looked across the wide fields. Beyond them he could see the slate roof of the Collier mansion, just visible above the trees.

The hand stirred in his pocket, touching and tickling and thrilling.

She had thrilled him unforgettably, that gentle child.

He spread his arms beneath the fire of the sun, for a vision came upon him. He saw all this land as it *would be*, cleansed in the fire, all these fields as black as death, and the house beyond the trees a smouldering ruin. 'On yonder hill,' he said, pointing directly at the roofs of the house, 'I will build my church.' And he saw it as clearly as could be: a fine brick church, with a tall steeple and a graceful portico. As proper a place of worship as Rugged Cross in Atlanta, a real House of the Lord, where His fire and His righteousness prevailed. 'Oh, the Lord has shown me such a sight. Rising from the ashes of the witch house, the triumph of His Name!'

'I hear something.' Deputy Benson pointed. In the silence that followed his words, Simon heard it also, human voices twisted to an unholy rhythm. 'Moom! Moom! Moom!' And within the longer notes, bright children's voices chanting faster, 'Moom moom moom! Moom moom moom!' There was another voice, this one single. An old woman was calling somebody.

'What's that name?'

'Amanda. She's calling the name Amanda.'

'Amanda Walker. The devil woman herself. The devil rider.'

'We're not certain it was her. It could have been any one of them.'

Simon turned on the deputy. He was getting tired of Benson's way of sapping energy with his satanic hesitation and questioning. 'Praise the Lord, Deputy!' He snatched up a bucket of the berries. 'For you.'

Benson was the kind of man who used to get into trouble in bars before he got himself saved and became a man of the law. He smiled past his false teeth. 'Sure, Brother. Praise the Lord.'

'Praise His Name!' This was an important moment. If Benson didn't pour out those blackberries –

He did it. He turned that bucket over and they spilled right into the road in a pretty pile. O Lord, wonderful are Thy ways! Just for good measure the deputy lifted his right foot and stepped carefully into the berries, crushing them good.

The Spirit of God came upon them all. Previously hesitant, the other men now went about eagerly destroying the rest of the blackberries. Brother Pierce kept an ear cocked to that devil chant. No telling how many demons were over there beyond that stand of dry cornstalks. He was not here in strength, not yet, and couldn't withstand a supernatural attack.

He did not want his people to end up having to run off this place. He wanted them to walk away.

You had to build a thing like this. Boldness would grow with success.

There were blackberries and blackberry juice all over the ground, staining the road, the dry grass beside it, and the shoes of some of the men. Simon could have kissed those stained shoes, and he would have been kissing the holy feet of the Lord. 'I think we oughta light the fire right over in that stubble. It'll spread to the standing corn on its own.'

'The ground's awful muddy,' Turner said.

'The sun's dried the stubble. We'll be okay.'

Turner hefted the five-gallon can of gasoline. 'I still think we oughta do it in the corn. We aren't gonna cause 'em any trouble burnin' a harvested field.'

'The fire will spread. The Lord doesn't want us to get too near the demons.' The chant made Simon's scalp tingle.

He walked a little distance into the field. The chant was hypnotic, intoxicating. They had to hurry. 'Okay, now, pour it out in a line right across the road. We're gonna be behind it, see. They'll come runnin' soon as they see the smoke. So the fire's gotta be between us and them.'

'Good tactics,' Deputy Benson commented. 'Let's not get caught.'

'We are doing the work of the Lord, Brother Benson. I am proud to be acting in His Name.'

'Yeah, but I still don't want to get caught by a bunch of damn witches.'

Simon allowed himself a small smile. Brother Benson would have a lot of trouble explaining himself to his boss. A lot of trouble, given that the sheriff was himself a witch. Who knew, maybe good Brother Benson was a spy for the witches.

The gasoline smelled nice. Simon had always liked the odour of it. When he was a very little boy and things were still good, and his dad would bring the DeSoto in hot from a long day on the road, Simon would like to sit on the bumper and smell the smell of gasoline fumes coming out of the grille. That was a wonderful odour, and he remembered it fondly even to this day.

'Step back,' Benson said. He had a match lit. He leaned forward and tossed it into the just-soaked grass. There was a crackling sound, and a wall of fire spread a hundred feet across the field and twenty feet into the air.

'Ohh! Oh – God, God, God!'

Turner was on fire! His arms and his chest blossomed with angry, orange flames. Frantic, he flapped his hands. The flames sounded like an awning fluttering in the wind.

Benson grabbed him – and got a fireball of a hand in the cheek. He jerked away, his own hair and shoulder burning.

'A curse, a witch curse on us!'

Turner was burning bad, his face a horrible mask of terror and agony, his chest and arms blazing. 'Help me! Oaaahhhh God! Aaaahhh!' He started running, then fell in the road. He was hitting his head with his fiery hands, and his hair was burning with blue spatters of flame.

Two of the men had their coats off. Then they were on top of Turner, smothering the flames. Greasy smoke came out from under their coats.

When he was put out, Simon rushed to his follower, knelt beside him. He almost screamed to see the hideous damage the fire had done. He had to force calm into his voice. 'You're gonna be all right,' he said, 'God will heal you.' But the man was far from all right. His hair was melted black, his cheeks and shoulders were livid red where they weren't crisped. And his hands, the poor man's hands were just two seared lumps.

Simon couldn't control himself anymore. He wept. Poor Turner's eyes rolled in his head.

'Hey! You men!'

A young woman in jeans leaped right through the fire they had set, followed by two more, and then three young men. Simon jumped to his feet. He was genuinely terrified now. It was a curse and a spell, too – those witches weren't even hurt by the fire. 'O Jesus, they're demons incarnate!'

Simon turned around, saw most of his men spread out along the road, running for all they were worth. First in line was Deputy Benson, clutching a handkerchief to the cheek Turner had burned.

Simon looked at the two men who had stayed with him. Then he looked down at Turner, whose eyes were rolling, whose legs were moving slowly, as if in some terrible dream he ran yet from the fire that had consumed him.

The witches had stopped. They were standing together, staring in surprise at the burned man. Simon saw hard, inhuman faces, evil grins. 'Let's get goin'!' he yelled.

'What about him?'

'He's a dead man.'

Three more witches jumped through the flames. They carried shovels. On the other side of the fire somebody was shouting instructions.

Simon gave way to the same kind of wild, panicky flight that had overcome the rest of the group. As he ran he heard his last two supporters, their feet pounding close behind.

Those witches were a well-organized bunch. They were already burying the flames, damn their black hearts. As Simon reached the gate he turned to see their progress – and his feet flew out from under him. He landed with a thud and a splash. He had slipped down in the blackberries. Davis and Nunnally raced past. For a moment Simon thought he was going to be caught by fierce witch women, who were coming up the road in their blowing cloaks. They waved long wooden staffs. He scrambled to his feet and hurried on. His right leg hurt like hell and his hands and clothing were stained purple.

'Simon,' he heard behind him, 'Simon Pierce, you fool.' It was a familiar voice, a very familiar voice. 'Don't run away from me! Don't be afraid.'

He hesitated. That was a voice from his own church! He had heard it raised in song and in prayer. He had heard that woman get saved. She was one of the ones who had walked out on her husband, taking her two youngest children. He turned around. 'Effie, by the love of Jesus, let me take you home.'

'Oh, Simon, no. I can't do that.' She came up to him, her cheeks flushed red, her eyes flashing. 'You're making a great mistake. These are God's people, too. We just worship in a different way.'

'The damned worship Satan different from the way the saved worship the Lord.'

'You don't understand. This is the best, the happiest, the most morally pure place I have ever been. I'm strong and healthy. Even my allergies have disappeared. And you ought to see Feather – that's little Sally's witch name – she's no longer the shy little girl her daddy used to beat. Now she's high priestess of the Children's Coven, and she's so devoted. Oh, Simon, this place is full of love, just as Christ is full of love. You cannot be Christian and have so much hate.'

'You serve the Devil!'

She raised her head, proud and defiant. 'No, sir, you are the one with the torch in your hand. If there is a Devil, you are the servant.'

Simon extended his hand to his lost follower, but she drew back from him. The other witches were crowding around, those who weren't back with Turner. Simon turned and walked briskly off their land.

The van was already in motion when he reached it. 'Stop! Wait for me!' Eddie Martin was driving; it was his van. Simon hit the gleaming black side of the thing. 'Eddie, please!'

Finally it stopped. The back door slid open and Simon pulled himself in. It was a comfortable van, with seats around the sides and a big cooler just behind the driver. Eddie would fill that cooler with Bud for hunting trips into Pennsylvania. You could shoot right through your limit of deer back there in the Endless Mountains.

'We left Turner! Oh, Jesus, we left Turner!'

'Take it easy, Benson,' Eddie said from behind the wheel.

'Look at it this way. We did damage to Satan's farm and most of us have lived to tell about it.'

Simon couldn't have said it better himself. Eddie was the Lord's kind of a man.

'The witches might have killed us all,' Simon added. 'Running is no shame in the service of the Lord, men. The important thing is that we will return!'

'A man is dead. There's gonna be all hell break loose around here. We ain't had a murder in Maywell in twenty years, not since Old Coughlin went around the bend and shot up the Unitarian Church.'

'Who said the word murder, Brother Benson?'

'The man was set on fire by – by a spell!'

'Here you are a man of the law and you don't even *know* the law. The State of New Jersey isn't gonna buy any stories about spells, true or not. The coroner will rule it an accident. We're the only ones who know what it *really* was, and we can't prove a thing, can we?'

'That mandrake thing. We'll go get that.'

'You'd still have to prove black magic, which has been around since the day Satan got thrown down into hell, and it ain't been proved yet. No, Brother, this is our own private problem. We know there was a spell worked, and a hex on that poor man of God, but the State of New Jersey doesn't know and doesn't care. Why do you think the state's got witches living in it anyway? Don't tell me the bureaucrats don't know about 'em. Those government people, they *like* the work of Satan being done in their midst! Sure they do! We are soldiers, every one of us, soldiers of the Lord. But you ask the State of New Jersey, and the state will say, an accident!'

There was a chorus of amens. Poor Turner had died hard in the service of the Lord, but he had given them all a great blessing. His death made him a martyr, and would be proof positive to the whole congregation that the witches were evil and had to be destroyed. Simon would create such a funeral for that fallen saint as Maywell had never seen before.

The Lord's people were not going to give up because of a martyrdom. Far from it, the tragedy would strengthen them. They had been plunged into the tempering bath of blood. Before this they had been a bunch of scared children.

Now they would become a fiery sword, wielded by the righteous hand of God.

CHAPTER 20

Torture

The bear was easy for Amanda to follow because it wore bells, and when it capered they jangled gaily. Summer airs danced about Amanda's head, and she went laughing behind the great black beast, through the alleyways and yards of her own early childhood.

They were going towards a certain gate, a very important one.

The little girl leading the bear stopped beside Dad's precious flowering plum tree, the one in Metuchen, in those fine days before they had come to Maywell.

She was sweet of face, her dress blue lace, her right hand always held behind her back, a charming pose. She beckoned with her left, and Amanda could not resist running towards the old back gate that led into their yard.

The old back gate, the old yard: here it was always a warm June day in about 1969, a year of highest happiness, long before the troubles started in Amanda's family.

She opened the gate and stepped through. Even the air smelled good! She was almost shaking with joy. Just around the corner of the house she could hear herself laughing, her own six-year-old voice, bell-high and full of joy. Her impulse was to hurry forward, but she hesitated. This was the wrong direction. She had to find the cauldron again, to get back into contact with the witches. Why had she followed the bear? Had she been hypnotized?

She turned around to go back. Instantly everything changed. There was a great screaming and clanking, walls arose, a raftered ceiling slammed down, and the next thing she knew she was upended and tied to a board in an echoing lumber mill. Logs thundered past on a flume. Down her belly there came a great ringing roar and she saw the blurry gleam of a saw and knew that it was going to chew her in half. She jerked, she writhed, she bellowed. At a far window she saw Tom, arching his back and spitting, then pacing behind the glass, his eyes terrible.

The little girl's right hand, detached from her body, appeared in the air and pulled a lever. The blare of the saw grew even more shrill and the board began to vibrate. Amanda soon felt wind tickling the bottoms of her feet, then sharp heat as the saw drew close.

Then it was between her legs, the spinning steel skinning her ankles and the sides of her knees.

She suddenly remembered herself when she was ten, reading *The Mad Monk* under the sheets, reading by flashlight the forbidden gore.

He had sawed a woman in half. He had done it slow.

And she, in her summer bed, had imagined not the hard screaming agony of being split asunder, but the softer terror of the breeze in intimate parts that signalled the approach of the whirling tool.

She felt that little wind now, right up at the top of her thighs. Hot sawdust was spewing up, then shifting down and tickling her belly. Soon the sound would deepen from the efficient pitch of steel cutting wood to a more liquid choffling.

The girl leaned her gentle face over Amanda and looked at her. Her eyes were no longer blue. They were the red of apple skin.

'Don't try to go back. You keep making that mistake. We don't want to hurt you, Amanda. We don't even dislike you. Far from it, we want to make you one of us.' And her eyes turned dead-water green.

Amanda was disgusted with herself. She had been deceived so easily. How stupid to follow a cheap carnival trick of a talking bear. But she would not relent, not even now.

She was, after all, dead. The saw and the body it was about to cut were both illusions.

But when the blade touched her and she felt the searing horror of its teeth in her secret skin, what resolve she had developed dissolved. 'I promise I won't go back!'

'I don't believe you.' The sound of the blade changed. Amanda felt as if she were being ruthlessly pinched, her skin being compressed to ridges and then torn off.

'I'll never go back! I'll obey you! I swear!'

'By what?'

'Oh, stop the saw. Stop it!'

'By what do you swear?'

'By – by –'

'By your own immortal soul?'

'By my soul! Oh, yes, by my soul!' Could a demon hear a lie? Amanda hoped not.

'Very well, I give you back your summer day.'

Instantly they were in the old yard again, Amanda and this strange little creature. As the girl walked along ahead of her, Amanda noticed that she had a stump at the end of the arm she usually kept hidden.

The girl didn't mention it and Amanda didn't dare, so they went on in silence. There was washing on the line, including Amanda's own very favourite pink flap-bottom pj's. 'Is childhood heaven?'

'Or hell. Whichever you prefer. Many a child has its own dead self as a silent observer of its life.'

'But time – the past – how –'

The little girl shrugged. 'It's not important.' She squatted down in the grass, motioned with her stub for Amanda to sit beside her. 'You made the right decision coming with me and Ursa. The witches call this place the Land of Summer. Christians know it as Heaven. And your old backyard is just the beginning. There are winged palaces the other side of the highway, and the pleasure of the sight of God just behind the drive-in bank.'

This wasn't heaven at all, and Amanda knew it. She looked sadly back towards the gate. Tom was gone. Beyond it was the long grey plain where her journey through death had begun. Ever so faintly she could hear the hoarse chanting of the witches.

'They need me. Without me they'll give up.'

'You don't have to go back there, Amanda. You've done your share for the witches.'

'But I've never been needed before, not like this. It's not because I'll feel guilty if I don't help them. I know I've already done a great deal in past lives, I've seen Moom. But I love them.'

For an instant the girl's eyes became as bright as bloody suns. 'Ursa,' she called, 'I need you.'

The bear came up, its bells jangling in a way that should have been merry. It leaned closer to Amanda. Its breath seemed sweet, or did it? When she smelled that thick, hot odour, she thought of night-blooming flowers, or perhaps of rotted ones.

'So *Leannan* and Constance succeeded in relieving your guilt, and yet you still want to go back. Strong girl.'

'I told you, I love my witches.'

'You love torture – because that's what you'll get if you go back.'

'Then that's what I'll get.'

The girl smiled. 'We're so much alike, you and I. You're a good magician, Amanda, and I'm a bad one.' She laughed a little. 'I was a monster by the age of eight, and dead from murder before I was thirteen.'

Amanda looked into the eyes. They were totally without depth. They seemed painted. She saw nothing, no wisdom, no help, not even any hate. Demons might sometimes look like people, and sometimes like nightmares, but they seemed, essentially, to be machines.

'Since you're so stubborn, Amanda, I'm going to show you a past very like the future you'll be facing if you go back.'

'You mean I have a choice? I can go back?'

'We serve you, Amanda. Your demons are part of you.'

'I'm going to go back.'

'I will show you the worst terror you can know.'

'No matter what, you won't stop me.'

'I will show you death by fire.'

'I've got to go – now!' Amanda leaped up.

'Ursa,' the girl said lazily, 'stop her, please.' The bear's claws came around her face like bars. Its immense force pulled her back to the soft grass.

'I said I would show you what will happen to you. You little fool, it's happened before. Just look!'

The voice was far bigger than the girl – even than the bear. It was as if the whole place, the grass, the trees, the sick yellow sky, had bellowed out the words. And the claws one by one popped through Amanda's skin and into her skull and sank coldly into her brain.

And brought with them visions.

She saw the earth as it was when the green muck first oozed upon it, a foaming cauldron of a planet, swept by bitter winds and howling in the agony of its birth, the sun blue and furious, comets and meteors swarming in unsettled splendour, the electric distempered sky striking life again and again into the ooze.

Ursa sent her forward through the cries and tinkling of five billion years, to a dripping afternoon on a hill overlooking a dark medieval town. There was a newly built manor nearby, with ugly little slits of windows and snapping red flags.

She no longer felt like a ghost.

But also, she was not her familiar old self, Amanda of the careful artist's fingers and the dreams. Her name here was Marian, and she despised that manor. It belonged to the Bishop of Lincoln, and she hated him even more than she did his house.

She sat upon her hill cursing the palace below her. She was the Lady of the Forest, the Queen of the Witches. The garters she wore were not so different from Moom's, but they were not on dirty naked legs. These garters reposed against skin as pale as cream.

She was the great ruler of the countryside. Her beauty melted the most violent hearts, and in this time there were many such. Her mother had reigned openly, but because of the Christians Marian was almost a fugitive, coming to her ceremonial hill only on the greatest occasions. The rest of the time she hid in Sherwood Forest, defended by Robin Goodfellow and his fairymen.

This special morning, though, she sat upon her stool and received her subjects. Last night had been Mayeve, and Robin as Godfather had drawn the moon down upon her. She had felt it come into her womb and shine there through the festivals of the dark. How the women had shrieked in the greenwood last night, while the pipes wailed and the drums mumbled low. Robin in his antlers had pranced and danced until his great stone of a devil's tail had stood straight up before him, and he and Marian had joined the common rapture.

The bishop, she knew, was in a fury about the rutting festival.

He had got a decree from Rome, he said, that proved she and hers were demons incarnate. She had not replied to him, that Sunday after Candlemas when he had challenged her from the steps of his miserable cathedral. She was Maid of England, after all. It was not for her to speak to a mere bishop; even the King knelt to her, did he not, in secret? Even Edward kissed her garters in Mab's cave, during the Mysteries.

So she sat upon Mabhill and let the wind flounce her hair, and handfasted those who had made merry in the night, and pretended not to notice the arrival of the bishop and his chain-mailed soldiery.

A youth saw him and raised a hand against him, saying, 'Kneel thou to the Maid of England.' In response the Bishop of Lincoln raised his eyes to the Silent God of the Catholics. The youth, who was of fairy blood and wide and short and strong, reached up and pushed the white mitre from the bishop's head.

He was bald but for his tonsure, and the long brown curls of it waggled in the wind. Goodfolk laughed, and when they did, one of the soldiers goosed the fairy with a dagger. The fairy staggered as blood spurted from the wound the point had made in his buttocks.

The bishop and his men had the laugh this time, and at the fairy's expense. Soon they left the hill and returned into the town, closing the gates behind them.

'The bishop has blooded a fairy,' people whispered. In the following days this terrifying news ran through the whole county, and soon all the churches, most of them so new their stones were yet white, became empty.

In the subsequent months the bishop fell into want and had to let many of his men at arms go.

Of those who remained, not a night passed that the fairy did not poison one with their tiny arrows. At Midsummer's Eve the bishop came and knelt to Marian and kissed the garters of the Maid of England.

Midsummer's Eve was a great joy that year of 1129, with all the handfasted couples from Mayeve leaping the fire, and the bishop and his priests dancing for the Goddess along with the goodfolk of the county.

But that bishop was a sly one. Never for a moment did he despair of the Silent God, nor forget his pope in the storied kingdom of Rome. There came a black ship into the harbour at Grimsby, sent up, it was said, from the great Catholic fortress of Canterbury. Upon this ship were seventy tall knights and seventy knaves, and horses for all. They took march across the Lincoln Wolds and climbed the Heights.

'My lady,' a fairy messenger said at last, 'they have crossed the Trent upon boats made from the sacred trees that grow on the bank.'

She only nodded, and let him withdraw before recommencing her weeping. None but she knew how she had prayed and spelled against these knights. And all for naught. That they were across the Trent meant only one thing: her hour was upon her. The Goddess was calling her Maid back to the red moon.

But her people needed her. Without her their faith would wither and die. They would become godless, or worse, Catholic. Alone in her palace, deep in Sherwood Forest, she waited and prayed. Her prayer took the form of a vision quest to the Cauldron of the Crone. She peered long into the bubbling stew of her own past.

Always before, this sort of quest had been rewarded with wisdom.

But not this time. No, her *lang syne* – the memory of her past lives – was closed to her.

And what of this fine palace of timber and wattle made, and her Robin? She sighed to think of the beams falling down, and becoming food for the termites and the fungi, and her marvellous dancing Robin stopped in his dance forever.

After the knights had crossed the Trent there came a week of slowly rising tension. They dared not enter the Maid's woodland domain, for even their hard armour would not be protection enough here, where her fairies could kill them as they slept or poison their food supplies.

But the knights did not need to come into the forest. They knew the cold truth: if they waited long enough, the Maid would be obliged to come to them.

The days grew shorter, and the deep wind of the north came back to Sherwood Forest. Robin made ceaseless forays into the camp of the black knights, but their defences were strong and always defeated him. Worse, the knights' sheet-metal armour was proof against even the most cunning fairy archers. Their straw-thin poisoned arrows could penetrate chain mail, but they bounced harmlessly off the sheet.

Hallows' drew nigh, and with it the timeless custom of the Maid's Progress. Never in remembered history had a Maid failed to carry out this ritual. To remain in hiding now would be to say that the Old Religion was powerless, or that its ceremonies did not matter more than the mere life of a Maid.

She could only hope that the Bishop of Lincoln would in the end hesitate to kill her, for fear that the country people would rise against him.

But he was such a clever man. To simple eyes it would seem that he had no part of these knights. The sheriff of Nottingham was his knave in the matter and commanded the troop. Few of the country folk knew the truth of who was really behind the expedition.

The red moon rose on Hallows' Eve and the fairy came with the silver carriage. It had been fashioned long ages ago by a fairy metalsmith. The carriage was a buttercup of silver, with silver wheels. It was drawn by eight fairy horses, small fellows but stronger even than their masters.

They travelled along the lower paths of the forest, where the trees were so tremendous that the ways between were barely wide enough for the fanciful vehicle.

She never reached Mabhill this Hallows' Eve. Just as they left the forest, the sheriff of Nottingham shouted from behind a long fence, 'Hallo, be ye the Queen of the Witches?'

She said nothing.

'If ye be or not, you cannot pass. I am seeking the Maid of England, to kiss her garters and make merry with her. Be ye she?'

She could not refuse his request; to do so would be heresy. 'I am the Maid, good sir,' she said, and raised her skirts for him.

But he did not come to her. Instead knights jumped out

of holes and bowers and laid steel hands on her. The fairy fought with their little swords, but they could not match lances. Two of the knights fell to poison by lucky shots against the cracks in their armour, but most of the arrows loosed from the protection of the woods fell harmlessly. 'Look how they fight us with twigs, the picts,' laughed the powerful Catholic soldiers.

The Silent God was not so weak as Marian had hoped.

They put her into a cage made of rushes and carried her all the night, arriving the next morning in Lincoln Town. The Maid had never actually been in a town before, and she was astonished to see the chickens and pigs swarming about right in the offal of the citizens. No wonder the people of the towns were sickly folk and given to riotings. Smoke hung low in the streets, and trolls wandered about snarling for farthings. Bread was stacked in great quantities in the houses, and bladders of wine lay by the doors. There were many barrels full of apples and cider. The sick lay about in corners, and filthy children ran back and forth with bits of garbage in their black little hands. She was most amazed, staring at the wonders and horrors of this place from her cramped cage.

At last the Bishop of Lincoln came down the way. He was preceded by blaring crumhorns and soldiers in white armour, riding upon a horse with his own chest gleaming gold and his helmet of burnished brass.

He might look grand, but Marian was the Maid of England, the Goddess Earth, and she met his eyes directly, even from the cage. He said naught, for he was proud in this place, and imagined that he had dominion over earth. But how was that? Would he build a prison around the greenwood or trap the sky? How did he intend to capture her?

They took her in procession, with dancing, up the muddy street and through the tall wooden gate of the bishop's palace. Upon that gate she saw a terrible sight, one that made her freeze inside. There were many spikes fitted to it, and on each spike was the head of a fairy. Some were black with rot and some gone to white bone, and others still dripped blood.

How dared this man kill fairy? They would set pox on him and all that was his. They would poison him.

But they had not managed it, for he rode fair and high, did he not?

No matter what, she would never pray to the Silent God. Her life belonged to the Goddess; indeed she was the Goddess. In the Mysteries it was revealed that every woman is the Goddess. She is water as well as thirsty throat; she is the quenching, too. And the Horned God, the Godfather whom the Catholics call the Devil, is Death her consort, both taker and giver of life.

The Catholics claimed that human beings were born of sin. But what was it? Marian had never seen any. Could it be poured from a cup or sold in the market? No. They said it lived in the soul, this sin. But where? The Crone of the Cauldron lived there, and the Cauldron contained only truth in its spiritual stew. She knew, she had tasted of it many times.

They carried her into a tall, dark hall most artfully wrought of stone. Compared with this, her own palace was rough indeed. But her home smelled at least of the forest, not as this did of greasy fires and sour beer.

'We will begin at once,' the bishop said. They took her down a winding stone stair. She was given a draught of milk by a young woman who worshipped her for a moment and then slipped away. Soon the bishop came prancing down the stairs. He had affected humble brown robes.

'Hangman, the first degree.'

She did not mind when they disrobed her. She was used to being naked before others. Clothes were only proof against the wind, after all. But when they laid hands on her garters, she at first almost swooned with astonishment. Then she fought their fumbling, clumsy fingers. She fought with all the fury of the legendary maid Boadicea who had fought the Romans, and did not stop fighting even when twenty of them sat upon her, laughing and flatulent, most of them stiff to wood from scuffling about with her.

In the end they took the ancient garters of the Goddess, and it was the first moment since time began that they had not been on the thighs of the Maid of England. She cried out and at last spoke to the Bishop. 'I command you, my knave, to have me unhanded, that I may replace the garters.'

'Rack her.'

There commenced an excruciation beyond belief. She was bound in a wooden bed so that she could not get up. It creaked, and when it did the most terrible pain came into her legs and arms. After a time it creaked again and hot agony shot down her spine. Her belly tore on its moorings. Bile came up, and when she spat it out, there was a great deal of laughter all about.

'Confess that you are a witch and a poisoner.'

'I am the Maid of England, sir. You must know I be a witch. Of course I am a witch!'

'You have poisoned the wells of Lincolnshire. Confess it.'

'The fairy poxed you, sir. Give them back their deadheads and make no more, and they will raise the curse soon enough.'

'The second degree, please, hangman.'

The men took her from the wooden bed and bade her stand, but she could not stand. So they made her kneel before the hangman while he cut off her tresses. How long and black they were, lying upon the vile stone floor. She sang to them a little and mourned that they would be with her no longer.

They poured a black liquor over her head and ignited it. The torment was awful, her ears and scalp raging with a pain as if the skin were being rubbed off the bone. Her body wanted to run, but she fell to the floor at once when she tried. There were great knots around her legs, and she could not move them for aught.

'I am broken,' she moaned.

'Then you say it, you are witch and poisoner. It is you who poisoned the wells of Lincolnshire, Lady!'

'I told you, give them their deadheads – oh, I hurt so, sir, really I do. Do you not know that I am the Goddess Consecrate? Oh, where are my garters?'

'The third degree.'

Her head ached so badly that she could hardly think anymore. She could still feel, though, as they lifted her high and put her wrists in rings. They horsewhipped her mercilessly. She fainted then, and the Goddess herself came to her and made her a promise that gave her courage. 'Only a little more will you suffer, my daughter. Your body will soon give up the ghost, and I will receive you.'

The Goddess appeared in her dream as bear. But when Marian awoke there was another animal present, a great black cat she knew well. He strode about the chamber snarling and spitting at the bishop.

'Look there – her familiar has come to save her! Capture it and we will burn it with her!'

The man who touched old Tom got the flesh ripped from the bone of his finger. Then Tom leaped into the rafters. Soon only his green eyes could be seen. Then with a flick of his tail and an angry scream he was gone. 'There you see, girl, your devil abandons you.'

'The Goddess cannot abandon me any more than the air can abandon me.'

'The fourth degree.'

They laid her in a wooden box made with boards between her legs. Then they hammered wedges between these boards and thus crushed and split the bones of her legs, causing her a torment that made her break her throat with shrieking.

'Say that you poisoned the wells.'

But she was insensible, and could say nothing.

She awoke to the distant crowing of cocks. A boy, most frightened, came to her and laid poultices upon her legs and back, and gave her thick beer, as much as she could drink, and worshipped her. 'Oh, Goddess,' he murmured, 'the peasants in the country weep that the townsfolk have got you.'

'My child.' She could say no more, and soon brought up the beer.

Then there was a dismal blast of crumhorns and sackbuts and the hangman returned. She screamed in terror to see him, but when they were alone he also worshipped her and wept bitterly. To let him know she shared his misfortune, she laid her hand upon his head, but she had not the strength to speak.

Soon the soldiers reappeared and put a conical crown of paper upon her head. Then they took her in hand and dragged her out into the misty morning. There was a stake erected in the middle of the bishop's close. The high sheriff of Lincoln and the sheriff of Nottingham both came, and other lords, and the high sheriff read aloud a charge:

'You have been found guilty of treason against the King, by calling yourself Queen of England, and have carried out a programme against his subjects by poisoning of wells and such-like, and you keep familiars and say you are a witch. By my authority as sheriff of this shire I command that you be tied upon this stake and burned forthwith for treason, and your ashes be cast into the river and never buried in consecrated ground, because you are a witch.'

She could not imagine a horror as great as being consumed by fire. She rolled her eyes with terror, she struggled despite the pain in her legs. She was weak from her injuries and could not get away. Soon she stood against the tall wooden stake, lashed so tightly there she thought she would be torn into parts. She wept openly before all the nobles and ladies of the shire, even many who had worshipped her, and forgot in her dread that she was Maid.

'Do not bring the torch,' she screamed. 'Oh, put it away! Put it away!' But the hangman, still weeping, laid it upon the faggots at her feet.

There was an awful time, watching the fire creep and grow in the wood.

Quite suddenly it pierced her feet as with hissing irons. She certainly could not bear it, and she shook what of her she could shake, which was her head. Then the flames caught to the robe they had wrapped her in and began eating her flesh.

'Oh, Goddess, Goddess!' She raised her face to the sky, to see if she could find the Lady of the Clouds – and she did. Yes, there, the Lady in her endless, ever-changing glory of forms, dancing across the morning as gaily as ever on a Mayfair's day.

While the flames devoured her she looked upon the white dancing shapes of the clouds, serene in endless blue.

Then she died.

And Amanda, lolling in the Land of Summer, understood the message of this memory. With twisting dread she foresaw what waited for her if she returned to life: another, slower fire.

CHAPTER 21

Constance stirred her cauldron with the fury of the possessed. She was old, though, and her body protested. These slack arms could not stir forever. 'Amanda, listen to me! Amanda!'

Despite all of her knowledge and her understanding of a situation she had in large measure created, Constance had not expected what was happening. Something immense and strange was coming down the road, a furious, disappointed little girl who somehow lived both in the other world and in this.

Her body was gone to rot but her spirit longed to finish its uncompleted life.

The moment Constance sensed this dead child's rage she knew she might never get Mandy back. There is no demon more angry than one who does not deserve its fate. The child had been cheated of her lifetime. Her bitterness made her want to hurt others. She had not yet understood the depth of compassion. Without life to teach her, she might never understand.

Why this demon was in Amanda's death Constance could not imagine. It was as if there were forces outside of Amanda's own soul commanding her to journey onward. And she was going. Constance could feel it. She stirred and groaned and sweated, but the veils between the worlds got thicker and thicker. She felt the loneliness that came when a spirit turned away from the circle. 'Amanda!'

The little girl was the key. But what had been done to her to make her as she was? Why was she still partly alive? And how could such a thing be? A child like that ought to be far, far into Summer by now.

The only explanation was that some part of her must still be in this world, by some rare process clinging to actual, physical life. Whatever it was, it kept her chained to bitter memories. The only protection from her would be to find out how to break this strange connection.

In her mind's eye Constance could see the child, pretty enough, dressed in blue – and bearing a stump where her right hand ought to be.

So that was it, the hand.

What gave it life, though? Only devotion and attention could do that, and what warped soul would have so intense a relationship with the severed hand of a dead child?

Dimly in her vision she could see Brother Pierce approaching. Yes, it was time for him. She had foreseen that correctly, in her long nights of meditation before the *Leannan*, submitting her mind to the shattering guidance of that powerful being. The *Leannan* could have met Constance anywhere, but their meetings took place in the Mabcave on the back of Stone Mountain. Constance preferred it that way. In her agony she was sometimes noisy. A glance from the *Leannan* could shatter the ego. Many times the *Leannan* had shown her the awful details of the death she had chosen for Constance. Not knowing the future is hard, but knowing it can be excruciation.

In her male form as the King of the Cats, the *Leannan* wove on the loom of time. She wove the life of Maywell just as she did the journey of Amanda. But it was a rough weave. The will and effort of humankind was what would make it fine.

Now came this angular, guilt-ridden man, straggling along with a few of his followers.

Tom, who had been stalking round and round the witches' circle, stopped and crouched to the ground. A glance at Constance told her everything: the hand was not expected. It contained a fury that did not belong to the world of the living.

314

It was capable of vast destruction.

A moment later flames roared to life on the far side of the cornfield. Despite them, and the screams that were uncoiling above their crackle, Constance and the Vine Coven tried to keep their circle.

'Moom moom moom moom moom moom,' went the chant, turning and flowing between the worlds, almost a thing apart from its creators. 'Moom moom moom moom.'

There was the barest chance that Constance could relieve the hate of the wronged child, but only if she could understand. To her it was obvious that the hand was connected to Brother Pierce. But why had he kept it? She rowed in the cauldron with her hazel staff, looking for answers.

Shadows flickered in the steamy water, bits and edges of the little girl's horror, her bitter runaway's life, and the man who had taken advantage of her dreams and then denied her everything.

Constance rowed and rowed, but she was old and used up, and the world in the water wasn't patient with her. Her muscles had been defeated ten minutes ago; only her will forced her on. Still, she got no specific vision of what had been done to the little girl to cause this rage. And where was the hand? On Brother Pierce's person. Good God, it was in his pocket.

She felt her life as a tattered edge; she wanted to drop the hazel rod. Tom glared at her. In his eyes she saw the *Leannan*'s image. *Leannan* whipped Constance with a vision of her own dying. Blue flames raced across a ceiling of her future, yellow flames spouted through a floor. The gnarling fire turned her to a black hump. She heard the crackling hiss of her own burning skin. Then there came the pain: she screamed in agony, terrifying the poor Vine Coven. 'Chant,' she shouted, 'chant for your lives!'

'Moom moom moom moom!'

Other witches began rushing past the Vine Coven, cloaks

315

and flaps of canvas grabbed from harvest wagons in their hands, running to the distant screams and flames. Nearby cornstalks were already rattling with wind from the inferno.

The cauldron circle wasn't strong enough to help the enraged child, and so there was little hope for Amanda. 'Moom moom moom moom, hear our call! Moom moom moom *moom*.'

There must be no end to the swirling of the cauldron or Amanda would be lost forever. Black wings beat in Constance's mind. 'I'm fainting! Help me!'

Tom jumped up on her head and dug his claws into her scalp. The pain of it would have kept Rip Van Winkle awake.

'Moom moom moom moom moom –'

The waters roiled and sputtered, deep with scent of herb and shape of frond, boiling-pot of a few common herbs, window into the human soul. Black, dangerous, interesting waters.

Constance was frantic. Even Tom's claws and his tail tickling her nose could not keep her conscious much longer.

'Moom moom moom moom!'

Black water covered Constance. Row, row, row your boat, gently down the stream. Merrily, merrily, merrily, life is but a dream.

She awoke a few seconds later to find the circle shattered, and with it Amanda's last contact with this world.

Why in the name of all holies didn't George Walker resuscitate her? He was supposed to have done it long before now. All of Constance's planning to create a safe journey through the netherworld had been useless. 'The only thing you are doing,' the *Leannan* had cautioned her, 'is sending Bonnie Haver to a terrible end. When you die yourself, how will you explain the arrogance of what you have done? Will you take her place in hell? What will you do, Constance? Look at you, holding your head high, you arrogant creature!

There is no guarantee for Amanda any more than there is for any shaman who attempts the journey. If there was a guarantee of her return, she wouldn't really be dead. You revolt me, not seeing that. How dare you be so stupid, so wilful, after all you have been taught. Amanda couldn't enter death if she had a guarantee. She'd come back with mere hallucinations. You're a shameful fool, Constance.'

That voice had cut more by its tone even than by its hard words. 'I give myself to your mercy,' Constance had murmured through her tears. The *Leannan*'s laughter had tinkled in the cave. Then Tom had come forth, great and roaring, a panther with teeth of steel, and driven her out.

There could be no guarantee. And, absent one, Amanda had died, finally and actually.

'Constance! There's a man on fire!'

She could smell the awful barbecue and gasoline of the burning man, and the matted stench of his burnt hair. They all smelled it.

'Moomoomoom – moom . . .'

'Chant!'

'Connie, we've lost her. She isn't here anymore.'

'Chant!'

Something awful happened. Tom leaped down into the cauldron, disappearing into its boiling interior with an awful howl. Then, rising from the water, came the little girl. She waved her stub of an arm, triumphant. *I am the hand, the hand that takes*.

'You poor child.'

A cry from beyond the cornfield and the smoke: 'Help us! Help us! This man is dying!' The Io Coven was out there. They had been in among the corn rows gathering culls for their pigs.

When the fire began crackling in nearby cornstalks, the Vine Coven finally gave up. Between Connie's exhaustion and Amanda's wandering, and now this little girl, they lost all hope.

317

But then things changed again. Brother Pierce was running, and taking the hand with him. As he ran, the little girl disappeared in a shower of sparks, her eyes flashing towards the departing figure.

Without the demon to block it, the way to Amanda was clear.

'We've still got a chance!'

'Moomoomoomoomoomoom . . .'

But there wasn't even a whisper of Amanda.

It really was a great blow. After Constance's own death the Covenstead would go on, but it would be a diminished thing indeed, weak and prone to the ordinary destructions of life. Without the wisdom of death and the connection to the old traditions Amanda would have brought back, it would last a generation, perhaps two, then fade away.

The Maywell Covenstead would not be the rebirth of a fine and peaceful old way of life after all. Mankind would continue as before, unable to stop the rape of war, the bleeding of the earth, moving helplessly towards the coming end.

'Help us,' came another call from the corn.

Joan and Joringel were carrying the burned man between them on a canvas tarp. The worst thing about him was his hands, flaking black lumps. 'Take him to the house,' Constance commanded.

'It's too far. He needs help *now*.'

Constance did not like the idea of an outsider, no matter how comatose, being in the village. Joan and Joringel went right past her, crashing through the cornfield, indifferent to the toppling stalks and the flying ears of the corn as yet unharvested.

Constance was wretched with despair over the loss of Amanda, but she had no choice. The situation demanded her presence. She broke circle and followed the others to the village.

Tom didn't follow, though, because he wasn't there anymore. As swift as smoke he had crossed Maywell to a certain house. He moved on soundless pads across the basement floor, coming swiftly to the Kitten Kate Room.

What a pleasure it was going to be to deal with this cat-hating maniac. George was going to die a most hideous and deserved death. Tom had planned it carefully.

But now was not quite the time. Not just yet.

He leaped up on the table where lay Mandy and George. The maniac was weeping softly as he caressed the body of his niece. The cat snuffled at his leg, looked long at his trembling, supine body.

Tom jumped down again and began circling the table. He was panting with rage. 'Meow.'

The sound penetrated George's trance deeply enough to wake him, but not so deeply that he was conscious of the presence of a cat. 'Uh? Oh, I'm – God, I passed right out!' He leaped from the table, ran over to his controls.

He felt the blood drain out of him. It had been fifteen minutes! Mandy was irretrievably dead.

Fifteen minutes of such ineffable sweetness. He had lain upon her, had kissed the stillness of her lips, had felt her eyebrows tickling his cheeks, had pressed his loins against the quieted sepulchre of her body.

He cried openly, to see what he had done. This had been a last chance, and he had been hypnotized with the pleasure of caressing her dead body. He had ruined everything for himself.

Now he was simply a murderer.

'Meow.'

What the hell was that? It couldn't be a cat, not in here, not alive.

He loathed the torture cats on the walls of this room, with their probing eyes and inflammable fur. But their feline skill at causing pain fascinated him.

Something was going very wrong. What if the torture cats were –

But they were just magazine cutouts. He had made them himself, selecting over the years the best and most dramatic of all the cat pictures he had seen.

A huge black Tom rushed along the floor – and with a faint hiss transformed itself into Silverbell at the moment of her burning.

'No! It's not you, you're not alive!' He backed away from Silverbell's blackened, smoking form.

Silverbell growled. She moved forward, wobbling slightly because one paw was burned off. She was between him and the door.

'Get away!'

He told himself she wasn't real. She was dead. Silverbell, who seemed to have forgotten this, growled again.

'Won't you ever forgive me? Please forgive me!'

'Forgive yourself,' snarled a tiny, extremely harsh woman's voice.

The voice was so small he could barely hear it, but it smashed into his soul with the force of a hurricane. Before such power only the truth was left him, and he screamed it out: 'I can't! Can't! Can't! Can't!'

The cat was close now, so close that he could see its smoked oyster of a tongue pressing between carbon-blacked teeth.

He kicked the cat hard, and its crisp skin shattered. But muscles and bones, even torn asunder, immediately took up the chase, oozing across the floor. 'God! Oh, God, I've gone nuts. I'm stark raving mad.'

He stomped on the crawling, sliding ruins of the cat, stomped and stomped until they were only wet marks on the floor. 'Jesus. That was a hell of a hallucination. I'll be needing a Thorazine drip if I keep this sort of thing up. I've got to get myself together. Come on, guy. You have a dead body to dispose of.'

There was another meow. Confused, George looked to the ceiling where it had come from.

It was a seething, squirming mass of living cats. George did not even have a chance to scream before they began dropping to the floor, screeching and spitting.

Next the walls came alive. As he watched, a huge Persian bulged and oozed into life and leaped at his throat. It grabbed his shoulders with strong claws. Then it sank its teeth into his neck. He felt them pop through his windpipe and deflect the passage of air.

Off the ceiling they came, out of the walls they came, all the cats he had ever known and feared, biting, scratching, squalling, killing him by their sheer suffocating numbers. When the smothering began to hurt, he threw some of them off. But more came, until he was nothing but a jerking hump in the swarm.

He was killed by the living flesh of his guilt.

The cats gobbled him, chewing and swallowing him in chunks, until at the end there was left only a belt, a pair of shoes, and three Bic pens.

The cats returned to the ceiling and the walls. The room grew quiet. Mandy lay in absolute stillness.

Some time later a fly entered the Kitten Kate Room. It circled for a few moments, seeking just the right place to undertake its project.

The fly landed on Mandy's upper lip. It preened itself carefully, then turned around and began to lay its eggs.

It laid them in the cathedral of her left nostril.

CHAPTER 22
Mother Star of the Sea

The thing the demons couldn't understand was that Marian hadn't died in despair any more than had Moom. She had seen visions of the Goddess from her pyre and been laid in Summer afterwards, where her soul had been renewed. Knowing that another fire awaited her return did not stop Amanda from wanting to go back to the Covenstead.

'But you can't, you're dead!'

'George will revive me.'

'It's too late for that. He's dead, too.'

The girl in blue waved her empty wrist, and a hole opened up in the ground. 'Go on, look. He's created a lovely hell for himself.'

Down the hole Amanda saw George laid out on an operating table, his whole belly opened, his pink insides exposed. She could see the froth of his screams, but thankfully was spared the sound.

Kittens were cavorting in his entrails, batting his intestines about as they might wriggling caterpillars.

She was stunned and appalled to see that she herself was his demon, standing over him with the scalpel that had opened him up. The demon image of herself looked up at her, smiled, and waved the scalpel like a child waving a treasured lollipop.

'Stop it! Please stop it!'

'How? Only he can do that, and he obviously doesn't want to.'

'But he can't have chosen such torture, and not from me. I don't hate him!'

The girl snickered. 'That image down there isn't you. It's part of him – his impression of you.'

'I'm not cruel, I could never do that. Why did he –'

'Demons serve their victims. Only a demon of you can punish away his guilt for murdering you.' A brush from her stub closed the hole. 'Enough of that. I can show you beautiful things, Amanda.'

'That's a lie.'

'I offer you the Land of Summer.'

'No. I'm going back.'

'Without the witches to guide you, you can't. And I destroyed their circle.' She held up her wrist. 'Something of me is left in the living world. My hand is still there, and it isn't dead. So I use it to manipulate life.' She laughed aloud, a harsh and bitter cackle.

As she did so, the illusion of the little girl shifted for a slight instant, and Amanda saw what *really* wore that frilly blue dress. It was a hard-shelled something, dark red and many-legged and misbegotten, and it bore the name of Abadon.

It looked at her through its many-lensed eyes, and in every lens she saw the gentle, smiling face of the *Leannan*. 'You! It's really you, it's all you!'

'No. All except you. I am not part of you.'

'You are my demon. You must be part of me.'

'Oh, the devil take you, Amanda! Why didn't you educate yourself more thoroughly? Don't you know that I'm not only *Leannan*, not only Tom, not only Abadon and not really any of them. See what sort of a cat I really am!' She changed again, spitting and grinning, sharp lightning sparking from the buzzing tips of her fur.

'Schrödinger's Cat!'

'That's only a concept. More than that.'

Was it against the law of the universe for anything to be only what it seemed?

'Nothing is against the law. The law is its own violation.

That is the core of all events, that is Schrödinger's Cat. Just relax. I'll take you farther than you ever could have gone yourself.' With that Abadon snapped his scorpion's tail, Tom hissed, and the conceptual cat spat, and the *Leannan* laughed a laugh so mean it startled Amanda.

She stepped back, stunned by the realization that the world of the dead was at least in part a great slaughterhouse for souls, and the handless child folded into all of these other forms was one of the master butchers. She was leading Amanda towards the clicking maw of something so remorseless that it was willing to devour the frail and precious immortal bits of human beings, a sort of predator of the netherworld, that ate all the best of men as men ate full-ripened fruit or the tenderest parts of animals.

Nothing any man had ever done to any man was as bad as this.

'We've got to get going,' the thing in the shape of the little girl said briskly. 'Oh, Amanda, you're just going to love deep Summer. It always makes me so glad when I can take somebody there. I really feel that it makes my job worthwhile.'

Amanda did the only thing she could do: she started to run away.

In an instant Abadon shed its disguise and leaped on her, grabbing her in enormous pincers and scuttling away with her.

Amanda fought it with teeth and fists. She had expected it to be impossibly strong, so she was surprised when huge plates of its shell came off in her hands. Then she discovered that it was no more difficult to open the pincers than it might be to push aside heavy doors.

When she freed herself, the thing slumped back, whipping its sting about and howling with rage and pain. 'You're a cheater, you don't play the game!'

'I told you, I'm going back.'

'You're dead, you haven't got the right! This is just the

border of hell, baby. There's terror beyond belief between here and life.'

'I'm going back, and that's that!'

'You are in violation of the law! Have you heard, ever, of anybody returning from the dead?'

'Osiris. Christ. Lazarus.'

'And little Amanda Walker from Maywell, New Jersey. Don't make me laugh. Now, come on, you're wanted elsewhere.'

Amanda strode back towards the garden gate, determined this time to go through it, and stay gone. She opened it and stepped forth.

Before her was a forest, a most unusual forest. From here it didn't look too nice. It seemed to be made of enormous human legs, festering with sores and ooze.

Amanda reached the gate. Behind her the girl in blue waved her ragged wrist and laughed her angry laugh.

The odour of the forest was pretty bad. Gas gangrene must smell like this, Amanda imagined, clinging to your nasal surfaces as oil clings to water.

'But I don't have nasal surfaces. I am dead. All of this is an illusion.'

From far behind her there came a shout: 'Give my regards to Mother Star of the Sea.' Then the *Leannan*'s needle-sharp laughter once again, merging with another very different sound.

This noise came from beyond the forest, and it was more welcome by far. One witch, still chanting.

Robin.

'I hear you! I'm coming back!'

But the chanting did not get stronger as Amanda entered the forest. The stumps grew taller and taller, absorbing all noises. She felt awful and alone and small. A little white bird fluttered gaily. 'Come with me, me, me!'

Of course the bird was trouble. Big trouble. But, at the same time, she was out of alternatives. The only place the forest opened up to let her through was where the bird went. She began to follow. It didn't seem likely but you never knew. Maybe she would get through.

It stank fantastically in among the towers of rotted flesh. They were too close together to pass without touching. Soon she was covered with ooze and scrapings. The bird flew eagerly ahead, deeper and deeper into the forest.

Amanda had to fight with all her strength to retain self-control. She was almost mad with revulsion. The wounds seemed to spit at her. And there was even a sense that unseen hands were caressing her from inside the cracks in the stumps.

What ungodly creatures must make their homes in these filthy things. 'Don't touch me!'

Nothing replied except the bird, which warbled furiously. 'Come on, on, on!'

Amanda couldn't stand any more. She stopped walking. She stared down at the ground.

And saw that it was a seething mat of long-bodied beetles. 'Oh, no! Oh, I can't bear any more of this! Why won't it stop? What have I done?'

'You didn't play the game! You won't judge yourself, not you! you! you!' The bird's eyes were silver pins of hate.

'I am not guilty, that's how I judge myself! Not guilty!' She stomped into the crunchy surface beneath her. 'My name is Amanda Walker and I am not guilty. My name is Maid Marian and I am not guilty. My name is All Women and I am not guilty!'

The beetles were beginning to bore into her feet. She hopped. 'I am Moom, full of blood and milk and babies!'

You, woman, are burning in the evidence of your name.

Amanda sank down into the crawling, hurrying masses of beetles. They swept over her like a wave but she just didn't care. Let the worst happen. She had got herself sent to a very special hell, the one hell not of the condemned's own making: the hell of those who refuse to face their own consciences.

'I don't deserve this! I do not!'

Somewhere far away, something tremendous and kind agreed with her and took an instant's pity on her. It allowed her to hear a music human beings almost never hear, the sublime harmony that rules and arranges all things.

The final government of the world is this music, coming from no throat nor bird, but from what fingers the harp of creation.

The blessed music of the *Leannan*'s harp faded into the rustle of the beetles. It wasn't much, but it suffused Amanda with a new and rare strength. Despite the beetles she raised herself to her full height. Even so, her face did not clear their mass. In these few seconds she had sunken deep into the hordes of them, so deep that she was swimming beneath their surface.

If she opened her mouth –

She raised her arms, she began to claw slippery handfuls of them, pulling herself upward, crushing hundreds of them at a time in her struggles.

Music, indeed! *This* part of creation at least was all disharmony.

The voice of the *Leannan*: 'You chose this, remember.'

Amanda's lips were tingling, and feelers were coming in between her teeth and tickling her tongue.

'I don't really have a body! So this isn't actually happening.'

But it felt more real than the sharpest living moment.

Her flailing right hand connected with something solid. She felt, she grabbed, she clutched. And she pulled herself out onto the root structure of one of the stumps. The bird was fluttering and shrieking. 'I thought you were a goner, goner, goner!'

Amanda dragged herself up out of the morass of beetles. As long as you stood *on* the darn things, they were no

327

problem. Just don't relax. Never relax, not if you are trying to cheat death.

Amanda took a deep breath, and when she did, became aware of a most perplexing new odour.

It was the tang of gingerbread.

She moved by her nose, in the direction of the smell. 'That's right, right, right,' the bird shrilled. Soon another scent was added, of warm chocolate. And then one of jelly beans. And then just a hint – wasn't it – of searing steak?

The bird darted, it flopped, it peered at her with its silver eyes. Amanda followed because the smells were from life. They brought tears of remembrance. She had loved gingerbread, and she had baked it often.

It was the essential smell of the best of her past, a mamma-smell from before Amanda could even talk. Poor Mamma. What a tragedy to leave life unatoned. It is so much harder later.

'Here we are, are, are!' The bird swooped off into a clearing. Amanda's eyes almost popped out when she saw what was there. Nestled in the centre of the clearing, in its own pool of thin yellow light, was a most charming little cottage. It was decorated with chocolate drops and jelly beans and taffy whorls. The walls and roof were made of slabs of gingerbread, the chimney was a gleaming liquorice top hat. Thick green smoke poured out of it, rising into the hazy air.

Amanda wondered who she saw moving behind that rock-candy window.

The trees pressed closer. The creature in the cottage bustled back and forth past the frosted window, and the smoke poured from the licorice chimney. The little bird spiralled up into the sky and disappeared. Lucky little bird.

Amanda had no intention of going into that cottage. But not to worry, the door was opening.

The wind curled some smoke across the clearing, and

Amanda caught a whiff of overcooked pork. A strangely familiar smell. School food.

There was a dark figure in the open doorway. Amanda stared, almost unable to believe what she was seeing, the long black dress, the white around the face, the silver cross on the breast.

What was a nun doing in a place like this?

'I'm Mother Star of the Sea. Glad you've come to see me.'

Amanda thought it better not to say hello.

'Come on in, Amanda, darling. Time for our lesson to begin.'

Oh, yes, it was her all right, despite the fact that she now had the rough voice of a stevedore.

'I think I'll stay out here.'

'Oh, no, my dear. Look, I've got all sorts of goodies for you – candies, cakes, gingerbread.'

'No, I'm okay out here.'

Mother Star of the Sea came forward, prancing, mincing, her arms akimbo, her head lolling from side to side, her jaw snapping.

Perhaps she intended to be amusing, but she could hardly have chosen a more unwelcome appearance. Ever since she was three and she'd been chased by a man dressed up as Mr Peanut, Amanda had loathed and despised all forms of puppets. Little puppets made her skin crawl, but big puppets – life-sized puppets – they rattled their grins in her nightmares.

Even though Mother Star of the Sea was a tremendous puppet, she moved with sinister human purpose. In another second she was going to grab Amanda with those intricate hinged hands.

Her painted eyes were blank, yet curiously avid.

When Amanda turned to run, she found herself pressing against the rubbery flesh of one of the trees that surrounded the cottage. The skin was grey and weak and it gave way.

Inside something sucked and swarmed about on itself – a

fat, brown serpent of a thing lubricated with yellow mucus.

It had the head of a human being. She thought, perhaps, the face was familiar. Was it Hitler? Stalin? She couldn't be sure. It bubbled words, 'Help me, he-e-e-lp me . . .' Then it snarled, its body whipped out, and in an instant coils as hard as iron had swarmed around her.

She saw flashes, she heard an old song, 'Lili Marlene,' a German song from World War II. And she felt hot wires digging into every part of her body, digging and exploring.

She felt herself disappearing, becoming less than nothing.

The wires were its teeth: it was eating her soul.

But then there came a rippling surge in the rock flesh, and the song changed to hissing, spitting invective, a Götter-dämmerung of gutter German. It spat.

Then Amanda was free.

Mother Star of the Sea: 'Don't go near those trees!'

'I didn't know!'

'Now, will you *please* come with me? The class is waiting.'

'The class?'

'Of course. Our Lady of Grace is a school, isn't it? There-fore we have classes, or haven't you put those two amazingly unrelated facts together yet, my bright girl?' She clamped Amanda's ear into one of her mechanical hands and started dragging her towards the cottage. 'These woods are really far more dangerous than any place on earth. There you can do no worse than die. But here – oh, dear!'

Our Lady of Grace had been a grim place, a Gothic pile full of pale nuns and semidelinquent girls in jumpers and oxford shoes. 'But I went to public school!'

'Not when you were eleven. We had you then.'

That was true. 'It was only a few months.' Mamma had gotten hepatitis that year and Dad couldn't begin to cope: they weren't Catholic, but Our Lady was the closest place Amanda could be stashed.

Mother Star of the Sea clapped her hands. 'I'm in the hells of all my girls! It's so *nice* to be needed.'

Amanda had hated Our Lady. Sausages were called bangers there and you had to eat them especially if you thought they were greasy and awful, and you had to kneel before the Madonna of the Upstairs Hall when you were bad. And they gave tongue-lashings that made you feel guilty for just being alive.

'You taught me music.'

'And you're still dancing to my tune!'

'No.'

'All right, now, in you go.'

The cottage was really a classroom. That classroom.

It was the most terrible place in her life, so terrible that she had crusted her memory of it with thick amnesia. There she had learned injustice, she had learned to hate, she had learned what evil is.

'Or was it that simple, my dear? Didn't I love you? Didn't I hold you when you cried, sent to school by your father with a black eye? Amanda, you've hurt me. You've wronged my lovely name. Aren't you ashamed?'

The chalk-dust smell of the classroom made her clench her fists. She remembered that Bonnie Haver had once stolen her crayons. When Amanda complained, Mother Star of the Sea blamed her for not finishing her work, and punished her while Bonnie went free.

'I was afraid of Bonnie, dear. She destroyed me, you know. I couldn't punish her, I had to let her go.'

That afternoon after gym Bonnie and two other girls, Daisy and Mary, had –

'They drew on me with crayons! They drew all over me and *you* made me kneel to the Madonna of the Hall because I was a filthy, dirty little girl. They drew on me with my own crayons, and you punished me, you punished me again and again and again, and I said one day I would see you burn in hell, you evil, sadistic old bag of bones!'

'So here you are, feeling guilty for hating me. As you

should. And punished you will be!' Her voice got lower, like the growl of a hunting cougar. 'Sit down.'

'The desks – they have straps. I don't think –'

'Have a goddamn seat! I'm your teacher. You're here to learn about yourself. Now, sit in the desk.'

Amanda sat. With a great clatter of fingers Mother Star of the Sea strapped her into the chair. 'There. Bonnie dear, time to come out and play.'

'Oh, no, not her. Not that –'

'Bully? Yes, she was a bully when she was eleven. Too bad you didn't know her more recently. She's gotten really mean.'

Amanda writhed. She really didn't understand this at all. Why was she here? This wasn't her hell. She hadn't done anything to be ashamed of at Our Lady. She'd been a good girl.

'You shouldn't have despised me. It's a sin called calumny.'

'You deserved it! You did!'

'I deserved compassion. It would have soothed me like rain.'

What little evil she had done, she had done in those months at Our Lady. There she had hated and hurt, and spread disappointment – but only because she was herself so sad.

Bonnie pranced down the aisle, blonde and delicious in her schoolgirl greens, her ponytail flouncing behind her, a vicious-looking ruler in her rattling hand.

'Open your palms.'

'I haven't done anything.'

'No, but I've got a right to my fun. Now, open your palms. This is going to hurt you more than it does me.'

This was crazy. She was getting the same kind of injustice she had gotten at Our Lady, and for no better reason.

'Both hands. Perhaps we can beat some sense into you. Remember, dear, we just *might* be your friends.'

Unwillingly, sure she was making a mistake, Amanda did as she was told. The ruler whistled a familiar tune, then came down cr-a-ack across two quivering palms.

'That's one!'

From the front of the classroom Mother Star of the Sea commenced a wooden rumble of applause.

Again the ruler snapped. Despite herself, Amanda yelled. It fell once more. Then another time and another and another. Her palms became purple. The room was echoing with her cries and the laughter of her tormentor.

'Oh,' Bonnie said, pushing an akimbo curl out of her left eye, 'that was fun.'

So this was how the demons torture the damned in hell, very artfully. 'Please let me out of here!'

'What? Let the pig out of the slaughterhouse? Come on, dear, there isn't a chance of escape. Smile, or we'll feed you to the trees.' Bonnie glared down at her with sparkling, furious eyes. 'This cottage is the heart of the forest. And Mother Star of the Sea – she's Satan herself.'

Amanda looked at her pulsing, agonized hands. 'If she's Satan, who are you?'

'I'm her wife.'

The straps were tight. Amanda bowed her head in defeat and sorrow. She wept, and her tears were real.

They were the first sign of life in the basement where her body lay, a miracle in the secret dark. They fell from the dead, open eyes of her corpse, rolled down her cold cheeks, and dripped onto one of the Bic pens George had dropped when he was doing his own dying.

They dripped also onto the Covenstead, in the sorrow of the afternoon, onto Ivy's cottage. They made their way through the thatch and pattered down in front of Robin, who sat frozen with grief, staring at the tabletop, and at nothing at all.

CHAPTER 23

As far as Ivy and Robin were concerned, a drip of perfectly ordinary water spattered on the oilcloth table that stood in the middle of Ivy's cottage. 'I hate thatch,' she muttered. From the hollow of his loss Robin lifted his eyes and watched his sister stomp about. 'Damn,' she said, 'double damn!'

'Water bind it, no one find it.'

'I'm not angry, Robin!'

'I didn't say you were.'

'Oh, no. You just recited the last two lines of the anger spell instead. Anyway you're right. Of course I'm mad. A man got burned to death and my thatch is leaking and we lost Amanda!'

Robin got up from the table and put his arms around her. He kissed the tears that were forming in her eyes. She laid her head against his chest. 'How are we going to go on without her?' she whispered.

The question intensified Robin's own grief. Outside, the evening wind whispered through the grass. Constance had carefully prepared him for her coming so that when he finally met her he felt a kind of ecstasy. She was a luminous woman, worth the year's anticipation, all the rituals, and the long hours of instruction. He did not love her, although she was physically appealing. Not until the Wild Hunt did his heart open to Amanda. It was not her increasing power that won him, but rather the open, innocent way she threw herself into the ritual hunt, doing her best to succeed. Her courage and her vulnerability were what made him love her, as well as the old tales and the dim memories . . . when he was Robin to Maid Marian, so very long ago.

Now she was dead, and his grief was like a brown cloud spreading not only through his new love but through his hopes for the future as well.

The unstated truth lay in the silence that had fallen between Robin and his sister. The combination of the pressures from Brother Pierce and the death of Amanda could kill the witches' dream. You could feel as a sort of weight on the air that the heart of this place was beating more weakly than it ever had before.

Robin took a deep breath. He could never stand this kind of silence for long. 'If we're *real* witches, maybe we can do something about it.'

'Like what, aside from burying Amanda?'

'What if we raised the cone of power?'

'In our present state of mind we'd never succeed.'

'Then we'd better change our state of mind! Look, what if the Vine Coven raised such a cone of power you could see it with your eyes closed on a sunny day. Then what?'

'So what do we do with it?'

'Don't you see – we raise it over Amanda's body, and we send a wish with it, for her to return to life.'

'Bill –'

'Please use my right name. We're still witches.'

'Sorry, Robin. Amanda Walker is really, truly dead. Her body is rotting in a basement over on Maple Lane. We don't even know if there *is* a life after death, in the final analysis.'

'You sensed her in the cauldron circle this morning. We all did.'

'We felt something. The same kind of strange, enigmatic something we always feel.'

'It was Amanda – I could even see her, sort of.'

'You understand, don't you, that this whole business of witchcraft could just be – I don't know – sort of self-hypnosis.'

'Oh, no, it's not. It isn't hypnosis at all. You know as well as I do that it's magical thinking, which is a very different

335

thing. The *Leannan*'s power stems from magical thinking. You and I can do it, to an extent. We can create vivid visions in our minds, which affect reality. You know, you do magic.'

'I know, I guess I'm just losing heart. I feel like I've been kicked in the stomach.'

'We've got to try!'

'But you're talking about raising the dead! That's a lot more than magical thinking. That'd be a true miracle.'

'I can't think of her as dead. She was so alive. When I heard her on the Wild Hunt, that unchained voice echoing through the whole of Maywell – well, I discovered how powerful a sudden love can be.'

'Robin, if we try and fail, don't you see that it'll demoralize the Covenstead even more? People are in despair. Not only that, they're scared to death of Brother Pierce. They're saying we're under a curse, and I for one think they're right.'

'Surely people who're willing to believe in curses are willing to believe the dead can be raised.'

'She's been dead for hours!'

'It's been done in history. Not often, but it has been done.'

'History is a tissue of lies.'

There were voices outside, latecomers back from their day's commute. Their laughter was comforting. As soon as they heard the news, though, they became as silent as the rest of the witches.

Soon the six o'clock gong rang. There were no cooking odours among the cottages, and no lights in the night of mourning.

Despite Ivy's arguments, Robin made the decision that they were going to try this impossible thing. But he had to be careful. Ivy wouldn't be alone in objecting. People didn't like to attempt things they thought were beyond their power. Failures weaken magic, and too many failures destroy it.

He had to handle this very carefully. 'It's time to go in

and get her,' he said, 'if we're going to bury her here on the Covenstead.'

'Up on the mountain. Near where she saw the *Leannan*.'

'Yes, there.'

He went out into the village, knocking on the doors of the dark houses until he had the Vine Coven assembled. Some of the others wanted to come, too, which was fine with him. The only trouble was a lack of transportation. 'Why don't the rest of you prepare a lying-in-state?'

'At the house?' a voice asked from the dark.

If he sent them up to the house, they would all discover the secret of how dejected Connie had become. She had retreated there, he knew, to hide that fact from her people. 'I have a feeling Amanda would have preferred it on the Fairy Stone.'

There was general agreement to that. The Vine Coven set off, going in the Covenstead's two station wagons. As they drove out through the silent farm, past the blackened field that Brother Pierce and his men had burned, Robin wondered if they might really have somehow brought a curse down upon themselves.

They reached the edge of the farm, then the limit of the estate itself. The lights of the cars played on the scar of the fire, and then on the purple stains in the road. He still had stickers in his hands from picking those blackberries.

There was a sharp *ping* from the hood.

Ivy, sitting beside him, peered forward. Just then there was another one. This time a long crack slit the windshield.

From the back seat somebody screamed.

Robin hit the horn to warn the wagon behind them and jammed the accelerator to the floor. The car lunged and slurried until the tyres caught the asphalt. Then it shot ahead, its old engine roaring and rattling.

Somebody shouted a charm. 'Things of the night, take flight.'

Robin was forced to slow down out of fear that he would

lose control in the turn. People in the car were silent, stunned by surprise and fear. 'They weren't actual bullets,' he said, 'or the windshield would be shattered. Pellets or even BB's. We weren't in any real danger.'

He did not add what they all knew, that it was only a matter of time before this sort of thing escalated to open warfare. The people lurking at the gates were building courage.

'They must have somebody there all the time. I hadn't realized that.'

'We'll post guards,' Wisteria said. 'We'll have to.'

Robin pulled over, motioned the following wagon to come parallel. 'You folks all right?'

Grape was driving. She gave him a tight smile. They went on, down West Street to Main, then up Main and across Bridge to The Lanes. There were a lot of cars in front of 24 Maple Lane.

From the house there came soft singing. The town covens must have assembled there spontaneously as soon as Constance had called them with news of the tragedy.

It occurred to Robin that he was going to have to see Amanda's dead body in a few minutes. He feared for his own ability to believe in her life, then. Ivy touched him. 'You're trembling, brother.'

From behind, Wisteria put her hand on his shoulder. 'We're all with you, Robin. Remember, she's in the Land of Summer now. The Goddess is taking care of her daughter.'

It was very hard, this new experience of grief.

Sky-flower opened his door for him. They had been initiated on the same day, he and she.

Robin began to approach the house. It was full of people, of course, not only the town witches but a large part of the Christian community as well. Most of the genuine Christians of Maywell viewed the witches with wary respect. Only Brother Pierce's followers hated, and Robin did not think of them as Christians.

A queen had died, and she would be honoured among all the good people of this town. He could hear that they were singing one of the Covenstead's own songs, one of the most beautiful.

> 'Somewhere there is a river
> Somewhere there is new youth.
> Oh, let me drink the cooling water
> Let me bathe my soul in truth.'

Just as the song ended, Sheriff Williams came tromping up the basement stairs. 'Evening, Robin,' he said. He embraced Robin, pressing him against his cigar-smelling shoulder.

'We got shot at, Sheriff. Just at the entrance to the estate.'

'I've got my deputy out there.'

'We didn't see him.'

'Well, I'll talk to him about it.' He looked at Robin out of stricken eyes. The sheriff had given up a great deal for his beliefs and his lifelong love of Constance Collier.

'You going down to the basement, Robin?'

'I'm going down.'

To get through the house they had to step over people, covens sitting close to one another, clustering around their priestesses and priests, and Catholics and Episcopalians and Methodists with their pastors. Even people who had not known her sensed the wonder of her.

When they reached the mudroom and Robin saw the ugly little hatch to the cellar, his throat constricted. She had gone down into that dark place to face death.

'She tried to get away,' the sheriff said laconically. 'Made it as far as her car. He dragged her back.'

Robin could hardly bear to listen.

'Fred, we're coming down.'

'Okay.'

'Robin?'

'Yes, Sheriff?'

'Look, it's kind of bad.'

'I want to. I've got to.'

The sheriff put a big hand on Robin's neck. 'In love with a witch. I know just what you're going through, boy.'

'We will gather at the river,
the beautiful, beautiful river . . .'

They were singing again, the strong voice of the Episcopal rector leading the rest.

The basement stank of dank earth and something else, something like overheated electrical wiring. Something awful. 'We haven't moved her, Robin,' Fred Harris said. 'We'll carry her up as soon as the casket comes.'

Casket. Robin hated that word. He remembered their one experience of lovemaking, upon the humid earth, the moon setting red and low, she so full of all the furious urgency of the hunt, her body running with sweat and slick with the oils of the ritual, reeking of horse and human heat and the thick scent of love.

Cold caressed Robin as he moved forward towards the little room where Mandy lay. Lights had been hung by the sheriff's people, and the place glared harshly.

'What is this? What are all these . . . cats?'

'He was crazy. We just didn't know how bad he was. Not even Connie.'

'Where is he, Sheriff?'

'We found his belt and some ballpoint pens down here. And there was blood on the floor. There's no sign of a body.'

'Why do you think he's dead?'

'She isn't wounded, so the blood must have come from him. He's dead, all right.' He gestured at the vast bloodstain. 'People don't bleed that much and live. Who killed him and what they did with the body we do not yet know.'

'This room is –'

'She had courage to come here.'

340

Robin could hardly bring himself to go to her, so hideous was the place, jammed with the jumble of George's strange scientific apparatus, haunted by the pictures of cats.

Robin forced himself to cross the basement, past the bulging furnace, to the little chamber. Closer, the profusion of cats was almost unbelievable. Perhaps because of all of the cat images, this place seemed connected to him, almost a part of him. 'Tom is a black spark,' Constance had once said, 'from the eye of Death.'

'Kate should have told us about this,' Robin said.

'She was probably afraid. Look at the place.'

When he thought about it, Robin realized that it was impossible that Kate Walker had kept this secret from Constance. Of course Connie knew all about it. She knew exactly how dangerous George Walker was.

When Robin peered into the death chamber, he felt the presence there as a thickening of the dark. 'Tom, is that you?'

'Who?'

'Connie's familiar. The one she was going to give to Mandy. I sense his presence.'

'There's nothing like that here, Robin.'

'I don't think Tom's going to show himself.'

'That cat scares the hell out of me. It's too old, for one thing. At least forty, by my count. In my time as a witch, it's appeared once when Connie was a girl and Hobbes shot her to make her a shaman – that was in the twenties, for God's sake – then when Simon Pierce came to town, and now I've seen it around, sulking along here and there.'

Robin didn't bother to mention that Connie owned a painting of Tom done in 1654.

He took a deep breath. He could delay no longer, and looked down at the form on the table.

Even in death she glowed. Her beauty, Robin thought, could defy the grave. Her face had been caught in a living expression. Her eyes were open, the fine brows knitted as if in puzzlement. Her hands were clasped in her lap. 'We removed the bindings,' Fred Harris said. 'She was tied to the table.'

Robin prayed in his own private, wordless way, to the Goddess who awed him and the God he loved. He let their images ride in his mind, the tall, pale Goddess and her shadowed consort, moving as ever in the Land of Summer. He wanted their comfort now.

Through the basement windows there came a honking of many horns and the ragged sound of human rage. 'Damn,' the sheriff said, 'they just ain't gonna leave us alone, are they?' The honking horns obtained an angry rhythm, their notes long and bitter.

'One of theirs died today, too.'

'Robin, that man was trying to burn down your farm!'

'He died a hard death.'

The people outside were literally growling, their voices dull and deep, as the fall of rain upon a place already drowned. 'I'd better get up there and give them a little hell,' the sheriff said. He hurried off across the basement.

Robin went around to the head of the table. He thought to close her eyes. 'You can't, buddy,' Fred Harris said. 'Too late to change the expression.'

He did not want her to stare like this. It wasn't a dead expression. Despite how cold it was, her body retained the suppleness of living muscle. In a way this was much more awful than the fixed stare of an ordinary corpse.

She was so obviously not at peace. 'Isn't there any way at all?'

'I can make 'em look closed, but I have to take her back to my workroom.'

Her eyes were the shade of the moon dimming towards morning. Constance had said: 'Every one of us has a hidden name, our *real* name. When you call her to the circle, call Moom.'

'Moon?' they had asked.

'No, with an "m." Moom is her real name. The *Leannan* calls her that.'

'Good-bye, Moom. Fare you well.' He visualized her on an old forest road, suitcase in hand, walking quickly away. Long breaths of sorrow filled him.

He was granted a vision of Moom: a dumpy little brown ball of a human being, reeking of fire smoke and rancid fat, full of thigh-slapping pride and laughter. That was the young Moom. Now the ancient soul seemed to stand over him, its face grave with the wisdom of very long time. 'I feel her. She's right in this room.'

'Come on, now, the casket's arrived.'

Robin wanted just another minute alone with her, but there were a whole lot of people waiting and outside the din was getting louder. There were thuds. Rocks hitting the house. Sheriff Williams could be heard shouting, but he wasn't having much effect. Upstairs the singing went on. 'Amazing Grace,' then the Pentagram Chant. 'Pentagram glow, bring us light and glow, oh, glow, pentagram glow . . .' Ivy led it in her powerful voice.

'You go on up, Robin. Tell some of my guys to come down and help me.'

'I'll help you.'

'You don't have to – I've got plenty of men upstairs.'

'I don't mind touching her. I want to.'

Her body was slack and cold. To put his hands on her like this, when in his imagination she was so warm and full of life, was really very difficult. But it was right. This was his responsibility, this body.

They got her strapped to the stretcher and carried her across the basement. Other hands took her up the ladder. When Robin arrived at the top, the stretcher was just going around the corner into the living room. The house was full of winking yellow light. The Bees had arrived with boxes of their handmade candles.

Others unstrapped her from the stretcher and laid her in the simple coffin favoured by the witches of Maywell, a box of hand-rubbed pine, lightly made. 'Let the flesh return quickly to the Mother,' Connie said. The box was a concession to state burial laws.

Ruby of the Rock Coven came to the head of the coffin. She looked long at Amanda. 'We'll go back in procession,' she said. 'Rock will carry her all the way to the mountain.'

They closed the coffin then, and Fred Harris bustled up. 'You're going to walk all that way? That's two miles.'

Ruby was Fred's daughter Sally in the outside world. Robin wouldn't have challenged her like that. 'There are plenty of us,' she snapped. 'We want to do it this way.'

'That crowd out there –'

'There's a crowd in here, too!'

'Okay, honey, I meant no offence. I was just pointing out the facts.'

'We want to show our strength. And to respect our dead.' With that Ruby was joined by the rest of her coven. They surrounded the coffin and took its gleaming brass handles. Others gathered before and behind them, witches and townspeople alike, all carrying candles.

The local churches preached acceptance, and the witches in turn respected them. Together the group, Christians and witches alike, filed out into the rage of the night.

Brother Pierce was standing in the back of a jeep, his jutting jaw flashing in the glare of gasoline lanterns and powerful searchlights. After the Israeli invasion of Lebanon in 1982 a wave of survivalism had swept his congregation. World War III had not broken out, but they had not abandoned their preparations. Station wagons, jeeps, pickups, and powerful four-wheel-drive trucks were their vehicles of choice.

'You are the harlot of the Devil,' he roared, pointing at the advancing procession. 'You killed a man today, you murdering demons!'

Ivy was the first to start singing. 'Amazing Grace, how sweet the sound, that saved a wretch like me. I once was lost but now am found, was blind but now I see.'

'You see nothing but the darkness and evil of your hearts! What are you doing – celebrating our sorrow?'

Brother Pierce and his flock had been attracted to the house by the crowd assembled there, not by any knowledge of what had happened to Amanda.

His spitting voice mingled with the hymn. For an instant Robin saw his face clearly in the sweep of a searchlight from one of the trucks. His expression was not one of hate. It was beyond that. You couldn't look at it.

The entire crowd lapsed to silence when the coffin was brought out of the door. In the back of his jeep Brother Pierce made a sullen hissing sound. Slowly one of the lights came about and fixed on the Rock Coven and its burden.

They were humming softly, a nameless song of woe.

Brother Pierce pointed at them. 'Rejoice, for death has taken one of the evil!' He hugged himself, twisting and smiling to the night sky. 'For wickedness burneth as the fire: it shall devour the briars and thorns, and shall kindle in the thickets of the forest, and they shall mount up like the lifting up of smoke! Oh glory, oh hallelujah!'

He began to clap, and each clap of his long, narrow hands exploded through Robin's sorrow. But Ruby had been right, so very right! They belonged here, with their burden.

A song burst from the throats of Brother Pierce's followers: 'We're gonna tell the world about this! We're gonna tell the nations about that! The battle's done, the victory's been won. There's joy, joy, joy in our hearts!'

How quickly they forgot their own dead.

The procession left the street at last, leaving Brother Pierce and his jubilant mob behind. Father Evans fell in beside Robin. 'I hope you can forgive them, Robin.' His head was bowed. 'I'm trying myself.'

'Are you succeeding?'

'No.'

'It's that much harder for us, Father. For me. I loved her, you know.'

'The rector told me how important she was to you. Still and all, that nude ride –'

'That's our way!'

'Okay, let's not get into that. Just know that it sure upset the Catholics. You oughtn't do things that violate the town ordinances.'

'We had a parade licence.'

'The nudity –'

Robin really didn't want to have an argument with Father Evans. 'I doubt if you'll see another Wild Hunt. This Covenstead will probably disband.'

'If I'm ever needed –'

'Thank you, Father.'

The procession straggled along, a bobbing line of lights, an occasional murmur of song. Up front the pallbearers were chanting quietly to keep themselves going. The Rock Coven was determined to carry her all the way. They were a heavy work team, building and maintaining roads on the estate, rooting stumps, making wattle and erecting cottages, hauling beams. Still, there was a weight in that box that must drag them down more by far than the heaviest stump.

As they marched they drew more and more people from their homes, until it seemed as if all the town that was not with Brother Pierce was in the procession.

'Are there any more candles?'

'Dad!'

'Connie called me. It's a terrible thing, son.'

Robin couldn't answer. His mother had come down from the house as well. She and Ivy were walking together just behind.

They entered the main gate of the estate, which had been thrown open for the occasion. 'Who was she, son, really?'

'She'd been coming to us for a long, long time. We belonged to her.'

The great old forest that separated the estate from Maywell was filled with the peace of nature. Some small creature screamed among the trees, and great wings swept away.

By the time they passed the house the procession was more tightly packed, in part because there were more people and in part because the Rock Coven, struggling at the front with the coffin, was slowing down.

The house was totally dark.

It was some little time before Robin saw Constance standing on the front porch. Around her the ravens clustered in unaccustomed silence. In her black cloak and hood she might have been a statue, faintly sinister in the light of the moon. She raised her head and Robin thought she might be about to speak. But then she came forward. She joined her people, and Robin was very glad.

The coveners had laid a way of hooded candles up the mountainside, each one carefully placed among stones to avoid the danger of fire. Even so, it was rough going, and not everybody was prepared for the journey. Even some of the town witches fell by the wayside. They joined others gathering in the fields, and as Robin negotiated the rough path he heard them beginning to sing together.

Ahead the Rock Coven struggled mightily with their burden.

When Robin reached the Fairy Stone, the coffin was already placed upon it. People made a ring of candles around it, which guttered in the wind, flickering reflections of the mourners in the polish of the casket. The witches formed a circle. Behind them the townspeople who had made it this far stood or sat.

A deep silence came. Far off the wind moaned, its voice echoing through all the Endless Mountains.

The moon stood bright and high amid the stars. Robin

347

looked up at it, and the living intensity of its gaze awed him. This night, he thought, the old moon is an eye into eternity.

CHAPTER 24
Requiem for a Witch

There had never before been a funeral like this in the Covenstead. In the deep silence there was a black flash of movement, then Tom jumped up and stood on the lid of the coffin.

His eyes were so fierce that Robin literally could not meet them for more than an instant. They burned green and they challenged, almost accused.

Constance Collier walked forward until she stood before the coffin, face-to-face with the huge, glaring creature that crouched upon it. The wind whipped her cloak. She spoke in a clear, soft voice, directly to Tom.

'O Great Irusan, King of the Cats, keeper of the doors of death, take this daughter of life safely through the shadowed abode. Keep her in your timeless kindness, lead her into the cleansing water. Smile upon the descent of the living, O Great God, as they go in thy lands of dark and laughter.'

She turned. 'Robin. Come here.'

He forced himself to approach her, and thus also the cat. Tom seemed to have become twice his normal size, the tips of his fur glowing blue, his claws digging into the lid of the coffin. 'We want you to invoke now, young man,' Constance said.

'Invoke?'

'Call Ama. The Dark Mother.'

Constance stood behind him, a trembling wraith, her breath rattling, her right hand steadily rustling the cloth of her cloak. The wind had been rising since they had arrived on the mountain. Now it seemed to gather itself and pour down upon them in a great, cold breath. Their candles spluttered and guttered out, the flames driven away by its enormous force.

Robin was not dressed for this; he was cold. Jeans and a sweater were never meant to keep out the breath of such things as were approaching this circle.

He searched his mind, but he could recall no familiar form for calling Ama. She was the aspect of the Goddess associated with empty fields and winter's waiting. She was also the mistress of secrets.

As best he could, he invented an invocation. 'I call to you, sterile Mother. I call to you, Ama of the empty fields. I call to you, mystery Mother. Take your daughter through Death's cold pleasure, lead her, gentle Mother, all the way to the Land of Summer.' His voice was snatched and harried by the wind. Without the candlelight the faces of those around him had been transformed by the moon, which hung more than half full, high over the mountains. Very faintly, from down in the valley, Robin could hear the others singing.

> 'Silver water of the sky
> Flow forever, flow forever
> Until I know why,
> Until I know why.'

The Song of Sorrows. It had not often been sung in this place.

Suddenly Father Evans began to speak. 'May I add something, Connie, on behalf of your visitors?'

'Of course, Al.'

'This is from Ecclesiastes. Take it as a message from my God to yours.' He bowed his head. 'In the day when the keepers of the house shall tremble, and the strong men shall bow themselves, and the grinders cease because they are few, and those that look out of the windows be darkened, and the doors shall be shut in the streets, when the sound of the grinding is low, and he shall rise up at the voice of the bird, and all the daughters of music shall be brought low:

'Also when they shall be afraid of that which is high, and fears shall be in the way, and the almond tree shall flourish, and the grasshopper shall be a burden, and desire shall fail: because man goeth to his long home, and the mourners go about the streets:

'Or even the silver cord be loosed, or the golden bowl be broken, or the pitcher be broken at the fountain, or the wheel broken at the cistern.

'Then shall the dust return to the earth as it was; and the spirit shall return to whom gave it.'

There was silence then, for a very long time.

Constance spoke again: 'Let us tell the story of the descent of the Goddess. Heed it well, for each of us shall go also upon that bourne.'

Always before Robin had heard this story in the joyous context of the Sabbats. He gave the opening: 'The Lord of the Flies, Godfather and Comforter, stood before the door into silence.'

All the witches responded: 'And the Lady came unto him, and sought the matter of the mystery of death; so she journeyed through the portal on behalf of those who had to die.'

'Strip thyself, Bejewelled Lady, for the cold is cold and thy bones are bones.'

Softly, gently, Tom began to howl. Only at the rarest of moments will a cat do this, in high sorrow and in the night.

Constance continued, her voice cast low beneath his keening cry. 'So she gave her clothing to the earth, and was bound with the memory of summer, and went thus with open eyes into the empty voice of the pit.

'She came before Death in the nakedness of her truth, and such was the beauty of her nakedness that Death knelt himself down, and lay at her feet as a gift the Sword of Changes.'

The witches sighed in unity with the wind, and one spoke for them all, 'Ours is the faith of the wind, ours the calling in the night.'

'Then Death kissed the feet of Summer, saying, "Blessed be the feet that brought you in the path of the Lord of Ice. Let me love thee, and warm myself in thee."'

The witches made a sound as of whispering snow.

'But Summer loved not the purple hour, and asked of him, why do you pin frost to my flowers?'

The witches were humming a wordless inner song. Behind them the townspeople glanced at each other in wonder, for they had never heard such a sound. High and yet vibrant, deep and yet full of laughter, and sorrowing with the sorrow we all know, but which is not named in any human language.

'"Lady," Death said, "I am helpless against the dropping web of time. All which comes to me, comes. And all which departs, departs. Lady, let me lie upon thee."'

The humming grew louder, merging with the cat's voice.

'The Lady said only, "I am Summer."'

'Then Death scourged her, and there were storms and ashes.'

The humming stopped. Tom crouched as if ready to spring at Constance's throat. She stood before him, her head high, the wind billowing her cloak.

'And she gave voice to her love in the fertile voice of the bee, and death was glad before her.'

'Now the mystery of mysteries: love death, ye who would find the portal of the moon, the door that leads back into life.'

All together: 'Upon us, O Summer, leave the five kisses of resurrection. Blessed be.'

Constance had thrown back her hood. 'Blessed be.' She glanced around. 'Cernnunos blows his horn this night, my children. Rocks, in the morning take her and bury her back in the mountains.'

'But the *Leannan* doesn't let us go beyond the Stone.'

'The law is lifted for this burial. She is wanted there.' She took Robin's hands in hers. 'You Vines, will you watch over her tonight?'

'I will,' Robin said. The other Vines joined him. They stood close together as the rest of the procession wound its way down among the rocks. Soon the last sound of the departing crowd was absorbed by the night.

All became silent but for the wind and the rustle of Tom puttering about in the dry brush. The coven joined hands.

It was not until Wisteria said in a soft voice, 'Look over by the rowan,' that Robin even thought of the fairy. But they had been here of course, observing everything. He saw them now, dark small shapes stealing forth from the great shrub. Their jackets and caps hardly reflected the moonlight at all.

Robin's heart began to pound. A chill swept his body. He reached out, and found the hands of other coveners waiting for his own.

The fairy came close, at least a dozen of them, pausing not ten feet in front of the coven. They had bows no more than a foot long, and arrows that looked insignificant to Robin's eyes. But he knew not to move an inch; those arrows were infamously lethal. Constance said that in the distant past they had killed mammoths with them.

The rustling grew louder.

The fairy smelled strong and sweet and nothing like human beings at all. Were they bearded or not? Young or old? He couldn't see.

Then there was a change. One moment the air was empty, the next a little woman was standing above the coffin. She shone in the moon, or perhaps she gave her own light. Robin looked upon her face, and saw in it such love and joy that he clapped like a delighted child, he could not help it.

Wisteria lifted shaking hands to her. She reached forward and touched Wisteria's fingers. Then the other Vines crowded close about the coffin, and each in turn was touched.

Close to her Robin could see the perfection of her body, the smooth, unearthly light of her skin. She came face-to-face with him. A thousand feelings roared through him: mad, lascivious passion, tender love, terror, lust, pleasure, laughter, all the wildest extremes of the heart.

She parted her lips and closed her eyes and raised her face to be kissed. He was shaking so badly he could hardly hold his lips open. He drew close to her, and into a scent that engaged his deepest, most private memories. In the single instant of that kiss he knew his whole *lang syne*, from the moment he had found Moom cracking walnuts in the forest to the awful night he had seen the bishop's men capture Marian, through the sad houses of all the years to now.

There was a rush of frowning forests and dances, and then the *Leannan* turned away from him and stepped off into the dark.

She seemed to go upward, and all eyes followed her. At first what they saw was incomprehensible. Then Grape screamed. Across the sky, enormous beyond understanding, blotting out the stars, were two enormous cat's eyes.

They glared until the witches hid their faces, and huddled like rabbits beneath a circling hawk.

It was some time before anybody moved or spoke. One by one, though, they looked up again.

They were alone with the night.

Robin was seething with an energy beyond anything he had ever felt before from even the most intense ritual. Around him the other coveners were the same, their eyes glowing with the light that had spread from the *Leannan*'s body.

He knew he had to act, or give up. 'Please,' he said, 'let's try to reach Amanda. Let's try the cone of power.'

Without a word of protest they made the circle. They were with him.

BOOK THREE

The Black Cat

Within that porch, across the way,
   I see two naked eyes this night;
Two eyes that neither shut nor blink,
   Searching my face with a green light.

But cats to me are very strange –
   I cannot sleep if one is near;
And though I'm sure I see those eyes
   I'm not so sure a body's there!

          – *William Henry Davis, 'The Cat'*

CHAPTER 25

The class of one sat before her teacher.

Mother Star of the Sea capered, her habit flying about her, wimple on the floor, naked wooden head bobbing, smile working as she darted in and out, pinching her student and scolding like a parrot.

Mandy was being pinched away by crumbs and bits. The worst part of it was how badly she missed herself!

'Somebody,' she wailed, 'somebody!'

'Will I do?' Bonnie Haver reappeared.

'Get me out of here! Somebody, please!'

Mother Star of the Sea rattled to attention. 'You vant out? Jawohl! Outenzee hellhole! Sure. You can be a ghost, you have that right. So, soul, take flight!'

Amazingly, Mandy was free! Blowing like a bit of pollen on the autumn wind, blowing through long black mountains.

Familiar mountains.

The Endless Mountains. And there was the Fairy Stone. Mandy's heart hurt to see the witches huddling together against the wind, and her own coffin.

It was high night in the Endless Mountains. Mandy had become one with the air, guttering the candles about the coffin, whistling through sweaters and under cloaks, caressing the ones she had loved and lost.

She was here, but she was helpless. So this was what ghosts were all about.

So close to her people and yet so separated, Mandy felt a desolation of loss. She could hardly stay still enough to touch her own clean coffin, much less return to the body that lay within. She slipped and eddied about while they prayed into the hollow darkness. She came close to Robin, and the grief in his face tormented her terribly.

'I love you,' she said, and the wind of her words made Robin shake in his sweater. 'I'm right here with you. Can't you hear me?'

He huddled into his clothing and lowered his head before the persistent gusts that were the spirit body of his lover.

She roared in anger because they could not see her, but only managed to put out all their candles. Then she quieted herself.

The night upon the mountain became as still as a bedroom. She heard their soft voices as they spoke encouragement to one another. How tired and beaten they were. Her heart suffered for them. She was so close, but so helpless.

In life we think of ghosts as rarities. We do not know that every rustle and squeak, every scratch of twig upon the screen or moan of wind along the eaves, is someone passing in the journeys of the night.

Mandy saw the first hopeful thing that had come to her since she died: Tom ran across the sky. His eyes were stars, his body the whole firmament, his tail the kink in the Milky Way.

Mandy wanted to hammer on her coffin, to dive into her body. Please! Let me go back to them!

As she flitted and blew along, she saw the *Leannan* coming across the mountain with her guards. As they crept into the rowan, Mandy had the odd thought that one could look on the fairy as a species that had developed a technology of the spiritual world, just as man has developed one of the physical. Using this magic, the Fairy Queen could rule here and also walk in the world of the dead. The science that supported her must be a strange and glorious thing – theories that were experienced as dreams; snatches of song that were powerful machines.

For her part, Mandy wasn't in control even of herself. One moment she could be close to the ground, the next high in the air. Then she might be in Robin's hair, then scudding among the stones.

Was the *Leannan* going to kiss him? She hoped so, that would help him! She began to plead on his behalf: 'Please, *Leannan* –'

Then she saw puppet grins nearby. 'No, not yet, don't take me back!'

'But Mandy, this is the perfect time.'

'You said I had the right!'

'You did, but you've used it up.'

No sooner could she smell the candy stink of the cottage than she felt herself falling down its liquorice chimney.

She was back in hell's schoolroom.

Robin heard the wind wailing, its voice echoing through the Endless Mountains to the north, and moaning south in the gentler reaches of the Peconics.

He couldn't even start the cone of power, so overcome he was by the *Leannan*'s kiss. Her loveliness had struck him temporarily dumb.

More than that, it had sent through him a current that seemed to have washed every cell of his flesh with new sensitivity. He looked out on the world from revised eyes, and the world was not the same. Beneath him the soil now seemed a surging flesh. Every stone was an eye, every blade of grass a nerve ending. Earth was not just alive, it was more than that: it was shockingly aware. It knew him as it knew every man, woman, and child, every tree and every animal that was resident upon its body. And it was watching them all, quietly, endlessly, like a mother dreaming over her children.

Wisteria began raising the cone of power, and Robin was grateful to her, to them all. Firm hands took his own. The coven was confident in their rituals; they had the balance of professionals. They raised the cone with a series of sounds, called the Chants of the Long Tones.

Wisteria started the whispery humming.

Soon other voices joined, each so familiar to Robin, each the voice of someone who was far more than a friend or even a lover. People who do real magic together become close in ways that words cannot say.

They chanted into the silence of the mountains, into the wind, into the living sky. Robin looked to the centre of the circle, just above the coffin, for the shimmering red moon the coven sometimes saw when they raised the cone of power, but only the darkness there returned his glance.

At first Mandy did not understand. What were those funny little joints her demons were putting together – wooden knuckles? They were building hands, arms, a new puppet.

Then she screamed, she pushed and struggled at the straps that bound her once again to her chair. Lying on teacher's desk was a gleaming, enamelled wooden head. And on that head was a caricature of her own face.

'I couldn't smile like that. I've never hated anybody enough!'

'Oh, no? We're *your* demons, Mandy. We make whatever serves your guilt. Do you think the real Mother Star of the Sea would be in hell – not that good woman, look!'

Suddenly there appeared in Mandy's lap a shimmering mirror, and in the mirror was an explosion of loveliness such as she had never imagined, smooth and cool and green, long hills and the perfect voice of joy, a young woman raising song. It hurt to see her, this real Mother Star of the Sea.

'She'll never know you chose her to be your demon.' The puppet Mother snapped her jaws. 'She's a saint! I'm your sin, not hers.'

Full of snide laughter, she and Bonnie assembled their new marionette. Mandy watched, slumped in her straps.

Mother Star of the Sea approached. She was wearing a surgeon's mask. In her hand was a hacksaw. 'I'm going to take out *your* brain and put it in *this* head.' Bonnie opened the hinged top of the noggin. 'Think of it, a miracle of modern science.'

Mandy looked desperately about. Bonnie was behind her now. Strong hands held her head steady. Mother Star of the Sea laid the saw against her temple.

This is just an illusion, she thought miserably. I don't have a body.

The first cut crunched through her hair. Then a prancing migraine – fire in her skull, nails being driven between bone and brain – made tears flow and her nose run. Her eyes rolled in agony with each rhythmic burr of the blade.

After this was done she was never, ever going to go back, she knew that. She was going to become some inconceivable part of hell.

She was dimly aware of three new schoolgirls at the front of the room testing the joints of the puppet, making it snap its jaw and rattle its fingers.

Somehow, in her agony and despair, she had an idea. What was the opposite of the demon's anger? Not love. They would jeer at that. It was compassion, rich, deep, abiding compassion. She could damp the fires of her own guilt with it.

She summoned up what strength lay at her command, she forced herself to think, to form words, to talk: 'I forgive you,' she said. 'I forgive all of you.'

The sawing stopped.

The girls playing with the puppet dropped it and stared at her, their eyes glassy.

Bonnie released her head.

'Damn,' Mother Star of the Sea said.

'I forgive you and I – I love you. I love you all no matter what you do to me.'

There was thick silence. Then Mother Star of the Sea burst out laughing. 'That old cliché! Love thy neighbour! What a load of crap!'

But she had thrown her saw to the floor.

'Unstrap me.'

Bonnie came dutifully forward. In a moment Mandy was free. She stood up, she turned.

There were tears in the eyes that watched her. These were all part of her, every one, no matter what else they had become.

'I'm sorry.' It was all she could say. To turn one's back on guilt is not difficult. After all, the deeds had been done, the wrongs committed. She understood how she had turned away from her mother and father when she could have embraced them in their need. But the past was the past, she did not need these demons to punish her. Mother and Dad were dead. Her best had not been good enough to heal their lives. Any effort she had made on their behalf would have failed. The lesson was, she should have tried.

The lesson had been learned. It was possible to melt the heat of Mother's anger with her own soul's spring. Compassion, acceptance of self. I did wrong, and now I have paid. She left the demon schoolroom.

Behind her there arose a great howling and clattering of puppet joints. She walked on, though. They were tragic and she could not help them, but she would never forget those parts of herself.

As she moved through the forest, the stumps shook and swayed and seemed to beckon her closer to their rotted sides.

Death never gave up.

'I am leaving you. I can't help you.'

Soon she came to the border of the terrible woods. Her heart pounded, her mind sang with her triumph.

The view before her was so vast, so extremely awesome, that she almost lost her balance.

Beyond the formless edge of the world of the dead a whole galaxy was revolving, its stars shining in colours too subtle and exquisite to be named. The light of stars is their voice; their language is the colour of that light.

The earth, a small green ball, lay in a tremendous, withered palm. Evil, huge beyond imagining.

I am the hand. The hand that takes.

All about wheeled other empires of stars. Hundreds of billions of fiery beings going in the orbits of their time, carrying planets and lives and rivers and storms.

The voices of the stars were raised in vespers, for the whole universe was at evening.

I am the hand.

But not only that. Death is also rebirth. In the very act of taking life, she returns it to the land. Spring flows from winter; the rose takes root in the rotted flesh of the shrew.

She may be the hand that takes, but she is also a little girl running along a lane between lilac hedges, beneath kindly old oaks, who converse as she passes new growth of purest green.

She could not see details of the earth below her. She did not even know what she might be standing on. She was just here, millions of miles out in space, lost.

Then she heard a familiar human sound, a vastly distant whisper of a chant.

The coven. But how could she hear them – from here the earth was no more than a pinprick in the night.

If she heard them, though, perhaps she might find them. Behind her was death, before her the whole gulf of space. She did the only thing she could: she jumped. She sailed out and down, trusting, hoping, that she would land in the right place.

There came a familiar girlish voice in her ear: 'I'm going right along with you. I'll be there waiting for you when you land. I am death, and you will not escape me.' The girl with the missing hand shot off, leaving a blazing track in the sky.

As she had at the moment of death, Mandy felt the awful, windless falling. She tried to will herself in the direction of the chant. There lay home.

High above the witches' circle a meteor passed in the sky, glowing across the face of the moon. They had been working for two hours, and still the cone had not appeared. Every few moments the Chant of the Long Tones was interrupted by the sound of Ivy clearing her throat. Grape was shivering. Earlier Wisteria had endured a coughing fit.

The wind pushed and challenged and demanded. Every time another frigid wave covered him Robin gasped, and for an instant forgot the chant.

But he tried, they all tried, and when it was right the chant was very, very strong, a sound that was wind and water, the grinding of the earth in the depths of a mine, the furious silence of the night-hunting bird.

Again Robin collected himself for another effort. He took a breath and closed his eyes, and expelled his tone from the bottom of his gut.

I am the hand.

The voice was not Mandy, but it was hovering just above the coffin. 'Who are you?' Grape whispered.

I am the hand that takes.

It was a freezing, bitter voice. Robin chanted on, filled with dread. This morning something had come into Vine's circle from the other world and displaced the wraith of Mandy. That other thing had been a little, maimed girl, who had jumped about the pentagram for a moment and then darted off again. Was she back?

The coveners chanted desperately, trying to keep the circle clear for Mandy.

A blizzard swarmed down the face of the mountain. Mandy's mind, her heart, her whole being, were now concentrated on one thing: find the circle.

Wisteria huddled in on herself. Grape and Ivy leaned against one another. Even clasped hands had grown cold. The moon had long ago crossed the top of the sky. There were no more meteors to bring an instant of wonder to this freezing effort.

The Chant of the Long Tones sank low, and still the spiral-ling cone of power did not appear.

Robin watched the sky for another sign and listened for another word.

But there was no sound, and the only lights in the sky were moon and stars.

Magic is just the physics of another reality, he told himself. It's perfectly believable. The physics would serve him when-ever he wanted it. But the cone of power just wouldn't appear. Magic. It encouraged you one moment, the next tried to convince you it didn't even exist.

If it is a physics, it is a damned contrary one.

Robin might have seen a cat crossing the sky. Might have seen a witch passing the moon. Might have heard a word.

It came again, very, very faint: 'Please . . .' That was all.

'Hey! Did anybody else hear that? Wasn't that Mandy's voice?'

'She's here.'

'Moom moom moom moom moom moom moom moooom!'

Oh yes I hear you yes I hear you down in hills in the dark. And I see you. This time, I haven't been sent and I can't be taken back. I got here on my own.

Mandy began to journey towards the faint glow that was the Vine Coven's circle. She was a wraith again, but now the circle directed her and helped her. The wind of her demons was not going to blow her aside.

Tom appeared ahead, switching his tail. When his eyes met Mandy's she came to a stop. She had never seen such menace. There was no way to move past that cat, not just yet.

After the one single, faint cry the witches had heard no more. They had tried and tried to chant it up again and finally exhausted themselves.

All of the Vine Coven but Robin slept. He sat rigid and still, facing the coffin through a rim of frozen tears.

Dawn was not far off. Robin stood up to gauge the time. Moonset had come and gone and only the stars lit the sky. He put his hand on the lid of the coffin, looked down at the constellation reflected in the wood. Ursa Major. The Great Bear, symbol of feminine courage.

The eastern sky was glowing now, just a little.

Robin wondered how he would face the day. Or the Vines, when they woke up all stiff and grumpy from their freezing vigil, and remembered how hard they had tried, and how completely they had failed.

A sound from the coffin startled him profoundly. He lifted his hand as if the lid were hot. It came again, louder. Of all the things it sounded like – a rattle, a mutter of thunder, gargling – it sounded most like a fart.

Robin's fingers went to the latches. He thought something must be going wrong with the body. He opened the coffin.

In the thin light he saw her, clear and pure, lying in her rumpled silk suit, her feet in gleaming Gucci pumps. But her face – he was shattered by its beauty. That such a creature could be a mere human seemed beyond possibility. A great, rasping sob escaped him.

If love killed, let it kill him now. Maybe they would be reunited in death.

She sighed then, and he realized what all the noises were – corpse gas.

With a thousand regrets he closed the lid and turned away. He was walking towards the rowan tree when a movement in its shadows startled him. Then he realized that the fairy had returned. All around they stood, and not five or six, but dozens and dozens of them, the men in black jackets, women in dark green gowns, and children everywhere, wee mischievous creatures darting about among their parents.

There were more than dozens – he could see them even on the far ridges, lining the naked cliffs like dark little clumps of shrub.

Come to do her honour, in some secret dawn ceremony of their own. Not even Constance had seen a fairy funeral. Who knew what their rituals were?

The coffin shifted. All around him the fairy clapped and laughed.

Robin knew, then, that this was not a funeral.

He grew afraid. The whole of the mystery had settled on this place and he had not even known it was coming. A wave of energy, tingling and electric, set all of his hairs to singing. He shuddered and turned around.

The coffin was still closed. But then thunder blasted in Robin's throat, a roar of astonished joy: sitting upon it was Amanda Walker.

He fell to his knees, he could not speak, could hardly bear to look at her. His mind didn't whirl with thoughts or fill with glee. On the contrary, he went quiet inside.

He heard a scrape as she came down from the coffin. 'Robin?'

A seizure took him. There was nothing he could do to avoid toppling forward. His fists came up to his chest, a sound between a grunt and a groan issued from between helplessly clenched teeth. He knew all that was happening, but from a distance, as if it were occurring on a stage.

She crouched down in front of him and took his face in her hands. Her touch was as wonderfully alive as the *Leannan*'s. He wanted to speak, but he couldn't. 'I'm here,' she said.

His emotions burst forth in him. Then he lifted his head and shouted glory. All around him the fairy were singing, a sound like the tumbling of small water.

Wisteria awoke. She smiled, and kept on smiling.

Then Ivy opened her eyes. When she saw Mandy she

screamed loud enough to rattle the mountains all the way to Pennsylvania.

That woke everybody else up, all except Grape. In the excitement they did not notice that she remained huddled where she was.

Amanda embraced them, one after the other, and after she had held them, each was sure that she or he felt noticeably warmer. When she slipped her hand into Robin's, there stirred in him the very laud of gladness. 'Let's go down,' Amanda said. 'We have to break the grief of the others as soon as we can.'

It was not until they started forward that Ivy noticed Grape. 'Robin, help me. If you can believe it, Grape's still asleep.'

'No,' Amanda said. 'I'm afraid she's dead.' Robin looked into Amanda's eyes, but only for an instant. There was no way to describe them. Simply put, they were terrifying.

'She's not dead, Amanda, she's just – Grape? Grape!'

The corpse fell over. It was already cold and stiff. Suddenly the fairy were all around. One of them did something to Robin's knee and made him fall back away from Grape.

'Let them take her.'

'She – why did she die?'

'She gave herself in return for me. Death cannot be cheated.'

Robin went close to Amanda. He wanted to kiss her, but he dared not, even though she seemed as sweet as woman-flesh could be. Light was hesitating in the sky when the coven started for the village. Already the east was yellow-green, Saturn a lantern in the last blue of night. As they walked, the fairy put Grape into the coffin that had been Amanda's and carried her off into the depths of the hills.

'Honour her, and be glad for her,' Amanda said.

On their way down the mountain a great happiness came upon them all and they began to sing.

'With a hey! and the sun.
With a hey! and the sun.
We go merry, we go gay,
We go in morning's way!'

Tom watched, with a fury of love in his green eyes. He lay where the night still lingered in the western sky.

His gaze shifted away from the triumphant procession, moving past the edge of the Collier estate and into the pre-dawn town. It went to a certain trailer behind a certain tabernacle and rested upon an object in the pyjama pocket of sleeping Brother Pierce. That object held the key to the end of the drama, the last confrontation.

There was movement in the pocket. Somebody besides Amanda had used the chant as a beacon. The owner of the hand had also returned. As nothing of her physical body remained but the hand itself, she was concentrating all her considerable energy there.

Already she was learning to use the old, dead flesh. Slowly, persistently, the withered, dead hand clutched and opened, then clutched again.

Brother Pierce slept on.

The hand opened. The hand clutched. As love had given Amanda new life, so hate was giving it to the hand. If hate had been visible, it would have appeared in the form of a murdered girl in a blue dress.

Or Abadon, the scorpion truth of Revelation.

I am the hand, the hand that takes.

The visible part, lying in the preacher's pocket, opened and clutched, opened and clutched, with a dry, crackling sound. Then it touched the preacher, caressed him.

It did not wake him, but it made him sigh.

CHAPTER 26

'You sure you want this thing open?'

Brother Pierce was getting exasperated with the funeral director. That question had come at least six times over the last half hour. 'His brothers and sisters in Christ want to say good-bye to him.'

'But I can't do anything with him.'

The man just would not see the point. 'All of that business with wax and face powder and whatnot – we don't hold with that.'

'I'll have to break his arms. You can't leave those fists like that, up against the face.'

'You'll do no such thing! Leave him just like he is.'

'Now, look here, Brother Pierce, I've got a reputation to uphold. I am not going to have a poor burned man go out of here for a viewing in that condition! He even smells burnt. No, sir, it's just unthinkable.'

Brother Pierce regarded Fred Harris. Your typical small-town businessman. Episcopalian. Daughter a witch. Probably a witch lover himself. Too bad he was the only funeral director in Maywell. 'I will have people *see* what those witches do to a good Christian soul! I will have them *see!*' The poor man had suffered terribly. Let it be a testament, let it be for a reason.

Harris sighed. 'The death was ruled accidental. If he hadn't had that gasoline –'

'You were not there. You did not witness –' Brother Pierce stopped himself. He was just about to say too much. So far nobody knew exactly who had been out there with Turner. The witches hadn't managed to give the sheriff's office any particularly clear descriptions. Simon had not needed to swear his own men to secrecy. The little community of the Tabernacle could be trusted to cling together in any trouble. He looked into the undertaker's suspicious eyes and prayed silently that the Lord might flood his starving soul with so much grace that he would lose his hatred of good Christian people. What a blessing it would be to see the stone fall away from the tomb of his heart, and Christ rise within as the lily in the spring.

Harris gave him a sharp, appraising look. Simon reached into his pocket, grasped the hand. It was there to remind him that he was full of sin, and for all his prayers no better than the worst sinner himself. That poor little girl's murder could never be atoned, but even so, he was determined to do only good with his life. Afterwards he would be glad to go to the hell he so richly deserved. 'We love you, Brother Harris, and we want your funeral home to have a fine reputation. But we also love Brother Turner and we cannot have communion with his martyrdom if it is hidden in makeup.'

Harris touched the coffin gingerly, with a respect that had not been there a moment ago, Simon thought. 'Even so, it's leaving here closed, Brother Pierce. What you do with it once you get it to your church is your business, I guess.' With that he lowered the lid on the staring, blackened corpse.

Brother Pierce stayed right with the coffin. He could honour the dead at least by constant attendance.

Harris's two assistants rolled the coffin into the funeral home's Cadillac hearse. Simon hated hearses, which were as black and lonely as the whole big sky. He kept his fist closed around the hand. Over the years the guilt it brought him had ceased to be a torture and become a comfort. When his punishment finally came, he would welcome it. The bottom of the pit would be a relief.

Riding towards the Tabernacle, his mind returned to

the accident. That fire had just jumped at poor Turner. Enveloped him. He saw it again, red and ugly, spreading all over the man. He saw the agony on Turner's face, the astonishment, the terror, most of all the sadness.

There came to Simon a shuddering thought. Wasn't it Turner who had first picked up the mandrake? Of course, yes. Turner. He must have been infected by the evil spell in it.

Sweat began to tickle Simon's neck. He clutched and rubbed at the hand. Could spells travel, jump across that long grey sky, maybe, and settle in the Tabernacle?

In his mind he saw flames leaping from every window of his church, and heard the hiss of the fire wind and the dreadful screams of his beloved people trapped inside. A gigantic, misshapen mandrake leaned in against the shaking, bulging door, holding it closed against the congregation.

'Brother Pierce!'

'Wha – what?'

'Are you all right?'

'Of course.'

They rode on. Simon was shaking, covered with sweat. What had he done to cause them to call out? Had he screamed, or maybe moaned? Yes, maybe that. He must have moaned.

'I feel such grief for my brother.'

'I'm sorry for you.'

Simon was very relieved when they reached the Tabernacle. He watched them take the coffin out of the hearse and roll it on the catafalque through the big double doors at the back. 'That's fine. I can take it from here.'

When they finally drove away, he could not have been more glad.

He looked fondly around the Tabernacle, the rows of pews he had bought from the closed Presbyterian church in Compton, the pulpit that had been a conference-room lectern, bought for eleven dollars at the Maywell Motel fire sale, the organ they had got full price from Wurlitzer, and the paint and the simulated stained glass and all the evidence everywhere of the hard work of the Lord's people.

No images, unless you counted the empty cross at the front. 'We keep his portrait in our hearts, brothers and sisters, that is the beginning and end of the images of the Lord.'

The Tabernacle was cold. He checked his watch. An hour to go before the funeral. He went to the thermostat and turned it up to seventy. By the time people arrived it would be comfortable enough. There was no reason for the oil bill to go above four hundred a month in autumn, not with all the body heat the congregation generated.

He rolled the catafalque to the front of the Tabernacle. His funerals were always simple, needing essentially no preparation. Simon required contributions to the Tabernacle in lieu of sending flowers, so there were no wreaths to worry about. For a moment he clasped his hands and thought of God sitting on his throne in heaven. God in heaven. 'O Lord, let me do right by you. Please, I love you so much.' He bowed his head. 'I'm sorry, Lord, to ask for help. I know I'm dirty in your eyes, but I'm still trying down here. Don't help me, but help my people. Give them the strength they need to get rid of the witches.'

The hand seemed almost to warm as he prayed. It helped him so much. Without it he'd be lost. He'd never know what moves to make. The hand was his guide.

He remembered it milky white, dangling from her smooth arm, the fingers tapering, nails bitten and lined with dirt from play. She was a picture, so pretty. She had come on to him, had snapped her gum and run her tongue along her teeth, and given him that steady, godless gaze.

If only he hadn't been so darned sad, so alone. When she snuggled close, he had embraced her right there and then in the middle of the foster-home rec room, and caressed her lank hair, and looked into her round blue eyes. 'Get me out of here,' she had murmured. 'It's such a dump.'

'I can't, hon, I'm just a social worker.' She had raised her face to him, and he had thought perhaps she was an angel, despite the chewing gum.

'Adopt me, Simon,' she had whispered.

'Oh, hon, I can't, I haven't got the money to raise a girl proper.'

'Simon, on the books I'd be your daughter, but I'd really be your wife.'

He remembered the smell of her breath, deep-sweet and juicy.

She had done things to him, things that felt so good he was as if tied in that chair. Never had he known the touch of such beauty. He had thought he was dying it was so good.

O Lord, I am Thy servant, and Thou art the kingdom and the power and the glory!

Afterward he just got so darn mad at her, she had damned his soul with those pretty white hands. She laughed at him and tossed her head like a little filly, and he took her by the neck and crushed the gristle of her windpipe, and all of a sudden her cream-perfect face was tight and blue.

Oh, God, he hadn't been able to get her breathing. Her throat was purple where his hands had been and she grabbed at it and her eyes rolled and she died right there and then.

He had tried to blow air into her lungs, to give her artificial respiration, but she wouldn't come back to life, so he was faced with this dead body.

'Lord, please, I've got to stop thinking about it!' If this kept up, he was sure to start hitting the bottle he kept in his trailer. It was less than half an hour before the congregation would start to arrive. Maybe one good drink would clear his head.

He went back to his trailer. Even though he usually didn't drink much, over the years the back of the trailer had become crowded with bottles. He couldn't very well throw them away.

Not that he pretended to be a teetotaller. But a preacher ought to be upright. So he kept his liquor to himself and followed even the smallest drink with a couple of peppermint Certs.

The opening of a fresh bottle was always a small festivity. He drank good whiskey. Twelve years old, smooth as a bunny's ears. 'Lord,' he said as always, 'forgive me what I cannot help.' He took a fair pull. Soon an echo of contentment was spreading through his body. 'Thank you, O Lord, for this gift.' He knelt on the floor of his trailer. 'Thank you for this kindness.'

Here he was, a preacher thanking Jesus for liquor. Now, there was something that would make a real man of God laugh out loud.

He lay back on his bed, reminding himself once again to change the sheets. He didn't have a maid – he never allowed people in here.

He took out the hand. It lay on his palm, small and complex, a thing of clutching angles. A cut-off thing. And yet, not cut off. In a way still alive.

Probably death was just nothing. The end. Sure there was a God, but God didn't give much of a damn. God was so very far away. Heaven was the other side of the sky, and the sky was too damn big to ever cross.

He looked quickly at the hand. Hadn't it moved just then, just when he thought how far away heaven was?

Sometimes he thought the hand could whisper to him.

He should have given her the knife and showed her how to cut a man's neck so the blood spurted out in a pulsating stream, and she'd move his hair aside and turn his head a little and – zip. She would have done it. She would have done anything for him.

'I am destruction.'

He was going to give them one hell of a funeral. Let's see,

how many Turners were there? Betty and – what – two kids? Three of 'em altogether. More than enough grief there for a fine show.

A change in the way the tight brown leather of the hand reflected the light startled him. He looked at it again. Was there subtle movement, or was that just the light flickering?

He put the hand down on the floor beside his cot and got the Bible from underneath. He'd do readings, the reference to death in Numbers, then the 116th Psalm, then the last and most important part, the Abadon passage from Revelation 9. The funeral would then wind its way down to the town graveyard just the other side of the Collier estate.

He was going to give fire to the faint of heart, he was going to burn wickedness in white heat.

He was going to burn the wickedness of the harlot in the hell of the flames, and at last destroy the abomination of the earth that infected this town and was tearing as a long-nailed claw tears at its God-fearing heart.

Another movement made him look again at the hand. What he saw shocked him. Always it had been closed. The thing was dry. And yet, as a flower of night, it had opened. He touched it in wonder, then picked it up. It was as stiff open as it had been closed.

He kissed the palm.

For a long time he lay inhaling its dry, faintly organic odour, remembering the salt-sweet smell of it in life, suffering an agony of helpless regret.

'Brother?'

He stuffed the hand in his pocket as he leaped off his cot. Had so much time passed? 'I'm sorry, Sister Winifred. I was resting in preparation for the service. I must have dropped off.' He smoothed back his hair, splashed some water on his face, and ate his Certs while Sister Winifred waited at the door of the trailer.

She had a look of quiet happiness about her. 'Brother,' she said as they went towards the Tabernacle, 'is there any provision we can make for those standing in the parking lot?'

He stopped. 'Wait a minute? Are you telling me I've got an overflow crowd?'

She nodded, at once pleased and solemn, remembering the nature of the occasion. Brother Pierce was careful to hide his own elation. One good thing about this witch business was that it was really an inspiration to the people. A man had lost his life, but the Lord willing, his sacrifice would not have been in vain.

'Tell you what you do, Sister. You stick that PA from the movie projector out on the front stoop. And leave the doors open. They'll hear us. They will hear the Word of the Lord.'

Shyly, and so quickly that he could hardly notice, she touched the bulge of the hand in his pocket. He was shocked, and drew back. There was on her face a knowing sort of a smile. 'Praise the Lord,' she whispered. Did she think it was his member?

The light of the packed Tabernacle washed him with energy. He was glad to see how intense those faces were today, and the sincerity in the tears. It humbled him to feel every stare upon himself when he mounted his pulpit.

He looked from face to face, nodding to the weeping Turner family. For the moment the coffin was closed. He would do the revelation after his first reading. 'Now we are gathered here to seek in the Kingdom of God for succour, my beloved brothers and sisters, for He who cherishes us shall now comfort us in our loss.'

'Oh, yes,' from a few mouths.

'For a man is dead, and he was a good man! Yes, he was a good man!'

'Oh, yes!'

'And this man was killed by the spell of the mandrake, a spell woven by witches against us, and he was burned in the fire of their evil hearts!'

'Oh, yes!'

379

'I tell you this: we will avenge his death, for the people of the Lord will not let the evil of witchcraft fester among them, growing out of all proportion as cancer grows, for in this congregation we have the power of His holy name, we have the cure for the cancer of evil!'

'We have the cure!'

'I recall from the Good Book, from the chapter of the Numbers where God spoke out of the mouth of Balak, and said, "Who can count the dust of Jacob, and the number of the fourth part of Israel? Let me die the death of the righteous, and let my last end be like his!" And I say to you, I say to you, I would join him in a minute if I thought it would bring us peace from the torment of these witches! Oh, these spellbinders and these devils are riding the horses of hell in our streets, and burning the fathers of our houses, for they are the very fire of evil!'

'Praise the Lord, praise His Name!'

'Now I am going to ask that you give one another the kiss of peace, and I am going to open this coffin, and I tell you this, Betty Turner, you are to come up here and embrace your husband, and each of your children will do it, too, for you must see and remember, all of you, the work of the dread hand of Satan, and bid good-bye to our lost brother.'

Something moved in his pocket. And in his mind he thought he heard whispered approval. The hand of the little girl, cut off for a lot of reasons. He told himself that he did it to prevent identification.

No, he remembered too well the work of the knife. It had been pleasure that animated him, a steaming pile of rotted pleasure, to take a part of her softness . . .

It was not soft now. It had become an instrument of the Lord's work. Praise be the hand, may it bring him his punishment in its curled, brown fingers.

He went down to the catafalque. The lid of the coffin opened smoothly. He could sense people craning to see, could hear the gasps, the stifled screams. Brother Turner lay, a blackened hulk of a thing, his head scorched bald, his carbonized fists raised before his chest. His eyes were half closed, his lips parted. He had died of suffocation, from seared lungs.

'The beautiful naked witch will burn as he has burned, in the slow fire of purification!'

It was all in planning, too. Simon did not make idle threats. He would at once avenge the lost brother and cleanse for them the souls of the witches.

Tomorrow night he would burn their elegant red brick devil-house with its fine white columns, the kind of house *exactly* that the filthy scum rich lived in back in Houston. Then he would take that woman of theirs, the one with the soft white hands and the flowing hair, the one who had abominated the streets of Maywell with her naked ride, and he would tie her up in her nakedness and burn her before the witness of his people.

Then he would say to the witches, disband. Be gone. God does not want you here.

The hand touched him so intimately that it almost made him cry out again, as it had so long ago in Houston.

'Betty Turner, come forward and embrace your husband!'

'Oh, please, I – we just can't!'

'You can and you must, for it is the will of God! I call on the rest of you, help her and her children to take courage! Come forward and embrace your brother, every one of you, embrace him and touch his agonized flesh and know what evil the witches do to the body of the lamb!'

Sister Winifred was the first to go. That was a plucky lady. She jerked back when she laid her cheek against the dead face and the dried crackling pricked her. Moving up and down the aisle, Simon exhorted.

'Here is the patience of the saints: here are they that keep the commandments of God and the faith of Jesus! Help them now, give them strength!'

The weeping of the Turner family filled the Tabernacle, that and the shuffling of the faithful up to the coffin.

'And I heard a voice from heaven saying unto me, Write, Blessed are the dead which die in the Lord from henceforth: Yea, saith the Spirit, that they may rest from their labours; and their works do follow them.'

Betty Turner clapped her hands to her face. 'Close it,' she wailed, 'please close it!'

'And I looked, and behold a white cloud, and upon the cloud one sat like unto the Son of man, having on his head a golden crown, and in his hand a sharp sickle.'

Some of the men began to push the open coffin towards the rear of the church so that more could embrace the dead saint.

'And another angel came out from the altar, which had power over fire; and cried with a loud cry to him that had the sharp sickle, saying, Thrust in thy sharp sickle, and gather the clusters of the vine of the earth; for her grapes are fully ripe.'

There began among the congregation soft clapping. Simon nodded to Winifred, who started the organ going, very low, 'Gather at the River.' Best to stick to the simple, familiar songs, Brother Pierce always maintained. That was the way into the most hearts and souls.

He was pleased with the strength of feeling in the congregation.

This funeral was going to give the men the courage they needed tomorrow night. It would take more than his pitiful sermonizing to inspire those men to face the witches again.

Harris signalled from the door. He was waiting with his hearse; the town graveyard closed at dusk.

'We will recite Psalm 116, brothers and sisters, as we go into the outer darkness, to return the flesh to the dust of the earth.'

He began the psalm.

'I love the Lord, because he hath heard my voice and my supplications.'

They put the coffin in the hearse. Simon rode in the funeral car with the Turners. Betty, a handsome woman, was flushed with her grief, her breasts heaving rhythmically beneath her black dress, her eye shadow running down her face. She had a golden harlot of a daughter, and a son of freckles and sandy hair, whose face shone with faith despite his grief. Simon read as the car moved off towards the graveyard.

'The sorrows of death compassed me, and the pains of hell got hold upon me: I found trouble and sorrow.'

Betty Turner leaned her head against Simon's shoulder. 'I'm sorry I couldn't hug him. But I just couldn't, and now I'll never see him again.'

Simon covered her hand with his.

'The Lord preserveth the simple: I was brought low, and he helped me.

'Return unto thy rest, O my soul; for the Lord hath dealt bountifully with thee.'

Betty Turner drew a ragged breath. Her daughter's eyes filmed. 'Now, don't start in again, honey,' Betty said. 'You'll start me, too.'

'Take comfort in the Word of the Lord,' Simon said. 'This is His Word also. "Precious in the sight of the Lord is the death of his saints." Your husband was a saint, my dear sister. A saint!'

The son's face clouded. Simon assumed he was remembering the truth of their private misery. That life with Turner had been miserable Simon had no doubt. Turner was a drunken, red-faced roach of a man with his hair full of grease, mean as a hog and twice as fat.

'Let Israel now say that his mercy endureth forever.'

'Brother Pierce,' the daughter asked, 'do you know the whole Bible?'

Simon smiled. It was such a simple, pure question, from

that darling, soft child. How could lips be so red, or eyes so blue, or hands so very smooth? He fought the ravening that he felt, and forced his face to gentleness.

The hand stirred.

He twisted and squirmed, but it remained close against him. He forced himself to answer the girl's question. 'I know about half. Every day I learn a new verse.'

'Is there anything,' the boy asked, 'that can make us proud of Dad?'

'Willy!'

'Sorry, Mom.'

'There is a verse, son, from the 119th Psalm. It goes like this. "This is my comfort in my affliction: for thy word hath quickened me. The proud have held me greatly in derision: yet I have not declined from thy law. I remembered thy judgments of old, O Lord, and have comforted myself." So we must all do the same, son.'

The boy thought about this. 'Can I watch,' he asked at last, 'when you burn the witch?'

'Oh, hush, now! Whoever said he was going to do such a thing?'

Simon felt himself grow cold. He had said little of his ideas, yet here they were coming out of the mouth of a child. There must be a lot of whispering going through the congregation. Sometimes he wondered who the leader was – himself or the intangible spirit of the group. 'Do not admonish your son, Sister Turner, for a child might speak in the tongue of the Lord.'

When the car stopped, dusk was already far advanced. Betty Turner sank back into her seat. 'I just don't know how I'm going to get through this! I dread the burial.' She looked at Simon with stricken eyes. 'There's no way you could call him a good man. He drank. He beat us up. He was lazy and he two-timed me. He left us poor. But he was a person.' She glanced out the rear window, towards the sunlight that still clung to the cliffs of Stone Mountain.

'Those witches killed him just when he was trying hardest to get himself saved. You see, that man wanted to live in the Lord. But the flesh is weak!'

She and her son and daughter, tears in their eyes, left the funeral car and walked towards the gravesite behind the coffin of the dead father.

Easily a hundred cars had come. Brother Pierce went to the grave, which had been lined with green artificial turf by Harris's people, and provided with a sling for the coffin. Simon saw that he had the biggest graveside turnout in the history of the Tabernacle. That was wonderful, but it meant that there might be spies in among the crowd, witches and people sent by the sheriff and such.

Very well. He would not threaten anybody, nor even mention the vision he was having, of that young naked-rider witch lying in the midst of a fire, and she can't get away, and she is burning and her screams are pealing through the night. And for just a few minutes, Simon is happy. He doesn't even need the hand. And it is because for these few minutes he is vanquishing the sin of that poor misguided girl.

He could only be at peace, he decided, when he was sending a soul to heaven.

She had shone in the night like a goddess, had Amanda of the long flowing hair. Of course it was her. He had noticed that hair when she visited the Tabernacle with her insane uncle. Oh, yes. The uncle was dead now, dead in that coffin they had taken from his house.

The deputy sheriff had said it was her in the coffin, but he was misled. She was young and perfect. No, it was him. If anybody were to dig up that coffin, they would find the old whoremaster of a scientist in it.

Simon stood in the thickening dark, among the dense crowd. The coffin was behind him, ready to be lowered into the grave. Betty Turner stood on his right, her daughter on his left, the son beside the daughter. Simon began reciting the familiar lines of Genesis 3:

'In the sweat of thy face shalt thou eat bread, till thou return unto the ground; for out of it wast thou taken: for dust thou art, and unto dust shalt thou return.'

He paused. The hand felt warm now, and heavier than it had been in years. It felt alive. He glanced down, but the bulge in his pocket was the same as ever. Best to put it down to nervousness and forget it. The witches had him spooked.

'Everybody knows why we are here. We are here to bury one of our own. And we are here to make a statement that those witches must not forget. We know you, and we burn with hatred for the evil that is in you, sons and daughters of Satan. For there is written upon your foreheads, "And they had tails like unto scorpions, and there were stings in their tails. And they had a king over them, which is the angel of the bottomless pit, whose name is Abadon."' He pointed past the tall shadow of the burial mound, towards the darkening mountain.

He remained silent, pointing.

Let the spies guess what it meant. His own people knew. It meant tomorrow night and fire.

He flipped the lever that set the coffin to lowering, then thrust into his pocket to reassure himself that there was nothing genuinely wrong with the hand.

Whereupon it twined its warm, living fingers in his own.

CHAPTER 27

On her way down the mountainside Amanda had become aware for the first time of the density of flesh. Every muscle and joint was stiff. The easy shorthand of movement she had enjoyed in the other world was replaced by a weighty crawling that she found most unnatural. Physical life was an astonishing limitation. She had never understood before the real effect of flesh on the soul, to stifle it in thick dying folds.

They had to carry her the final distance to the house. She had slept deeply, without dreaming. She was awakened by the whisper of the sun's return. She could hear its light sweeping into the room. It poured across the floor, yellowing the damask curtains of the bed. She slipped from beneath the covers and parted the curtains, letting in the golden haze.

The quality of the light reminded her of where she had been and, above all, what she had learned. The whole secret carnival paraded in her mind's eye. It was impossibly beautiful, a series of images acutely charged with meaning. There were the terrors, Bonnie and the demon-girl Abadon, and of course Mother Star of the Sea. There were also her two fleeting moments of heaven, and in retrospect they had far more impact on her than did her long journey through her own guilt. Her few moments in the old backyard of her childhood were suffused in memory with the richest light that could be imagined, a light that illuminated both physically and emotionally. To know that she had left this light caused her the most intense suffering. She twisted and turned in the bed, experiencing her body as a tangle of iron chains.

Then there was that short flash of Mother Star of the Sea's real fate, her own heaven. Hidden in her had been a great and compassionate spirit, trying by sheer strength of will to save the souls of the girls she was teaching. Did she know that she had become their demon, the arbiter of their guilt?

Yes, she knew, and upon that knowledge rested the palace of her happiness. For she also knew that she provided them with a safe means of working through the sour material of conscience after death. They used their memories of their stern, uncompromising teacher when they died to cleanse their souls for heaven. Because they had her, their work went quickly. To give them this enormous blessing, she had sacrificed love on earth and accepted a lonely death.

She understood the silence of Lazarus. How could you make voice from the air of so dun a world as this, after heaven? And she had seen only the edges, not the whole light of it. She felt actual physical pain, as if the air were being crushed by very longing from her lungs, and her blood boiling with a need beyond addiction.

She wanted nothing so much as to tighten into a little knotted ball and wait until she could return.

A shadow bulged in the canopy above her. 'Tom?'

He didn't stir. Nor did he purr. She found him awesome now, having seen him out of disguise. She wished she could thank him, but she had no idea how. She could hardly give him, say, a catnip mouse.

She looked down at her own flushed nakedness. It might be heavy and coarse, but she could still love this body of hers. Her blood sang in her veins, her skin thrilled at the simple contact of the air. She touched her own thigh, sensing the electricity of the contact between flesh and flesh.

There was also something else, a new and more objective awareness of the world around her. She saw the Covenstead as a tiny eccentricity of life, a final refuge of magical thinking. In her own mind she could see the blue stretches of reason and the bright shapes that defined the inner realm of her magic. She had acquired access to more of her mind than she had previously known. Her attention rushed into this vast new space. In it she saw Constance, who looked up at her with hollow, awestruck eyes. Instantly she *knew* Constance. Her knowledge was not verbal, but it was total. The experience had a powerful emotional impact on her. Without being able to say how, she understood the hidden meaning of this tragic and enigmatic figure.

Constance stared at her, and she was shocked to realize that this was a shared experience. They were somehow linked. Then Amanda saw Ivy, then Kate, then Robin. His love poured out of his eyes, a perfumed glow. He was coming towards this room, bringing his innocence and his helplessness. She wanted to cherish and protect him. But for Constance, none of them were aware of her careful scrutiny. Their attentions were not strong enough to enable them to see by this other light.

Outside the bed there was a small voice. 'Amanda?'

She pushed back the covers and raised her head into the full light of the sun. Beside her bed stood Robin, just as she had known he would. Instantly she knew what troubled him. Her heart opened to him. 'Look at me,' she said.

He raised his eyes. His sense of rejection was easy to read. After his initial jubilation at her return, he had begun to see her as unreachably strange. There was nothing she could do but show him that she valued him and needed him. 'Please,' she said, 'kiss me.'

A peck.

So he was not so much awed as angry. 'Robin?'

'Your breakfast is ready.'

She got out of the bed and put on her robe, which she found neatly folded across the back of the big blue chair. 'Robin, I love you.'

'Thank you. I love you, too. We all do.'

She felt a sharpness within her, a taste of salt. 'I mean I

love *you*.' She looked at him. 'Holly King.' Did he know how long was their association, through how many lives they had danced together? No, not really. He had been told, but his awareness lay at the side of his mind, shrouded in dark curtains of doubt and confusion. The trouble with reason is that it is only one part of the mind. In him, as in all of them except Constance, it was a great, central bulk of a thing, condemning them to perceiving only the linear and the expected.

She saw that mankind was exactly like the dinosaurs. The reptiles had chosen physical overgrowth at the expense of all other development and so had perished. So also mankind, since the beginning of recorded history, has been crushing all parts of the mind except the reason, until this excessive mental growth threatens him with extinction.

Reason is useful for building buildings, but it cannot build a happy life, nor enable a human being to see the sacredness or the richness of the earth. It cannot allow him to feel with his own blood just how painful it is to hurt the land. We live in maya, the world of illusion. There is no need for most of what we have, not for all these transformations of material that we have accomplished.

We have built a civilization that is exactly like a poison in the earth, or a viral growth, or an exploding cancer.

Amanda saw it all so clearly, and as well that the Covenstead might be tiny – just a few people, after all – but because it stood against this terrible, fundamental human mistake, it was incredibly important. May the idea of the Covenstead, rich and open and unchained by the hungers of the consuming society, spread through the world, freeing man from his own mind, and the terrible hypnosis that is going to extinguish the species if it is not broken soon.

'Amanda!'

Robin's voice interrupted her. She was breathing hard, staring. 'Sorry. I'm fine. I was in another world.'

Slumping in his black sweatshirt and faded jeans, his

muddy working boots, he could not have looked more forlorn. 'I'm sure.'

'No, I don't mean – oh, Robin, I was preoccupied.' How could she tell him what wonders she now perceived? The mists had lifted from her vision. To her, people had been revealed as magic architectures of almost unbelievable beauty, and him especially.

She went to him, gathered his unresponsive body in her arms. 'Please kiss me.' She opened her lips and waited, remembering the hungry passion of the kisses they had traded at the culmination of the Wild Hunt.

He held her stiffly.

'I'm only a person, Robin.'

'I know that. It's just that – I saw you –'

She put her finger over his lips. 'You don't know what you saw.'

'The hell I don't. I saw you dead!'

What could she do to bring him back to her? Nobody could be natural and at ease with a miracle.

She realized, as the strengthening sunlight set her blood to racing, that they were all going to react much the same way. 'The last thing I need is worship. I'm still me, Robin. And I love you exactly as I did before. Or no, that's a lie.'

'I'm sure it is.'

'I love you a million times more. More than you can possibly imagine!'

His expression closed. How stupid of her to say that! But the words were already out. They swarmed in the air, vibrating his whole being to a sort of brown despair. He was thinking he'd like to get this over with and get out to the fields. 'I don't want to keep you from the harvest,' she said.

'You can even read my mind. What are you, Amanda?'

She had asked that same question of Constance. From this side it was a bitter question to hear. 'I know that I love you.'

'Quit patronizing me! I mean, what happened to you? What did you find out?'

She wondered how she could ever tell it. If death is truly what one makes it, then there was little to say. 'Something's out there,' she said. He raised his eyebrows. 'Surprise is important. I can't deny you that.'

Robin held out his hands to her. She went to him, but she was little comforted by his stiff, nervous hug.

'Tell me anyway.'

'There is another world. It grows out of the mind when it is freed from the body. When you die you find your conscience waiting for you. It cannot lie. If you suffer then, it is because you choose to do so. If you go on into the highlands, it is because you feel ready to accept the joy of heaven.'

'Am I ready?'

She could see so easily into his soul. Like her own, his guilts seemed terribly small. He was unsure that it was right to leave his parents, and he worried about not being able to provide for them in their old age. She slipped her hand into his. 'You should reconcile yourself with your parents. Growth for you lies in the direction of understanding how you really feel about them.'

'We've come to a pretty good understanding already.' She heard the lie. But it was not her place to correct him. He had to travel his own path. 'Robin, I have so much to tell you. I relived our past together.'

On the surface he barely heard her, so preoccupied was he by what he imagined as the distance between them. But his essence heard, and looked out of his eyes with graceful eagerness. 'May I know?' he asked. The acid in his voice, so contrived, seemed silly to her, but she did not laugh.

'You didn't choose the name Robin by accident. It's been your name before. We were lovers a long time ago, when I had a house in the forest.'

How they had loved, in the warm Sherwood nights, when

the cat watched from the branch, and the stars coursed beyond the treetops.

'I don't remember.'

Oh, but she knew that was a lie. He did remember, and very well. She saw it in his eyes. 'The log palace? The fairy? The coming of the sheriff of Nottingham?'

'You're telling me I was Robin Hood?'

'Yes. You were Robin Hood.'

He looked askance at her. He smiled just a little.

'You really were.'

He burst out laughing, and when he did the wall between them fell at last. He kissed her easily, and there was hunger in it, the real hunger of essence seeking essence. 'Oh, Amanda, I'm so glad you came back! We tried all night, we raised the cone of power, but nothing seemed to help. I worked and worked and worked and I was sure I had lost you. Then the *Leannan* came and a little while later there you were!' He was covering her face with kisses now, and they were kisses of passion. 'You're so beautiful, I love you so much, I didn't think I could live without you!'

She delivered herself to his embraces. They went back into the bed and she drew down his pants and underpants and opened her robe to him. There, in the secrecy of the curtained bed, they made furious, shaking, gleeful love, laughing and kissing as they did it. She opened herself to him and let him seek the centre of her pleasure.

When he spent himself, she attained a level of ecstasy so intense that for an instant she blacked out. Afterwards it was as if the rich dark of her womb was vibrating, announcing the presence of new life.

They had conceived a baby just then, she knew. But that was for another phase of life in the Covenstead. Just now, she would keep her condition a secret.

They lay awhile, linked. She followed his semen on its journey, feeling it struggle up her fallopian tubes, a swirling, struggling cataclysm in the dark, until finally one bright speck of him reached the egg, and there burst forth a light that sang. The connection to the egg held, and a new voice jabbered up in her. She smiled, beatified by her womanhood. 'Can you keep a secret?'

'Of course.'

She saw how thin was his real ability to do this. Keeping a secret is one of the most difficult of disciplines. 'You must keep it for about three days. Can you do that?'

'Certainly. Come on, tell me.'

'You made it,' she said. 'I just got pregnant.'

His eyes widened. 'How –'

'I felt it all. The whole thing.'

He fell on her in a wild excess of passion. 'I was scared of you, my love. I was scared to death, but you cured me of it. You opened me up somehow.'

'You opened yourself up. When you saw there was still room to laugh.'

He laid his mouth on hers. She touched him all over, feeling every delicious inch of him.

Robin's kiss went on and on, lingering now, probing now, seeking in the miracle of their joined selves.

Finally he cuddled beside her. There came from him a whisper so soft it was almost unarticulated . . . a thought. 'Was it just dark, death? Were you telling me the truth?'

She hugged him. 'You can look forward to great wonders.'

He went up on an elbow. 'I still can't believe it. You actually came back to life. This is a scientific fact. And you have memories, knowledge from the world of the dead. This is incredible.'

She had to forgive him; he did not mean to make her feel lonely. 'The better you know yourself before you die, the better off you'll be.'

'Is there a moral order? Such a thing as sin? Is there a hell?'

'As far as moral orders are concerned, we make our own choices. We are our own judges. And we are never wrong.'

'So, like, if Hitler *thinks* he's doing good, then he goes to heaven? Is that right?'

'After death, all illusions fall away. We know ourselves, exactly as we are. I think I had a glimpse of Hitler.'

'In heaven?'

The memory so thoroughly revolted her that she almost screamed. 'No.'

Tom's head appeared between the curtains. For a moment the two of them just looked at it. It was much too far from the floor, and he certainly wasn't dangling from the canopy.

'Is there a chair out there?' Robin asked nervously.

'Not that I recall.'

Tom extended his tongue and slowly, sensuously, licked his chops.

'He must be – he has to be –'

'I think it's his idea of a joke. Don't let it upset you.'

'The cat is floating in midair and you tell me not to get upset! Jesus! Scat, damn you!'

Instead Tom came in, rolling and playing in the air.

'I think he's celebrating.'

He floated past and out the other side of the curtains.

Robin was silent for some little time. Once or twice he started to talk. Then he shook his head. 'As I recall,' he said at last, 'you like pancakes.'

'This is truth.'

'Would you like some now?'

She regarded him with deep fondness. 'Would I ever.'

They both dressed, and she brushed her hair and washed her face, and they went down to the kitchen. She had expected light and activity, but the room was cold.

'They're all down at the village,' Robin said. 'They've made a feast for you. As you might imagine, there is a great deal of excitement. Only the Vine Coven's really greeted you.'

'I barely remember coming down the mountain. I was terribly tired.'

'You walked like a zombie.' He hesitated at his own words, then looked away, as if he had unthinkingly called attention to some deformity of hers.

The two of them went out into the morning.

There was more than one veteran in Simon's congregation. His call had been heard, as a matter of fact, by no fewer than seven vets, three of them tough young steelworkers on indefinite layoff. All had been trained in modern infiltration techniques during the Vietnam War.

At Betty Turner's request the command post was in her home. Simon sat before his makeshift desk in the family room, which had been renamed the Operations Room.

'I got the radios, Brother,' Tim Faulkner said. He put a big box down on the floor. 'Just what the doctor ordered. Three hand-held CBs, all tuned to the same channel.'

Charlie Reilly tromped in with a map, which he proceeded to unroll against the wall. 'Give me a hand, Tim, I want to tape this thing up.'

Simon had never seen such an elaborate topographical map. It showed contour in great detail, brown lines against the various shades of background colour.

'This is the National Guard '63 update of the Geodetic Survey map of the Maywell Quadrant,' Reilly said. He and Tim Faulkner finished taping it to the wall.

It brought a military look to this headquarters. Simon took pleasure in the calm and professional atmosphere. He had been trying not to think about the hand coming to life. It was almost the only thing he *could* think about. Either it was a miracle to proclaim or a spell from which he must protect his people. But which?

'Davis is down at the County Courthouse,' Deputy Peters said, 'getting the blueprints of the Collier place. Once we have those we'll be ready to get this operation set.'

Eddie Martin spoke up. He was wearing green army fatigues and a camouflage flak vest. 'I want to develop a mission analysis with detailed operational orders. And I don't want anybody handling weapons or gasoline who doesn't know what they're doing. We're not a bunch of assholes. We're organized, we've got struchure, and we're in the right. So let's act that way.'

Even Simon's original men had acquired new efficiency. He had little to do but watch. The martyrdom had filled his people with the grace of God. How he loved these people, deeply, abidingly, with his whole soul. They would help themselves and the witches, too. Let the poor people suffer in this life so that they would be happy in the next. Only one person among them all would not be going to heaven. Such was his joy and his deep, inner sadness that Simon wept quietly, the tears moving coldly down his cheeks. He sat hunched at his card table, nervously touching what was in his pocket.

The witches' barn was crowded. In the centre was a great circular table, heaped with all kinds of food. People stood around it or sat on the floor. When Amanda and Robin came in, there was an intense stir, suddenly hushed.

Amanda was not surprised to see Constance a miserable shadow of herself sitting off in a corner. She would need much support and reassurance. Her fate was upon her, visible to Amanda as a sizzling, burning finger that pointed directly at the centre of the old woman's skull.

'Connie?'

When Constance met her eyes, Amanda knew at once that she was aware of it, too.

After a life lived between the worlds, the old woman was afraid of death. Connie's black ravens stood in a line along a rafter above her.

Amanda made her way through the silent, watching crowd of people to her benefactor. She sat down on the floor in front of her. 'Connie, how can I help –'

'I'm not afraid of death. It's pain.' She saw Connie burning

397

in agony, her ravens swarming, their wings dipped in blue flames.

'Oh, Connie!'

'Whisper!'

'Can't you stop it? There must be some way, surely.'

'When my fire burns, I'll be there. Nothing can change it.'

Amanda saw that. The closer the future comes to the present, the more possibilities become probable. Then they become inevitable.

Connie smiled, a study in sadness. 'Nature must feed, Amanda.'

'Yes, Connie. You can lean on me now. You can tell me all your fears. Nothing is hidden from me.'

Constance seemed to sag. In her eyes there was incredible gratitude. 'I need you. I've needed you for years.'

She would have taken the old woman in her arms there and then, but a woman came up, offering Amanda a bowl of sweet yogurt, all but bowing and scraping. Constance looked very sad. 'It takes an independent spirit to do magic. They won't be witches long if they become your followers, young woman.'

'I don't want that.'

'You certainly don't! They're awed of your knowledge of death, but they all have the same information hidden in their hearts. We just forget it for a little while, so don't take advantage of your fellow man's poor memory.'

'I'll try not to.' Rather than have the woman grovel there, she took the proffered bowl and ate it while the whole of the Io Coven, who managed the dairy, looked on with pride. 'It is human nature to seek the confirmation of princes,' she said. 'That's why royal families are forced to spend so much time making inspections. I can teach them not to regard me as a royal person.'

'Let them be in awe of you, but let them make their own decisions. It'll be hard, especially when you can see farther than they can. But they must learn from their own mistakes.'

'I know. We can't teach people anything. They have to have their experience.'

Constance moved her hands beneath her dress and brought out a blackened, ancient garter. 'This is yours,' she said. 'I've been keeping it for you.' And so, without ceremony, she was being offered the very garter of Maidenhood. She recognized it of old, and took it. The leather was very, very old, as black as carbon. The clasp was of bone. Dimly, as if she were an echo of a cry, Amanda remembered Moom. Moom's laughter, Moom's pain, Moom's courage. She had given birth to six children and died before she was fifteen.

Moom had owned two garters. And so had Marian. 'Where's my other garter, Connie?'

Constance waved her hand. 'Lost to fire during the time of Innocent VIII.' The room was stuffy, the smell of the food heavy. Two children, Ariadne and Feather, actually knelt when they brought a plate of pancakes.

Amanda knew that she had to act, and quickly, to avoid becoming the resident Goddess-Queen. It was right for the witches to have a queen, but she must be no more than first among equals.

She held up the garter. 'I've been given this. It belongs to the Covenstead and it can only be worn by an initiated priestess. Am I right?'

There were murmurs of agreement.

'Fine. Initiate me just as you would any apprentice. And if you elect me, I will wear your garter to the best of my ability.' She thought of Moom, who would have torn any woman apart who had tried to take this garter. And Marian, to whom the sacrilege of removing it was unthinkable. She put it in her pocket and took Connie's hand. 'You want anything from the table, Connie?'

'No.' Her voice dropped. 'You know what I'm going through.'

'Yes, Connie.'

'I wish you could hold me.'

'I will, Connie, when we're alone. As long as you want me to. I'll be with you, Connie, even at the very end.'

'I feel so strange without the garter! So sad.'

She took Connie's hand, for a moment held it tightly. The moment between them seemed to deepen. But Amanda knew that she had to break the moment. As much as she wanted to comfort Connie, this time belonged to the Covenstead. 'If I don't go over to that table and serve myself, I'm going to get more of bowing and scraping.'

'You don't need that. Go, do your duty.'

There were pitchers of apple cider and a little blackberry juice. No whole berries, though. Too bad. Amanda had seen them on the bushes, fat and delicious-looking. There were elder-blow pancakes and pumpkin pies and squash cooked in herbs and honey, huge loaves of dark bread and white goat's milk cheese. There were pitchers of cream and milk and pots of pungent tea. Slabs of the pig Hiram's bacon. Long before she had tasted it all, Amanda had managed to satisfy even her fierce appetite. Her body wanted to confirm its renewed connection to life, and it did that by eating.

She moved through a fog of silent, fascinated stares. 'I haven't eaten since yesterday morning,' she said. 'If you ever resurrect anybody else, don't forget to feed them. You come back hungry.'

A little nervous laughter, as lame as her attempt to relieve the tension. Connie put a gentle hand on Amanda's arm, drew her aside. 'Take a lesson from Marian. She was very clever at being queen. She knew how to rule without co-ercion, and reign without causing awe. But even when she played hide and seek with the children or raced horses with the men, nobody ever forgot she was queen. It's a trick, Amanda, to be first and equal at the same time.' Then Connie said something that disquieted Amanda. 'It's an illusion, just as the peace and happiness of this moment are an illusion.'

'What do you mean?'

'Go outside and look at the sky. Look with your new eyes.'

Amanda stood up, told Robin to stay behind, and went out on her own into the quiet village. A drift of smoke rose from the sweat-lodge chimney.

As her eyes followed the smoke into the sky, she almost fell over backward with terror and shock. She was looking up the side of a towering leg covered with gleaming black fur. It was so tremendous that it was almost beyond seeing.

She looked up and up the rippling, muscular sweep of black fur to the vast, expanding chest perhaps a thousand feet above, and right into the grinning Cheshire face of the largest and most menacing black cat she had ever seen.

And Tom was looking straight back at her. There was instantaneous communication between them, deeper than spoken words. Tom was at once a part of what menaced the Covenstead and what protected it. The aim of the *Leannan* was to test the witches. The aim of that other darkness, that which controlled Brother Pierce, was to destroy them, as it was to destroy everything that gave mankind a chance of survival and growth.

This *Samhain* was indeed a season of learning and of dying.

That which menaced the Covenstead was far larger than Tom. Indeed, it towered over him, an immense presence of hate that swept up from Maywell and across the sky, drawing its strength from the immense heart of evil, and all the smaller hearts of men and women who would kill what they do not understand, who would despise ways which are not their own. She saw it clearly, even as it shrank back from her. What had possessed Brother Pierce and those like him fed on fear, and hated both man and God.

'This long central hallway suggests to me that the way to go is to jemmy the front door and work through with the gasoline sprayers until we reach the kitchen, here. Then we get the hell out. On a radio signal the fire team goes through the same way. We put a two-minute timer on the fuses. By the time the place starts burning we're approximately three hundred yards away, just at the edge of the forest.'

'I'd rather you had three minutes,' Brother Pierce said. He did not want another Turner.

'If we leave it go too long, they'll smell the fumes.'

'How many people altogether on the place?' Bill Peters asked.

Bob Krueger answered. 'There's twenty-one commuters to Philly and New York. Plus they're running a damn good three-hundred-acre farm using only hand tools. We can't see they have less than seventy people working that land. Add in children and boost the total ten percent to be on the safe side, and a reasonable guess is a hundred and thirty.'

Bill rubbed his cheek with his right hand. 'Where the hell do they live?'

'They're out there,' Eddie Martin said. 'Got to be. We've targeted twenty-three houses in town as witch-owned, but the estate witches ain't living there, or we'd see 'em move out to the farm every day.'

Bill thumped the blueprint. 'They sure as hell don't live in this house. Not unless they're jamming together.'

'They might be. Anyway, I don't think it's a concern.'

'It's a concern, all right. We've got to know where these people are. You're talkin' sixteen guys in our group. We're no match for over a hundred. If we aren't careful, we could all end up captured or worse. With these people, maybe a lot worse.'

Simon thought of the house burning and lowered his eyes, praying once again to the Lord for guidance. They were witches and they must be evil, but was it his place to pass sentence on them? He was tempted just to say the whole attack was cancelled and that the Lord had given him a better idea.

Unfortunately the Lord was quiet, and Simon had no better idea. 'Please, Lord,' he called in his heart, 'help me to do your will. Help me, O Lord.' But the Lord remained silent. The planning session went on.

Amanda looked up at the creature above her. Its great eyes glared down. It was waiting, and she had the feeling that there was very little time. But what did it want her to do?

She looked into the eyes. They were too knowing to be safe, but they were also very, very good. There was even humour there somewhere. In a flash he crouched down.

Amanda backed up. She could see the huge face superimposed on the village, hear the breathing, even hear the damp sound when he blinked. She could feel he was calling to her. Despite all his awesome power, he could not succeed without her.

'How can I help? Please tell me!'

In his eyes she saw men running on dark streets, she saw gasoline tins and roiling orange fire, and she heard Constance screaming in agony.

'Can't you stop them, Tom?'

Then in the cat's gleaming eyes Amanda saw the whole Covenstead on fire. She was so horrified she jumped back and fell down.

She stared into the morning sky. And sure enough, what she feared to see was there. Poised over the barn was a flaming finger exactly like the one that threatened Constance.

Amanda went back to the barn and drank a long draught of cider. People gathered round her then, and began kissing her one after another. She kissed them all, soft lips of women, thin lips of men, wet lips of children. She kissed them as openly and intimately as she had Robin, and shared her breath with them all.

Some went away shocked, all silent.

None but Amanda and Constance saw the fingers, and Constance kept to her corner, from time to time jerking her head as if to get out from under the thing that hissed in the air above her.

But that was not the way to escape. Amanda's mind was tormented with the problem. This was why she had been returned to her people. She was here to save their way of life.

There seemed to be no direction in which to turn. She sensed that she might as well try to change the course of the Amazon as alter the fate that overhung the Covenstead.

She knew the emotion that came to fill her, knew it all too well. It was absolute and unreasoning. She fought it but it would not subside. Her fear was like ice in the depths of her belly, freezing everything, freezing hope. She could see Brother Pierce as if through a vault of night, his spirit tortured, his mind made up. He personified man's deep, visceral fear of the unknown. There was so much hate and so much ignorance. She had no power against it.

But she had to have power. Somehow she had to save the Covenstead. She saw Simon Pierce standing alone in the centre of his night. In his hand was a torch, and fire was in his eye.

CHAPTER 28

Night on the Surface of a Star

In the hush of afternoon Amanda went alone to the ruins of the fairy village. She needed time alone to think about the Covenstead's problem. Tom had communicated to her that there was no escape from fate. They had to live through whatever lay ahead, or die in it.

She climbed a hummock until she was isolated, as Maid Marian had been so long ago, overlooking her dominion. A small black stone came to hand. It was smooth with time, a thing aged to gentleness.

In it she could feel the record of all it had ever known, whole aeons collapsed to sighs. The stone was wise, and it had a message for her.

The stone said: you must embrace the fire.

Amanda saw the whole Covenstead consumed by quick red flames.

The leaves, the stems, rustled with a hurrying breeze. 'Act,' it whispered, 'act.'

The secret is –

She saw the horses kicking in the barn as their manes began to smoke and curl.

The Fairy Queen spoke: 'This is the destiny of the night: you are warned that children of the fairy danced here once, but they do not dance now. The demon has different forms in different times, but it kills the same way. It is the hammer of witches.'

'How do I stop it? Tell me how!'

She saw the *Leannan* for a moment, standing in among a tangle of weeds. 'I don't know. If I did, my fairy would be able to reclaim this place, and they cannot.'

405

'Why not? What stands against you?'

There was no answer.

Amanda sat a long time, her eyes closed, listening to her body work and to the breeze worrying the dry grass. The body may be heavy and slow and coarse, but it was so wonderfully real. Once tasted, the life of the flesh could never be forgotten.

Destruction, wars, fire . . .

Had Brother Pierce no epiphany?

When she opened her eyes, she was astonished to find how long the shadows had got. So many hours, so little time.

Her people had come. They formed a circle around the base of the hummock. They chanted her name. 'Amanda, Amanda, Amanda, Amanda.'

It was deeply moving to hear the word of the smell and taste and look of herself. Moom, also, had been thus moved, and Marian.

You must act, the wind had said.

But how?

The stone educated her. Images, words, thoughts, poured through her mind. She saw the whole massive mechanism of oppression. It came not only from the sorrowful heart of Brother Pierce but from the bleak, loveless minds of fundamentalist legislators assaulting witchcraft in Congress, and their followers persecuting witches in the dark of night. It was as if some great consciousness had possessed them and perverted their desire to do good, sweeping a black hand across their eyes.

Then the stone showed her the condition of other witches in the world, the desecrated Grove of the Unicorn in Georgia, being vandalized by fundamentalist Christians before television cameras, the act gleefully broadcast on an evening news programme. She saw Oz, a witch in New Mexico, being slandered on a 'Christian' television programme, and more: she saw the restless, questing hatred that animated this new persecution of the Old Religion, the articulate men in their fine suits arguing in Congress, and the spreading madness of the Brother Pierces of the world, and the sadness hidden in the hearts of them all as they prayed to the Risen Lord even as their hate chained them to the service of the Dark One *Leannan* would not name.

Then she saw the future, as it might very well be, a future so hard that she must not even share it with Constance. She saw prisons full of witches, steel bars and raping guards, and long, agonizing laws on the shimmering digital books of tomorrow, and she saw the glimmer of coals where witch places had been.

She knew with steel clarity and a gentle heart what she had to do. 'Take me to the children,' she said. 'I want them to initiate me.'

Ivy: 'Amanda, that isn't the way we ought to do it. You're to be welcomed, not initiated. Death initiated you. And the honour goes to the Vines.'

Robin: 'We have it all planned. We've invented a really beautiful ritual.'

She went back to the village.

People there were preparing for the rite, which was to take place at moonrise in the stone circle the Covenstead used for its major rituals.

An awesome ceremonial was not right. If the kids made up a ritual, it was bound to be simple and full of fun, and so powerful and rich with real magic.

On a small wooden table in the middle of the circle were Ivy's athame, cup, cord, and scourge, the traditional tools of initiation.

A group of six or seven people were making decorative sheaves of wheat to dress the altar. A crown of rowan had been woven for Amanda.

'Windwalker, will you round up the children for me?'

He looked up from his work. By day he was an advertising executive. His mundane name was Bernie Katz. He worked with the children's coven. 'They're halfway between here and the mountain. There's a game of follow the leader going on.'

'That makes it easy. Find the leader.'

He went off through the village calling the name of Ariadne. She was one of the middle girls, a gangling child of eleven, brown of eye and quick to smile. Amanda remembered her kneeling with her plate of pancakes, like an Egyptian slave girl.

A perfect choice for high priestess of the initiation.

Soon she appeared at a flamboyant run, her green skirt whipping about her legs, her hair flying behind her. She came up, wide-eyed, just managing to stop at the edge of the circle. 'It's not cast,' Amanda said. 'Come on in.'

Behind her, straggling along, were the rest of the children of the Covenstead, twenty-eight kids in all.

'Good game?'

Ariadne nodded. She was breathing hard. 'Up to the Fairy Stone, then back down the mountain.'

Amanda remembered Grape, gone forever beyond the Stone. There had been a quiet ceremony in the Covenstead just after dawn, but they had not awakened her for it. What had happened to Grape? Did she also wander, as Amanda had, in hard kingdoms?

The *Leannan* spoke again in Amanda's mind, this time testily. 'She's in the Land of Summer. She's perfectly happy.' Amanda was startled to hear the voice so close. It was like wind or remembered melody. Anyone could have heard it had they known what to listen for.

Amanda spoke to the children. 'Come and sit around me, all of you. I have something I want you to do.' They gathered round, all freckles and smears and wide eyes. 'All right, now listen closely. I'm going to be initiated after we go to sweat lodge.'

'You're the Maiden already.' This from a grave boy, dark hair, thin, intense face.

'But I'm not a member of your Covenstead. I don't belong to you, not yet. You have to initiate me first. And I want you kids to do it, as a very special favour to me.'

They stared at her, waiting for more.

'You need to select a priestess.'

There was silence.

'Come on, discuss it. Do you want Ariadne? Or maybe somebody else?'

'I want Feather,' came a soft voice.

'Wait a minute,' Ariadne said, 'you can't say that. You *are* Feather!'

'I'm a better witch, Ariadne, you know I am.'

'But you can't choose yourself! It's not fair. I'm the high priestess of the children's coven.'

Feather was a girl with a smile hidden in her face and the glow of early puberty about her.

'I want Feather, too,' a boy said.

'Ariadne,' another replied. 'It ought to be her.'

'Feather is nicer.'

'Ariadne pulled you out of the bog last month.'

'All right, kids,' Amanda said, 'you can have an election. All in favour of Ariadne, raise your hands.'

She counted fourteen.

'And in favour of Feather.'

Fourteen again. Both girls had voted for themselves. Amanda could not imagine a better outcome. 'Very well, you'll do it together. Which of you knows best the Way of the Altar?'

Ariadne nodded to Feather.

'Feather will be first priestess, then. Will the two of you choose a priest?'

They consulted for some time in whispers, laughing frequently as they went through the list of boys.

'We choose Robin,' Feather told her.

'Robin? You mean the adult Robin?'

'You should always be initiated by your lover, don't you know that?'

'I have a lot to learn about witchcraft.' But even as she spoke the words, she knew they were not true. In Marian's memory alone there was a vast amount of lore, of the herbs and the spells and the ways of the forest. From Moom came the simple heart of it all, the chants and dances.

Somebody was banging the gong for sweat lodge. Amanda went with the children to the wide foyer of the building. Smoke was rising from both chimneys, and the wooden flaps covered the windows. The adult witches were gathering at the lodge entrance, hanging up their clothes and pulling off their workboots.

Long shadows were creeping from under trees and around the corners of buildings as the witches passed into the big lodge. The steam had been filled with the aroma of the forest, drawn from damp herbs laid on the hot rocks.

Amanda strode naked into the centre of the room and lay on one of the long benches. The children went first to the stone tubs and crowded in together, squealing and laughing as they attacked one another with soap and rush broom.

Amanda contemplated them, the fire-marked children. Why must there be such hate for such happiness?

'Hey, lazy!' She looked up, startled. Ivy proceeded to shove her down the bench. 'Give me some room there, Maiden.' Ivy lay down beside her. 'I understand the point you're trying to make with the kid's initiation,' she said. 'It's a good idea.' She laughed. 'A lot of the coveners from the town and some of the Christians are coming. What we had planned was a procession around the estate, with you riding a horse.'

It was Amanda's turn to laugh. 'You're not serious?'

'Not entirely.' She gave Amanda an arch look. 'You really are rather awesome. The Catholics are calling you a miracle. I think the Episcopals favour a medical explanation. But everybody agrees, you're something quite unusual.'

'I'm just me.'

Ivy smiled at her. 'An awful lot of people saw you dead. Now you're alive again, walking around. Naturally there is a little awe.'

Amanda thought of the finger in the sky. 'I'm not nearly as powerful as you think.'

'Don't patronize.'

There came in the splashing of the children's water a sparkling whisper, 'Hurry, Amanda, every moment counts.'

'Surely, *Leannan*, there is still time.'

'No. There is no time.'

'I think we gotta give 'em warning,' Deputy Peters said. His eyes were red, his face was perspiring. Simon watched him carefully. Bill Peters was so damn afraid. Even the tone of his voice could cause people to lose their courage.

'We can't, Bill, we'll risk a fight.' Eddie Martin was certainly more Simon's sort of man. Strong, decisive, looked like he'd beat hell out of the first person to cross him. His wife had complained of him once in a private session with Simon. 'You cleave to him,' Simon had told her. 'The Good Book says a man's supposed to cleave to his wife,' she had replied, 'not the wife to her husband. You men just read it backwards. And anyway, he doesn't cleave. He hollers.' A decent girl, Simon had tried to treat her kindly. He had blessed her and told her to place her troubles in the hands of the Lord.

'We are talking about murder, you guys! My God, if we burn a hundred and thirty people – we can't risk it, we're crazy.'

Simon listened, but at the same time did not. The meeting had been going on for some time, and he suspected that it was going to resolve itself no matter what he said.

Lately he found himself turning more and more to his past, as if the approaching crisis was returning him to his own great guilt, and to the hand. He had only known her for a few days, but he had thousands and thousands of detailed memories of her, of how she had laughed and what hopes she had cherished, and what she had enjoyed. She wanted to be a lawyer, and her favourite thing in the world was Double Bubble bubble gum. He remembered her talk, her ideas and ways, the anger and the bitterness at a fate she could not control, and how very much she had wanted to be held.

He was snapped back to the meeting by Eddie Martin's voice. 'Now, look here, Deputy, we are talking about something that has to be done! This town's got cancer. If you want to get rid of cancer, you take a burning brand and you just burn it right out.'

'I'm telling you, if we burn that house, old Williams is going to be pretty mad, but in the end he's going to give up on it. But if even one person goes up, he'll have the state police in here and every damn one of us'll be in jail within the week.'

Simon spoke mildly, softly. 'Thou shalt not suffer a witch to live.'

Eddie Martin slapped his fist against the table.

Hard silence followed.

'But also, "Let none of you imagine evil against his neighbour." We must punish them until they come to their senses, and when they do, then let us love them.'

Feet shuffled. There were a few coughs. Simon sensed that they did not really understand him, and that was sad. He knew the truth about Christianity, its deep, inner decency and tolerance. Why, when he preached, didn't it come out that way? He just couldn't figure it out. But here they were. Would Jesus be comfortable in this meeting?

Bob Krueger spoke a compromise. 'We set everything up, then we pull back almost to the road, see. Then we fire a few shots into the air with a shotgun. That'll wake up every damn witch from here to hell. They'll have time to get out of the house but not time to catch us. Or even see us.'

'That's a good idea,' Deputy Peters said.

'Vote,' Eddie Martin said.

They tied it up. Eddie looked long at Simon. 'You gotta break it, Brother.' If he were to vote against Eddie's wishes, how would he take it?

'I must seek the counsel of the Lord.'

Just then Mrs Turner came in with two big pizza boxes. Her son followed with three six-packs of beer. There was no merriment as the men began to eat. Simon had never been in battle, but he could imagine that men must be like this the night before an assault.

As they dug into the food, Simon left the room to pray in private. Unfortunately Eddie Martin followed him. They went together into the garage. Eddie was stiff with rage. 'I'm not satisfied, Brother Pierce. Seven of 'em voted against me. Seven cowards.'

'They'd call themselves prudent.'

Eddie sucked in breath. 'What do *you* call them, Brother?'

Now, this had to be handled very, very carefully. He didn't want to lose either half of the group. 'Brother Martin, I think we are walking in the way of the Lord, and we are doing His work, in His vineyard. I trust in His wisdom.'

'I trust in His wisdom, too. That's why we gotta do things the rough way. Burn 'em. Make sure the survivors leave and *never* come back – if there are any damn survivors.'

'Williams was already over to my place, asking all kinds of questions about poor Brother Turner, rest his soul. If the witches die, there'll be no doubt in his mind about who did it. And it will be a crime of national importance. We'll look evil, and they will look like martyrs.'

'We're about to burn down a house worth an easy quarter million dollars. Probably more. Williams is gonna be asking questions anyway.' Eddie Martin came close to Simon. He stank of machine oil from cleaning guns. His eyes were bloodshot. 'I'll tell you what we ought to do. We ought to capture every one of those bitches and all the little toads they got as men, and have us a public execution. And then when Williams pokes his nose around – just blow his head right off. I'd do it myself, and I'd be proud!'

This was too much, and Simon knew it. He had never seen a look like the one in Eddie Martin's eyes. 'Have a caution, Brother.'

'Why? You know you got more than half this town on your side? Sure you do! Even got some of the Episcopals, who don't hold with the town covens meeting in their damn basement. And Catholics who got upset about that nude ride. Hell, you got every law enforcement person except the sheriff himself. And Tom Murphy, he's state police major up to Elsemere, runs the whole damn county. He's been around the Tabernacle a couple of times. I seen that man prayin' his heart out with you, Brother Pierce.'

Everything Eddie said was true. The more public the witches became, the more powerful Simon got. He knew that, but he did not know just how to handle this situation. If he voted to warn the witches, he lost Eddie and his six supporters for sure. If he voted against warning, he probably wouldn't lose the others.

But they risked committing a crime of extraordinary ferocity, one that could not be justified anywhere in the Bible. Or could it? 'Thou shalt not suffer a witch to live.'

Eddie had been out here long enough. Simon wanted to take this before the Lord. 'Where lives are involved, Brother Martin, I have to pray. Please leave me alone for a few minutes.'

After Eddie left, Simon knelt down beside the Turners' old Dodge wagon, facing the back door of the garage. A tattered toy puppet lay on the floor between him and the door, its head cut open, no doubt in some childhood game. He noticed then that there were a number of other dolls lying on a shelf near the door, all with their heads in disrepair. A lot of anger in the Turner house.

'O Lord,' he whispered, 'please help me now. It is in my

power to send the witches into the fire of your divine justice. Hear me, O Lord, and let me know what to do.' He knelt there, staring at the dolls. Soon the concrete floor started hurting his knees. 'O Lord, just send me some kind of a sign.'

There was nothing. Simon knelt a while longer, his mind full of wordless prayer. At last, sorry that his need had been too little to interest the Lord, he began to rise. Just then he heard something odd – a mewing sound on the far side of the garage. He peered around the car.

The sound came again, much louder this time. He couldn't see anything over the top of the car. But when he looked under it, he saw well enough.

There was a black panther in this garage with him.

Even as he started to get to his feet, it sailed soundlessly across the hood of the car and blocked his way. There it stood, huge, its massive, kinked tail flicking, its one good ear cocked towards him.

He was dumbfounded. There weren't any panthers in Maywell. 'Help!'

It growled and leaped at his throat. The thing almost knocked his breath out of him. Then it was on him. He couldn't believe this.

A panther with terrible eyes, laughing and green and cruel. 'Help me!'

'We're coming!'

The men came through the door in a bunch and stopped, shocked. The panther had Simon down. He knew it was about to kill him.

'What the hell –'

'Get a gun. It's gonna tear me apart any second.' He could smell its breath, an odour like rotten meat. He tried to control his shaking, because it seemed to excite the cat, which began to breathe harder and harder, washing him with the foul stink.

Suddenly the cat yowled. Something invisible was pulling

at its powerful neck, forcing its head back away from Simon.

Well, glory be, he understood now. The cat was a witch spell and the Lord was protecting him from it.

His men were bunched up at the door. They had guns, but Simon knew that bullets wouldn't hurt this panther. It was a spirit thing, had to be – despite the torn ear and busted tail.

'Brace yourself!'

When the bolts clicked, the panther didn't even bat an eye. Instead it opened its mouth wide and with a lunging motion went for Simon's jugular. 'Oh, God!'

It stood gagging, unable to reach him. He could see the faint outlines of immense fingers around the thing's neck. And a tremendous, dark, *something* standing behind it, holding it back.

The sheer strangeness of it all terrified him. A shot exploded over the sound of his screams.

The big cat leaped straight up into the air shrieking in rage. And the shadowy form leaped right after it.

Simon sat up. He felt his throat. No injury. 'O my dear Lord,' he said. His heart was thundering, his blood roaring in his veins.

'It's up in the rafters,' Tom Faulkner said softly. 'Nobody move.' He cast the beam of his flashlight towards the dark directly above Simon, who was still sitting on the floor.

Tom was the first to cry out. Then Bill Peters took it up, then they were all shouting, backing towards the door, and Simon himself was scuttling along the floor, trying to get to his feet, too terrified to make his body work right.

The only thing left up there was a pair of eyes and a big cat grin. Then the eyes closed, and the grin faded.

'It's gone,' Eddie Martin cried. 'The damn thing just evaporated!'

The beams of half a dozen flashlights confirmed that the garage was empty.

'That, my friends, was what you call a witch spell. Praise

God, it was a thing sent after us from the depths of hell! And the Lord Himself saved me from it. The Lord *saved* me. Glory hallelujah, I have seen the hand of God.'

Now Simon knew exactly what God wanted.

Thou shalt not suffer a witch to live!

CHAPTER 29
Daughter of the Moon

'When we were kids we used to try to imagine what death was like. Like an explosion, a little girl – I think her name was Nancy – said. Nothing, one boy said. He was killed in the Great War, which was just as well. From his idea of death you can see he was an afflicted bore.'

'Connie, you must collect yourself.'

Constance's reply was bitter. 'Thank you, Amanda. I need advice from someone older and wiser. I'm very grateful.'

'I've come up here to invite you to attend my initiation.'

'Ah! Into what? Fire?'

'Into the Covenstead.'

'I can't get that *thing* to go away that's over my head!'

'Oh, Connie!'

'Don't pity me, you little whelp! Pity yourself. You've got one, too. We all do. The whole Covenstead's as good as dead.'

'Connie, *please*!'

'I'm only telling you the truth. Here, take a pull.' She started to hand Amanda a bottle of Madeira, then stared at it fixedly for a moment. 'Old women can get drunk on any damn thing.' She laughed. 'Something's in the air. Don't you smell it – burning hair?' She got up from her bed and came to Amanda, put her head on her shoulder. Amanda embraced her. 'I am not afraid of death, but of the manner of dying. I don't want to burn.' She moaned, nuzzling into Amanda's shirt. 'You're so young and warm and strong. But be clever. Even you cannot resist it.'

'I've got to save the Covenstead.'

'Yes. That's why you've been dead. You've passed all the

tests. You have the strength and the wisdom.' She was shaking. 'Oh, Amanda, I'm so frightened.'

Constance had always been her strength and her support. To be witness to the old woman's terror was itself terrifying. But Amanda kept her feelings to herself. She held Constance in strong arms. 'The Covenstead will survive.'

'The Covenstead is to be tested by fire. Remember that the *Leannan* is as much with you as she is against you. If the Covenstead proves itself weak, it will certainly die.'

Compared with what she had been through with Mother Star of the Sea and Bonnie, the onslaught of Brother Pierce did not seem so terrible. After all, he was a mere wave from the outside, expending itself on the outside. Her demons had come from within her own soul. 'We will not die. I'm stronger than Pierce.'

Connie clutched her. 'You have come to us as a warrior Maiden, to see the witches through another era of persecution. The fundamentalists will grow and grow in power, and they are the direct agents of darkness.' She sobbed. 'They're so innocent, and so deceived. Brother Pierce may well fail. You *are* strong. But what about the next, and the one after that, and the one following? Will you still be strong, ten years from now, twenty? Will you be strong in prison, or in exile? What if you lose your freedoms, your right to a fair trial, your right to due process? Believe me, Amanda, there is a dark time for witches coming, and we have never been more necessary.'

'I am not afraid.'

Connie hugged her more tightly. 'All power to you then, Maiden. I don't know where you get your courage.'

'Well, one place I get it is out of being sensible.' She moved away from Constance and picked up the telephone. She dialled the sheriff's office. 'Sheriff Williams, please.'

'May I say who's calling?'

'Just say it's important.'

He came on the line.

'Sheriff, this is Amanda Walker.'

'Oh! I heard about last night. Amanda, I was so deeply moved. I'm sorry I won't be at your welcoming, but I don't trust my deputy anymore and I've got to stick close to the office.'

'Never mind that right now. I'm calling you to tell you that this Covenstead is in danger.'

'I know that. Simon Pierce is after you.'

'I want you to deputize everybody in the town you feel you can trust, and bring them out here tonight with all the weapons at their disposal. Some people are already coming to the initiation, but they won't be enough.'

'I'd better call in the state police.'

'Do that if you think it'll help. But get people out here no later than nine. I want all the approaches guarded.' She looked at Constance, who was nodding on her bed, about to slump over onto her side. 'And I want you to personally guard Connie. I want you right in the room with her at all times, do you understand that?'

'I'm already moving.'

'Sheriff, thank you. I love you. I love all of you so much.' She hung up the phone. Where was the self-involved little artist of a week ago, the one who used to paint pictures of imaginary elves? If she spent the rest of her artistic career painting a portrait of the *Leannan* and captured a tenth of her beauty, her career would be a success. Or if she painted Tom somewhat as he was, or Raven as he had been.

But it wasn't time to think about that now. She had to go back to the village and go through her ritual initiation.

Getting Connie settled, she wished she could relieve some of the poor woman's terror. To know when you are going to die is a hard thing, but to know that it is going to be by fire must be very much worse.

The gong sounded. Amanda tucked the quilt around Connie's chin, kissed her head, and quietly left the room.

'I'm telling you, we go late. Catch 'em all sleeping.'

'Early. We'll take 'em by surprise.'

'When they're not asleep? They'll be all over the place. The house'll be full of 'em.'

'They'll be out in the fields. It's harvest time and they've still got a lot of standing corn.'

The group had been arguing ever since the appearance of the thing in the garage. Again Simon saw those eyes. Despite the help of the Lord, he was, quite frankly, frightened. There were real supernatural events happening in Maywell. Opposition to the witches had become far more than a means of ensuring the loyalty of his own congregation. The Christian brotherhood itself was at stake in this little town. The witches could command real, live demons with green eyes and the bodies of panthers.

The demon had been terrible, but the Lord had shown He was stronger. Simon was a sinner, too, of course, but his own crime must seem small to God beside that of the witches, who were willing to call hell-things into the world. 'We've got to destroy them!'

A chorus of Amens.

The beeper Deputy Peters carried at his waist started warbling. 'Gotta call in,' he said. Everybody fell silent as he made contact with the sheriff's office. He said a few words, listened, hung up. He looked towards them, his face pale. 'I just got told to get down to the office by nine P.M. I'm on desk duty all night.'

'He wants to keep tabs on you.'

'Which means he suspects something. But he suspects it for later. After nine.'

Brother Pierce spoke. 'That decides it. We move as soon as the sun goes down. We move fast, and we hit 'em hard.'

Eddie Martin rolled up his maps. Other men began assembling the equipment.

Afterwards Brother Pierce led them all in prayer.

The sun rode the edge of the sky. All the Covenstead and many of its friends and supporters crowded around Amanda, except for the children, who sat in the circle they had cast. Robin and Ivy's father Steven was there, and the Episcopal rector and Father Evans.

They intended a Christian presence here, no doubt as a gentle reminder to the witches that they could always return to the Church. Amanda accepted that. Between them they had brought twenty parishioners.

For the past hour the children's coven had been working furiously and noisily, creating their ritual. Ariadne and Feather stood in the centre of the circle now, Robin behind them. The great sword of the Covenstead lay on the ground before the two girls. Ariadne held the cords, Feather the scourge. Robin took the athame from the small table they were using as an altar and used it to symbolically open the circle for Amanda to enter.

The Christians began the ritual with a benediction. 'O Lord,' Father Evans prayed, 'let the light enter their hearts, let thy hand touch them in blessing.'

At the same moment that the sun touched the edge of the horizon Amanda stepped into the circle. Previous to her experience in death, she had considered the circle a symbolic place. But the symbols of this world are the concrete reality of the other. She vividly recalled the cauldron circle, and Connie stirring and calling. The cauldron, full of the energy of the spells that had been cast into it, had been as real as a rock, the people around it vague, flickering shadows.

Robin stepped forward between the two girls. All three dropped their cloaks to the ground. Amanda did likewise. The four of them stood naked in the crisp air. Amanda felt goose bumps rising on her skin. Because of the cold, the rest of the coveners remained clothed. Steven was just outside the circle, watching his son. Father Evans had a bemused expression on his face.

Feather gave Robin a sheet of loose-leaf paper on which

a dozen different young hands had written in red pencil. Robin read:

'This is the Charge of the Coven:

Keep our secrets hidden in your heart,
Master our ways; if you cannot do it do not start.

Perfect your inner sight
That you may to the circle add your light.

The Craft of the Wise is sought, not found.
It is everywhere, so look around.

Tonight you will vow before the Goddess and the God
To give your all to the hidden synod.

Will you answer this Charge?'

Amanda nodded. 'I will.'

Feather spoke. 'Then kneel and take our pentacle.' She handed Amanda a five-pointed star of silver, enclosed in a circle of gold. 'Say with me, I have heard the Charge of the Coven. Before the Goddess and the God and all the wise, I swear I have taken it into my heart.'

Amanda felt the presence of the witches around her, the whispering power of the circle, the nearness of the *Leannan*. Full of joy, she swore.

The gong of the Covenstead sounded.

Robin took the paper on which the charge had been written and burned it in a little golden bowl. 'By smoke, by fire, fix these words. By wind, by air, by earth be it done!'

He came and knelt beside Amanda. Feather stood behind her and Ariadne knelt on the other side. They made a circle, Ariadne and Robin clasping their left hands before her knees and their right hands on the back of her head. Feather laid hers on theirs. The three spoke together. 'Do you to the Goddess and the God give all between these hands, without reservation or hesitation?'

'I do.'

'Say it then: I am a child of Earth and Sun, I am daughter of the Moon.'

Amanda said the words.

'I love the planet of my birth, and the star of my life, and the moon who granted me my humanity.'

Amanda repeated after them.

The whole circle spoke. 'By our will and the goodness of the Goddess, may all the powers of the craft enter your body, and especially the secret wisdom of our coven.' Their voices dropped to a whisper. 'Be as the animals. Their simplicity makes their anger small, their love great.'

Silence fell.

Amanda could hear the wind bothering the weeds, and the silver cries of birds at evening.

From behind her Feather spoke: 'Stand up. I'm going to mark you as a witch.' She took herbed oil that smelled of rust and peppermint, and made an X on Amanda's lips. 'Blessed be the mouth that speaks its love of the earth.' Then she marked Amanda's breasts. 'Blessed be the heart that beats its love of life.' Then she marked Amanda's genitals. 'Blessed be the loins that give birth to the world.'

Amanda thought of the life growing inside her. Just barely there, but so very there. Her darkness was flowering.

Ariadne took the scourge. 'This is the Charge of Remembrance.' She hit Amanda across the buttocks with it, just hard enough to sting. 'Remember that you belong to the dust and will return.' Again she struck her. 'Remember that you belong to the coven and will never leave.' Again the cords touched Amanda's flesh. 'Remember that you are daughter of the moon.'

Three more times the gong rang, its voice echoing off the vastness of Stone Mountain.

'Guess what,' Feather said, 'you're a real, live witch.' She smiled. 'It's official.'

The children's coven crowded around her, laughing, hugging her and one another. Nearby a harp began to play. As the rhythm grew more and more intricate and faster and faster, it beckoned, then demanded that there be dancing.

They went round and round together, Amanda and Robin and the children, the other witches and their guests joining outside the circle. The harp sang to quicken blood. The moon, fat and red, slipped swiftly up the purple sky.

The last of Simon's men scaled the wall and dropped down into the leaves below. 'We're clear,' Simon whispered to the others. 'Let's go.'

Eddie Martin led. They filed along the inside of the wall, seeking the road that led into the estate from the main gate. The darkness was almost absolute, and dry twigs kept brushing Simon's face, scratching at him. This must be virgin forest on this side of the wall. The trees were giants, ready to crush you.

There were fifteen men divided into three groups of five each. The lead group Eddie called the Suppression Team. Their job was to pin down any opposition on the way in. The second group was the Fire Team. Three of them carried gasoline in five-gallon sprayers. The other two were responsible for the timed fuses. The last group was the Support Team, and Simon was part of this. Their mission was to remain a few hundred yards behind the others, providing cover and diversions – if necessary drawing fire.

Even though the sun was just down and the moon rising, the forest was so dark that Eddie from time to time had to flicker his flashlight ahead. Simon, running along among his men, was not surprised to find himself afraid. They all were. Somehow the fear made the Lord's work seem even more important.

There came a soft word from ahead. The road had been

found. The group gathered itself together. Simon was cold, and confused about directions. Fortunately Eddie Martin and the others were good at this sort of thing. They knew exactly what they were doing.

'Okay, everybody gather round.' There was warmth in the little group huddling around Eddie. 'We have to move fast. We could be under surveillance even now.'

Silently, feverishly, Simon said a prayer: 'Lord, let thy will be done.' He said it again and again and again as they moved along. The witches were human beings, he couldn't forget that. He touched the hand.

'Suppression Team, front and centre.' There was shuffling movement among the shadowy forms. 'Lemme set my watch. Okay, you've got two minutes lead, then the Fire Team will follow. Take off!'

They hurried away, their footsteps muffled by the leaves that littered the road. A flicker of light from time to time marked their progress. 'Damn that Faulkner,' Eddie murmured, 'he can't stay away from his light!' Soon his watch peeped. 'All right, Fire Team, let's go.' As they trotted into the dark, Bob Krueger set his own watch. He was deputy leader of the Support Team. Simon was content to let him do the commanding. Give him a pulpit and Simon could convince turnips to dance, but he was no good at military manoeuvres. Back in 1962 he had failed his induction physical for reasons the draft board had refused to disclose, even to him.

The next thing Simon knew they were marching up a slight incline. The smell of the woods was almost overpowering. The presence of the witches in Maywell had sensitized Simon to the devil's ways, and this wood was definitely infested with demonic force.

They went farther and farther, deeper and deeper into the forest. Simon could sense the unseen things crowding about them. It was all he could do not to take a shotgun from one of the men and start blasting away.

As they reached the top of the rise they had been climbing, the blackness ahead began to change, then to lighten. They were coming to the end of the woods.

'What the hell is that?'

'Quiet!'

'Something's moving.'

Simon couldn't tell who was talking, but he could hear the slow dragging shuffle. It was emerging from the forest, parallel with them. 'Oh, God.'

'Be quiet.'

A light snaked out.

There was nothing there. The light moved left, right, left again. Then Simon saw it – a stone statuette of a broad-shouldered man no more than three feet tall, a powerful little man with a furious, grimacing face.

'It's some kind of a charm. Pass it by.'

They kept on walking. Simon looked back once only. He might have seen the shadow of the thing moving slowly up the road.

'Okay, halt,' Krueger said. They had come into a pasture. Now all that separated them from the house was a few hundred yards of field.

The moon was riding the treetops. It cast its pale light upon the scene below: empty, disused fields crossed by the road. And on that road two clumps of dark figures, spaced a few hundred yards apart, going forward at a steady pace.

'Okay, guys, it's our turn. Move out.'

The Support Team started off. Simon felt the moonlight on the back of his neck like a living finger. The darkness had been hard, but this was harder. 'O Lord,' he prayed, 'thy rod and thy staff –'

Far in the distance crows began to call. Their voices shattered the silence, echoing up and down the valley. Simon actually ducked. He remembered those damned birds, and somebody should have thought of them before. During that nude ride the other night they had saved the witches with their fierce pecking attacks.

Their noise grew more intense as the Support Team reached the house. The crows were swooping and flapping frantically in the front yard, but they didn't attack. When Simon stepped up onto the porch, he sensed the charged presence of the house.

In among the gracious columns he could see that the front door was gaping. From the shadows within there came a powerful odour of gasoline.

CHAPTER 30

After the initiation the group retired to the barn. Carpets had been laid on the floor and a fire built in the central fireplace. The room was warm, tenderly lit by the flames. Incense scented the air. One of the members of the Vine Coven played the panpipes, the long, sweet notes swelling in the quiet. The Christian delegations were gone. After the ceremony their cars had moved slowly off across the farm. For the sake of the witches' safety Amanda would have preferred them to stay, but they could not be allowed to witness this.

Amanda had never known that there could be such intimacy among a large group of people. They were deeply in love with one another, all of them. It was upon this foundation that their society rested. How anybody could find such gentleness threatening was beyond Amanda's comprehension. And yet she herself would once have been shocked at the spectacle before her.

Even though it was an act shared among many people, it was as intensely private as a wedding night.

Robin lay beside Amanda, his hand resting on her thigh, his eyes closed. She turned on her side and regarded him. 'Are you asleep?'

'Hardly.'

'Robin. I'm so happy.'

He kissed her cheek. 'You belong to us now.'

'I feel that.'

'There was dissension about you once, when you first came here. A couple of covens even thought about leaving the Covenstead.'

'What kind of dissension?'

'Over you being an outsider.'

'I'm not an outsider.'

He smiled at her, leaned over, and began kissing her.

She could see a vague, colourful haze around most of the people here. Where the lights of the couples touched there played deep blue of heartrending beauty. She remembered that colour: it was the same as the sky of the Land of Summer. Love, she now understood, was so connected to death that the two were like an old married couple, serenely embracing.

Amanda gazed at Robin, enjoying the wonder of him. 'You raised the cone of power. Without you I couldn't have found my way back.'

'Vine Coven did it.'

'Each did it, and all. If you're a witch, everything you do is magic. The craft of the wise is the art of expressing the true relationship between humanity and the earth.'

'Which is?'

'I can't explain magic any more than a Japanese monk can explain Zen. Every human being is a hologram of the whole species. Each contains all. That's the basis of magic. And earth is not an inert ball of rock. It is aware, it thinks, it knows we're here. That's magic, too.'

'Why do I find that thought chilling?'

'The earth will give back exactly what it gets.' She was silent a moment. 'Humanity is supposed to function as a single being, the brain of the planet. Instead we are all scattered, each going his own selfish way. The earth gets selfishness, it will return selfishness of its own. You have to feel the world as a whole, mankind as a whole. Let illusion drop away. Differences, ideologies, fears, all disappear. Hate evaporates with the rest of illusion. Only love remains.' His expression was blank. 'Don't you sense it? The love, the compassion?'

'I can hardly imagine what your perceptions must be.'

A disquiet came upon her. How could such a simple thing be so opaque to him? But what about her, a week ago? She had to bring what she had learned into the world. But not now. There was work yet to do. Brother Pierce and his followers would come once deep night had fallen, she felt sure of it.

And yet, in her mind's eye she saw him moving through the woods, saw him approaching the house in darkness . . . as if he was already there.

It was not long after eight, though. She must be projecting images from later tonight. Surely they weren't already here, when it was still gloaming. Soon the sheriff would come and the danger would be over. Even so, she heard the hissing fire that still lingered above the Covenstead. The thought of it made her dig her fingernails into her palms. If all was well, why did danger still point its finger?

Robin was aware of none of this. She returned his smile, all the while feeling the most acute loneliness. She and she alone understood enough to protect this place. She was very uneasy.

Outside there was a dull boom, followed at once by a low, steady roar. Amanda started, then raised her head. 'No, be quiet. It's only a jet.'

She saw fire.

Somebody started humming. Others took it up, and soon the whole room was filled with a gentle, human music. It was the sound of over a hundred people all married together. For a little while it seemed as if the marriage was even bigger than the Covenstead, that it extended forever outward, covering the whole earth and including everything – air, rocks, plants, all matter living and otherwise, and all people whose hearts could join.

When the hum died away, the roar did not. It had got louder and was now punctuated by deep crackling sounds.

Amanda's throat almost closed, her breath came in a long

gasp. Everybody in the room knew at once what it was. Somewhere on the estate there was a great fire.

People jumped up in their fright and rushed naked for the door. A mistake, and Amanda acted instantly. 'Stop! All of you!' They froze, turned, their faces tormented by their feelings. 'We get our clothes on first. We do not panic.'

'I think it's the house,' Robin said as he fumbled with his jeans.

Amanda got jeans and sweatshirt on, and jammed her feet into her boots. She was among the first through the door.

Red, flickering reflections covered Stone Mountain. From the direction of the main house there arose a tower of sparks. Smoke was billowing up into the sky. 'Connie!'

As she ran, Amanda felt a fool. Why had she not heeded the warning of her own mind, then her own ears? She had been seduced by the moment. She raced frantically across the hummocks, her legs pumping. 'Connie!'

Flames were literally bursting out of every downstairs window, snatching and licking at the bricks. The upstairs windows glowed.

Smoke shot from the chimneys. Sparks climbed in whorls and eddies up the sky.

She had never before realized how long the distance was between the house and the village. She ran and ran and yet seemed never to get any closer. Her wind began to come hard and her legs to ache.

At last she reached the edge of the herb garden. The tang of smoke was heavy on the air. Wood and something else.

Gasoline.

'You're killing her, you're killing her!'

Connie's crows were flying round and round the house, screaming horribly whenever they went through the flames. When they saw Amanda, they came and fluttered and shrieked about her head. She rushed straight to the kitchen door.

A blistering wave of heat slammed her back. The kitchen

432

was blazing. Beyond it was a sea of flames. She couldn't get in that way. 'Connie!'

She ran around to the front.

Flames had climbed the columns of the portico. The front door itself was gone. She could see inside, to the black profiles of the hall furniture. As she watched, a chunk of ceiling collapsed into the hall and was lost in sparks.

She backed away, shielding her face. Robin came rushing up, followed by half a dozen others. Three of them went to hook up garden hoses.

The crows were throwing themselves against the window of Connie's bedroom. 'She's in there, Robin!'

His arm came around her waist.

She broke away. 'I'm not going to let her burn!'

'There's no way –'

If only she had asked the sheriff to come at eight instead of nine. A thousand if-onlys, and the hell with them all. She was going to do her best. Others were trying to save what they could from the library. One group was looking for a ladder in the toolshed. They dared not try to get the one in the basement. Amanda began climbing a gutter. The bricks behind it were hot to the touch. Smoke was coming out around some of them.

The wall was bulging, ready to collapse, and the gutter was loose. Amanda climbed anyway, hand over hand, her feet barely able to keep her from slipping back down.

'Amanda, stop! It's too dangerous.'

Struggling with the shaky gutter, she continued up. Beside her the downstairs window belched flames. She could smell her own hair beginning to burn. A few feet farther up, the crows were hurling themselves again and again against a window. She felt something cold running down her back, saw water steaming on the bricks around her. They were trying to protect her with the garden hoses.

What a fool she had been not to have got things organized before! Wasting time with rituals and pleasures.

She was now parallel with the window. The crows flew madly about in a stink of burning feathers. She reached out and tried to get her fingers under the edge of the window frame. No luck, it was too tight. She climbed a little farther. Water played around her, making things dangerously slick. But the others weren't thinking of that. They were afraid she would burn.

How could anybody believe that other human beings could deserve a horror such as this? She hammered with her one free hand on the glass. 'Connie! Connie!'

Slowly, unwillingly, the glass began to give way. Again and again Amanda slapped at it. Finally lines of fracture started to cross its surface.

The gutter made a scraping sound. Amanda felt it sway outward, away from the wall. 'It's falling,' Robin bellowed. 'You've got to come down!'

The glass shattered. Amanda cleaned out the shards and, levering on the window frame, was able to pull herself over onto the sill. The crows flew past her into the room.

Connie lay on her bed with her hands folded neatly on her breast. Her face was in repose. Flames were popping up through the floorboards. The doorway was a sheet of fire. Even as Amanda watched, the bedclothes caught with a snapping sound.

The crows rushed madly about in the room, becoming smoking, blazing meteors in the superheated air near the ceiling. Their voices high with suffering, they tried to protect Connie with their bodies.

'Connie, wake up!'

The combination of the crows and Amanda's screaming did it at last. Connie's eyes opened. For a long moment she simply stared at the ceiling, which was shot with fingers of red flame from the doorway. 'Connie, come to me! Quick!'

Her eyes met Amanda's. 'Don't be a fool. You can't protect me from my fate. Get out of here!'

'Come with me.'

She sat up on the bed, and when she did, something terrible happened to her. There must have been a layer of superheated air in the room just above the level of the bed. Her hair burst into flames.

She screamed then and began beating her burning scalp. Then she leaped to the floor. Her eyes were wide, her lips twisted away from clenched teeth. 'Goddess!'

The whole top half of her body started on fire. She danced. She made barking noises. Urine sprayed around her. Then she pitched back onto the floor, burning fiercely. Her legs hammered, her arms moved in slow arcs.

A white-hot stone of grief and rage slammed into Amanda's heart. Robin screamed above the roar of the fire. 'Hurry, Amanda! The wall's caving in!'

The frantic voices and the heat compelled her to turn away from Connie. To keep from catching fire herself she had to crouch low. In seconds the room was going to be a mass of fire.

She reached the window, climbed out, swung to the gutter. With a wrenching scrape it separated from the wall. The ground whirled beneath her. Bits of burning tar from the roof dropped past her like meteors. If she didn't get away from here, she was going to become a torch.

Dark figures raced about in the reflection of the flames. The garden hoses played frantically. Excruciating pain stabbed her shoulder. There was fire on her but she couldn't even slap at it without losing her precarious grip on the gutter.

Flames now poured out of the window of Connie's room. Above the window the roof was a pillar of fire.

The hoses had managed to put out the fire on her shoulder, but another brand of tar hit her arm. She screamed in agony. The gutter began to break. She braced for a thirty-foot fall to the ground.

Then there were arms around her, big, burly arms.

Robin and Ivy's dad. 'Steven!' He was on top of the

435

longest free-standing ladder they had been able to find. Balancing, grunting with effort, he carried her down.

Then she was being dragged away by grasping, struggling people. She managed to get up and run with them, and not a moment too soon. With a roar and a great burst of withering heat the whole side of the house gave way.

They went far out into the herb garden before they turned around. The house was an inferno.

Beyond it red lights twinkled. The township's volunteer fire department was arriving.

Silence settled over the witches. There was nothing they could do, nothing the firemen could do beyond making sure that the conflagration didn't spread to forest and field. They stopped their truck in the front yard and began deploying hoses.

Amanda felt tears on her cheeks. She was not sad so much as bitter, and incredibly angry with herself for being so careless. Despite the clearest portents and warnings, she had underestimated Brother Pierce and his followers.

Sheriff Williams came running up, his pistol in his hand. His eyes were stricken. 'Did they get her? Is she killed?'

Their faces told him. He dropped his pistol and sank to his knees, shaking hands covering his face. 'I love you, Constance! I love you! O Goddess, help me!'

Steven held Amanda, and Robin kissed her face, kissed it frantically. His eyes spoke the terror he had known when she was in the house.

Ivy came rushing up and put a salve on her arm and shoulder. 'Third degree on the arm,' she muttered. 'Not too much of it, though.'

The salve helped.

Father Evans was back, and most of the others who had attended the initiation. 'My dear girl, I'm so sorry for you all. I just want you to know that it wasn't my people who did this, not a bit of it! I have preached to them that you aren't evil, that you are simply doing things differently from

436

us.' He faced the ruin of the house. 'Please forgive them, Lord, those who did this thing.'

'It was Simon Pierce,' Sheriff Williams said. 'I'm going to put that man away for the rest of his life! And I'm going to disband that Tabernacle of his as a menace to the public safety.'

'You do that,' Amanda said. Her heart was full of woe and fierce hate for the ones who were oppressing the Covenstead. She intended to make Maywell safe for the people she loved. They had as much a right to the freedom of their practice as anybody, and they were not going to be denied that freedom.

After his speech, the sheriff had bowed his head and covered his face with his hands. He stood swaying and silent. 'Sheriff Williams,' she said. She put her arm around his shoulder. 'Come on. We need you now.'

'She's dead! I loved her, you know. I loved her every day of my life for fifty years. She was a wonderful woman. Truly, one of the greats.'

'I know how much you loved her. And I respect it enormously.'

'I hope she's happy. I have faith that she is.'

'I know where she went,' Amanda said. 'I can tell you for certain that she's happy.'

'You –'

'I do know.'

'That means an awful lot to me. Thank you for saying that.' He was silent a moment. 'I remember her first coven. Back in 1931 it was. We were just kids! Hell, I wasn't even twenty. That was the Appletree Coven. We met around a crab apple tree out by the edge of the woods.' He gestured off towards the dark. 'Hobbes and her and Jack and me and five or six others. It was quite a secret.' He stopped. His shoulders shook. 'She was so beautiful. Like you are. Her skin was like pearl. I just fell for her. Totally and completely. I've been on her side ever since.' He hugged himself. 'She was the Goddess personified, as far as I was concerned.' There was a long silence. 'Oh . . . all that went so bad . . . there were terrible times! Hobbes –' The sheriff sobbed. 'Why couldn't she have gone peacefully? Why did she have to burn?'

'I saw it happen. She didn't even know. She never felt a thing.' Best to keep the truth to herself. She needed this man to get himself together. He was very important to them now.

He took something from his pocket. 'I keep these as trouble stones,' he said, hefting a small object in his hand. 'To me trouble is a piece of flint.' He threw the stone. 'Earth bind it, no one find it!'

He took a deep breath and contained his grief, at least for the time being. 'Okay, let's get to work. Can I assume arson?'

Robin spoke. 'The whole downstairs caught at the same time. And we all smelled burning gasoline.'

The sheriff went to his car. He spoke into the radio. 'This is Williams. Constance Collier's just been killed in an arson fire. I want you to go get that Brother Pierce of yours and lock him up until I get back to question him.'

'On what charge?'

'Murder one! Now, move or it's your ass!' He put the microphone back on its dashboard hook. 'I shoulda gotten rid of that damn Peters months ago.' He shook his head. 'Who'd have known how crazy they really were. How damn crazy!'

The house now consisted of five standing chimneys and two blackened columns. The rest was flaring rubble.

Amanda thought of the treasures that had been lost with Connie. The library now consisted of a couple of stacks of scorched, sodden books. The magnificent Hobbes *Faery* was not among them.

Steven remained close beside Amanda. She suspected that he was as drawn to her as his son. 'Thank you,' she said, and kissed his cheek. She tasted the tears there.

438

Robin hugged her.

Amanda realized that the whole Covenstead had gathered around her. For a moment she was afraid, but then her ages of experience came to her aid. On behalf of all the witches she spoke:

'We've had a loss. A terrible loss. But I want all of you to think not of what has been taken from us, but of what Constance Collier gave us before she died. And what she would want us to do. What she would demand of us if she were here. We all want to mourn. I'd like to go crawl under a rock somewhere and just forget this world exists for a while.

'But we cannot do that, not one of us. Connie would scorn us if we did. We've got to save this Covenstead, and the way to start is to protect it from further damage right now, tonight. I don't think we can assume that Pierce will give up until the whole place is destroyed.

'Nor can we assume that he's gone. Every one of us is in danger. So I want every coven to be aware of where all of its members are at all times. Nobody wanders off.' She motioned to Sheriff Williams. 'Before we organize, find out if anybody's missing. Look around you. Are you all accounted for?'

There was general movement. 'The Nighthawks are in the volunteer fire department. They're over by the pumper.'

'Except for the Nighthawks? Good. Now I want everybody who knows how to handle a pistol or a rifle to step forward.' About a third of the coveners, most of them from the town, gathered around Amanda and the sheriff. Generally the town witches kept guns. What weapons were on the Covenstead had been stored in the house. 'Deputize them.'

'I did that before I came out, like you said on the phone. I was just finishing up when the fire alarm came through. We were planning to get here a little early, just to be on the safe side.'

It hurt to hear that. But Amanda continued. 'I think we ought to divide up. The main group will go to the village, some people armed. And get some fire extinguishers from the truck. I'm sure they've got them. That thatch could go up in a matter of seconds if our friends manage to get to it with a torch. I want the Rock Coven to stay with me.'

'If you shoot,' Sheriff Williams said, 'do so only in self-defence.'

Most of the coveners went off towards the village. Amanda watched them go, the moonlight gleaming off their weapons long after they themselves could no longer be seen.

'Now I want the rest of you to guard the Covenstead. That means the main gate, the West Street entrance near the blackberry patch, and the old road through the grave-yard.' She left them to do their own organizing and went over to the pumper. A couple of the firemen were sitting on the running board drinking coffee. 'How long do you intend to stay?'

'Until we're sure it isn't going to flare up again. Probably means all night, a fire this big.'

'Good. Watch the horizon, too. Especially towards the fields and off in the direction of the village. The same people who started this fire might not be finished.' With that she went back to the sheriff.

'Amanda,' he said, 'I wish I could convince you to hide out in town until I have Pierce behind bars.'

That was out of the question. 'I can't leave the Co-venstead.'

'I know that. Just wishin' out loud.'

'Robin and Ivy, let's go back to the village. That's where I belong.'

They crossed the path through the herb garden and de-scended into the dark of the fairy mounds. The moon rode the middle sky.

On their way Amanda cried, silently, privately. Without speaking Ivy and Robin took her hands.

The village was very quiet.

'Where are they?' Ivy asked, standing among the cottages. 'Hello?'

'Don't move an inch. Don't even breathe.'

The voice was hard and scared and mean. A man came hesitantly forward from between two cottages. In one hand he held a shotgun. A flashlight flickered, paused a moment on Amanda's face. Her throat tightened, her tongue felt thick in her mouth. They were being captured, right in the middle of their own village.

'Well, look what we got,' said another voice. It was terrible to hear, mad but powerful, cruel but ever so smooth. She remembered it well. Hate came forth in the shape of a man, smiling. 'The rest of your people are under guard in that barn over there,' Brother Pierce said. He was Alis of the Alesians, he was the Bishop of Lincoln.

Other men were bringing the three guard covens towards the village. 'Looks like we got the drop on you folks,' Brother Pierce said. 'We've just been waiting and watching. We knew you'd fall into our trap.' He motioned them into the barn with the others, but when Amanda started to follow, he put his hand on her shoulder. 'Not you, young woman. You're coming with me. There's a lesson I want to teach you.'

Brother Simon Pierce put a rope around Amanda's neck, knotted it, and led her off towards the dark face of Stone Mountain.

CHAPTER 31

In the dark Amanda stumbled and fell hard against her burned arm. The pain drew an involuntary shriek. She hadn't wanted to scream, she had wanted to go in silence.

Nothing was served by this man seeing her weakness. He stood over her, his rifle crossing his chest, a tower in the moonlight. She looked up at the gleaming face, the amethyst eyes. Did he, too, remember the other times, when he was other men . . . Did he know the kinship between the two of them, the long association. In some ways he was as much the dark side of her own spirit as Tom was of the *Leannan*'s.

How had so few of them managed to capture so many witches? For a moment it seemed almost impossible, even with the advantage of surprise.

Then she saw the help they had.

It was visible as thin smoke, hanging just beside him, the handless girl and also something else, at one glance lace and blue, at another slow-clicking claws.

'Abadon.'

'That's one of God's words. Don't you make a spell with it!' He brandished his rifle. 'I'll blow your brains out right here and now!' She fought her panic back just enough for silence.

The ghostly child whispered in his ear, and after a moment he spoke again. 'Let me tell you something, Miss Witch Woman, so you understand. Get on your feet.' She stood up.

There must be some way to communicate with him. 'Do you know what's there, attached to what you carry in your pocket? Surely you do. It's talking to you –'

He slapped her across the mouth. The blow hit with a bright yellow flash. As best she could, she swallowed her anger.

She was unable to look for more than an instant into his eyes. They were sheened with hurt, not hate. She could hardly bear to imagine the suffering of this man.

They reminded her of other eyes – Mother Star of the Sea's. They were desolate buttons, the eyes of an abandoned doll, the eyes of guilt. The *Leannan*'s voice came as a murmur of wind: 'Remember that Mother Star of the Sea is part of you. Remember, she is your guilt.' The voice faded, and Amanda considered its message. If she could release herself from her own guilt, she could release this man from his. Had she the compassion to love somebody who had so hurt her, and was about to hurt her more? Fighting him could not save her now. Only love could do that.

'You come with me, and you come fast. If I don't get back to your village inside of an hour, my men are going to set that round cow barn of yours on fire, and all the devils in the damn thing are going to burn and their children with them. So I suggest we get a move on.'

The night was growing much colder. Amanda shuddered and set off, walking quickly. Tears obscured her vision. She told herself to be calm, but it was very hard. They had not climbed long before he spoke again, his voice rough. 'Stop here.'

He was walking behind her. She felt him draw close, felt his rifle between their bodies. His breath trembled down her neck.

'What do you know about spells?'

'You are one.'

'If there is anything, any black panther or walking statue or anything at all like that, I am going to let them burn your people. And I am going to burn you very, very slowly. Do you understand that?'

She saw Tom in the tangle of brush at the foot of Stone Mountain, saw him by his moonlit eyes. It was all she could do not to call to him.

She expected him to spring at Brother Pierce's throat, to kill him, or at the very least to grow enormous and scare him away.

Tom's eyes were fixed on her. He was panting.

There was a long silence. Pierce's lips came close to her ear. 'Listen, you and me, we have a problem. My people are kind of like, they're out for blood.'

'You burned Constance Collier to death!'

'There was a sign from the Lord.'

They were very close to Tom now. Amanda could just see his crouched form in among the rocks. Any moment he would spring.

Closer they came. Now she could see his tail switching in the moonlight. She moved forward more quickly, to give him room for his jump.

But something happened to prevent him. It was very quick and very damaging: a needle of a claw sliced out from the ghost child and narrowly missed blinding Tom. With a scream he bounded off into the darkness.

'What the hell –'

'It was just a cat. I saw it.'

'Just a cat! You people got a few cats, don't you?' After a moment of studying the brush Pierce continued on, pushing her with the side of his gun.

Dread filled Amanda. Hate dominated love. The flower always died. Every birth ends in death. Perhaps that was the true lesson of the Sabbat that was upon them. *Samhain* is about the tragedy of the dead, not their persistence in the spirit world.

As she had on other last journeys, Amanda sought solace in the sky. The sweep of the heavens reminded her that peace, in the end, would come. Worse things than this have happened, and better things, and as does joy, sorrow has an end. Nobody will ever know all of the secrets in the stars, the worlds that have come and gone.

They were more than halfway to the Fairy Stone. No matter his reluctance she knew that she would soon be burning again, and he tending her fire. It was a cruel homecoming for them both. His guilt came along beside him and he didn't even see her. The little murdered girl glared at him, but he was blind to her childish stare. In her form Amanda could see the flickering image of the blood-red scorpion, Abadon. It seemed an amazingly dangerous thing, this creature. Was this a denizen of some real and final hell she had not suspected before? Abadon was not an invention of Brother Pierce's guilt. It had an independent life of its own. The way it looked at him, so steadily, so . . . carefully, suggested that it thought it would soon devour his soul.

The wind hit them as they reached the rocky crest. Amanda began to shiver uncontrollably. A sweatshirt was no proof against this cold.

The wind sighed in the bare trees and whistled across the stones. Listen as she might, she heard no words in it. There was only the peace of its movement, as it flowed its own secret way.

Ahead, glowing in the moonlight, she saw the Fairy Stone, and before it the gangling rowan bush.

'Get to work, sweetheart.'

'Doing what?'

'Gathering firewood! It's as cold as the devil's behind up here.'

He was going to make her build her own pyre. Would he also make her light it? An awful quivering started inside, in the skin and meat that would soon be dripping grease. The stake was an agony beyond the conception of those who had never endured it. Her legs resisted by growing heavy, her hands by getting clumsy. The branches and twigs she was gathering seemed to cling to her like claws.

Before, she had always defied him. Now she must attempt

something new. Was there enough love in her to include this evil being? 'You can be free of your guilt,' she said miserably, hopelessly. 'I can help you.' She knew that he had murdered the little girl, she could see it in his eyes, marked indelibly there, that one moment repeating and repeating in their glassy reflection. 'She will forgive you, Simon. She has already forgiven you.'

'How the hell do you know about that? Devil musta told you!' The butt of his rifle whistled in the wind, then she was flying against the Fairy Stone, her kindling flung about her. 'Pick it up! Load it up on that rock. I want the whole country to see this fire. It's a beacon to the people of the Lord, that they have been made free!'

She scuttled around gathering twigs. Her side hurt where he had hit her, her shoulder and arm where she had been burned earlier. So much pain.

She had to get through to him. There was no other hope. 'Simon –'

'You shut your mouth and keep working!'

He feared, therefore he hated. On the surface he hated women, deeper inside he hated the woman in himself. At his core he hated life.

Mistakes, recriminations, and guilt are the central bondage of evil. Finally she had a good-sized pile of brush and kindling. 'Come here, witch.'

She went to him. She looked straight into the desolation of his eyes.

I am trapped, those eyes said. And I hate you for it.

The wind scurried, hissing against the Fairy Stone. *I am the hand that takes*. The sheer power of his own guilt was opening the stiff fist in Brother Pierce's pocket, opening it and clutching his thigh with the bony fingers. A question, dark with terror, concentrated in Pierce's eyes. She could see the moonlight reflecting on them as on two brown glass balls.

'I can free you, Simon. I have the power to forgive sin.'

446

The eyes narrowed. 'You're crazy.'

'The hand is alive. I can see it moving in your pocket. Not only that, I can see what it's attached to – a little girl you once knew.' She spoke softly, trying to calm him with her tone. Carefully she reached towards him. 'Face the wrong you did her and forgiveness will come.'

'Wrong *I* did? We aren't exactly here to talk about my guilt, are we? You're the witch, the spellmaker, the devil worshipper.' He snorted, trying to deride her. 'You're evil incarnate.'

'I'm just a woman. What you've got in your pocket might well be evil incarnate.'

'You shut your mouth about that, Miss Witch!'

'For heaven's sake, Simon, you're carrying the hand of a murdered child. You can't tell me what's evil and what's not.'

He looked at her out of eyes sharp with suspicion. 'You know too damn much,' he murmured. 'Maybe you'd better go over and lie down in that kindling now.'

That terrible command brought back the harshest of memories: the feel of the cage that had held Moom, the way the bars had bent but never broken; the hideous three minutes that Marian's fire took to crawl to her through the wood, then the swooning torment when it first touched her feet.

She told herself that she was reconciled. Beyond death, this time, she knew that Summer awaited. She could smell the air of it, and already hear the music.

Even so the command made her sink helplessly to the ground. Her mind might be reconciled, but her body refused to go willingly into such torture. 'I'm sorry.'

He twined his fingers in her hair and dragged her to the pyre. 'Put your arms over your head.' When he grasped her wrists, a shock of knowledge swept through her. She saw the guilt that lay yet in his hands.

'You murdered that little girl and cut off her hands so

447

they couldn't identify the body. Then you kept one of them. You did that, didn't you?'

'I am a man of God! How dare you blaspheme me!'

'You can still find your way out of this.'

'You're a lying witch and you're gonna burn!'

He crossed her wrists and wound the end of a long leash around them. Then he looped wire around her ankles.

She remembered how as Marian she had watched the clouds. She would do the same with the stars.

He tightened the leash. As long as he kept it taut, she could struggle all she wanted, but she could not get away.

Even as he worked, she saw the sadness in his eyes. His surface personality might really hate her, might really be about to burn her, but his deeper essence loathed what he was doing. She got a flickering image of herself escaping across Stone Mountain. 'You were going to let me go. Why have you changed your mind?'

'How come you know so much about me? Nobody in the world knows what you know.'

She remembered Connie beating at her flaming head.

Why do they burn us? They want to banish the dark.

And Moom thinks: 'But I *am* the dark. I give life in the dark. What comes from me, comes from there. Babies come from the dark!'

The voice of Grape: 'I'm waiting for you, Amanda. This time you will not wander the underworld. You're coming home.'

'Stop that heathen muttering. I warned you, no witch spells!'

She felt her soul gathering the memories it would take on its journey, pausing at the door that leads out of the body. 'Goddess,' she whispered, 'open it fast once the fire starts. Please don't let me suffer long.'

He twisted his leash tighter around her wrists. Her hands bulged from the pressure. For a time she was silent. A moan escaped on an exhaled breath. The next one became a sob. 'You killed a child, Simon. But you can atone, even for that. I can help you atone.'

'I am not guilty! Before God, praise His Name, I am not!'

He looked at her, into her eyes. 'Could you really help me?'

'Of course I could. Of course!'

The torment of the leash grew less. By the Goddess he was letting her go. Then he sighed a long sigh, tightened the leash again, and laid her face-up in the dry brush and sticks.

Her disappointment made her burst into tears. Through her own suffering, though, she kept trying to understand him, to find the insight that was the key to his need. He wanted her help, she could see that. Why wouldn't he allow himself to accept it?

Then she saw into the nature of the hell he was inventing for himself. In the heart of his guilt he would be forever devoured. It was surprising that he could not yet see the shadow of his demon, the ghost child, for the more hatred Simon conjured in himself the more real she became. From all around them there came the scuttling of Abadon's long, jointed legs.

He was the first human being she had encountered who had condemned himself to the eternal hell.

Tom hovered just at the horizon, huge in the mountains, his black shape like a cloud along the ridges. He gazed at her with fixed intensity.

Amanda kept on trying to reach Simon. 'The child will let you atone.'

He peered down into her face. There was a distinct odour of pizza on his breath. 'I'm sorry I did it. I just – all of a sudden, she touched me and it felt too good, and all of a sudden – oh, God, she was just lyin' there dead. A kid and dead.'

He clasped his hands together and looked into Amanda's

eyes. His essence seemed to call out to her, 'Help me, don't let me do this to myself. Help me!'

The clicking of Abadon's pincers mingled with the wind-clatter of the rowan's limbs.

Amanda's tight-bound arms hurt so terribly that she had to force herself not to bellow. There was only one way for her to save herself: she had to save this man.

'I cut off her hands and tossed her in a river. I couldn't have any ID. But I'm sorry, damned sorry.' Even his sorrow was ugly.

'You don't have to endure your guilt. You can relieve it if you've got the courage.'

'I'm so scared,' he whispered. 'I deserve eternal damnation for what I did.'

'You deserve what you choose to deserve. Your guilt can end, Simon. Untie me and we'll talk.'

For some time he didn't move. At least there was a struggle going on in him, or so it appeared.

She kept hoping, but when finally he met her eyes, the pity she saw filled her with despair. He would not look so sorrowful if he had decided to set her free. 'You're right to think this is hard for me. I don't enjoy making people suffer. In fact I'd like nothing better than to let you free. But I'd be doing a real sin then. You need the suffering I'm going to give you. I'll spare you God's fire by burning you in mine. You see, you don't understand that this is a good deed I'm doing. When you're dead and in heaven you'll thank me. Fifteen minutes of torment will save you from an eternity of spiritual fire.'

With a little, fascinated smile on his face, he began to spark his cigarette lighter. Amanda turned away. Her stomach churned, her womb contracted around the tiny life within it.

She thought of the Covenstead. This was to be their last *Samhain*, then. Where had they erred? Why had the powers abandoned them?

With a click and an orange flicker, then another click, Simon got his lighter going. He cradled the whipping flame in his hands, then applied it to some dry leaves at the edge of her pyre.

'I'll pray with you as long as I can.'

'Put it out!'

'As the fire burneth, let her soul be cleansed, O Lord.'

She tried to roll away but she couldn't. She twisted and groaned. Remembering Marian's death, she concentrated on the sky. Summer is waiting, she told herself. The flames rose from blue to orange and began to dance in the wind. When the first heat touched her, the fire was perhaps three inches from her thigh.

The little girl came close then. It was amazing that Simon could not yet see her. Amanda looked right at her. Her eyes were so still, so knowing, so very angry. By moonlight Amanda could see the freckles on her nose.

'You think you're going to hell, don't you, Simon? You think there's no way out for you. There is a way out.'

A flicker of interest registered in Simon's eyes.

The fire came closer. He tightened his leash until she thought her arms would break. She began to cough in the tangy smoke. She could see coals raging in the centre of the spreading flames. Sparks flew to the sky when she struggled.

'Simon! The Lord wants you in heaven. He wants everybody, doesn't he?'

The heat was rising fast.

'O Lord, on behalf of this your daughter I ask mercy and forgiveness in this time of her agony. Let your purifying fire cleanse her of the sins of the earth.'

Tom paced just beyond the circle of firelight. She screamed at him. 'Please help me!'

Simon licked dry lips. His eyes reflected the fire. The heat against her thigh was becoming a torment. Her clothes were smoking. Simon had started to shake.

'You ask God to forgive me, but you're the one who needs

forgiveness. You're the sinner here, Simon. The hand is proof of that.'

'I am the light –'

'You're no better than the rest of us! Scared and guilty and lost. Now put out this fire and rejoin the human race.'

'I killed her. I admit it, sure I do. I confess it. But what's the good, she's still dead.'

'Worse sins have been forgiven. If you have courage, you can atone – oh, for the love of all that's holy I'm catching on fire!'

The wind was making the fire caress her hip. 'I beg you, I beg you, please stop!'

'I'm sorry! I'm so sorry!'

Miserably Amanda writhed. There must be some way to reach this man. 'Oh, please!' In another moment the flames were going to cover her.

Simon's face in the firelight was that of a little boy.

She squirmed, she kicked, she shrieked.

Watching her, his expression changed. There came into it a glimmer of something she hadn't seen there before, that might be remorse. 'The hand is –'

'Guilt. Your guilt. But you can atone for your crime. I can show you how!' The flames were licking along her leg.

'I can't! I can't ever atone!'

'Put the fire out! That's a start.'

The flames spread to her shirt.

'Oh, put it out! *Put it out!*'

He was divided, his hands alternately reaching for her then pulling away. The heat was starting to drive him back.

'You'd be free, Simon! Free of your guilt!' Her body wanted to give up to the maddening anguish of the fire, but she had to keep trying. 'Think of it, Simon. All these years you haven't slept a peaceful night! You could, Simon, you could have peace!'

'O God –' He burst into tears. Then he was moving, he was coming forward, his hand shielding his face, and suddenly the leash was loose and she was able to leap up, to roll, to free herself.

Pain boiled in her chest and leg but it had worked. She was free, she was not being burned anymore and Simon Pierce was kneeling among the broken coals, fumbling in his pocket, then bringing out something small and strange, the hand, dead but splotched with areas of living skin.

He held it cupped in his two palms.

Amanda backed away, for something beyond conception was happening beside him. The air filled with a sighing sound as of a thousand children murmuring for home, as by threads and tatters a girl of twelve spun into final, true, and absolute reality.

A small, dark shape scuttled towards the rowan. Fairy were here, maybe even the *Leannan*.

The girl reached out and took the hand from Simon. 'Oh, no,' he said. 'Oh, Betty. Oh, no.'

The girl twirled in the firelight. Her hands, both attached again, were spread wide. She was not smiling.

'You've got to forgive me, darlin'. It was one of those crimes of passion, like they say. But you're dead, darlin'. Please, I don't want to see you like this! You're dead.'

A great roar of wind came sweeping out of the sky and with it a raging, furious voice screaming every foul word in every language of man.

The murdered child's fury slammed across the landscape, echoing from valley to valley. Simon cringed before her, who bellowed loud enough to break rock.

Then silence came again, filled only by his shaking breaths. 'She's the Devil! Lord, O Lord, she's the Devil come after me!'

'I'm not the Devil,' she said. 'I loved you, I really did.' She drew his face up by the chin, making him meet her eyes.

Amanda could see Abadon hiding in the body of the child, ready to burst out and grab him and drag him down. She had to help him. 'You're guilty, but not eternally guilty, Simon! Nobody is eternally guilty.'

There came a ringing as of great bells back in the chambers of the mountains. With each tintinnabulation a flock of unlived days fluttered by on moth's wings. The life that the girl had been denied, the nights exquisite, the wearing days, the hard incredible pain of birthing, the old shadow again and the reaped field of experience, all came up and sank back again, dissolving into a powder of shadows.

Simon saw what he had denied her, and Abadon began to flex in her body. 'She'll have another life, many lives. She has time.' He sank down, he covered his head, he made a long sound beyond a sob. 'Betty,' he whispered, 'Betty, Betty, Betty. I can't give you back your life, Betty. I can't give you back what I took.'

'Simon, think how many others have taken lives. Millions. You aren't alone and you don't deserve eternal damnation for it. Accept your guilt and atone, but don't pretend it's worse than it is.'

'Atone? My atonement is hell eternal.'

'Your atonement is what satisfies her, and she won't keep you for all eternity. You are not that bad.'

He looked at Amanda with gratitude, and in that moment Amanda knew that he had accepted that his own guilt had limits.

From the shadows came a strange fairy music, not the harp, but a harsher sound as if of drums and bells and rattling stalks. This music made Simon look curiously in the direction of the rowan.

But there was nothing to be seen, not to his untrained eye. Amanda saw it all, though.

He gasped. A shaking hand went up to touch his hair as his gun, forgotten, clattered to the ground.

Off in the dark the fairy musicians pointed horns at him. They did not make a sound that could be heard, but Amanda could feel it in the air all around her. Simon put his hands

454

to his ears and crumpled forward. Rendered white and narrow as silk, his hair fell away.

He uttered a sound like wind spending itself. His flesh sloughed from his bones, his fingernails grew long. His eyes sank, his hands became crone claws.

Amanda remembered him at the Tabernacle, pointing and shouting a terrible sentence from the Book of Revelation. She spoke aloud, but her voice was small: 'And they had tails like unto scorpions, and there were stings in their tails. And they had a king over them, which is the angel of the bottomless pit, whose name is Abadon.'

The horns made great brown noises, which sucked the youth from him. He fell forward, already little more than a terribly aged skeleton.

The girl murmured a pitying word and caught him, cradling him in her arms. There was something like satisfaction in her face. Her overseeing his hell would in the end relieve the suffering of them both, her anger and his guilt.

Amanda could hear the snap of his skeletal jaw, a noise no bigger than somebody clicking the teeth of a comb.

The girl carried her burden away across the Fairy Stone, in among the crowd of fairy that lined the far ridge of the mountain.

When Tom came bounding up at last, Amanda at first wanted to greet him, then felt anger as sharp as cut glass. 'You old cat, why didn't you help me?' She looked out into the dark, at the departing shadows of the fairy. 'And you, why did you wait so long!'

She knew, of course. They had not been able to do anything to Brother Pierce as long as he wanted eternal damnation, for they could not be a part of his hate. It was ironic that his own self-loathing protected him from his destruction. As soon as he found the least glimpse of his good core, though, he could not condemn himself for eternity. Then they could become a part of his justice.

Amanda followed the progress of the girl climbing into the mountains, still carrying her burden. As they went, the girl changed. She became like smoke, then more solid, until she was the *Leannan* sweeping through the heights and glens, carrying an extraordinarily shrunken man in her arms.

When she realized that the ghost child had also been the Queen of the Fairy, she knew that the last test was over. They had all been tempered in the *Leannan*'s terrible fire. The strength and wisdom Amanda had been given were her weapons against the coming age of persecution, of which Brother Pierce was only the beginning.

She began making her way down the mountain, thinking of the other witches. Her injuries made her progress slow, and as she moved along, she heard gunfire and the roaring of some great animal, shouts and finally screams as high as wind in wire. Pain or no pain, there was only one thing for her to do. She leaped ahead, rushing along the rough path as fast as she could. Her injuries screamed, almost rendering her insensible, but she ran on.

She looked around for Tom, who had been slinking ahead through the undergrowth. 'Help us,' she screamed. 'Help us!' He was nowhere to be seen.

Terrible imaginings of the murder of her people swam through her mind, of Kate being shot, of Robin burning and Ivy burning and all the Covenstead in ruins, of animals kicking at fire in their stalls.

By the time she entered the village her head was crashing with pain and exhaustion. She needed medical attention, and soon.

An awful silence had settled on the Covenstead. The village stood in darkness, in shadows. She saw nobody.

She went close to the barn.

A faint sound came from within – singing, low and sad. The people were alive, at least. But their tone said all: they were preparing to die.

She peered down the pathway between the cottages.

Where were Brother Pierce's men? There wasn't a soul around.

Then she noticed Tom. He crouched low, facing the shadows beside the sweat lodge. He was huge, and amazingly terrifying, a great, black lion with a flowing mane and golden eyes. He was the size of a car. Huddled before him were Brother Pierce's men.

Tom yawned. Nearby the *Leannan*'s harp began to play. It was odd, to think of her at once back on the mountain with Simon, playing her harp in these shadows, and stalking about as Tom. Amanda loved the *Leannan Sidhe*, and the warmth in her heart made the music grow sweeter. Is it that God is lonely? Is that why we exist?

Amanda saw what had happened here. Their usefulness expended, the *Leannan* could have taken Brother Pierce's men, too. Or could she? Maybe she had not the right; maybe it was not their time to die.

Tom gazed at Amanda and swished his broken tail. His pink tongue appeared for a moment between his teeth, and he licked his whiskered cheeks. She picked up a discarded .30–30, found it to be empty, and tried a shotgun. It had two shells left. When she pointed it at Pierce's silent, staring men, Tom leaped up in a shower of sparks and became a cat again. Then he closed his eyes and soon was purring the first purr she had ever heard from him.

She threw open the door of the barn with a shout of joy. 'We're free! We've won!' Robin swept her into his arms.

There followed a time of people holding one another close, joyous in their lives but remembering their dead. Sheriff Williams was called, and Brother Pierce's men were led off to the county jail.

The silence of the night engulfed the village and soon brought rest to the exhausted little group.

As far as Brother Pierce himself was concerned, a search was mounted for him the next day by the sheriff's office and the state police. Nothing was found, not so much as a discarded gum wrapper.

Over subsequent weeks wells were sounded, Maywell Pond was dragged, and the mountains were walked.

Tom would scamper along with the searchers, his tail bobbing in the tall grass, his good ear pricked to any sound.

But nothing was ever heard, nothing found.

Simon Pierce was never seen again.

The world's greatest science fiction authors now available in paperback from Grafton Books

Samuel R Delaney
Stars in My Pocket Like Grains of Sand   £2.95   ☐

William Gibson
Neuromancer   £2.95   ☐

Sterling E Lanier
Menace Under Marswood   £1.95   ☐
The Unforsaken Hiero   £2.50   ☐
Hiero's Journey   £2.50   ☐

Ian Watson
Chekhov's Journey   £1.95   ☐
The Book of Being   £1.95   ☐
The Book of the River   £1.95   ☐
The Book of the Stars   £2.50   ☐

Kevin O'Donnell Jr
Ora:cle   £2.95   ☐

Robert Sheckley
Mindswap   £1.95   ☐
Dimension of Miracles   £2.50   ☐
Options   £2.50   ☐

To order direct from the publisher just tick the titles you want and fill in the order form.   SF1382

The world's greatest science fiction authors now available in paperback from Grafton Books

Bob Shaw
One Million Tomorrows	£1.50	☐
A Better Mantrap	£1.50	☐
Orbitsville	£1.95	☐
Orbitsville Departure	£1.95	☐
Fire Pattern	£1.95	☐
The Palace of Eternity	£2.50	☐

Arthur C Clarke
1984: Spring (non-fiction)	£2.50	☐
The Sentinel	£2.95	☐
2010 Odyssey Two	£1.95	☐

Harry Harrison
West of Eden	£2.50	☐
Skyfall	£2.50	☐
Captive Universe	£1.50	☐
You Can be the Stainless Steel Rat: An Interactive Game Book	£1.95	☐
Rebel in Time	£2.50	☐

'To The Stars' Trilogy
Homeworld	£1.95	☐
Wheelworld	£1.95	☐
Starworld	£2.50	☐

Doris Lessing
'Canopus in Argos: Archives'
Shikasta	£2.95	☐
The Marriage Between Zones Three, Four, and Five	£2.50	☐
The Sirian Experiments	£2.95	☐
The Making of the Representative for Planet 8	£2.50	☐
Documents Relating to the Sentimental Agents in the Volyen Empire	£2.50	☐

David Mace
Demon 4	£1.95	☐
Nightrider	£1.95	☐
Firelance	£2.50	☐

To order direct from the publisher just tick the titles you want and fill in the order form.

Fantasy authors in paperback from Grafton Books

Raymond E Feist

Magician	£3.50	☐
Silverthorn	£2.95	☐

Richard Ford

Quest for the Faradawn	£2.50	☐
Melvaig's Vision	£2.50	☐

Robert Holdstock

Mythago Wood	£2.50	☐

Michael Shea

Nifft the Lean	£2.50	☐
A Quest for Simbilis	£1.95	☐

Tim Powers

The Anubis Gates	£2.95	☐

Patricia Kennealy

The Copper Crown	£2.95	☐

Fritz Leiber
'Swords' Series

Swords and Deviltry	£2.50	☐
Swords against Death	£2.50	☐
Swords in the Mist	£2.50	☐
Swords against Wizardry	£2.50	☐
The Swords of Lankhmar	£2.50	☐
Swords and Ice Magic	£2.50	☐

To order direct from the publisher just tick the titles you want and fill in the order form.　　　　SF1482

The world's greatest science fiction authors now available in paperback from Grafton Books

Piers Anthony
'Cluster' Series

Vicinity Cluster	£1.95 ☐
Chaining the Lady	£1.95 ☐
Kirlian Quest	£1.95 ☐
Viscous Circle	£2.50 ☐
Thousandstar	£1.95 ☐

'Tarot' Series

God of Tarot	£2.50 ☐
Vision of Tarot	£2.50 ☐
Faith of Tarot	£2.50 ☐

'Split Infinity' Series

Split Infinity	£2.50 ☐
Blue Adept	£2.50 ☐
Juxtaposition	£2.95 ☐

'Bio of a Space Tyrant' Series

Refugee	£2.95 ☐
Mercenary	£2.95 ☐
Politician	£2.95 ☐
Executive	£2.95 ☐

'Incarnations of Immortality' Series

On a Pale Horse	£2.50 ☐
Bearing an Hourglass	£2.50 ☐
With a Tangled Skein	£2.95 ☐

Other Titles

Anthology	£2.95 ☐
Steppe	£2.50 ☐
Phthor	£2.50 ☐
Chthon	£2.50 ☐

To order direct from the publisher just tick the titles you want and fill in the order form.

All these books are available at your local bookshop or newsagent, or can be ordered direct from the publisher.

To order direct from the publishers just tick the titles you want and fill in the form below.

Name _____

Address _____

_____